THE
SECOND
REBEL

Also by Linden A. Lewis

The First Sister

THE
SECOND
REBEL

LINDEN A.LEWIS

HODDER &
STOUGHTON

First published in Great Britain in 2021 by Hodder & Stoughton
An Hachette UK company

1

Copyright © Linden A. Lewis 2021

A CIP catalogue record for this title is available from the British Library

Hardback ISBN 978 1 529 38695 0
Trade Paperback ISBN 978 1 529 38696 7

Printed and bound in Great Britain by Clays Ltd, Elcograf S.p.A.

Hodder & Stoughton policy is to use papers that are natural, renewable
and recyclable products and made from wood grown in sustainable
forests. The logging and manufacturing processes are expected to conform
to the environmental regulations of the country of origin.

Hodder & Stoughton Ltd
Carmelite House
50 Victoria Embankment
London EC4Y 0DZ

www.hodder.co.uk

To Connor, the brother who saw and loved me as I am

CHAPTER 1

LITO

One may look at Val Akira Labs and see only its array of products and services. Another may look and see a legacy of scientific progress dating back to the discovery of hermium. But when I look, I see the cornerstone of mankind's future, a map through which humanity will achieve true transcendence and the resulting immortality.

> Souji val Akira, CEO of Val Akira Labs, End of Venus
> Rotation Shareholders Report

I can't move in my coffin. Arms stuck to my sides, legs straight beneath me, toes pointed at ninety degrees. Glass mere centimeters from my nose. Beyond that, black. Trapped, and unable to do a damn thing about it.

Whenever the panic comes like an overwhelming wave, I do as Ofiera taught me: I take a deep breath and blow it out slowly. Of course, then I think of how I have at most fifteen minutes of air inside the cryo chamber and that makes the anxiety, and my breathing, heavier. Now it's more tempting than ever to rely on my implant to erase my emotions. But for the mission, I need to be able to feel.

If Ofiera can do this, so can I.

Cold burning my lungs, muscles seizing as they reawaken, eyes adjusting from bright white lights to a hard face. A voice calls my name: "Oh-feaaaaaaaaar-uhhhhh."

No, not me. Ofiera's memories that I haven't let go of after we shared thoughts through her faulty neural implant. They're recalled more easily now than ever. A chamber just like this was her tomb, the ice box they locked her in whenever she finished her assigned missions, only now we're both being wheeled into Val Akira Labs' R&D facility in cryo chambers. Though we're fully awake. That's different, at least.

We had concerns with Hemlock's plan, but we realized its brilliance at the same time. We couldn't disappear without putting Sorrel at risk, and there was no way we could fight our way into the labs, get what we came for, and fight our way out. The odds were too overwhelming. So, during our trip from Ceres to Mercury, we fabricated false reports for Command, tales of Gean patrols that necessitated longer routes. Between the current rotation of planets and the speed of the retrofitted grasshopper, we bought ourselves four weeks.

They expected us to return to Cytherea, but at the end of those four weeks, we landed on Spero, where Hemlock had empty cryo pods and Aster agents at the ready. Each pod had an encrypted ID tag corresponding to the person to be delivered to the lab, only we would be taking their place. As I crawled into the pod, I wondered but couldn't bring myself to ask what they'd done with the bodies.

The air is thin now, my breathing short. My legs cramp, aching to bend, but I don't move, even for relief. It's only been about ten minutes, not long enough for us to reach the inner labs, but there's no telling our location when I can't see out of the black canvas bag they have the chambers wrapped in. Instead of the mission, I think of the sea, the rolling of the waves as they wash in and out, brushing against the sand . . . a comforting thought, and one that settled me when I was a child watching holovids until I fell asleep.

As if I summon the sea itself, the pod around me hisses, spraying a wet mist over me. I suck in a sharp breath at the cold, only to hear it as a wheeze—the air is too thin, I can't fill my lungs. Something even colder hits me—first on my sides, then pooling at my lower back—and while my muscles stiffen in response, I have nowhere I can move to get away from the liquid.

Shit—the damned cryo chamber has turned on. More frigid fluid pours into my pod, and I can't get away from it—there's nowhere for me to go—

I suck in my last breath, knowing I may never wake again. I sink into the liquid, letting it arrest the blood in my veins, my heart—

No, I'm not calm—I'm not Ofiera, and these are not my memories.

The sludge quickly fills the small space as I gasp for air and find none—it's being pumped out as the liquid comes in. Instinct kicks in and I try to take one last breath before I'm submerged, but there's no air—*no air at all*—and the icy solution, thick and stinging, rushes up over my head—I fight not to breathe it in—not to suck it into my lungs—I can't hold on—I can't—

I breathe in the liquid, freezing me from the inside out. My thoughts turn sluggish, ice crawling across my skin, stilling motor functions.

This feels like death.

Am I dying?

Then even that thought is lost.

WHEN I COME to, my last thought is my first.

Am I dying?

Then I correct myself: *Am I dead?*

The world around me is a bright light. Slowly other things filter into focus as my consciousness expands—my body, shivering. Voices, echoing as if underwater. Movement, zipping past the corner of my eye.

Not dead. No matter which stories you listened to, the Thousand Gods Below the Sun never described an afterlife like this.

I cough, and that vile, thick liquid stings coming up my throat, just as cold going out as it was coming in. I turn my head to spit, and my eyes slowly adjust to the figures—two Asters in charcoal-gray maintenance uniforms and one blessedly familiar face.

"O-O-Of-Offf—" I can't manage her name.

Oh-feaaaaaaaaar-uhhhhh. I struggle against her memories.

"It's okay," she says. "It's okay, Lito."

She's just as naked and sticky as I am, but she ignores her own state as the Asters—Peony and Elm, two of Hemlock's agents on Spero—bring me a silver shock blanket. They wrap it around me, but it does little to help.

The smell of my sister's coconut shampoo hits me. "Luce?" I manage through my raw throat.

"It's okay," Ofiera says again, and this time I believe her. At least, I can hear her better. "It's hard coming out of cryo the first few times."

Gods, the thought of experiencing this a *few times* . . .

"Your neurons fire strangely, make your memory play tricks on you."

The scent of Luce still dances on the air. I close my eyes and try to focus on the warmth of the blanket instead.

"You'll continue to improve over the next hour."

Do we have an hour to spare? I don't know. I don't even know how long we've been under. Hours? *Days?*

As I suck in lungfuls of air and the control of my body and mind returns to me piece by piece, I run through what I know: Ofiera fon Bain is my Dagger. I was tasked with killing my former partner, Hiro val Akira. I followed Hiro to Ceres, where they were supposed to kill the Mother, the leader of the Sisterhood. When I found them, I discovered Hiro had been geneassisted into Saito Ren, a Gean captain. Together we killed the Mother and escaped to the Under with Hemlock's help.

And that bastard Hemlock is the reason I'm here in Val Akira Labs, coming out of a frozen coma . . .

I sit up once I feel able to. By now, Ofiera has dressed in the same charcoal maintenance uniform that the Asters wear and is pulling her shoulder-length brown hair into its usual messy bun. "There's a towel and some clothes beside you."

"You're way better at this than I am . . ." I slip off the table and force myself to drop the blanket. I shiver as soon as it's gone.

"Practice makes perfect, as the old phrase goes," Ofiera says wryly.

"Look at you, making a joke." I towel the remaining cold slime off of me, and as my muscles work, I feel more in control of them. "Why did the cryo chambers turn on? That was only supposed to happen in cases of—"

"Emergency," Elm confirms. He's stocky and thick-shouldered for an Aster, making him appear more intimidating than he is. His voice is the exact opposite: soft and sibilant. "We ran into trouble. Had to store you until we could come back for you."

"'Trouble'?" I repeat. It could be anything from nosy guards to Souji val Akira himself.

"It would be easier to show you . . . Just a second while I connect. Can't be too forceful or they'll notice we've tapped the cameras." Elm's fingers drum on a compad, its screen reflected in the lenses of his goggles.

As he works, I pull on the waiting clothes, loving every stitch of them despite the Val Akira Labs logo embroidered on the chest. After the cryo chamber, I'd be happy to wear rags. At least they're warm.

"Are we in the inner labs?" Ofiera asks.

Peony, who keeps her Aster-plaited white hair wrapped about her neck like a scarf, nods. "Main lab is just down the hall."

"Good," Ofiera replies. "That's where military assets are kept." Assets like Sorrel.

"And that's where we'll be able to plant the relay." If the trouble Elm mentioned isn't too bad . . . My brain may be sluggish, but I still remember that our mission here is twofold. If we can successfully install a relay for Hemlock, he'll be able to snatch precious data right out from under Souji val Akira's nose.

"That's the problem," Elm says.

I can feel Ofiera's emotions spike through the implant. "What?" she asks in a low voice, doing her best to keep calm.

Elm hands his compad over to Ofiera, and I huddle close to watch over her shoulder. The video starts with a wide shot of a laboratory. In one room, a group of scientists in lab coats monitor screens; in the other, through a wall of glass, a figure sits in a cruel-looking metal chair.

"Is this live?" I ask.

Elm shifts from foot to foot. "Yeah, a live view of the main lab."

Shit. Packed room like this means we aren't getting in to plant the relay unless we can somehow get the scientists out. We were brought in during late evening. According to the clock, it's just past midnight. We were supposed to be able to sneak through the lab without running into employees. "What the hell are they doing?"

No one answers me, and as I watch, my throat tightens. The footage zooms in to focus on the lab's glass wall. As the lighting adjusts, I make out an Aster in the chair, the top of their skull removed, their brain exposed. At intervals, their eyes shoot wide before falling sleepily, back and forth, switching between exhausted and terrified. Strangely, it's the Aster's silence that sends a shiver down my spine. From the trembling that shoots through their body, arms straining against the straps that tie them down, open mouth gasping, they look like they want to scream but . . . can't.

This has to be one of the off-the-books experiments; Hemlock will want us to gather proof for later. If we could just get the relay in place . . .

"We have to cancel the op," Elm says, halting my thoughts. "There are too many people here. There's no way someone won't spot us if we try to pull Sorrel *or* plant the relay."

"There has to be another lab where we can pull military assets," Ofiera says, and the heat in her tone says she's not giving up.

Elm looks to Peony. "There is," she says, slender fingers picking at the fabric of her uniform. "But with the test happening, lab security is heavier than expected."

We should call the op off. It would be the safest thing to do. But we can't reenter cryo sleep and wait until a better time. The longer we're here, the higher a chance that someone discovers we're not the people who're supposed to be in the pods. We can't plant the relay with the main lab occupied. We can get Sorrel out, but only if we're willing to deal with security while we have no weapons and our clothes aren't shielded. One shot, and we're dead. The best option is to leave empty-handed and try again at another time.

I turn to Ofiera, and her yearning reaches me through the implant, impatience to be reunited with Sorrel warring with the need to keep him safe—*so close, we're so close.* Leaving has its drawbacks too. If we don't show up in Cytherea within the next couple of days, High Commander Beron val Bellator's going to know we've gone rogue, and the punishment for Ofiera failing her mission has always been Sorrel's demise. That's not a factor either of us wants to play with.

"Up for risking your life?" I ask Ofiera.

Her eyes narrow as she senses my determination through the implant. "Always."

WE MOVE THROUGH the white hallways on light feet. The recessed lighting is turned low, a golden glow the only thing fighting back the overwhelming shadows. The corridors are nearly identical and the doors are labeled with both numbers and symbols, making the building look more like a maze than a sprawling laboratory. If not for Elm and Peony's instructions, we would no doubt be lost in minutes.

We come to a T junction, but as I start to turn the last corner before we reach the secondary cryo lab, Ofiera reaches out through the implant and screams a warning. I hear the noise that alerted her a second too late, two sets of shoes clipping against the polished floor toward us. I press myself against the wall and freeze; the human eye has always been drawn to movement, easily missing people who hold perfectly still. I hope with all my might that they don't turn down our hallway, that security doesn't have heat scanners, as if I could impress my will on the universe through desperation alone. Though we're wearing the maintenance uniforms, our faces aren't in the system, so all it'd take to screw our entire plan is someone with com-lenses identifying us as outsiders.

The two people come to the T junction, walking slowly. They're in lab coats—scientists. I hold my breath as one looks down the hallway, and my heart speeds as I feel his eyes land directly on me—but he doesn't stop. Doesn't *really* see me. In the dark uniform, completely still, I blend into the shadows.

They continue on and, within seconds, are gone.

Still, if security has noticed us skulking about in the dark, it's only a matter of time before we're hunted down . . . Tempted to erase my anxiety with the implant, I instead release a long, shuddering breath and steel myself. Ofiera nudges me forward.

We turn left, the direction the passing scientists came from. We don't have to go far before we reach a door labeled 18C. My throat tightens as I press the compad Elm left with me before he and Peony returned to work, unable to risk themselves further, to the bioscanner. I wait for either the click of an unlocking door or the blare of alarms.

The door clicks. Ofiera enters, and I follow after.

Inside is a room similar to the main lab but far smaller. Rows of monitors wait in the dark like sleeping sentinels. The glass between the observation area and the temperature-controlled chamber is fogged from the cold. On the other side are rows and rows of cryo chambers hanging from hooks on the ceiling. From just a quick glance, I calculate that there are hundreds of them in this lab alone.

"Thousand gods," I murmur.

Ofiera is silent as she crosses the room and approaches the glass. Set before it is a hulking control panel with a screen that wakes at her touch. As if she knows what she's doing—she's probably seen scientists do this before—she types a string of numbers, 4757828, into the field labeled ASSET.

The pods swing into motion, the belt on the ceiling shuffling the frozen occupants like they're no more than clothes in a closet. I stiffen at the unholy amount of noise in the otherwise silent lab, expecting any second to be the one security comes to check out our unscheduled work. Finally the machine halts on one pod in particular, and the hook brings it forward, close to the glass, so that we can see who rests inside.

Ofiera's emotions are like an electric shock through the implant. A pain in my chest grows at the sight before me. And though he looks different than in Ofiera's memories—older, wearier, his white hair shaved close to his scalp—I'd know him all the same from her response: Sorrel.

My feelings rise to take the place of Ofiera's. Outrage battles with guilt. Cryo ads always promise a peaceful slumber, but Sorrel's face is contorted in a rictus of pain. I doubt he's known peace for many years.

Ofiera jerks into motion, fingers on the screen again. Sorrel sways away from the glass and disappears in the shuffle of pods.

"What're you doing?" I ask.

"We can't wake him here. Security is too thick. But we came in on a ship marked for loading and unloading, so from here, we can send his cryo pod into our ship's hold. We'll wake him once we're in orbit." Over her shoulder I see her selecting a delivery route for Sorrel's pod to dock three, the place our ship is parked. At the same time, a vibration in my pocket grabs my attention.

I pull out Elm's hacked compad, slaved to the Val Akira Labs security system. There are no alarms blaring, no flashing lights—but there don't need to be.

Ofiera—

I swallow her name, tilting the compad toward her so she can see.

Moving Sorrel, an important military asset, has alerted lab security. The cameras capture the flurry of the guards' movements.

They hunt through the hallways. They have guns at the ready. They're moving in for the kill. And we have nothing but a hacked compad and our lives to lose.

CHAPTER 2

ASTRID

It is with my abundant thanks that I receive your offer, Aunt Margaret. My affirmation on Olympus Mons cannot be postponed. However, if you are to oversee the Temple of Ceres and its Sisters, let me be clear: Because of the tragic passing of Mother Isabel III, may the Goddess welcome her into the Eternal Garden, no one has imparted the proper conduct to our dear First Sister of Ceres. She needs your guidance—your *stern* guidance, and a watchful eye.

Message excerpt from Aunt Marshae, head of the Order of Cassiopeia

olden light falls through the greenhouse windows, tumbling through the leaves of tall trees and climbing ivy. Below, kneeling amidst the roots and stems, I am bathed in a calming green glow and wrapped in the loamy scent of wet earth. The morning broadcast, coming from a compad I left near the entrance, softly filters through the foliage and fills the air with swaying orchestral music. I am, in this place, in this moment, perfectly happy.

Of course, all things must end, and as the melody comes to a close, it is replaced by the dulcet tones of an Aunt. "Today, let us consider the Meditations," a woman I instantly recognize as Aunt Margaret says. The broadcast must be an old recording, since Aunt Margaret is here on Ceres and not on Mars. "Specifically, chapter one, verse twelve." She speaks clearly and forcefully for the recording; in person, she talks with a Gean clip, putting the onus of understanding squarely on the listener's shoulders. Still, she is a welcome change from Aunt Marshae. By comparison to the Auntie in charge of me on the *Juno*, Aunt Margaret is as gentle as the Marian's Fire roses I tend with their gentle yellow centers and orangey-red exteriors.

The recording catches the sound of turning pages. Aunt Margaret must be preparing to read from the Canon, as opposed to quoting from memory. But I know Meditations 1:12 by heart, and while I used to solely consider the scriptures in my head, now, with my voice, I join in as she reads. "'Nature may be bent by mankind,'" I quote alongside Aunt Margaret, "'but never broken.'"

While Aunt Margaret closes the Canon with a thump and goes on to speak of tenacity and faith, all the usual things associated with the verse, I continue to Meditations 1:13. "'What is plucked may yet bloom. What is burned may yet nourish. What lies fallow may yet grow.'" They are words that have come to mean much and more to me on Ceres as the months have passed. As trials, one after the other, have set themselves before me.

This is what the people know: Four months ago, Mother Isabel III was slain by Saito Ren, the captain of the *Juno* gone rogue, in a protest against the Annexation of Ceres. This was a shock to everyone, but particularly the Sisterhood. Before her death, the Mother named me the First Sister of Ceres because of my valiant attempt to unmask the traitor Ren, with help from Aunt Marshae.

Those are all lies from the Agora, the seven Aunts who lead the Sisterhood. This is the truth: The Sisterhood suspected something traitorous about Saito Ren from the beginning and hoped to embarrass Warlord Vaughn, who had traded highly valuable political prisoners to the Icarii for her release, by proving it. Aunt Marshae and the Mother assigned me to spy on Saito Ren, but I never gave them the information they wanted. Undeterred, Aunt Marshae lied to her superiors to make herself look good and made me desirable as a side effect. She was named

Aunt Edith's replacement as the head of the Order of Cassiopeia, and I became the First Sister of Ceres. She is even now, I'm sure, working to undo my appointment as part of the Agora on Mars.

Perhaps the most startling facts are the ones that only I know. The person called Saito Ren was actually Hiro val Akira, an Icarii gene-assisted into Ren. They had come not only to assassinate Mother Isabel III, but to influence someone who might rise to the status of Mother who aimed for peace between the Icarii and Geans. Someone like me.

Only Hiro did not kill the Mother. They failed in that task. The Mother was murdered by my hand.

After she revealed the illegal usage of Icarii neural implants within the Sisterhood to take away our voices—well. To say I reacted poorly would be an understatement.

My hands slip from the soil to the pocket of my dress. I feel the outline of the ring box there, a shape and weight that brings instant relief. After the Mother's implant was turned over to me as First Sister of Ceres, I feared losing it, as small as it is, so I decided to keep it in something larger. But I fear to leave the box anywhere, knowing that, even now, secrets are hard to keep.

The door to the greenhouse opens with a whoosh, releasing both pressure and heat. Whoever has come, she—as only Sisters are allowed here—lets the stresses of the world in as well, and I am reminded of everything I must do. Everything I must be. She turns the compad's volume down until I can no longer hear the morning broadcast, but it is not until the visitor says my name that the tension releases from my shoulders.

"Astrid." My secret name. The name I have chosen, since I cannot remember the one I was born with.

"Good morning, Eden." The Second Sister of Ceres, who was also my Second on the *Juno*, moves until her shadow falls over me. At one time we were enemies, but fate—disguised in the actions of Hiro val Akira—brought us together. Then we realized who our real enemies were.

"It's after noon, Astrid, not morning." When I look up at her, I see she is diplomatically keeping her face pleasantly blank. She is beautiful, my Second, as most who advance in the Sisterhood are, but her fiery-red hair and emerald-green eyes are particularly noteworthy on Ceres, where few look like her. "You're due at the dedication ceremony in less than an hour . . . and you're wrist-deep in dirt." Ah, *there's* the judgment in her tone I know so well.

I gently pat the earth over the newly planted rose seeds and clap my hands to rid them of excess soil. My fingernails are ragged, though; there's no hiding that. "I can wear gloves," I say with a shrug. Eden sighs, so I add, "Tending a garden is an important part of my worship."

"I've been meaning to talk to you," Eden begins, playing with a pair of gardening gloves I abandoned, "but it's hard to get you alone lately."

She has no idea. "About what? Caring for my hands?"

"No, no." Eden tosses the gloves aside. "About the communications tower. I want to earmark some funding for it so we can improve the transmission speed between Mars and Ceres." I keep quiet while I pretend to think about it. "Then perhaps you'd get your morning broadcasts in the morning instead of the afternoon."

I cannot help but laugh at that. I have lost track of time in the greenhouse, and the broadcast didn't help. "I'm sorry, Eden, but the next month's budget has already been approved."

Eden jerks upright. "What're you spending it on?"

I take in a deep breath before I speak again. "I promised Lily she could build the shelter for Asters displaced during the Annexation of Ceres."

I expect Eden's scoff, so I'm not hurt by it. "It's always her."

I level a hard look at Eden. We have had this conversation many times, and I refuse to have it again. Aunt Marshae may have left for Mars to be trained and confirmed as Aunt Edith's replacement, but that does not mean she didn't leave eyes on Ceres. Keeping Lily happy with her pet projects ensures that, if she is reporting to Aunt Marshae, she will be more favorable toward me. Placating an asset is the first way of turning them. I learned that directly from Hiro.

"I should get ready," I tell Eden as I stand up and brush by her, not inviting her to follow but not barring her either. After a moment, she falls in step beside me, and we walk companionably out of the greenhouse situated in the inner courtyard and across what we have renamed the Cloisters, filled with tilled rows of vegetables and skinny-trunked fruit trees. Eden plucks an apple, pink as her lips, as we pass through the miniature orchard and into the high-ceilinged stone hallways of the Temple of Ceres.

The Temple, once a building that housed the Icarii Senate, is the center of Gean worship on Ceres and the seat of my power. Perhaps that is why I feel kinship with it. Or perhaps it is that I aim to build myself in its image: to appear as one thing, but be another.

Eden takes a bite out of her apple, juice dripping down her chin, and tosses the rest to me with a playful smile.

THE PILOT WHO navigates our podcar through the streets of Ceres is unnecessary when the programming of the vehicle does all of the work, requiring him to simply watch the screens in silence, but we Geans adhere to one of the oldest Sisterhood laws: *May no machine be set above a human.* At least, openly we do. My right hand finds the square shape in my pocket, and even through my gloves, the feeling of the box is pleasing.

Step by step, I work toward becoming the next Mother. Step by step, I will make these neural implants illegal. I will change the Sisterhood, and the Geans, for the better.

Already I have left my mark. Ceres is much improved from when I took power four months ago. The streets are no longer rubble-strewn, the buildings no longer pockmarked from Gean bombs. Shelters have been opened for those displaced in the Annexation. Unemployment is lower than on both Earth and Mars; I wasted no time getting the people to work on rebuilding their communities. And Aunt Margaret brought Sisters to the city and helped me start the Green Garden Initiative. Even now, passing through rows of commercial buildings, I see the fruits of our labors: metal trellises amidst strips of green, covered in reaching tomato and cucumber plants. The GGI works on multiple levels but, at its most basic, ensures that Ceres produces its own food and no one goes hungry.

The months have not been without troubles, of course. The destruction of the Icarii warship *Leander* had many on Ceres fearing life in the asteroid belt. But if the Gean military knows what happened to the *Leander*, they have not felt the need to share it with the Sisterhood, and so I focused on increasing patrols around Ceres as opposed to panicking about the unknown *something* out there that destroyed the *Leander*. For all we know, it was an accident. Now the Leander Incident is but a memory.

Still, I believe my greatest achievement was my first. When I was the First Sister of the *Juno*, six Icarii quicksilver warriors boarded the ship looking for Saito Ren. After the battle was over and the Geans stood victorious, Ren decided to cage the warriors as opposed to killing them—the Warlord's preferred method for dealing with prisoners. But then the Mother was assassinated, and the six Icarii were forgotten.

Except I didn't forget. As soon as I had the power to do so, I released them with an unallied ship and sent them back to the Icarii bearing a message of peace. With one gesture, I opened a dialogue of friend-ship between us, resulting in the current cease-fire as our heads of state debate terms for a peace treaty.

Perhaps their release is the reason broken manacles have become the symbol of my rule of Ceres. As our podcar slows to a halt at our destination, I spot the sigil on flags and handmade posters throughout the gathered crowd: two manacles connected by a circle of chains, bro-ken. Snapped in two. Fragmented, and thus useless. A symbol of freedom.

The pilot gets out to open the door for us. In our brief moment alone, Eden nudges me and gestures to the banner hanging from a lamppost, the chains a dark gray against the white background. "I'm sure that'll thrill Aunt Margaret," she says wryly.

I have no chance to respond—that it is not Aunt Margaret I am worried about—before the pilot opens the door and the noise of the crowd assaults us. As I step out, the cheers turn wild. Packed shoul-der to shoulder, the people are barely restrained behind stanchions and thick velvet ropes. It is only the presence of soldiers that keeps them in their place, though a few residents reach across the line, hands desperately grasping for me as if power flows from a mere touch. I gesture at my bristling soldiers to leave them be.

Eden and I walk single-file on the packed-earth path beneath a wrought iron gate, away from the chaos of the crowd. Around us, the stretches of green hills are dotted with leafy chestnut and almond trees, while the trail is lined with cypresses, offering both shade and shelter. Above, the projected sky is bright blue and calm, a perfect day to dedicate a new park.

Before I've even found peace in the nature surrounding us, we break from the tree line into a stretch of field where a wide stage has been set. More stanchions guarded by soldiers keep the attendees on one side, while Eden and I approach from the other. I can hear a ripple pass through the crowd as a few spot us, but it is little more than low chatter from this distance. They are excited, and that is a good thing; it won't be hard to whip them into a frenzy.

At the back of the stage, Aunt Margaret waits for us. Now that Aunt Edith has retired, Aunt Margaret is the eldest member of the Agora. With her short gray hair like the coat of a sheep and wrinkled, rosy cheeks, it would be easy to think of her as a grandmother figure and nothing more, but I know firsthand it would be foolishness to mistake her old age for softness. She has ruled the Order of Pyxis for the past twenty years, like steel thorns beneath silken petals. The golden medallion she wears around her neck, one of only seven, is evidence of her membership in the Agora.

Aunt Margaret gestures for the soldiers to leave us alone. They back away, but not far enough for me to speak openly; while Aunt Margaret knows I have been released from the oppression of my neural implant, its very use in the Sisterhood is still a secret to most. "Did you see them waving that symbol of yours, shouting, 'Unchained! Unchained!' like a bunch of idiots?" she asks.

Eden's elbow digs into my side as if to say *I told you so.*

I lift my hands and flex my fingers. *I had nothing to do with that,* I sign. It feels strange using the hand language of the Sisterhood now that I am free, but sometimes I must.

"Well, letting them get away with it isn't doing you any favors on Mars," she says.

I've heard what they whisper on Mars, that the symbol of the broken manacles is meant as a reprisal against the Order of Andromeda's chain-wrapped stone. Being that I am from that Order, it is almost as likely as the story that freeing the quicksilver warriors gave me the symbol. But truthfully, though I do not know where it came from, I like it, and so I cannot bring myself to do away with it.

What would you advise me to do? I ask instead.

"Bah," Aunt Margaret spits. "It doesn't matter now. After all this is over, we have more important things to focus on." She pats my arm with a soft smile, once more calling forth the image of a doting grandmother—or what I would imagine one would be like; being an orphan, I wouldn't know. "Afterward, we'll talk. All of us."

All of us, as in her, Eden, and me? But no, as she steps toward the stairs leading onto the stage, I spot the small Sister lingering in her shadow.

I shoot a look at Lily—short, plain Lily with her brown hair cut in a childish bob at her chin. Of all the people here, Lily is the *only* one who looks unhappy. Because Aunt Marshae is displeased, or because of the news Aunt Margaret wishes to share?

I do not have time to think about it. Aunt Margaret gestures for me to follow her up onto the stage. "Pull your head out of your ass, girl," she says before offering me her arm. Onstage, she'll affect an elderly shuffle, allowing me to brace her, to really pull at the crowd's hearts. It is a song and dance we have done before, and one I am sure we will do again.

We have been planning this dedication ceremony for the past month, and today it comes to fruition. Everything goes smoothly, for once.

After Aunt Margaret says a few words and leads the crowd in prayer, we each take our place on either side of a silk-covered figure and grab hold of the golden ropes that hang beside the statue. Aunt Margaret nods at me, and we pull together without a word.

The sheet falls, revealing a statue with the likeness of our late Mother Isabel III. The crowd applauds politely, a few cheering in fervor for the Sisterhood.

And, with a beautiful smile on my face, I stare into the stone eyes of the woman I killed, knowing I would do it again if given half the chance.

BACK IN MY chambers at the Temple of Ceres, my ears ring with the thrum of the crowd, but better that than the overwhelming memories of the past. Though I have done my utmost to make the space mine, pulling down priceless icons and paintings and hanging plants in their place, this is the very room where the Mother greeted me four months ago and taught me that I could speak. The stark, hard leather chairs have been exchanged for comfortable divans and sprawling couches, but this was the sitting room where she forced her will upon mine and controlled my body.

The space does bring comfort at times, with its shelves of books in a variety of languages, its private bedroom with a spacious bed and bathroom with a deep tub, its office with its real wooden desk and glass doors that open onto the courtyard. But while the blood has been washed away, the memories remain.

Just there, I shot the Mother. Over there, Eden and I wrapped the rope around her neck to hang her body from the balcony. And there . . .

That is the place I stood as I discovered Ringer was not real.

There is no point in thinking about him, I chide myself. Hringar Grimson, the specter soldier, was created thanks to the neural damage from the Icarii implant the Sisterhood put inside my brain. But there is no need to consider his ghost, no need to ruin a good day such as this with thoughts of the harm done to me by the Agora.

I close my eyes and try to recall the overwhelming peace and happiness from the greenhouse this morning, but there is no chance of finding it when the day is far from over. Now that the dedication ceremony is behind us, we still have to meet with Aunt Margaret to hear the news. My head begins to spin when Eden sits at my side and tosses something into my lap. When I look down, I see her bare feet on my skirt. She wiggles her toes. "Rub them," she says.

I snort a laugh. "Eden!"

"Pleeeeease."

Still, she has coaxed a smile from me. "Only if you rub mine."

"Deal," she says, patting her lap, "but I want you to rub my feet like you hate them."

The two of us are giggling when the knock on the door comes. We sober at once, and Eden jerks upright as Aunt Margaret enters, escorted by Lily. Guards are stationed farther down the hallway, but none of them would dare stop an Auntie from going where she pleases. "Oh, stuff your formality," Aunt Margaret says. "Sit down and relax."

Still, when Eden settles at my side, she's much stiffer than before. I fight the urge to reach for the little box in my pocket, to rub it in my anxiousness. "Can I offer you something to drink?" I ask. "I can call for some tea or lemon water."

"Bah, at my age, if I drink anything, I'll have to piss two minutes later." Aunt Margaret sits on the sofa facing mine and Eden's, Lily beside her.

The shorter girl straightens her skirt over her legs with fingers covered in itchy-looking pale patches. When she sees me noticing the scaly clusters, she shoves her hands beneath her thighs.

"Let's get to business," Aunt Margaret says, pulling my attention from Lily. "I've called you all together—First Sister, Second, and Third—because I have news about the future of Ceres."

I rarely think of Lily as the Third Sister of Ceres, though she is. "Go on, Aunt Margaret," I coax, as Lily turns her big doe eyes to me.

"The Agora has sent word that it will convene to consider the matter of choosing the next Mother." I lean forward, unable to help myself. "Which means, as one of the sitting members of the Agora and head of the Order of Pyxis, I must go to Olympus Mons."

Aunt Margaret's green eyes sparkle with a mischief that belongs to a woman half her age, and I know she is not here merely to inform us that she is leaving Ceres. Anyone with sense can see that I aim to become the next Mother, and Aunt Margaret is a clever woman who has worked alongside me for the past four months.

"What advice would you give those who wish to put forward their name before the Agora for consideration?" I ask, keeping my tone light.

"Usually succession is a straightforward matter." Aunt Margaret adopts the same inflection, a teacher explaining to her students. "The Mother chooses her successor and trains her for a period of years. Her second shadows her, gets to know the Agora, and learns how to rule. Of course, this time, with the tragic way Mother Isabel III passed, we have no successor."

"Things," Lily chimes in, her voice airy, "will not be straightforward this time."

Aunt Margaret continues as if Lily did not speak. "Now, for the Agora to consider someone, their name will need to be brought forward by an Aunt."

Eden leans forward as well until we sit shoulder to shoulder. Her warmth is a comfort to me. "*Any* Aunt, or an Aunt of the Agora?"

Aunt Margaret smiles as if pleased by the question. "Any Aunt may make a suggestion, but recommendation from an Aunt of the Agora will carry a certain weight."

"It makes one a stronger candidate," Lily says.

"Or a target," Eden whispers.

Lily turns her swallowing gaze to Eden. "Yes, there are rivalries among Aunts of the Agora. One Aunt's choice may automatically be dismissed by another, simply because of bad blood between them—"

"*Politics*," Eden scoffs, cutting her off.

"However," Lily continues, louder than before, "it still stands that a recommendation from an Aunt of the Agora draws attention, and one needs that to make a good impression. It requires at least four votes of yes for a Sister to become the next Mother."

There is no chance that Aunt Marshae would ever recommend me for the position of Mother. Perhaps Aunt Delilah, my Auntie from when I was a Little Sister, would, but it has been years since we worked together. But if Aunt Margaret is taking the time to explain this to me, it must be for a reason.

I sit up straight, tilting my head to feign curiosity and smiling to encourage her to speak the truth. "Whom do you favor for the position, Aunt Margaret?"

"That depends," Aunt Margaret says, "on what the candidate could offer me."

Ah, yes. *Politics.* I look between Aunt Margaret and Lily. Surely Aunt Margaret would not back her over someone like me when I both outrank her and have successes to my name. No, this is just a negotiation dressed up as a discussion.

"What is it that you want, Aunt Margaret?" My curiosity is gone; now there is only the shrewdness that she has perhaps come to associate with me.

Aunt Margaret chuckles. "I admire your tact even when there's no need for it. We stand at a river's edge, and the only way to cross is together. So let's be blunt." She points a withered finger at me. "You want to be the next Mother?"

I do not hesitate in my answer. "Yes."

She points at Eden. "And you?"

Eden looks between me and Aunt Margaret. There are things she could never tell—that she wishes to avenge Paola, the girl she loved on the *Juno*, and that she wants to make the neural implants illegal like I do—so instead, she focuses on what an Aunt would understand: power. "I want to be her second." After a moment, she rephrases. "The Mother's second."

"And Lily wants to be the First Sister of Ceres," Aunt Margaret says as she leans back into the sofa.

That is news to me. I do my best to keep the surprise from my face.

As if Lily is not sitting right beside her, Aunt Margaret goes on. "Lily was, at one time, Mother Isabel III's second. It was Lily, through her outreach missions, who put the Mother into contact with the Asters of Ceres, and it was Lily who oversaw the negotiations that led to the Annexation."

Now I *know* my face betrays my surprise. I had heard rumors, but had never given any heed to them. Lily is awkward at best, no grace to her at all; I could not imagine what the Mother saw in her. Knowing that it was not her but what she offered helps me to understand. "But she was not the Mother's second when Isabel passed," I say.

"Suffice it to say they no longer saw eye to eye after Ceres was annexed," Aunt Margaret summarizes, but Lily clears her throat to get our collective attention.

"The Mother went back on her promises to the Asters," Lily explains. "It was a point of contention. And I was assigned to . . . other duties."

So goes absolute authority. Still, she could have supporters in the Agora who know of her and would make her the Mother now. But no . . . Aunt Margaret specifically said that Lily wants to be the First Sister of Ceres. Well, whatever her reason, I am fine with that.

"If I were the Mother, naming Lily the First Sister of Ceres would be easy to arrange." I let my gaze flow from Lily to Aunt Margaret. "But I have yet to hear what *you* want, Auntie."

Again Aunt Margaret chuckles. "I've seen your work these past four months. The Green Garden Initiative. The Mother Isabel III Memorial Park. You think like one of the Order of Pyxis." I hold my tongue, knowing that she will go on if only I am patient. "I want a guarantee that you will increase our budget. I want to bring the same hope to Mars that you have given to Ceres."

Eden stiffens at my side, but the request is a simple one for me. The Order of Pyxis, in charge of establishing gardens, farms, and parks, is one that I favor regardless of Aunt Margaret's influence. I know I cannot guarantee what Aunt Margaret will do with the budget increase right now, but with careful wording in the future as the Mother, I might.

"It will be done, Auntie," I say with a smile.

Like a businesswoman of old, Aunt Margaret holds out a hand. I take it, and, palm to palm like equals, we shake. "Pack your bags then, First Sister of Ceres. We're going to Mars."

CHAPTER 3
HIRO

We are not ruled by archaic laws, set in place by those who consider their words more important than an individual life. We give credence to common sense and the belief that every person, whether from a planet or the asteroid belt, has a right to govern themselves in a way they so choose.

From *The Declaration of Autarkeia* by Dire of the Belt

The target takes his sweet fucking time getting home, leaving me to stew in a closet filled with his stiff shirts that reek of smoke and sweat. Dire gave me a file with basic information on him—Alessandro Rossi, age sixty-three, former Gean military, now a weapons dealer—and I've filled in the gaps after a week of tailing the guy. He leaves his house at a quarter to eight, stops for a coffee, and walks to his warehouse rental while smoking. He has a dozen or so people working for him, and since this isn't Cytherea, where I can tap the feed for their names, genders, or occupations, I have zero clue who they are, but they all clear out around six. After Rossi locks up, he heads to a bar for exactly two Martian whiskies before returning home around ten. He never drinks alone, always surrounded by friends his own age—playing cards and gossiping about so-and-so's niece—and he never answers his compad when he's off work.

For a guy doing illegal shit, he's pretty chill.

Only now it's half past ten, and I'm still waiting for him to get home. Of all the days for him to drink late, it *had* to be the one when I'd broken into his apartment and crammed myself somewhere small and stinky. Unless he knows I've been tailing him, suspects his living space is compromised, and has gotten the hell out of town . . .

I make myself a deal. If he hasn't come home by midnight, I'll sneak back out. That only leaves . . . an hour and a half of standing in a smelly closet. *Oh, fuck me.* I bite my cheek as I remind myself that no one said being a Dagger was a glamorous life.

As time drags its feet, I do my best not to think of upsetting things. Not to think of fire-blue eyes and golden-blond hair and a warm, gray-clad body against mine. The way she glared at me with hatred and told me I was as bad as the Sisterhood. *Was I?*

Not to think of the scenes of my life that appear in my nightmares: the Fall of Ceres, my father's fox smile, the look of my body as I wake and find it's not mine, Saito Ren's face staring back at me in the mirror, First Sister's screams, Lito's broken grin.

Not to think of the agony pulsing around my prosthetic arm and leg. The phantom pains always sneak up on me and linger until I want to bash my head against a wall, unable to massage a limb that's no longer there. There's also the burning that comes from flesh grinding against metal.

But stuck as I am, there's not much else to think about.

I've never in my life been more excited to hear a drunk man stumble home. It's eleven at night—not that *night* means anything on this station—and every light in the apartment turns on as the system registers his presence. With walls as thin as paper, I hear him rustling around in the kitchen, but when he emerges, he doesn't come into the bedroom to change out of his work clothes as I thought he would. Instead, his heavy footsteps take him into the generous living area, where, with a grunt, he plops onto his couch and turns on the holovid screen. After that, there's nothing but five minutes of listening to the swaying, grim music of a war serial and the annoying, openmouthed chewing of some crunchy snack.

As quietly as I can, I emerge from the closet, wipe my clammy palm against my pant leg, and reach for my mercurial blade before second-guessing. This is a stealth operation, and that sword is a dead giveaway, practically shouting *Look at me, I'm Icarii!* I go for a switchblade instead, hoping that the knife favored by street kids system-wide might keep me anonymous.

Outside the bedroom, I stop at the end of the hallway and peer around the corner. The old guy's sitting in a chair so worn I first mistook it for a pile of dirty clothes. He's scarfing down something brown, oblivious to everything but what he's watching. I can't help the ripple of confidence I feel as I make one last check of the cloth covering my face and slip out of the shadows.

Just as I'm reaching around the back of the chair to press the knife to his throat, the bowl of snacks goes flying into the air. くそ. The chips fall in a rain of salt and crumbs, and before the last one hits the ground, Rossi, like a man a quarter of his age, is up on his feet and pointing something at me—*fuck, a gun!*—and I hit the floor and roll as he fires at me.

The laser burns a hole in the wall I was standing in front of moments ago. The sound is covered by the program he's watching—was he expecting me?—and when I push myself back to my feet, he trains the barrel of the HEL gun on me with expert precision. While the room is large by station standards, it's not a lot of space for a fight. I reverse directions—a shot goes wide to my left, almost takes out his holoprojector—and I rush at him, aiming to neutralize that pistol before it blasts my face off.

He tries to step away, to keep enough room between us to shoot, but can't because of the chair he's using to cover his back. I jab the knife at his forearm, but he moves at the last second, and the blade goes directly into his wrist as he stumbles over the chair. As he falls, the knife is jerked out of my grip.

"Fuck!" he screams from the floor, but he hasn't dropped the gun.

Dripping blood, his hand comes up again, and I grab the only thing I have left and ignite my mercurial blade in standard formation.

His eyes immediately snap to it, the silver glow harshening the lines of his face as well as illuminating the dreary apartment, but he doesn't fire. Instead, his face takes on a layer of confusion.

"You're no Gean assassin," he spits. He's got the gruff voice of a man who stopped giving a fuck about three minutes after he was born.

"Good guess. You must've been a great intelligence officer when you worked on Mars."

He snorts. "Smartass."

"I've been called worse."

"I believe it." He holds both hands up as he stands, then sets the gun in the ass-grooves of his old chair, a good move now that he knows he's facing down a duelist with no way to deflect my blade. Still, I don't underestimate the old fucker for a second, not after he caught me off guard the first time with chips. "Look, I really don't want to bleed out. Can I take care of this? I got pelospray. It's in the end table there." He nods to it.

"Yeah, just don't try anything stupid." Like call for backup. Not that there's any form of law enforcement here—or even laws—I just don't want him to summon gun-toting friends.

He moves slowly so I can watch him. With his un-stabbed hand, he opens the drawer and pulls out the pelospray, then grabs a blanket that looks far too dirty for my taste. Before I can stop him, he yanks the switchblade out and wraps his hand in the blanket. *Agh—what the fuck, why bother with the pelospray if you're going to put something dirty on your wound?* I feel like I should complain even though I'm the one who stabbed him.

"This is my home, I have to live here, and I really don't want to paint the walls with your blood," he says, and I drag my eyes back to his face. "So if you're not here to kill me—and I'm thinking you're not, since you came at me with that dinky-ass knife first—what the hell do you want?"

Without looking away from him, I pull out a compad with my left hand and toss it to him. It hits his belly and bounces to the floor.

"For fuck's sake—" I sigh.

"You stabbed me *in the hand*, and now you want me to catch something with no warning? Goddess's tits . . ." He stoops to pick up the compad and checks what I want him to see.

I've memorized the screengrabs he's now flipping through. Every single image is of the same girl with a half-shaved head. What hair she does have is long and black and straight. No matter where she appears, she's always hidden behind someone or something bigger, taller, more vibrant. She dresses in dark, somber colors. In some pictures she looks like a teenager, much younger than me. In others, she looks like a grown woman. The most distinguishing feature about her is something that, on this station, doesn't warrant a second glance: the part of her head that looks shaved is actually metal, some sort of implant or enhancement.

He reaches the last pic and, if anything, looks more confused. "The fuck you want with her?"

"So you've seen her."

His face takes on an entirely new aspect. He shakes his head, paler even than when I stabbed him. "Seen her? Yeah, we've seen her. *Only* seen her."

I'm not sure what that means, so I stay quiet. Like most people who enjoy the sound of their own voice, he fills the silence.

"Who sent you?" he asks.

I fight back a scoff. "Do you really think I'm going to answer that?"

"Fine, I'll just assume you know what I do around here." I nod for him to go on. "Bunch of my people saw her poking around our warehouse. Told 'em the next time they saw her to grab her and bring her to me."

I lean forward, trying not to tip my hand. This could be it—exactly what I came for.

"Only they couldn't grab her, no matter how many times they tried. And I don't work with people who can't lift fifty pounds—nature of the job and all that—so I send 'em after her. They should be able to take care of a slip of a girl like that. You'd think, anyway."

My excitement is squashed flat. I know what he's going to say before he says it.

"Every time someone spots her snooping around, they try to grab her and she disappears—poof—like a fucking ghost."

Just like everyone else who's dealt with her . . .

Fuck, this is another dead end. This whole night—this whole *week* of following him—is a waste.

"When you tripped my alarm tonight, I thought for sure it was her, that she'd come to kill me."

So he *did* know I was here. He must have motion sensors on the windows I didn't spot. "Why'd you come back here alone, then?" I ask, curiosity getting the better of me.

He hefts his blocky shoulders in something like a shrug. "I'm an old man. Pissed off a lot of folks on Mars on my way out. And my people are good people. Loyal people. They're the next generation of the belt, and I'm not going to ask them to take a bullet for me. But hey, if you're not here to kill me, I'm more than happy to give you some useless information—not that I want to see you hanging around my warehouse again, got it?"

"Got it," I say concisely, more than ready to leave.

But Rossi looks at me, one fuzzy caterpillar of an eyebrow inching up his forehead. "Why're the Icarii after the girl?"

"I'm Icarii the same way you're Gean."

That doesn't seem to satisfy Rossi. "Is she Gean, or is she some new kind of Icarii spy?"

If only those were the two choices, dude. If only.

"Thanks for the info." I back toward the living room's window and slide one leg out. I don't put away my mercurial blade until I'm ready to drop to the alleyway a story below so that, even if he reaches for his gun, I'll be ready to jump out of his range.

"That's it?" he asks incredulously.

Well, there is one last thing. "You should think about washing that wound before using the pelospray."

And then I jump.

. . . .

BACK TO SQUARE one, and nothing to show for it. I move away from Rossi's apartment, pulling my mask down and letting the fabric pool around my neck like a scarf. Disappointment washes over me at the same time as the noises of the night, but even the chaos of this commercial district doesn't serve to distract me from the facts. Hemlock sent me here a month ago, and I'm still no closer to finding our target than the day I arrived.

I come to the end of the alley and dive into the fray. The disorder that is the outlaw station Autarkeia swallows me alive.

The only word to describe this place is *clusterfuck*. The station is a giant cylinder, rotating to create gravity, and while the interior is built like a cityscape, there is little that is homelike about it. There's only night here, the black of space permeating every corner. What light exists burns brightly, hot splashes of neon used more to illuminate sections of the street than to brighten the whole settlement. Above, there's no false sky, no barrier dome like I'm used to. There's just more city, only from this direction it looks upside down.

The people who live here are just as outlandish as the city. Skin in a rainbow of unnatural colors presses against me, red and blue and purple on this street alone. Wings flutter, scales shimmer, and tails twitch in the shadows. Extra arms flex, digitigrade legs paw the ground, bone-like spurs protrude. Cybernetic enhancements in craniums—eyes like camera lenses, heads plugged with tubes—and prosthetics are everywhere. I make no mistake in believing they're just limb replacements; I've seen people pull weapons out of hidden compartments in their mechanical arms or legs. Even those without all the extra bells and whistles have unique body art—glowing strips of light or ink billowing into different shapes across skin.

Every corner would give a member of the AEGIS heart palpitations for illegal body modification. The majority of these genetic enhancements are considered dangerous since there's no guarantee they won't affect the germ line and thus be passed on to children, and there's no telling how that'd turn out.

I cut down a narrow street and cross into a more residential area.

The buildings look the same—squat and flat with a cold metal sheen, built with necessity in mind as opposed to beauty—but the smells of various home-cooked dishes reach me—boiled cabbage, baked bread, some sort of grilled protein—and my stomach growls. Drones of various sizes zip by, not just the hand-sized ones we use in Cytherea; some are as big as a cat. The lowest floors of most buildings house shops, their windows a riot of holographic advertising, selling ship parts and "reclaimed" goods. Sound pulls at me from all directions, various discordant genres of music competing against each other, people in the midst of their lives shouting, laughing, fighting.

Finally, half an hour after I leave Rossi's apartment, I reach the boundary where new meets old. Without much thought, I cross the invisible line and enter into the shadow of an industrial plant, once the heart of the Synthetic empire.

Or perhaps I should call it the womb. While no space is wasted in Autarkeia—with a million people, there's none to waste—the industrial plants that built Synthetics during the Dead Century War, scattered throughout Autarkeia, are looked at with a sort of superstition and avoided. A few still work to power the station, but the majority are mere husks, whatever nuclear fission machines they housed long since gone to sleep.

While haphazard buildings are clustered next to them, even butting up against them at some points, the factories themselves remain untouched. They loom like organs in the torso of a fallen giant, silver rib-like structures reaching up to cradle the central dome of the plant. In their shadow, thin streets serpentine, forming circuitous alleyways that lead to what residents consider safer neighborhoods.

I can tell from the lack of noise that this plant is dead, a tombstone in the Synthetic graveyard that is Autarkeia.

On the opposite side of the dead plant, I come to a colorful building painted different shades of fading purple, and while I can hear the roar of the crowd a street over, the only people here are the harsh-eyed elderly sitting quietly on their balconies above. An orange cat with golden eyes yowls at me before running off. Next to the door is a sign in warped handwriting: DON'T PISS HERE!

From inside my jacket, I produce a key—a physical card key, as Autarkeia seems to run on ancient tech—and press it to the door. With a click, it unlocks. Inside, lights wake, sensing my movement and illuminating the hallway. At the first door on my left, I swipe the card again and enter what currently passes for my living space.

I've always had a complex relationship with the word *home*. While some think of their childhood house with their parents or siblings as home, I think of the Ceres barracks where I lived with Lito. Not much else has felt like home since then—

No, not true, a part of me whispers. For a time, home had been a person with golden hair and blue eyes . . . One I refuse to think about now, because she fell in love not with me, but with someone who doesn't even exist.

"ただいま," I call into the darkness.

"おかえりなさい," a deep voice responds as the lights turn on, and I nearly shit my pants.

"Oh, what the fuck!"

Dire uncurls from my bed, and while the man holds his laughter hostage, he's got a smirk on his face that threatens a chuckle.

"Not funny, man," I spit, pulling my hair back from my sweaty forehead and tying it in a ponytail. It's getting long and slightly annoying, but I don't want to cut it because *Saito Ren* wore her hair short, and I refuse to be her anymore.

"You're late," Dire says, all business. With the light on, I look around the room. It's small, a simple square layout without a single window. I can kick the toilet from the end of the bed. There's an industrial drain in the corner circled by a tattered curtain that works as a shower. A little kitchenette takes up the rest of the gray wall. And in the corner, a small end table laden with personal items . . .

My face burns with embarrassment as I look over the sad little shrine I've erected: spent incense, a chipped bowl of rice, a fresh but small orange, and a static holoimage of my mother, my father cropped out—things I've spent precious funds acquiring.

My mother once told me a shrine was meant to reflect on our lost loved ones, but I can't help feeling that she deserves better than what I'm able to give her.

I put my back to the shrine and finish the patrol of my flat. There's nowhere for anyone to even possibly hide.

"Your shadow not here?" I ask, looking for the tall, axe-faced man who follows Dire around like a bodyguard despite being smaller than him.

"Falchion is not my shadow."

Probably outside, then. "Guessing you want to hear about how this *also* ended in failure?"

Dire steps right into my space, looming over me like a tree. If, you know, trees were sexy. He's taller than Lito. Dark brown skin, an intense gaze, hair in locs run through with white. Not from a sense of fashion, though—it's pure aging. He's as old as my father, which I have to remind myself daily, because *godsdamn*, he should be on Cytherean billboards, not stuck at the ass end of space.

"Failure?" he mutters, assessing me coldly, stomping any sexy thoughts I have flat. I know what he sees: a person as patchwork as Autarkeia. Auburn hair with my natural black roots starting to show. Long legs stretched to match Ren's. A sculpted face with my hard jaw and Ren's soft cheeks. I'm just thankful he can't see beneath the baggy flight suit to the real monster show beneath: A rib cage too narrow for my hips. Puckered scars where skin meets prosthetic. A body I can't bring myself to recognize and don't want to touch.

His gaze is so intense, I clear my throat and drop my eyes.

Weak, Hiro. Just pathetic.

"Another digital ghost," Dire says, crossing his arms, one a shimmering gold prosthetic. It's an older model than mine but still moving smoothly thanks to regular maintenance.

I shift around him and sit down on my bed—which now uncomfortably smells like him. "Please don't give me another name to chase down. This is the fifth person, and he was just as useless as all the rest."

"Not a name. Not this time. I've got something new to show you."

"Oh?" And here comes the curiosity, welling up inside me despite my better judgment.

"I need to make a call first. You came home late, and I have to make sure everything's still ready." Dire's eyes flick back and forth as he makes a selection on his com-lenses. Just as I settle in to snoop, he crosses the room in two purposeful strides and exits my studio.

"Bye, I guess," I call after him. He'll be back. I wonder if he's calling Hemlock. I lean back on my bed and prepare to wait. At least I'm not in a cramped, smelly closet this time.

I never did get the whole story from Hemlock—does anyone ever?—but he and Dire go way back, and, contrary to all the tales of Dire being some sort of ex-military Martian built for command, Hemlock was actually the man in the shadows who helped Dire set up his smuggling operation to bring goods from both Gean and Icarii space to the outlaws. It's not surprising then that Dire became part of Autarkeia's leadership; he had access to stuff everyone wanted.

Of course, Dire's thieving from Val Akira Labs caught him a lot of heat, and the Icarii are nothing if not consistent; they don't acknowledge the Asters as threats because of how utterly powerless the majority of them are, and they focus on Dire because he's a human and people listen to him. They think *he's* the reason a few Asters have turned into bad seeds, which suits Hemlock just fine, because he'd rather no one saw him coming.

As for the station, Autarkeia used to be a Synthetic-abandoned squatter's paradise in gray space, that area between the asteroid belt and the rotation of Jupiter. It was through Dire's leadership that the station became what it is now—not just a place for the lawless to live, but an actual outlaw kingdom, welcoming anyone who wants to live free and eschew the governmental structures of both the Geans and Icarii. And, with Hemlock's influence, Asters are welcome here too, living and working alongside groups of people who would shun them on any other planet.

Dire and Hemlock's cooperation is, consequently, the reason I'm here. At some point during my career as Captain Saito Ren, Dire reported a problem to Hemlock: he was being watched.

I know, I know. *No shit*, right? But the ones watching him weren't Gean or Icarii, and while Hemlock and Dire have pulled most of the people of the belt into the Alliance of Autarkeia, there are some who might still be working to undermine their goal, which is, as far as I can tell, independence of the belt from the tyranny of the other governments and fair treatment of the Asters as their own sovereign people.

With that in mind, Hemlock needed someone to root out the group spying on Dire's operation, and who better than an Icarii Dagger? Good thing Hemlock had one just lying around.

I was a bit skeptical when I first arrived. Dire passed me a compad of the same pictures I showed Rossi tonight, as well as a sparse file on the target, and all I could wonder was why the outlaws couldn't deal with one person. But now, after four weeks of trying to chase her down, I understand the inherent threat. If this girl is checking into Autarkeia's offensive and defensive capabilities while only appearing as a data ghost on the com-lenses of people working in key areas around the station, it's not just her who is the problem. It's who she represents.

Because there's only one group powerful enough to perform the kind of trick that allows an agent to roam unfettered, gathering information without even needing a body that could fall into enemy hands: the Synthetics.

And if one Synthetic knows, they all do, connected as they are through the shared consciousness known as the Singularity. Problem is, if the Synthetics have taken an interest in Autarkeia, that's something that could fuck up not just Hemlock's overarching plan but the entire galaxy as we know it.

I sit back up when I hear my door unlock. Dire enters like a thunderstorm.

"How's Hemlock?" I ask, but I swallow my playful tone when I notice Falchion in his long black coat on Dire's heels. He's brought his shadow after all.

Falchion finds a corner of the room to loom in like an ugly vulture. The guy's in his fifties with salt-and-pepper hair and scowls like he's paid to. But we both know what he's really paid for. Inside that coat he's got a dozen ways to kill a man—and that's without counting the guns.

"Get up." Dire nudges my foot with his own. "There's something you need to see."

I don't move. "You can't just show me on a compad?"

"No." His tone is flat, not to be argued with. "I have two witnesses you need to talk to."

So that's who he was calling. "Witnesses to what?"

"The Synthetic contacted us." I bolt upright. Dire's face is a closed book despite the significant news. "She left us a message, and we need to respond."

It takes me no time at all to answer. With things finally turning in my favor, I'm out of the bed and striding for the door. "Let's go."

CHAPTER 4

LUCE

FLAGGED: The sky is captured in heavy streaks of white and gray, calling forth the image of an oncoming storm. An untamed ocean crashes against the rocky shore, reaching up the stones like greedy fingers. A single figure, completely in shadow, scrambles toward a small opening in the rocks. The viewer is left with the impression that it is the darkness, not the ocean, that brings the woman comfort. POSSIBLE LOCATION OF INTEREST?

Description of *The Sea Cave*, painting by Lucinia sol Lucius

I wait until the peacekeeper turns down Clerk-Maxwell Street and starts his slow meander through the neighborhood of the same name before I clutch my bag closer to my chest and leave the shadowed alley. We have twenty minutes before he returns, so we have to move quickly. Isa is behind me, Shad behind her, and following him are a handful of other Keres members I don't know beyond their faces. We move in a line until we reach our target: a squat, blocky building butted up next to one taller by half. Despite the height difference, down here on the bottommost layer of Cytherea, the construction is identical, sharp shapes in neutral grays, reflective windows in thin strips. There's nothing beautiful about the headquarters of the Maintenance Guild.

Shad gestures to one of the guys, and the boy, not even old enough to need geneassisting for his facial hair, pulls off his backpack and fishes out a collapsible ladder. He sets it against the base of the building and presses a button; the ladder snaps securely to the stony surface and extends until it reaches the roof. I'm surprised when Shad gestures for Isa to go first, but then his eyes find mine, hand absently fiddling with the point of his beard, and I know I'm next. As soon as Isa's far enough up, I grab the rungs and start climbing, the ladder as secure as if it'd been built onto the side of the building.

With my heart beating so hard I feel it in my hands, I reach the roof and survey the space. Other than the wiring and one skylight we'll have to avoid, it's flat. There's a square shack in the corner, containing either access to stairs or some kind of maintenance supplies. I don't spot any cameras, but that doesn't mean they're not here.

I crouch behind a humming generator next to Isa, her rose-gold hair hidden beneath a black scarf, same as my recognizable purple. She winks at me, and I cross my eyes and stick out my tongue. She smiles like she's holding back a laugh. We used to egg each other on during classes at the Cytherean College of Art and Design, twisting expressions like cartoon characters as our professors critiqued our work. Our instructors said they were teaching us how to accept criticism by being so harsh, but all it taught Isa and me was how to make silly faces without getting caught.

It's because of Isa that I'm here tonight. The Keres Art Collective doesn't accept just anyone, but she knew Shad, an upperclassman who graduated three years before us, and arranged for us to meet at a café. I was invited to join the collective later that evening. That was two months ago, and I'm still not sure how I feel about Shad. Despite how Isa talks like he put all the colors in the rainbow, he was rude to me at first, either cutting me off or ignoring me. He didn't even seem impressed by my portfolio. It wasn't until he heard my name—sol Lucius, with its inferior nobiliary particle—that I seemed to interest him at all.

Now it's different; as the rest of the Keres group reaches the roof, they float toward me as if pulled by magnetism. Thanks to Lito, I've become something of a minor celebrity among them.

Until yesterday morning, the news only talked about the miraculously returned duelists carrying a message of peace from the Geans. Then came the break-in at Val Akira Labs. Reports of the Gean-Icarii cease-fire disappeared. Forgotten was the possible peace treaty. In its place was my brother's face on every stream and feed.

Shad is the last up the ladder. After checking the roof, he kneels next to me. "Spread out along the face of Building B," he says, pointing to the taller construction at the back of the building we stand on. "Do the work just like we talked about it. No surprises." He casts a quick glance at his wrist, where he wears an antique watch he likes to flash. It projects the time in a blue holograph above its thin black band. "We have eighteen minutes. Go."

Like duelists, we split up into pairs and spread out along the face of the second building. Isa is my partner, of course, and we've practiced the design until we've gotten the timing down to fifteen minutes. But now that we're doing it for real, my heart is pounding with adrenaline. I force myself to take a deep breath in and release it slowly; anxiety makes for shaky hands, and we don't have any room for error.

"Time to get to work, Luce," I tell myself.

Isa sets up our stools as I unzip my bag. Inside is my entire collection of airpens in a variety of colors. I grab the white first to lay down a base over the smooth stone of the building, while Isa selects a yellow since the background of the painting will be the sickly sky of Venus, not the lie of the dome around us. Almost as soon as the airpen is in my hand, my heart steadies; I fall into the familiar rhythm of painting.

The airpen mists swaths of the wall a blank white, and as soon as I finish, Isa steps into my place with her yellow to paint atmospheric clouds. I select an orange and follow along with her, shaping a planet most Icarii never see. After the background is done, we choose some blues—this time she's the base and I'm the shadows—and begin the figure of the woman who is the calling card of the Keres Art Collective.

As she begins to take shape, I wonder if Shad intentionally designed her to look both Icarii and Aster. Even in college, Shad's work focused on the poor treatment of lowlevels, Asters included. But as we move from the figure's slender body to her outstretched gray wings, she loses any resemblance she had to humanity. With a shadow there, her mouth gapes a little too wide, her teeth jut a little too sharp. With a highlight there, her fingers end in ragged claws.

"Eight minutes left," Isa says, but I'm feeling good about our time. And the Keres is *looking* good, even if the design Shad chose for Isa and me isn't one I would've picked. But after assignments went out, Isa made it clear she didn't want to argue with him.

"If we impress him with this, we'll get to do other things," she explained, and since I love Isa, I bit my tongue. I didn't want to tell her the real reason we got stuck painting the Keres was because I refused to paint Lito.

Lito, the Icarii traitor.

Every Icarii from Spero to Cytherea has seen the news—and we all know what the stories say. Lito sol Lucius, radicalized by an Aster terrorist cell, broke into Val Akira Labs on Mercury to steal sensitive Icarii data. And as everyone I knew at work, from my manager to the interns, began to look at me with suspicion, the members of Keres built me into someone one step away from greatness.

"Your brother is the symbol we need," Shad told me last night as he planned the strike against the Maintenance Guild on lowlevel Cytherea. He'd brought up my online portfolio from CCAD on his compad and was flipping through various paintings I'd done of Lito for classes. I was more shocked he remembered my work at all than that he was talking about Lito—*everyone* was talking about Lito at that point. "He speaks for true Icarii freedom. His is the path Keres should follow."

I was too angry to point out that Lito didn't *say* anything, that his path was unknowable to anyone but him. The news could say whatever it wanted; that didn't make it true. And while I could absolutely see

Lito getting caught up in something crazy because of Hiro—my brother had always been willing to follow Hiro through the thousand hells—I doubted he was targeting the average Cytherean citizen. Besides, how was Lito's break-in at the labs tied to justice for the lowlevel people of Cytherea? Wasn't that Keres's mission statement? I asked Shad, but he didn't seem to care. "Just think about painting Lito for us," he said, waving my concerns away. I agreed, if only to get him off my back.

When we met up earlier tonight, Shad didn't mention Lito again. I guess he'd found something else to occupy his short attention span.

"Three minutes left," Isa says, tenser than before, but as I finish the last white streak of the Keres woman's hair, I step back to survey the whole painting and realize—we're finished. All things considered, she looks good. Maybe even better than she does when other Keres artists paint her. Though . . . it probably helps that Isa and I aren't painting her to look sexy like some of the guys do.

Movement above catches my eye. I freeze, breath caught in my throat. On the top of Building B, a figure prowls. A peacekeeper?

But just when I'm about to shout, the cry fizzles out. The fluid way the person moves doesn't scream *security* to me. Another artist, then? Besides, what security wears a hooded jacket to hide their face? The figure puts a leg on the lip of the building and leans over. I feel like they're looking directly at me. *Watching* me.

"Isa . . ."

"What?" Isa steps to my side and follows my gaze. She doesn't seem nearly as startled as I am. "Probably just a fucking junkie, Luce."

The words sting unexpectedly. It's easy to forget Isa's surname has a *val* attached to it, that I'm the only one here who actually came from this level.

"Come on, Luce, we have to go," Isa says, calling me back to the roof. She's tossed all the airpens into my bag and is zipping it up. Right. She's totally right, especially if someone is up there and has called security on us. I grab my bag, pull the strap over my head, and start toward the others.

They're finishing paintings of their own, recalling their personal drones, and putting away paints and tools. The word CROOKED blazes in red letters, dripping like blood. Another duo has painted three sets of lungs stacked on top of each other. The top set is clean, the middle slightly faded, and the lungs on the bottom are withered and brown. CLEAN AIR IS A RIGHT is painted above it in the stiff typeface of a personal drone.

"Isn't that yours?" I ask Isa, but she doesn't meet my eyes. She shrugs like she doesn't know or like it doesn't matter, but I know Isa's designs like I know my own. Why didn't Shad have her work on that when she was the original artist?

"All done?" Shad asks with a smile when we approach him and his partner. His fingers are stained with ink, signs of his guilt. Mine are too, now that I think to look. But all of that is forgotten when I see Shad's painting.

Blue-black hair like a crow's feathers. Dark eyes reflecting the clouds of the Cytherean dome. His face in profile, showing off the same prominent nose that I have. A painting so much like *my* painting, but wrong—so much of it *wrong*—that my anger bubbles up hot and fast.

"What the fuck, Shad?" There's no moderation to my voice. The entire group spins in our direction, faces paling. But I don't care. Let them look. He stole my art. He plagiarized my painting. He took my brother's *face*—

"Your brother now belongs to the people, Lucinia," Shad says, cold and distant. "He is a symbol for so much."

"But that's *my* painting," I say, and I know he knows what I'm talking about. It's one of the best pieces in my CCAD portfolio. "His face isn't even *right*—"

"We can talk about this when we're not trespassing on the roof of a building right next to our illegal artwork," he grinds out. To the others, he gestures toward the ladder. "Let's get out of here."

I unzip my bag of airpens. I'm reaching for a soft brown when Isa's hand shoots out to grab mine. "Luce, what are you doing?"

"Fixing this fucking mess," I say, pointing with my chin at the image of Lito.

"Are you serious?" She looks like I slapped her.

"It's not right. It doesn't look anything like my brother. His cheekbones—those aren't his cheekbones. And his jawline—"

"Leave her, Isa!" Shad calls. "If she's going to be a stubborn bitch, let her get caught."

It's only now that I remember the figure on the roof above us and realize how loud our shouting has become. But it doesn't matter. If they've called the peacekeepers, they're already on their way. I'll just have to work faster. I can't leave Lito looking like this.

"If we go and you stay, how're you going to get down?" Isa asks.

"Leave the ladder," I say.

Shad scoffs. "You'll just lose it when you get arrested."

"Then I'll buy you a new one," I snarl.

Shad quirks a brow. The ladders aren't cheap, and while he has money—his *parents* have money—I have a job that earns me an annual salary that makes ends meet.

"I'll buy you two, then! I don't fucking care." I have no idea how I'll make good on this promise, but it doesn't matter right now.

"Whatever." That seems to convince him. "Isa, let's go." He follows after the other members to leave.

For a moment, I look at Isa and think she'll stay to help me. We're a pair, after all, two artists working in sync. And if anyone understands what it feels like to see Shad co-opting her artwork, it'd be her. But then, at last, she releases my hand and backs away. "Please call me later to let me know you're safe," she says, and I murmur some sort of assent, knowing it's a lie.

I don't look back at her as she leaves.

I grab several colors at once, shadows and highlights for Lito's skin, then set to work. I try to focus on what's in front of me, on putting down one line at a time, instead of the racing of my heart. My compad vibrates in my jacket, but I ignore it. I don't want to know how much time has passed. I sharpen his jaw. I lift his cheekbones. I add the hook to his nose that Shad ignored in favor of making him pretty. If my brother is going to be on this building, I want him to be *Lito*, not some idealized version of him.

I take a step back to check my progress. Lito's profile takes up two square meters of space, big enough that, without a stool, I can't reach the top. But now it's beginning to look more like my original painting. Though Lito's face is upturned, most is in shadow, only the curve of his nose and the downturn of his lips highlighted from the background of a Venusian sunset in yellow, orange, and purple. Rising from his head is a crown of gold. As soon as the dome wakes and light hits the gold, it will glow, alive and warm. It just needs a little thickening of his brows—

I hear a whistle above me and look up. It's the figure in the hooded jacket again, still watching me. I want to shout at them to fuck off and leave me alone, but I see their hand come up and point at something. I follow it to the little shack in the corner of the building, the one that probably holds maintenance equipment.

The door opens.

Shit. Not maintenance equipment. Stairs to the building below.

"¡Oye tú! ¡Estate quieta!" someone shouts as a light hits me and Lito, almost blinding as the gold paint flares. "Stop right there!"

I snatch up my bag. A couple of airpens slip out, but I don't have time to stop and grab them. I run as fast as my legs will carry me across the roof and swing myself onto the ladder. I slip on a rung, cling with my hands, and skid down. The ground comes up fast, and I land on my ankle wrong and stumble. The skin of my hands is scraped clean off.

Though it stings enough to bring tears to my eyes, I lean down and press a button to release the ladder. But the ladder doesn't move, and when I look up, I see why. The man from the roof—a peacekeeper, my com-lenses note—is already coming down after me.

Forget the ladder, then. I take off at a run, darting out of the alley and across the street, my ankle shooting hot fire up my leg with every step. In the alley we had hidden in before, I hoist myself over a fence and ignore the pain shooting white stars across my vision.

A quick look over my shoulder tells me the peacekeeper is following, so I consider my options as to where I can lie low. What's still open at this time of night? Restaurants? Too few people to blend in. A nightclub? Perfect.

I leave the alley as the peacekeeper hits the fence and starts to scramble over. If it weren't for my ankle, I'd be able to outrun him easily with my longer legs, but I have to settle for taking what ground I can. I'm going to hurt tomorrow, I know; I'm making my ankle worse with every step I take, but it's better than being arrested.

I can't be arrested. I *can't* be. I have a promising job as an artist at Val Akira Geneassists. I love my apartment. And after working on my relationship with my parents, I can safely say it's been smooth sailing for at least a month. Well, three weeks, but I am optimistic. Getting arrested will ruin all that. My parents would be so furious, I'd become like Lito to them, a disappointing child with a rotten end. I'd lose my apartment on the upper level of Cytherea. I'd get fired and prove to all my coworkers that they were right to suspect me simply because Lito is my brother.

Maybe you should've thought about that before you were willing to throw everything away for a painting of Lito, my logical mind hisses.

I run another three blocks before rounding a corner onto Avenida Ramón y Cajal. As soon as I'm out of sight of the pursuing officer, I strip off my jacket, shove it into my bag, and toss the whole thing into a dumpster, airpens and all. I can't worry about my things right now; I'll have to come back for them later . . .

I know there's a discoteca at the end of this street, the wild music reaching me even here. A sweaty girl in streetwear won't look suspicious there, so I hurry down the adjoining alleyway, paint-streaked and bleeding hands shoved in my pockets, adjusting my stride so that I'm just a young adult eager for a party. My breath is coming in heaving gasps. The air is so thin down here. It takes all my willpower to slow my breathing.

I hear heavy footsteps behind me. The sound of something metal, and then a click. Something odd. Something dangerous. And though I shouldn't turn back, though it makes me look guilty, I can't help it— curiosity seizes my limbs and turns my head and—

"Put your hands up!" the peacekeeper yells, pointing a HEL gun at me.

"Shit!" My heart beats hard in my throat.

Thousand gods, please don't kill me—

"You're under arrest—"

Movement above me. A shadow falls.

I clap my hands over my mouth as something lands on the peacekeeper—no, some*one*. The officer goes down, HEL gun skidding to land at the toes of my boots. The figure in the black coat—it's the same one from the Maintenance Guild building—reaches down and presses something over the peacekeeper's mouth, and then he stops struggling.

My jaw works, chewing on question after question, *Is he dead?* first among them. But then the figure stands straight—taller than me—and pulls back the hood of their jacket, and I'm greeted with a purple-tinted face and half-curled lips and shimmering golden eyes like a Venusian sunset.

An Aster. An Aster *saving* me, and I'm too stunned to say anything, to *do* anything, other than stare.

"Hi," the Aster says, pointed teeth peeking out from a wide mouth, "I'm Castor." A finger indicates the guy on the ground. "He's not the only peacekeeper around here." Then a gesture back the way I came. "And we should go."

Stunned, I sputter for a second before finding my voice. "'We'?" I repeat.

The Aster shrugs. "Unless you're *not* interested in a message from your brother."

Lito, part of an Aster terrorist cell, or so said the news. I never thought it could be true, but now . . .

Swallowing my fear, I run to catch up to the Aster. "This way."

THERE'S A SMALL part of me that remembers Isa's request to call her when I got home safe—*if* I got home safe. Then there's a much larger part drowning in questions, like did the peacekeeper see my face? Am

I a wanted figure across Cytherea? Is security on their way to my home even now? But all of that is overwhelmed by the simple sight of an Aster in my apartment.

My apartment, because I wasn't about to follow a stranger to a place I wasn't comfortable. And I want that message from Lito—no denying that.

We talked little on our way back—simple introductions; Castor said it wasn't safe to explain things out in the open—but when he opens his mouth to say something, I press my paint-stained fingers over his lips and bite back a hiss at the sting of my tattered palm. I'm accustomed to being one of the tallest people in the room, but he makes me feel small and compact in a way I never have before. He says nothing when I drop my hand, and I wrestle my compad out of my jacket and swipe a quick message I don't send.

Apt could be bugged, I write, turning the screen to him when I'm finished.

"Doesn't matter." He pulls a little silver device from his pocket and waggles it. I have no idea what it is but instantly relax at the assurance that we're safe speaking here.

"Since the thing with"—safe or not, I still can't say my brother's name—"the labs, I've noticed someone tailing me to and from work. Not sure how in-depth they're watching me."

His sharp teeth make another appearance in a half smile. "You have a tail, and you still went out to paint with your friends?"

I shrug, trying not to let his words embarrass me. "I know how to lose people moving between levels. I know the bottom level of Cytherea better than most."

"Still needed my help tonight," he says. Of course he won't let that slide. I would've been fine if my ankle hadn't been twisted. He checks a compad of his own. "You can relax about that, by the way. Looks like they didn't identify you or your friends. The all-ports warning is vague, looking for two individuals without many details."

I want to ask him how he could possibly have access to that data—

want to demand Lito's message—but now that I'm home, my wounds pick away at my attention. "I'll be back in a second," I tell him, then excuse myself. The kitchen is off to the right, my bedroom at the end of the hallway, but I head for the bathroom on the left, wash my hands of paint and dirt, and, ignoring the sting, grab a first aid kit from beneath the sink. When I return, Castor is looking over my makeshift studio in the corner, the holoprojector with network access shoved aside and forgotten.

I try to experience my apartment the way an outsider would, the sharp smell of turpentine in the air, a freshly stretched canvas on my easel, my brushes resting in recycled cans like tiny flags claiming this space as *mine, mine, mine.* He looks at the rough sketch on the canvas—a planned landscape—before turning to the desk and the supplies I use to make my own paint—powders, shells, and various dried flowers. His eyes light up as he spots my finished paintings leaned against the wall.

He is sure of himself as he moves through my apartment, past spaces Lito and Hiro shared. The shabbiness of my living room falls away—the battered couch, the faded carpet, the walls I slapped a coat of lavender paint on when I moved in—until there is only him.

He picks up a painting of Lito—*the* painting of Lito with his crown of gold—and smiles at it. "The original," he says. "That idiot's painting didn't look anything like Lito."

His words bring back the bitterness I felt earlier tonight. Fucking Shad, stealing my art, using my brother's face for his own gain. And fucking it up, adding insult to injury. But the thought also helps to center me. I should ask Castor for my brother's message now, but I'm halfway scared of what it'll say. How much of what the news said about Lito is true? How well—or how poorly—did I really know my brother?

Instead, I sit on the couch, gingerly pull off my boot, and dig out a theracast from the first aid kit. My ankle is fat with swelling, but whether it's broken or sprained, the theracast will fix it.

"Let me help." Castor's at my side in an instant, kneeling before me like a duelist offering the use of his blade. He takes the theracast packaging from me, opens it with his teeth, and pulls out the soft binding. I suck in a little gasp of surprise when his hands—long-fingered, callused but elegant—lift my foot and begin to wrap my ankle. The theracast is cold, but his touch is warm.

I lean into the silence, my face burning at the strangeness of it all. I've never seen an Aster without their wraps and goggles, not in person anyway, and I've never seen an Aster like him. His hair is white, like all Asters', but not long enough to be plaited; though it's tied at the nape of his neck, much of it has fallen loose and frames his face. His skin has the softest hint of purple, darkening in places like his lips and beneath his eyes. And while his eyes are large, they're not the swallowing black I thought they'd be, but slitted pupils surrounded by molten gold.

Castor catches me staring at him and smirks. I forcefully look away, focusing on my hands. "You don't need goggles?" I ask, hoping the question isn't offensive as I hit my palms with a dose of pelospray. The burn is even worse than when I washed them, and I bite my lip against the pain as Castor answers.

"Geneassist modification." He looks at my face instead of my ankle as if to prove a point. "I needed to be able to reliably work in Icarii lighting." The theracast starts to harden, and Castor moves to sit on the opposite end of the couch.

Now that the moment has come, I want to ask about anything other than Lito. "How long have you been following me?" I ask. Maybe he's the tail I've been glimpsing since yesterday afternoon.

"Just tonight."

"Before or after I met up with Keres?"

He scoffs. "I have no fucking interest in Keres, if that's what you're thinking. Those kids are too busy jerking each oth—" He clears his throat at my glare. "Too busy playing in the sandbox to do anything useful."

I swallow the insult, and it bubbles in my stomach like poison. I'm one of Keres too. Though after tonight, after what Shad did and how I was almost arrested, I'm not sure I want to be.

"You're well-connected," I say. "You have someone backing you." I gesture to his pocket and the silver device there, trying to think of how to ask him about who he works for in a way he'll answer.

But before I can, he quirks an eyebrow at me. "Is there a reason you're asking about everything *other* than Lito?"

I freeze just like I did when I spotted the peacekeeper's HEL gun. What if Castor gives me Lito's message, and I find out he really *has* been radicalized by terrorists? What if my parents and coworkers are *right* about all the terrible things they accuse Lito of?

I'm scared—no halfway about it.

In the silence, Castor offers me his compad. I take it from him, fingers lingering a bit too long. Then I see the first line on the screen.

Luce, it begins. Already I feel like I've been slapped.

I turn my body away from Castor, not wanting him to see the tears in my eyes as I read.

Luce,

I'm sorry. I love you. I found our old friend the nine-tailed fox, and heard a thousand stories that are truer than myths. I don't know what they will tell you, so I want you to hear it from me: I chose this, because it is what I believe is right. I can no longer ignore what is happening every day in Cytherea and Spero, on the planets of Earth and Mars. Please be cautious in your new job for Val Akira Labs. Souji val Akira will do whatever he can to control you and, by extension, me. If you can, run. If you can't . . . or you don't want to . . . disavow me. Tell them everything you know, even show them this message if you have to. And be careful.

One day when there is peace, I hope our paths cross again.

All my love,
Lito

I read it once, then again. Read it one more time for good measure, then hold the compad to my chest.

He's still the Lito I know. The brother I love. He's fighting for goodness. My parents and coworkers are wrong.

Reality slowly leaks back in. Not caring if Castor sees the naked relief in my eyes, I turn back toward him.

"You're working with Lito?"

His eyes burn with something like offense. "Lito works with us."

Semantics, but I don't argue. "Who's 'us'?"

"Asters. People who want the Icarii to play fairly." Castor cocks his head, watching me intently when he says the next name. "Hiro."

"Hiro val Akira is part of your"—I hesitate, not knowing what to call it—"group?" I shouldn't be surprised. When my brother told me of his mission to hunt down and kill his former partner, I knew he wouldn't have trouble finding Hiro. But killing them? I feared it was far more likely that Hiro would kill Lito—or convince him to join their cause. Perhaps that's why I mourned Lito leaving Cytherea; a part of me knew it was the end of the lives we'd built on the top level.

"That's not all, though. I didn't come all this way just to deliver a message."

"What, then?"

His pupils widen as he focuses on my face. "We need your help, Luce."

A tremor runs through my hands. "Don't call me that," I say softly. "Only Lito calls me that . . ."

"Lucinia sol Lucius." He says my name like he's tasting it. "Would you prefer 'Lulu'?"

I roll my eyes. "Only if you go by 'Castor the Aster.'"

He snorts. "Fair enough."

"What do you want from me?" I gesture to my apartment to remind him of who I am—an artist, not a duelist like Lito.

"We want certain files from Val Akira Labs, data Lito tried, but failed, to get."

"The news said he stole confidential information—"

"Not true," he snaps. "They're fucking liars when it comes to this stuff."

"You know I'm a first-tier artist at Val Akira Geneassists, right? It's just a subsidiary of the labs. I'm not a scientist. I'm not trusted. I'm sure you've read Lito's letter—you know I'm being watched."

"Yes, but you're also in the perfect position to watch them back." His golden eyes burn with a righteous anger, smoldering coals in the heart of a fire.

I sigh. It's obvious he won't be put off by me or the lack of status at my job. "What information are you looking for?"

"Proof that Souji val Akira is a hypocrite, a liar, and a mass murderer. Evidence that will take down Val Akira Labs when released to the public." He straightens as he speaks. Even sitting, he towers over me. "We know the AEGIS isn't bothered by the slaughter of a few thousand Asters, but the people of Cytherea can *force* them to care."

"Is that all?" I ask, trying not to let on how overwhelming the request is. Attempting to control the Agency for Ethical Guidance of Icarii Science sounds impossible.

"We also hope to recover some Aster research confiscated by Val Akira Labs," he says, either missing my sarcasm or outright ignoring it. "We'd made strides into gene research that could help our people afflicted by experiments and other diseases, but Souji val Akira labeled the information dangerous and sealed it away."

"Oh, so you want me to personally take on Souji val Akira? No problem," I say with a heavy shrug. "Let me make a few calls. I'll have it done by Tuesday."

He glares at me. "Maybe you don't understand just how bad things are for us. Maybe you're like those art school jackoffs who pay lip service to a war they don't have the spines to fight."

Guilt and anger battle inside me, the words hitting far too close to home. When the peacekeeper was after me, all I could think of was the things I'd lose—my nice apartment, my good job, my parents' respect. I didn't spare a thought for why I was down there painting in the first place.

"I'm from the lowest level of Cytherea," I say, letting the heat color my tone in response to his. "Why do you think we targeted the Maintenance Guild down there? I've seen the way you can slip credits to the right official and jump the line for home repairs. I've seen the neglect of the air filters compared to the higher levels, felt that tightness when breathing."

"But some things you've only seen, not felt," he says. "Like the Asters on that level, bandages yellow with weeping sores, sleeping on streets until peacekeepers make them disappear." His lips twist. "You can't know the pain of that."

My first response is offense, but I smother it, letting out a shuddering breath. "At least I don't avert my eyes like other Icarii. Maybe that's all I can do."

"You can do more. You can help us now," he says, denying me even the slightest comfort. "You want to help the Asters and the lowlevels, then help me. You say that you see the problem—then look at my request as a solution."

I'm struck silent. The worst part is that he's right. I thought I was helping, thought I could make a change by spray-painting slogans on buildings, but I've been—what did Castor say?—playing in a sandbox.

"I'm not Lito," I say for what feels like the hundredth time. "I'm not a duelist."

"And my sister isn't me," Castor says, "but we both do what we can."

The moment stretches. Faint footfalls and muted voices from adjacent apartments break the monotonous electronic hum of devices and appliances. I let out a long, shuddering sigh.

"How can I help?"

Castor's smile is wide and bright like day breaking across his face. "All Val Akira companies, whether subsidiary or parent, use the same servers." He pulls something small and black out of his pocket, a naildrive balanced between his thumb and forefinger. "Plug this into a computer at work. It'll break into the server and get the information we need."

"I don't know," I say, and my face burns with shame. My apartment, my job, my family—they're all still haunting me. It's hard to give up things you've always wanted and have finally gotten.

"You will." He says it like he says everything else: Confidently. Stubbornly. Almost like he can will me into acceptance with his naked belief. "The compad I gave you with Lito's message? Keep it. You can contact me through it. Don't say anything you wouldn't want your enemy reading, so use a code." He rattles off the list like I've already agreed to his terms.

"And if I don't want to contact you?" I snap.

He touches the compad, our fingers brushing once more. The heat isn't just in his voice, it's in his body, and I am warmed against the night's chill.

"There are recordings on this compad." He says it softly, as if there is something even he fears. "Hiro's recordings they made for Lito."

His words jerk me through time. Back to the morning of Lito's departure from Cytherea with his new partner to hunt down his old one. I'd opened my door to find an unfamiliar package on my doorstep. There'd been no warning, no drones alerting me to a mail drop, but the box was there all the same. I'd opened it and found an out-of-date pink playback device, and though curiosity got the better of me and I'd started to listen, Hiro's voice—*"Fucking gods, I've started this recording over a hundred times now"*—had me yanking the device off and shutting it away again.

It was for Lito. I knew it was. And I knew I wanted nothing to do with it.

But as the weeks wore on and Lito didn't come home, I knew I'd made a mistake. What had Hiro said? Where had they gone? The device could have offered answers I would otherwise never have.

And now they're back in my hand.

By the time my shock fades, Castor's at the door. "Later," he says, as if my helping him is a foregone conclusion, and then he's gone and my apartment is exactly the same as it was before this disastrous night.

I should take a shower. Go to bed. I have work in the morning. But the compad in my hand sings me a siren song, and my fingers dance across the screen until I find the saved recordings.

I press play.

CHAPTER 5

LITO

Asset #4757828 "SORREL": Aster male, 215 cm, 95 kg. Clearance requirement: BLACK. Known aliases: HARBINGER, THE. Special notes: DO NOT, UNDER ANY CIRCUMSTANCES, WAKE SUBJECT WITHOUT ASSET #5403210 "OFIERA," OR THE PRESENCE OF A MINIMUM OF TWO SECURITY TEAMS.

Assessment of Asset #4757828 in Val Akira Labs computers

There's no time to waste. The longer it takes to get out of the labs, the more security will come down on us. With no weapons and Elm's hacked compad as our only means of defense, we are rapidly running out of options. Ofiera brings up a map of the facility, memorizes a route to the docks, and guides us out of cryo storage and into the unending white hallways.

Not one corridor over, the heavy stomp of boots halts our progress. I quickly press the compad to the nearest door's bioscanner and lead Ofiera into a darkened side room, what looks like a tiered lecture hall devoid of furniture. We wait until the sound fades, security rushing past us to the cryo storage we were in moments ago, before we emerge and continue our escape.

When we reach a crossroads, Ofiera nudges me through the implant, telling me which way to go. It becomes clear after the third turn that the route we're taking is indirect in the hopes that we'll run into less security. But it also keeps us in the labs longer, which only serves to increase my worry about how many guns will be waiting for us at the docks.

A faint voice reaches us from around a corner—"the sweep"— muffled words I can't make out—"continuing route."

I press the compad to the nearest door, hoping to repeat our previous strategy, but the bioscanner turns red with a warning message: UNAUTHORIZED.

Shit—obviously whoever's ID Elm spoofed for this compad doesn't have clearance to go everywhere.

Ofiera pulls my attention through the implant and gestures to the door she crouches by. I toss her the compad. She snatches it out of midair and presses it to the bioscanner by her head. It lights up green. Swiftly she opens the door and disappears inside.

The security guard is turning down our hallway as I roll across the floor. I slip through the doorway just as he hits a switch, flooding the corridor in pale fluorescence.

There's no sound of him alerting his comrades, no sound of boots running in our direction. I don't think he saw us, but . . . the door is still ajar. He'd be blind not to notice that. I look at the room we've trapped ourselves in. It's little more than a supply closet, full of the shadowy forms of cleaning drones. Though they vary in size, their bodies have been tightly packed together, leaving nowhere for us to properly hide.

I look at Ofiera, and she at me. I can tell through the implant that we're both thinking the same thing: if there's no chance at flight, we have to fight.

With what? the part of me that's a soldier snaps.

With what we have is the only answer.

I track the guard by the light tap of his boots. Every second he comes closer to where Ofiera and I hide. He stops just outside the door. He has to be suspicious, but does he know that we're inside? I hear a metallic click, and I know immediately what it is: he's turned off his gun's safety.

Now! I send to Ofiera.

She kicks the door with all her might, and it slams into the man on the other side. He stumbles back, righting his gun—a heavy HEL rifle that could blast us into pieces—but I'm out of the closet by then, a meter-long cleaning droid held above my head. I slam the droid against his hands; the machine shatters, and he drops the rifle. He dives for it without a second thought, but I do as well.

Then Ofiera is on him, one knee in his back, his neck in the crook of her elbow. His fingers scrabble for his gun, but I pull it out of his reach. He struggles, trying to headbutt Ofiera or kick backward, but she holds tightly until, eventually, his movements soften and then stop altogether. With a grunt, she releases him once he's unconscious.

Now in the silence, I hear a voice coming from the compad on his belt. "Report, Kristoff." I look at Ofiera, my guts sinking. "Kristoff?"

"Let's move," she says out loud. No point in being silent after the noise of our fight.

But I hesitate, looking between the HEL rifle I hold and the guard.

"What are you . . ." She trails off, but I know what she's thinking: the gun is of no use to us when all Icarii weapons have a fingerprint lock.

"We need a weapon," I say, not adding that without one, we're not getting out of here.

Her eyebrows shoot up to her hairline when she takes my meaning. Without a word of recrimination, she turns away and searches for something sharp from the destroyed cleaning droid. When she returns, I've already pulled the guard's arm straight and spread his fingers, and she bends over him, the shard of metal gleaming in the hallway lights. She presses the tip of her makeshift shiv to the knuckle of his trigger finger.

"Wait," I say.

"Want the whole thing?" she asks, moving the blade to his wrist.

"No, just . . . I saw a first aid kit in the closet." I slip back into the shadows of our hiding place.

If she thinks I'm being stupid for wanting to cut off a man's finger but not let him bleed to death, she doesn't say. "Well, hurry up. I need you to hold his mouth, because he's going to scream."

I return from the closet with bandages and pelospray. "Right . . ."

Sorry, Kristoff.

THE HEL RIFLE is a heavy comfort in my arms. Kristoff's finger, taped atop mine, isn't.

Along with the sharp metal piece, now wrapped in medical tape, Ofiera carries other supplies from the closet at my insistence. I hope we don't have to use them, but it's better to have them than to need them.

Now that we're armed, we make a straight shot for the docks. We come across a patrolling duo of guards, but after I pop off a few rounds, hitting one in the foot, they retreat, shocked that we have a weapon and calling for backup while we rush on.

We slow when we reach a heavy metal door, different from all the other nondescript white ones. "The loading dock is just through here," Ofiera says in a whisper.

A part of me feels relieved that we've made it this far, but I quickly quash that feeling. This is no time for anything but focus. Who knows how many guards are in position at the docks, waiting for us to step through this door?

We take cover on either side of the doorway. "Ready?" she asks, and when I meet her eyes, I think of all the other times we've been through hell together—stealing the grasshopper from outlaws, finding Hiro, killing the Mother, escaping Ceres pursued by Ironskins. All that's left is for us to make this instance one more link in the chain of our victories.

"Ready," I say without hesitation.

She presses Elm's compad to the bioscanner, and the door opens with a heavy metallic thunk. I peek out from cover, my heart dropping at what I gather from a quick glance.

Six people, all armed and wearing silver-trimmed military blacks, stand between us and our ship. "Peacekeepers," I spit like a curse. That means they'll have shields, which we'll have to wear down if we even want to scratch them.

"They're at loading dock three!" one shouts, undoubtedly connected to other security throughout the premises.

"Open fire!" another cries, and then the air is filled with the sound of burning HEL rifles. The open wall across from us is scorched black from the laser blasts.

We have minutes, at best, to get out of here before other security, perhaps even more peacekeepers, arrive. But every step we take is one closer to our ship, and as I look at Ofiera across the doorway gap, I feel her determination through my implant.

"Hold!" a peacekeeper calls. My ears ring in the silence. A moment later, another order follows. "Advance!"

Now, Ofiera sends through the implant.

I briefly step out of cover, and the guard in front—a tall woman—raises her weapon to shoot. I throw a dusty piece of the cleaning drone in her direction and it hits the ground in a cloud of gray. "Gas grenade!" she screams, terror in her voice—there's nothing a shield can do against something breathable.

"Masks!" another peacekeeper cries as they dive behind boxes labeled with the Val Akira Labs logo.

It's not a grenade, but it's enough to create an opening for Ofiera. By the time the peacekeepers realize I've bullshitted them, Ofiera's inside the range of the point woman's gun, fist bunching in her uniform and knife digging into her shield. Ofiera blocks most of my view of her, locked together as they are, but I take shots at what I can—her leg, her shoulder—running down her shield while keeping my cover.

The other peacekeepers hesitate, unable to get a clean shot at Ofiera. When the woman's shield finally flickers and dies, Ofiera's makeshift knife slices through the tendons on the back of her hand. With a scream, she drops her rifle in what feels like slow motion.

For a moment, we have a clear shot across the docks. Then one of the peacekeepers bellows, "Rush her!"

"Don't!" the woman responds, Ofiera's knife at her neck a strong deterrent. The peacekeepers hold position, torn between commands, but I'm not about to give them time to figure it out.

I step through the doorway and lay down suppressive fire, shields rippling with each hit. *Go*, I send Ofiera, and she hauls the woman over her shoulder and pushes toward the open cargo bay of our ship. Together, we run.

"Fire!" one of the peacekeepers screams. The air fills with heat and sound, and though I shoot back wildly as I serpentine, my focus is my movement.

Ofiera reaches the ramp and tosses the peacekeeper aside before rushing into the cargo bay. I hurry after her. As I approach the doorway, something heavy slams me sideways. My leg burns like it's been set ablaze. I do my best to ignore it as I fire off another round, limping backward up the ramp.

As soon as I'm through the door, Ofiera punches a nearby button, and the bay slams closed. I ease myself to the deck, my scar from the Fall of Ceres aching in my memory. Just above my knee, my inner thigh is scorched from a laser blast.

"No!" A scream reaches us over the livecam. I watch the peacekeepers amassing, very few focusing on their fallen comrade. One's face contorts with rage and despair. Anger at losing us. Fear at what Souji val Akira will do to him now that we've slipped through his fingers.

Ofiera kneels to check my wound, but it's her appearance that shocks me. She's covered in blood.

"Ofiera—"

I run my hands over her but find nothing. No holes in her clothing, no wounds. Then I realize . . . the blood isn't hers.

"They shot the peacekeeper," Ofiera says, tossing her makeshift knife aside. My stomach twists. How badly did they want to capture us to shoot one of their own?

Ofiera pulls out the pelospray we brought with us and hits my leg with a blast. I suck my teeth at the way it stings. "How bad is it?" I manage.

"It just grazed you." She smirks. "Don't be a baby."

Job done, Ofiera moves deeper into the cargo bay. I give myself a few additional seconds, allowing the pelospray to seal my wound, before I push myself to my feet and follow her.

I find her leaning over the cryo pod. Her face is inches from his, separated only by the sweating glass. How familiar this must feel to her, after all the years of only being able to see each other this way.

I don't have the heart to call her away from him. Besides, it doesn't take two of us to launch the ship.

I leave her alone and head to the command center.

AFTER WE LAUNCH from the docks, I set a course for an automated gate that will pass us through the hermium barrier so we can leave Mercury. Compared to our last ship, retrofitted in order to smuggle medicine from Val Akira Labs, this thing is a hunk of junk. Sure, the grasshopper's layout is more or less the same, but this one looks like it hasn't been cleaned in the last century, and a sharp smell like old cheese permeates everything.

I dump myself into a command chair and check my leg. The pain lingers, but Ofiera was right—it was just a graze, and the pelospray has done its work. The wound looks more like a burn than the remnants of a laser blast. With nothing left to do, I turn to the screens. On one monitor, a program of Hemlock's runs to spoof a proper gate code for us that I can only hope will hold up. On the others, Spero passes beneath us.

Compared to the great city that is Cytherea, Spero is a sleepy town, its traditional graystone buildings blocky and low. The streets are cobbled with the same material, broken up by rolling fields of green and thick clusters of trees. A fat river lazily winds through the center, propelling boats beneath stately arched bridges.

It's come a long way from what it used to be. Mercury was seeded out of necessity when peaceful scientists left Mars during the Dead Century War in hopes of creating a utopia, and while it remains a planet dedicated to industry and knowledge, it has become one that boasts of Icarii prowess. The hermium-powered dome over Spero projects calm blue skies and soft fluffy clouds, making it easy to forget that Mercury is an inhospitable wasteland.

It also works to make me forget that we're being hunted. While it doesn't look like we're being tailed from the basic radar this grasshopper has, there's no doubt in my mind that Command has every available ship in the area out searching for us. I imagine them like a pack of wolves, noses to the ground, teeth bared and sharp. Right now we're barely a step ahead. Stumble, and that's our end.

I try to get some rest, knowing the alarms will wake me if there's an emergency, but for the two hours we travel across Spero, I'm on the edge of my chair with anxiety. Ten minutes out from the gate, Hemlock's program chimes, signaling that it's finished our code. Still no sign of an Icarii ship, but that's about to change. Every gate, automated or not, has security.

I cut on the intercom. "We're approaching," I say, and my voice echoes through the ship back to me. "We should buckle up . . . just in case." Just in case our ID doesn't hold up and we have to burn hard in hopes of somehow escaping.

I settle into one of the empty chairs and strap in. Ofiera enters the command center as I'm getting comfortable. Her eyes are red, but I don't comment on the fact. I'd be crying my eyes out in relief too if my partner had been held hostage for two hundred years and just released.

Our ship slows to a crawl as we approach the gate and join the queue. With a tap to the console in front of my chair, I forward the spoofed code to the basic AI in charge. It issues us a number as we wait our turn.

I focus on my breathing. In and out. In and out. Seconds pass too slowly.

"We're next," Ofiera says.

In and out, in and out . . .

Now that the automated gate is checking our ID, I find all the anxiety I thought I left behind at Val Akira Labs. It all comes down to this.

We pass. The main screen scrolls a farewell message: *We hope you enjoyed your stay in Spero!*

I release a long, shuddering breath as we move through the gate and into the eternity of space. Ofiera pats my hand, and I smile at her.

A button on the command panel lights up. I almost shoot out of my chair, but the straps stop me.

"Someone's hailing us."

"The make of our ship must've been flagged." The fear in Ofiera's voice matches the shadow in my chest.

"Ship number GR9873," a control officer says, reading our spoofed ship number, "hold for secondary check."

I unstrap myself and move to the command panels. I open a return channel to respond. "Copy, tower. Can you clarify secondary check?"

"Hold for boarding."

I look at Ofiera. We both know there's no way we can risk a boarding party.

We have to run.

I close the comm channel, then furiously type in a new command. The ship reacts sluggishly, and for a moment, I fear that something has gone wrong with the engine, but then the entire thing jerks, and we rocket forward.

I barely make it back to my seat before I'm slammed by the pressure. I bite my own tongue and taste blood. I close my eyes for a second before remembering that I need to pay attention to the screens. Though we've already passed through the checkpoint, we need to monitor the other ships around us.

For a heartbeat, the screen is clear, the dots of other ships being left behind. But it's only a heartbeat.

"Lito!" Ofiera cries. "Ship coming up fast!"

"Shit! I see it!" It's not the ship that hailed us, but another is on our tail with ease—security from the checkpoint, no doubt. It's faster than we, in this shoddy little grasshopper, could ever be.

"A *Nyx*-class," Ofiera says softly, and it feels like gravity doubles at her words.

It's an Icarii spy craft. There's nothing else it could be, and there's no way we can outrun it. They're armed while we're not. Our rickety grasshopper will fall apart with the first missile. If they shoot, we're dead, no question.

"They're in range," Ofiera says, and I brace myself for our sudden end—

Only it never comes.

The *Nyx*-class ship appears next to us on the radar. It must be matching our speed, but it hasn't launched a missile. And if it hasn't shot us down, then . . .

"They want us alive." I shove myself out of the chair and leave the command center. Everything within me pushes me back toward the hold.

"Lito, what are you doing?" Ofiera yells after me.

I don't answer, but I'm not surprised to hear her following me. I slide down the ladder, not bothering to take it slowly, and stop only once I'm in front of Sorrel's pod.

"Lito." A hint of a warning comes to me over Ofiera's implant. She's beside me in an instant, hand grabbing mine as I reach out to touch the pod. "Talk to me."

"We have to fight. We can't flee. And if they've matched our speed, they plan on boarding—" The ship rocks as if to prove my point. The *Nyx* has connected to our grasshopper. The sound of rending metal fills the air.

"You can't wake him." Her eyes widen with something unnamed— dread? Fear? "Not yet. Not here."

I fix her with a hard stare.

"You don't understand," she goes on. "When he comes out of cryo—"

"Either he wakes up and fights with us," I say, cutting her off, "or he's collateral in the battle that's coming."

She stops. Releases a deep, slow breath. And though she still looks worried, she releases my hand.

I know she's afraid, but we don't have any other choice.

I slam the emergency evacuation button on Sorrel's cryo pod. With a hiss of steam and the whine of an alarm, the blue sludge inside begins to drain.

CHAPTER 6

ASTRID

Whenever I allow myself to remember Paola, I try to think of the way her hair felt, like silk slipping through my fingers. The smell of her skin, like lavender. But in the end, I only remember her shaking hands, frantically signing as the soldiers backed her toward the hermium barrier at gunpoint. *Trapped*, she signed, her eyes on me. *Trapped.* Even now, that's how I feel.

From the diary of Eden

The preparations for our journey to Mars are made hastily. Aunt Margaret decides the majority of things, consulting me for little. When the name of the vessel that will take us from Ceres is announced, fear, hot and stifling, seizes me at once. I will be returning to Olympus Mons on the very ship that took me away from it: the *Juno*.

Sleep becomes difficult. I easily lose focus on my daily tasks. Even my mornings in the greenhouse do not soothe me. Logically, I know traveling on the *Juno* will not be the same as being assigned to it, but there is a voice in my chest that whispers through the slats of my ribs of times I wish I could forget. I never intended to return there. I don't even want to set foot on board. But as the days pass and the moment to leave comes closer, I resign myself to going, walking side by side with my dread.

THERE IS NO space elevator on Ceres. There is no need for one with the Icarii's hermium-powered barrier technology. The four of us—Aunt Margaret, Lily, Eden, and I—board a dropship on the Ceres docks, slip through the glowing dome, and emerge into the swallowing black of space. I watch the dwarf planet recede on the screens. In our absence, an Aunt assigned by Margaret will oversee the programs I began. I have confidence that she is up to the overwhelming task that is vibrant Ceres. Within minutes, the pilot announces that we are approaching our destination.

The *Juno* waits, a slumbering black beast, its open mouth ready to devour. Our ship, quite roomy despite its model, feels like a gnat compared to such a warship. As the pilot maneuvers us through the bright blue hermium barrier into the hangar, memories assault me. This place is all too familiar.

This is where the amber-eyed girl who was Second Sister—Paola—was punished. Killed because of Sisterhood laws. Thrown into space to asphyxiate and boil alive from the inside out.

This is where I discovered that Arturo had left me behind. Where I learned that no one would save me from the Sisterhood, and that I must save myself.

And the worst thought of all: *This is where I first met Saito Ren.*

The dropship lands. The doors open. I exit first, as befits my station as the First Sister of Ceres.

But as soon as my foot touches the metal floor, my legs grow weak beneath me. Inside, I crumble. Stripped away are my titles, my achievements. Gone is my symbol, the broken manacles. I am reduced to the frightened girl I was when I first came here.

I am nothing. I am no one. And being here reminds me that no matter how far I've come, the Agora can take it all away with a few words.

Eden touches my shoulder. I turn to her, see from her pale freckled face that she feels as I do. We were enemies on this ship, once upon a time; Aunt Marshae pitted us against each other with our looks, our service, our bodies. We almost destroyed each other to spy on Saito Ren, to discover who they really were.

She slips her arm through mine, holds me up as I wobble. I feel faint. Ill. I do not want to be here. But she, at least, is a comfort.

Until we come around the dropship, where all relief fades away. Standing in neatly filed lines are the soldiers I never wanted to see again, clustered as they were all those months ago when Saito Ren led the punishment against Paola. Only now I am on the dais. I stand where Aunt Marshae stood. Where Ren stood.

"Isn't this an honor?" Aunt Margaret says, smiling in that affable way of hers that clashes with her sharp eyes. It is only in her gaze that you can see that this soft flower of a woman is covered in thorns. "They've all gathered here for you, First Sister of Ceres."

I force myself to look at them, at the soldiers waiting expectantly. At their new captain, a man dressed as Ren did in the formal navy-and-gold Gean uniform. And among them, I see one soldier who does not belong, who does not watch me like I am something special. Towering above the others at six and a half feet, with shoulders as wide as the ancient carved doors to the Temple of Mars, Ringer stares at me as he always has: as if I am nothing more than human.

Once I spot him, he is all I can see. He looks no different from when I saw him last—does he ever age or change?—blond hair shaved to his scalp, thick black eyebrows shadowing silver eyes. He stands out among them, the perfect Gean soldier. Only now I know he is not real.

My shaking hand slips into my pocket. The box containing the Mother's implant is there, and I grip it tightly, like a talisman. I remember what I did to get it, what I did to make it this far. *You are not the sniveling girl who was first assigned here*, I tell myself. *You do not need Ringer, and you do not need coddling.*

I extricate myself from Eden, step to the edge of the dais, and smile.

Hold up my hands as if blessing the soldiers. And the captain, a gruff man with thinning red hair, starts the applause, but within seconds, everyone on board is clapping for me.

All save Ringer.

AFTER THE CAPTAIN dismisses the soldiers and they all trail out—Ringer included—only the Sisters remain. There are more of them than I recall, faces I do not recognize from my time here, but the First Sister of the *Juno* is someone I remember well; she had been Third Sister when I was First.

She looks healthy, her dark brown skin glowing, and happy with her big smile. She signs to us with excited, flashing hands, but it is difficult to pay attention to her words when she wears the armband of the captain, a golden oak leaf on a white field with three stars denoting the captain's rank. He has claimed her, that redheaded man twice her age.

She sees me noticing and straightens proudly. *The captain says he loves me*, she signs.

For a moment, I want to hit her, to wipe that sappy look off her face. Does she really believe he loves her, that he feels anything for her other than lust or ownership? Then I realize it is not her I want to hit; I want to hurt the captain. I want to hurt every person in power who thinks they have a right to demand a woman's body, a change in her appearance, her hobbies, or her personality for their benefit.

You are not palatable, they say, and we Sisters must change or suffer. *Smile prettily. Brush your hair. Wear cosmetics, but not too much. Touch us, but not with too much enthusiasm. Tempt us, but do not look as if you want to tempt us.*

I want to scream. But here I must pretend to be voiceless.

Do you believe him? I sign.

First Sister's hands, held before her, are still. Did she expect me to praise her as Aunt Margaret did? Did she expect me to be impressed with the suffering she must endure for her position?

Are you happy? I ask.

Her eyes widen with concern. With worry *for me.* Doesn't she know she should be more concerned about herself?

First Sister, she says, addressing me but using the exact same signs that make up her own name, *is there something I can do for you?*

That is answer enough; the difference between being happy and simply surviving.

Before I can respond, Aunt Margaret seizes one of my hands. "My dear First Sister of Ceres," she says, "you must be tired. Let's get you settled into your room."

I look at the First Sister of the *Juno*, at the girl I used to be, and dip my head in assent.

I am more than tired; I am already exhausted, and this journey has hardly begun.

REGARDLESS OF WHO is in charge, the *Juno* has always run on a clock that matches the time at Olympus Mons. I withdraw into my assigned chambers during the day cycle and task my guard with turning away anyone but Aunt Margaret, hoping this will keep Ringer, who always acted like any other soldier, from appearing again. Only once we are deep into the night cycle, when the majority of soldiers and Sisters are in their bunks, do I emerge from my room.

While I have been assigned quarters in the guest wing, a deck set apart from the crew of the ship, I go to the communal shower on one of the Sisterhood levels for its familiarity. I know there are no cameras or listening devices here, and while my guard—a young soldier boy— follows me, he halts just outside the entrance to wait for my return. The showers are abandoned at such a late hour, giving me all the privacy I require.

I choose a stall and turn the water as cold as it will go. Step under the stream, and let it prickle my flesh. Submerge myself beneath it as it caresses my hair, softer than fingers.

Such torture, this cold, and yet it clears my head. I become silence and stillness, a winter unto myself, until I am as clean and pure as an ancient Earthen stream.

But the peace does not last. Before I have even had time to consider the problem of Ringer, a second stream of water joins the sound of mine. A suspicion forms in me, hard and heavy as a stone.

I lean down and look beneath the dividers. Two stalls down, I spy small feet amidst steam.

I do not take my towel. Do not turn off my water. I simply move like a storm and throw open the door to her stall. Lily spins to face me and gasps, eyes wide and red. She drops something as I push her against the wall, my hand on her collarbone.

Close to her throat.

"Why are you following me?" I spit. Her head is of a height with my shoulder, and I wonder at how such a little thing could pose such a large problem for me.

"Astrid—" she begins, but I cut her off.

"Are you trying to record me?" I gesture to the thing that fell to the tile.

"I have allergies, Astrid. They're eye drops for—"

"What on the Goddess's green Earth could you *possibly* hope to discover in the shower?" A part of me knows that this outburst is far more than she would have gotten had I just stayed in my own stall, but I do not want to spend my entire trip to Mars looking over my shoulder, watching for Lily in the *Juno*'s hallways when I must already worry about Ringer. I am haunted enough.

Her gaze flashes toward the door. "Can we lower our voices?" she asks.

I cast a quick look over her naked body. She holds her hands before her, weaponless. Her breasts are small and high, her hips narrow. Between that and her big doe eyes, red with irritation as if she's been crying, she looks more like a girl on the verge of womanhood than one old enough to have achieved her rank.

But then smaller details come into focus: the pale, scaly patches on her skin. The scars on her arms and legs, clustered at her joints. The stiff way she shifts her weight from foot to foot. What has happened to her, this scarred girl?

All at once, I understand why she followed me: No Sisterhood stands between us now, no rank. We are, both of us, women stripped to our skin. Where else could we speak like this, woman to woman instead of Sister to Sister? Where else could we go where no one would overhear us or record us?

I release her, bend to pick up her eye drops, and return them to her. "You followed me because you want to talk off the record? Then talk."

She takes the eye drops from me, gaze never wavering from my face. "I came to warn you."

My defensiveness rises. "Warn me of what?"

"The Agora," she says, as if I need a warning about the danger they pose. "As soon as we land, they'll call you before them, but not for the reasons you want." With the smoothness of someone who has done it a thousand times, she squeezes a drop of the medicine into each eye and closes them. "Regardless of the cease-fire, they want to hold an inquiry into your release of the Icarii warriors."

The air comes rushing out of me. "Goddess wither it . . ."

When she opens her eyes again, the redness has lessened. "The Agora is efficient at stamping out rebelliousness, and they believe you've overstepped your authority."

My hands curl into fists. Suspicion still rises strong within me. "And how did you come by this information?"

I don't expect her to answer, and am pleasantly surprised when she does. "It was part of the same message that recalled Aunt Margaret to Mars," she says. "But Aunt Margaret can't be seen to do you any favors, such as warning you about this."

"She didn't want to tell me? You are not here on her errand?"

"No," Lily says, "she wished to keep the Agora's plans quiet. However, I disagree with that approach."

I look at her. Really *look* at her. "Why go against Aunt Margaret's wishes, then? Why help me?"

She shakes her head, wet hair clinging to her cheeks. "Because I want to give you enough time to form a response. Because I think you deserve that."

I cross my arms. "It will seem like Aunt Margaret warned me now, you know."

"Then make sure your response doesn't sound overly rehearsed." Lily says it like it's simple. "If you need me to—"

I scoff, and she stops midsentence.

She actually looks offended when she finds her train of thought again. "Regardless of what you think, Astrid," she says, "I want you to succeed."

Of course, because when I am named the Mother, she will become First Sister of Ceres.

"Anything else?" I ask.

When she answers, her voice is low. Cutting, in a way I never expected from her. "You think I don't know my own limitations? You think you have none?" Her lip curls. "You are a good First Sister of Ceres, Astrid, but you will need support if you are to become the next Mother. You want to believe people can't help you without getting something out of it? Fine, look at my offer like this: I'll help you navigate the Agora, and you teach me so that I can become as good a First Sister of Ceres as you are. And make no mistake, I *can* help you. You've never dealt with the Agora before, and I have. We can help each other. We *should* help each other."

I want to put my hand against her neck again. Want to tell her that I believe her offer is useless. But a part of me whispers that I should see what she can offer me, should count every small advantage I have in a battle against people who outnumber and outrank me. "How can you help me? What could you know about the Agora that other Sisters don't?"

She does not fidget or flush when she speaks. "There is talk within the Sisterhood about the Aunts of the Agora. I know of things you could look into, knowledge that would prove advantageous to you."

A sinking feeling steals over me. "'Knowledge'?"

"Blackmail." There is so little of the child I thought she resembled in her hard eyes when she says it. "You could blackmail individual Agora members, Astrid."

For a moment, we stand quietly, the only noise the running of the showers. That dark whisper, caged behind my ribs, rumbles in my core. The knowledge could be an advantage in my dealings with the Agora, one tool in my arsenal against them. Could it truly be as simple as helping her become the First Sister of Ceres, or is this a poisoned gift? If I seem interested, will she report that to Aunt Margaret—or worse, Aunt Marshae?

In my silence, she reaches behind her and turns off the hot water. "Think about it," she whispers. Wrapping herself in a robe, hiding her scarred, scaly skin, she strides past me.

"I will," I say to her back, an ambiguous answer for an uncertain proposition. She pauses, but her only response is the slightest dip of her head.

Then she is gone, leaving me alone in the showers once more.

I RETURN TO my assigned quarters with the soldier boy at my heels, my mind swarming with questions and emotions I wish I could shut out. Could I work with Lily? Should I? Is Ringer waiting for me just around the corner? How will I answer the accusations of the Agora?

I do not find Ringer in my room, but my skin still itches with discomfort. The chamber is spacious, larger than my chambers were as First Sister of the ship, and it infuriates me that this room, so elegant, is kept empty most of the time. Certainly other girls could use its space for their own, especially as cramped as the Sisterhood dormitories are belowdecks.

"First Sister," the soldier boy says, standing in the doorway. His nervous eyes sweep the floor. "Will you . . . pray for me?"

This is not a chapel; I am not one of the *Juno*'s Sisters. He should take his place guarding the hallway. I should shut the door. But then I would be alone with my overwhelming thoughts and worries about the days ahead.

I look him over, this boy. Two years younger than me, but only in time. A lifetime apart in experience. He is tall and blue-eyed, his brown hair in regulation cut. He looks like he just joined up, and my attention catches on his wrists, thin and strangely elegant.

I gesture him into the room, and he kneels before me. It has been a long time since I prayed with a soldier like this. A longer time since I wanted to.

My hand against his head, I intercede with the Goddess on his behalf, begging Her for his forgiveness. For Her protection. For his worries to be soothed. When I finish, I let my fingers trail over his temple and down his cheek to his chin, and he looks up at me with soft blue eyes.

He reminds me of no one.

I lean down and kiss him gently. Chastely. When I pull back, even his ears have turned red with a blush.

He could say something in complaint. Could say no. He has a voice, after all. But he doesn't. He stands only to close the door behind him. He stays. And with trembling hands outstretched, he closes the gap between us.

His fingers thread into my damp hair. He tries to kiss me again. I don't allow him to. I turn my head so that he kisses my cheek, my ear, my neck. I unbutton my dress, drop it to the floor. I take a step back to the bed, and he follows eagerly.

He starts to undo his belt, but I stop him. When I lean back on the bed and part my legs, he seems to understand. He kneels before me.

"Tell me what you want," he says, and I fight the laughter bubbling in my throat because this boy, while well-intentioned, is so naive.

I pull him toward me. Take his hand, show him what I want. Where I want to be touched. And when his mouth joins his hand, when his tongue sends shivers of pleasure through me, I can forget.

I gasp in the cool air, but even it cannot fight the fire building within me. As I move against him, I bite my lip to keep from crying out. I increase the pace, moving to my own rhythm, focusing only on the way it makes my legs tingle and my belly pull taut.

Until that moment when I tumble over the edge, the muscles of my thighs tight, and I toss my head back in the perfect mix of ecstasy and relief.

I lie still, breathing heavily. The pressure weighing me down is gone. I am, for a time, weightless.

But of course, that moment is over too soon.

He says something that I don't catch. Asking a question, maybe. Making a comment. It brings the rest of the world back into focus.

I remember again.

Saito Ren. The waiting Agora. Aunt Marshae's sharp nails. Hiro val Akira's smirk. Lily's unknown loyalties. The endless war, spread out before me like text on a page.

"Should I go?" the boy asks, standing.

I roll onto my side, turn my back on him.

Let that be my answer.

CHAPTER 7

HIRO

The Alliance of Autarkeia is not so much a government as it is a statement of purpose. It is a guarantee that we will favor no one person over another, for it is this type of selective tyranny, one based on race, class, gender, and genetics, that we aim to eliminate completely in Autarkeia.

From *The Declaration of Autarkeia* by Dire of the Belt

Sandwiched between Dire and Falchion, I feel like I'm about to become part of a holoseries trope where the Icarii who dares to trust the outlaws dies a terribly violent death, bleeding out as they express their regret. The fact that they say nothing contributes to the scene, leaving only the wash of tumultuous noise from the main streets to reach us and echo down the narrow corridors we take.

Dire sticks to a map only he seems to have access to, choosing paths so narrow as to be almost unnoticeable and forcing him to turn sideways in order for his wide shoulders to pass. Even I find myself uncomfortable at times, walls pressing in on both sides of my body, the only light one Dire carries, and a smell like stale water permeating the air. But Falchion slips through like thread through a needle, like he was born in these labyrinthine alleys.

Our destination isn't what I expect. One moment we're in a claustrophobic tunnel between buildings; the next we've emerged into a commercial district decorated with red neon so bright it hurts my eyes. Despite the press of bodies, the street smells sweet, like incense, and with a sinking feeling, I know exactly where we are.

"We're going to a chopshop?" I ask, but Dire only shoots me a narrow-eyed glare over his shoulder and keeps moving. Everywhere I look, stores promise the most cutting-edge bodymods. Prosthetics hang like freshly cut meat in windows, and geneassisted models beckon toward open doors. A person with skin as red as the neon and elegant horns rising from their forehead like an 鬼 from Japanese mythology reaches out to touch me before I slip out of the way. I swallow down the bad memories and hope we're only passing through.

No luck. Dire stops at a dark shop front, the windows pasted over with hand-drawn artwork, and shoos away a group of teens who have perched there to smoke. At first they square up like they're ready to fight, but as soon as they spot Dire's golden arm and realize who he is, they're out of there with smiles. "Whoa, was that really him?" I hear one whisper to another.

Dire knocks on the door four times, pauses, then twice more. After a moment of fighting with the manual locks, a person on the other side opens the door for us and welcomes us into the light.

The shop isn't like one I've been to before. More artwork is pasted over every space on the walls. Behind the front counter is a piece of furniture that's a cross between a table and a bed. Nearby are a metal cabinet and a table laden with little bottles of various colored inks. A sheet hung like a shower curtain partitions off a back room. Despite the cluttered atmosphere, the whole place, including the floor, looks clean enough to eat off of.

Dire motions for Falchion to guard the door, while the person who let us in—an Aster, I now see in the light—sits down on a stool. Their shirt is plain black with sharp white text that reads FAST AIN'T GOOD, AND GOOD AIN'T FAST. "You must be Hiro," they say with a smile. They wear their hair cut in a short bob, unlike most Asters I know, who wear it long, and beneath their black eyes are two strips of metal, some sort of mod so they don't have to wear goggles, I'd bet.

"That's me."

"Dandelion," they say, and hold out a hand. I shake. "They call me Dandy around here. Welcome to my shop."

I gesture to our surroundings. "Is it a—"

"Tattoo parlor," Dandy says, almost too excitedly. "We do them by hand here. Old-style, you know?"

"Huh." I look at the art on the walls, at landscapes and portraits and geometric designs, all well drawn. "This your work?"

"Yep," Dandy says.

I'm just about to tell them how amazing it all is when the sheet to the back room parts and I come face-to-face with the one person on this godsdamned station I never wanted to see again. くそ.

"Sorry," Sigma says, "had to take a shit."

He's dressed like a tourist on vacation in his stained, oversized shirt. His receding hairline gives him a huge forehead, and his eyes bulge like twin marbles. His lips have a fishy quality to them, barely hiding crooked teeth. Maybe I wouldn't think so poorly of him if the first time we met didn't haunt me, but, believe it or not, this person is supposedly the greatest geneassist Autarkeia has to offer.

Sigma sees me and smiles. "Well, if it isn't Hiro." He says it like *Hero*.

I pin him with a look. "Hiro. Hi. Ro. There's a subtle difference, though a lot of native English speakers miss it—" He stares at me like he's not listening, and all I can remember is the way he looked me up and down at my first geneassist appointment and dismissed me.

There's no going back, kid, he told me, like he didn't care that he was delivering bad news. Val Akira Labs had placed an encrypted genelock on the changes they made to me, and only Val Akira Labs could unravel that piece of IP. *I've done weird shit for Hemlock before, but unless you can get a copy of your old genetic profile, you're stuck with pieces of Saito Ren's DNA.*

And while I could make little changes here and there—sharpening my jawline, widening my mouth as opposed to Ren's pointed pout—I still had remnants of her in me. I still felt like I was wearing her skin.

"You got anything to drink, Dandy?" Sigma asks, and Dandy points with their foot to a little fridge nearby.

Sigma kneels to rummage through the options, little glass bottles filled with colorful liquids, but slams the door after a few seconds. "Of course he doesn't have anything good," he mumbles.

"'She' today," Dandy clarifies.

"*Of course* she doesn't have anything good!" Sigma laments louder.

"Can we begin, or do you two want to continue your little theater play?" Dire holds his prosthetic wrist with his flesh hand.

Dandy chuckles, and Sigma waves a hand for Dire to get on with it.

"I thought we were going to talk to witnesses regarding the Synthetic contact." The words slip out before I can bite them back. I look between the strange Aster, the old geneassist, and Falchion, who leans against the door with his eyes closed, as if he's not part of this.

"We are, so listen up," Dire says, but I can hear from his tone he's not happy. "First, you need an explanation about some tech on Autarkeia."

He has my attention now. Finally I feel like I can adequately ignore Sigma. Of course, it helps that I don't have to look at him when I take a seat next to Dandy. "So explain it to me."

"When you first arrived, I gave you a set of com-lenses connected to Autarkeia's network."

Something I thought would be more helpful than they turned out to be. Cytherea's feed has access to maps and the identity documents of citizens, but Autarkeia doesn't even have security cameras on the streets. Its network is more a selection of Gean and Icarii news along with communications channels to reach various contacts. Whoever lives here does so in privacy, and not even Dire could provide a list of their names.

"The com-lenses are an example of connecting via external hardware," Dire says, and I feel like he's explaining this to a Gean child.

"Neural implants that connect to the feed are an example of internal hardware."

"We have both examples on Cytherea too," I say. "Get to the point."

Dire's nostrils flare as if he's fighting back the urge to yell at me. "The majority of Icarii who come here choose to have their neural implants replaced," he says louder, daring me to interrupt him. "The interior hardware we use here is proprietary."

Whoa, whoa, whoa. Back up. "Autarkeia has its own version of the neural implant?"

"Built by yours truly," Dandy says with a smile.

"I put them in," Sigma says. "Though most people who want to connect via internal hardware are the extreme modders who get them as part of a package deal with some other prosthetic." Like the people with tubes in their heads and cybernetic eyes . . .

I knew from the briefing on the Synthetic agent that anyone who was seeing and capturing imagery of her had access to the network. She moved like a data ghost through connections, appearing and disappearing at will. "So the Synthetic is in the Autarkeia network." Could that be why, with my Icarii neural implant, she hasn't appeared to me? Though I do wear com-lenses with access to Autarkeia's network . . .

"Yes, we believe that she's accessed Autarkeia's network in order to gather more intel about us," Dire says. "However, if she were just accessing the network, we would be able to push updates to our tech to force her out—at least for a brief time."

Yeah, because I doubt anyone here would be able to outcode a Synthetic. There's no firewall high enough. And if she is just data, there's no way to capture her and interrogate her about what she wants.

"I told you when you first arrived that we had evidence the Synthetic agent was on the station physically," Dire says. "Now we're going to show you that evidence. Dandy?"

She hops up from the stool. From inside the metal cabinet, she pulls a compad that she then offers me. The first image is of an assembly line. If I didn't know any better, I'd say it was an Icarii factory making neural implants, but now that I know Autarkeia has its own version, I'm sure this is wherever they manufacture their tech. The biggest difference is the lack of lighting and the older machines that are making the implants. Val Akira Labs would never use such machines.

Then *she* appears. I feel like I could draw her with my eyes closed, I've stared at images of her for so long. In this picture, the Synthetic girl stands before a wall, holding something . . . a tube of some sort? On the wall behind her, black drips against silver.

The next image zooms out to take in the whole room, and—oh. *Oh!* She's painting the wall with a black airpen. The drawing is of a cartoony rat, its wide, shining eyes watching over the factory.

"That's vaguely threatening," I mutter.

The images that follow are blurry. Whoever took them chases after the Synthetic, but she slips outside the factory and disappears into the chaos of the Autarkeia streets. The final picture is of the rat she left behind, a hand smudging the line of its little foot, fingers stained black. Proof that the paint is real. Proof that she was physically there.

"Who took these?" I ask.

"Me," Sigma says. "I saw her when I was there to pick up some new implants. It was almost like . . . she was waiting for me." I hear the shudder he fights off. "She *wanted* me to see her."

I back through the pictures to the one of the rat looming over the factory. "She wants us to know that she's watching." No one answers me. "I want access to the factory."

"No," Dire says without hesitation.

"But—"

"No one is allowed in the factories except for me, Dandy, and Sigma." He pulls out his compad and, with the flick of a finger, sends another image to Dandy's compad. I magnify it. "This is what I want you to focus on."

Another painting of a rat, but not in the factory. This time the rat is on the outside of a building that looks like a group of storage units or a motel with wide doors. It stands on its hind feet, eating a piece of cheese held in its front paws. Beside it is an empty trap, untriggered. This must be the new message from the Synthetic.

"She's taunting us," I say, and I can't help but smile.

"I found it earlier tonight, around ten," Dandy says, looking at the image over my shoulder. It's well past midnight now that I've trekked all over the station. "The paint was still fresh."

So the Synthetic was painting it while I was dealing with Rossi . . . I revise my thought: *Is she taunting* me?

This time when I make my request, I know Dire will grant it. "Tell me where the new painting is and get me an airpen."

IT'S THREE IN the morning by the time I find the building with the painting of the rat beside the door. Autarkeia's signs are absolutely useless, all Synthetic symbols with half-erased chalk written on top of them in an attempt to translate. I have to stop and ask a couple of people for directions before I wind up in the right place.

When I first arrive, I walk the street twice, keeping my eyes peeled for any hint of someone watching me, but the whole area looks abandoned. And that's weird enough in a place like Autarkeia, with people literally crammed on top of each other. Usually it's only the Synthetic factories people avoid.

On my third pass, I stop at the painting of the rat and pull out my airpen. I'm not a painter, but my subpar skills will have to do. Beside the Synthetic's art, I spray a rat of my own, not nearly as cute but one that is offering her rat cheese in its outstretched paws. I have no idea if this will work, but if she's trying to communicate with us through her drawings, hopefully this will inspire something.

My exhaustion level tells me to go home and check on it tomorrow, but if the Synthetic is watching us, I don't want to miss her response to my offer of friendship. Though the biggest part of me chafes at the sheer grunt work of it, I prepare to stake out the unit.

The storage units stretch down both sides of the street, but above them are squat apartments that match the rest of Autarkeia's buildings. I lurk at the door to the one across from the painting of the rats, half-hidden behind a closed dumpster where an orange cat rests with a single golden eye open, and when an elderly man comes shuffling out, I slip in the door before it closes. I check each floor and find the perfect window to monitor the paintings on the second. With my shoulder and hip joint aching from my prosthetics, I gingerly settle on the windowsill. After that, all I can do is wait.

I guess it's not so bad when I have my com-lenses. Thanks to an Icarii satellite station in the belt, abandoned after the Fall of Ceres, Autarkeia has access to Cytherean news feeds. I check up on the Gean-Icarii cease-fire—which, despite the sharp nostalgia that comes with remembering First Sister, makes me think the universe isn't completely terrible.

The temptation to drift is strong. My fatigue becomes overwhelming. The burn in my shoulder and hip becomes so unbearable, I force myself to stand and pace. Only once the news changes with an emergency update am I able to ignore the exhaustion and pain.

Lito sol Lucius's face is everywhere.

It doesn't take me long to see through the bullshit, especially since I know his goal was to liberate Sorrel. But as for whether they escaped Icarii pursuers? I can't find a single thing.

A little less than an hour later at five minutes before six, my com-lenses alert me to someone walking down the alley. I swipe away the page I was reading and lean closer to the window.

Only it's not the Synthetic, as I hoped. It's a pair I never thought I'd see again in my life. And for a horrifying moment, I am back on Ceres in the dark shadows of Mithridatism before I ever met Hemlock.

Noa sol Romero and Nadyn val Lancer.

The two of them are dressed in street clothes, but I recognize them all the same: they still carry themselves like they're in the military.

Nadyn is the Dagger of the pair, short geneassisted navy hair framing a beautiful heart-shaped face. She's taller than Noa but leans toward them like she orbits their gravity.

Noa is the Rapier and stands like it. They're exactly as I remember them with their coppery dark brown skin and hair cut into a flattop.

Then Noa turns to look down the street, and I see just how much they've changed.

One of Noa's eyes is the deep brown I remember, but the other is a stark blue so bright it almost matches the white of the rest of their eye. And that side of their face is mutilated with puckered skin, melted like a wax candle. I'd heard Noa lost their life in the Fall of Ceres. Is this what they lost instead?

A sharp stabbing pain hits my wrist—the one that isn't there—like someone slipped a knife into it. For a moment, I lose track of Noa and Nadyn, grabbing my prosthetic arm hard as if I could stop the phantom pain. Nothing helps, but I don't want to lose track of them, so I bite my lip and force myself to look at the street.

They're leaving. Fuck, they're leaving the alley and heading gods know where.

I want to follow them. Want to know what they're doing here. But that's not my mission. I'm supposed to be finding the Synthetic, not following a couple of duelists I thought were dead. But if they're here . . . are they trying to find her too? What did Rossi say? *"Why're the Icarii after the girl?"* Did he know?

I'm on the line to Dire within seconds.

"Hiro?" he answers.

"There are a couple of duelists on Autarkeia," I say, and while my tone is frantic, I don't rein it in. Let him hear how afraid I am, I don't give a shit. "I know them from my posting on Ceres, and they were poking around the painting of the rat—"

"Slow down."

I suck in a deep breath and let it out slowly. It doesn't help my mood that my missing leg has decided to act up like my hand and feels like it's on fire. Fucking shit prosthetics . . .

"There are Icarii duelists on Autarkeia," I say again.

"That's what you're calling to report?"

"Um, yeah? Seemed pretty fucking important."

"We know."

I feel like he's reached across the line and slapped me. He didn't even ask what they looked like. "How many duelists are here?" I'm surprised by how calm I sound.

"We've spotted a total of five, two pairs and one Command."

I don't care to explain that someone in Command isn't considered a duelist; it only reminds me that I was once Icarii and now I'm not, and if *any* of these people find me here, I'm fucked. *Beyond* fucked.

They'll drag me back to the Icarii in chains and throw me before my father to be executed.

"I've gotta go." I've made my decision; I'm not going to let them out of my sight.

"Hiro—" Dire starts, but I don't let him finish. I cut the connection.

As I head down the stairs, I try to shove away my anger and confusion. Why didn't he tell me about the duelists? And even more concerning: What do the Icarii want with the Synthetic?

My limbs aching, I hit the alley and lengthen my stride in an attempt to catch up with Noa and Nadyn. Though the pain slows me, they weren't walking fast, and I find them on the next street over, meandering in a residential neighborhood. This early in the morning, the sidewalks are almost empty except for people on their way to work. I pull up the hood of my jacket and the cloth of my mask-slash-scarf and dive into the street.

I can't possibly hear what they're trying to say from this distance. I'd have to get closer, but getting anywhere near them would mean they might recognize me . . .

No, they think I'm dead. And technically, Hiro val Akira *is* dead. I'm Saito Ren now, so as I slip after them, I straighten to my full height.

Just as I'm getting close enough to hear them, Nadyn turns right and Noa turns left. *Fuck.* Do they know they're being followed? I have a split second to decide, and I choose to follow Noa. We butted heads when we were both stationed on Ceres, but at least I felt like I knew them, as opposed to Nadyn, who always acted like she was wearing a mask of kindness to hide her razor teeth.

As soon as I turn after Noa, I know I've made a mistake. There's no sight of them in the looming darkness, and I didn't bring a light source with me. I hesitate halfway down the alleyway and turn back, hoping I can catch up with Nadyn instead. But there, at the mouth of the alley, is a shadowy figure . . .

Nadyn or Noa?

No, it can't be either of them. Noa is shorter, Nadyn taller.

"Who . . ." My tongue feels fat in my mouth, words refusing to form.

"What . . . is . . ." My vision darkens at the corners, and my entire body trembles beneath me.

I can't even finish my question. My breath comes in ragged gasps.

And a horrible realization hits me as I try to take a step forward and my body refuses: Have I been poisoned?

How?

I hit the ground with a pain that feels far off.

"I'm sorry," a small voice says, echoing around me.

I look up as the figure strides toward me. I see nothing but a shimmering blur.

Someone leans down, reaching toward me.

Then I see nothing at all.

CHAPTER 8

LUCE

My Castor: It's said that when each child of Śouji val Akira was born, he took them into his arms, pressed his lips to their heads, and whispered a single phrase to them: "You were born to guide this world." What, then, have we been born for?

Message on Hemlock's private server from Pollux

My Pollux: Fuck being guides. We were born to shatter worlds.

Message on Hemlock's private server from Castor

◇———◈◈———◇

I'm so exhausted on my way to work the next morning, I stumble like a drunk. I bump into others on my way out of the Newton Street Station, apologizing as I move. "Disculpe. I'm so sorry. Lo siento." I never spot my tail, if I have one.

When I reach the trendy Tesla Gardens section of Cytherea's top level, I stop for coffee at a shop so small it fits only a handful of people, giving it a feeling of exclusivity. The wait is abysmal, but the coffee isn't just a perk for the day; it's a necessity when I spent the entire night listening to Hiro's recordings.

Every time I think about what I heard, a numbness creeps in. Everything that Hiro suffered at the hands of their father . . . everything they endured. Everything they *did*. The numbness becomes a fog.

It's no wonder Lito joined them, a part of me thinks.

A woman in a flexglass coat behind me nudges me with her purse. "Order or move," she says. The barista stares at me, patience waning. Shit, how long have I been staring at the ceiling?

"I'd like two large cups of coffee—one black with no sugar, one with four sugars." I rattle off my order, falling into routine.

After grabbing my coffees, I fight to keep my mind from slipping back into that fog. My walk from the shop to the office isn't long, but there are a lot of people already in the wide pedestrian street, and with two hot Verdad cafés taking up both my hands, I have to carefully maneuver around them. Tesla Gardens Street is a main artery of Cytherea's heart, a place where Paragon influencers dress in the latest fashions, their glass-walled homes and offices decorated with highly exclusive, expensive furniture and electronics. Anyone can walk down the street and watch them living their lives, every item on display, including them, just a query on the feed away from a wealth of information—brand, cost, sizing, whatever. But only the lucky few can secure appointments with the Paragons, have them act as style guides and personal shoppers.

I can't believe I wanted to be a Paragon when I was younger. They have zero privacy. Now the idea of anyone watching me that closely makes my skin feel prickly with anxiety. *Especially* if that someone is military.

I reach the sculpturesque entrance to Val Akira Geneassists and juggle my coffees to pull my pass from my purse. For a moment, my fingers fumble over the compad Castor gave me and my heart speeds, but I ignore it and a moment later, I find my identification card—imprinted with my name, gender marker, and a picture of myself, all information that we're required to keep up-to-date. After a quick scan, I press my palm to the biometric reader. With a soft chime of acceptance, the flexglass doors slide up and out like a bird spreading its wings, admitting me to my place of work.

Inside is a posh waiting area with white walls, flexglass furniture, and soft golden lighting. I march past the empty reception desk and into the back, where patient consultation rooms flank either side of the hallway. "Good morning, Jun!" I call.

"In room three!" Jun val Akira replies.

"Anyone else here?" I ask, following Jun's voice straight to her. "I brought you a Verdad café, but I only have two."

"Gimme, gimme!" Jun perks up as soon as she sees the coffees, coming around the desk and forgetting the screen she was so focused on. "How many sugars?" She pops off the cap and inhales the curling steam that radiates from the hot liquid. Her pageboy haircut falls into her eyes, but she ignores it.

"Four, of course."

"One of the many reasons you're my favorite employee."

I try not to flinch at her words, thinking of Lito's note—*Please be cautious in your new job for Val Akira Labs. Souji val Akira will do whatever he can to control you and, by extension, me.* I never doubted she was watching me—she's the branch's manager, after all—but I don't think I realized until today just who she reported to.

I try not to think about that, or about the compad in my purse, but instead focus on Jun. She's never more at peace than when she has her first sip of coffee in the morning, and in that moment, her expression makes her look so much like Hiro that I'm transported back to my apartment, where Lito, Hiro, and I would talk about something pointless. The latest interactive theater performance that Hiro wanted to play and Lito wanted nothing to do with. Or the newest Shimmer val Valentine song that Hiro and I adored and Lito pretended not to nod his head to.

"You okay?" Jun asks, jerking me back to the present. "You look . . ."

"I didn't sleep well," I admit, though I know I can't tell her the truth about why, and if I don't come up with an excuse she'll think it's because of Lito on the news. I wish we could go back to talking about the Gean-Icarii cease-fire, but instead, I grasp for something else. "Had an argument with my mother. She thinks I should get a neural implant."

"I'll never understand why you don't have one. You're, like, the *only* person our age who doesn't."

I shrug. It confuses a lot of people that I don't have a neural implant, but I saw what it did to Lito, and that scared me too much to want one of my own. He was an emotional child—crying, screaming, always fighting—and after they put one of those things in him at the Academy, he became so *different*.

"I just . . . want to make my own decisions about things," I say, surprising even myself with my honesty. "Like, I hate it when my mother tells me what to do with *my* body."

"Tell me about it." Jun leans toward me conspiratorially. "My dad threatened to strap me to the geneassist chair and crank up my metabolism if I don't quote-unquote 'pay more attention to intake.'" She pinches her belly fat. "Like I'm some sort of robot or something."

Just the mention of Souji throws me off. "He wouldn't actually do that, would he?" I ask, hoping my anxiety doesn't leak into my tone.

Jun takes just a little too long in answering. "Of course not."

"I should get to work," I say, glancing at the clock. Our coworkers will be arriving any minute. "See you later."

"Wait a second," Jun calls as I reach the door. "The client coming in at two—Harmony val White—I want you in the room during her consultation."

Her words knock everything else out of my head. "What? Why?" We get a lot of big-name clients, but I've never been in the room with someone like Harmony, a highly demanded theater actress.

"You're the one who did the artwork for her new face." Jun shrugs like it's no big deal, but it feels *huge* to me. "She might want to talk to you, or ask for some adjustments. She's, let's say, 'highly opinionated.'"

With money like she's spending, she can afford to be so. "Are you sure?"

"Yeah, of course." Jun takes another sip of coffee. "Plus, if you can impress her, we can move you up to a second-tier worker."

I force myself to nod. "Yeah, okay. See you at two, then."

On my way to the back, I straighten my bright blue uniform coat. Past the client consultation rooms is an open office, rows of desks below jewel-colored hanging plants. A couple of my coworkers are here so far, and I offer them a little wave, only for them to ignore me. Such has been the dynamic since news of Lito broke . . .

While we don't have assigned seats, I settle at my usual place, slipping my purse inside the sliding drawer and setting my coffee on the decorative coaster with the Val Akira Labs logo. To log in to the computer, I scan my identification card and fingerprint. A heartbeat later, my virtual desktop appears with a chipper flash of *Good morning, Lucinia!* All my files hover before me, projected above my desk, ready for input.

If I chose to help Castor, how would that work? Would my limited access to the server meet his needs? Would I simply plug that naildrive he showed me into my computer tower, or would I need to use someone else's identification—someone higher up, like Jun?

I smell my boss before I see him, his cologne a musky scent that makes my nose burn. He places his hands on the desk beside mine and leans toward me, crowding into my space. I do my best not to shrink into my chair and give him what he wants. For someone in middle management, he's quite muscular. "Lucinia." Mathieu says my name with the same gravity he would use to announce a murder; he supervises the first-tier workers—college students and new hires like me—with the severity of an Academy drill sergeant. "Why were you late this morning?"

My eyes shoot to the clock. Five minutes until eight. "Mathieu, I'm early—"

He cuts me off, speaking loud enough for our craning coworkers to hear. "On days you're going to sit in on client meetings, you have to be here fifteen minutes before the hour."

I suck in a deep breath through my nose and slowly release it, doing my best not to let my anger answer him. I can't wait for when I'm a second-tier worker and don't have to deal with him anymore. "I didn't know I was meeting with a client until this morning." And even so, I didn't know the rule . . .

Mathieu's face, normally attractive beneath his mop of golden-blond curls, twists like I stink. "Lucinia, please tell me you're not going to use that as an excuse."

"I—"

"Because if that was your excuse, you're basically admitting that you're not checking your company messages."

My face burns, though I don't know why I feel so ashamed. I checked my messages before I went out with Keres, but after that—painting Lito, running from the peacekeeper, meeting Castor, listening to Hiro's recordings—I neglected everything. But I didn't meet up with Keres until midnight, so when is Mathieu expecting me to sleep? Am I *always* supposed to be connected to the company feed?

He glares at me, waiting for an answer, and I know anything I offer him will be shoved aside as not good enough. No, what he really wants is an apology.

So, though it twists my stomach, I give it to him. "I'm sorry, Mathieu."

"I hate to do this, but I'm going to have to mark you up for it," he says. *Sure you do,* I think. Too many marks as a first-tier worker, and I'll get fired. "Come see me before you meet with the client. We clearly need to review the proper procedures."

And with that, he's gone, leaving me to slump in my chair and feel like an absolute idiot.

HARMONY VAL WHITE arrives a little after two, but the entire office is at a standstill waiting for her. As soon as she enters, we usher her into the back. No waiting for someone of her status.

I take my place beside Jun in the consultation room, my artwork projected large on the wall. Harmony's a woman in her sixties who looks not a day over thirty, and the digital painting I drew up has her age brought down even lower—early twenties, twenty-five at most—for her newest role.

"Welcome back to Val Akira Geneassists," Jun says with a shining smile. "Can we offer you something to drink?"

Harmony doesn't answer, just shoves her coat into my chest. I scramble to find a gentle way to hold the jacket, an expensive biodome made of flexglass and filled with blue liquid and living, growing strawberries. I would kill for a biodome coat, but even if I could afford one—I can't—I certainly couldn't keep up with maintenance payments on it. I hang the jacket behind the door as Harmony settles in the reclining chair in the middle of the room.

"Get my face off the wall," she snaps, and Jun complies with ease. My artwork disappears. "Let me see it." Jun places a company compad into Harmony's waiting palms.

I stand in the corner with my hands clasped in front of my pelvis, an appropriate waiting pose, according to Mathieu. Harmony surveys her new face in silence. Just imagining being promoted—and free from Mathieu—makes me so nervous that I fear I'm going to be sick.

"My eyes," she says after what feels like the three longest minutes of my life. "You've done something different with them. A hint of gold?"

"If there's anything you're not happy with," Jun says, "we can change it before implementation."

"Who did my artwork?" Harmony asks, looking up at Jun.

"Lucinia did." Jun gestures to me, and I take one step forward.

Harmony looks me over from toes to head, stopping at critical intervals—my flexglass-heeled boots, my slender hips, my glitter-freckled cheeks, my purple hair—never meeting my eyes. I've been careful to cultivate an image that says I'm fashionable and use Val Akira Geneassists myself, while trying not to outshine our clients.

"What's your name?" she asks when she finishes her assessment.

"Lucinia," I say.

She stares down her nose at me. "Introduce yourself properly."

I try to ignore the growing lump in my throat. I know what she wants, but hesitate to give it. "My name is Lucinia sol Lucius."

Her face never changes, yet I see something within her shift. She looks away from me to the artwork. "The gold is gaudy," she says, and my heart falls. "The skin is inexpert." She holds the compad out to Jun. "I don't like it."

Jun rushes to take the compad from her, never glancing in my direction. "I understand. I'll call for our art director immediately."

I was a fool to think I could be in this room, that my name would go unnoticed. Harmony *val* White. Jun *val* Akira. Is it because of the *sol* in my name, that inferior nobiliary particle, or is it my connection with Lito that offends her?

"They'll come to speak with you about—"

But I don't hear the rest, because I open the door and step out.

The lump in my throat makes it impossible to breathe, and my face heats as my eyes water. *Don't cry*, I coach myself. *Don't give them the satisfaction of seeing you break.*

But it hurts. It hurts so fucking much to hear someone reject my art simply because of who I am.

Mathieu's cologne assaults me. I turn to face him, and he takes me by the shoulder and guides me away from Harmony's room. The touch of his strangely callused hands is soft and caring, and I wonder, for a moment, if he sympathizes with me. Then he speaks. "Excuse me, Lucinia, I've got to go fetch the art director to clean up your mess."

My lips tremble, but I manage to bite back anything I might say.

"Go back to your desk until you're called for," he whispers, and I'm all too happy to comply.

OVER THE NEXT few hours, I try to keep myself from thinking about Harmony val White, but perhaps because of the lack of sleep, everything else in my life is just as upsetting.

I joined the Keres Art Collective because of the disrespect I've faced as a lowlevel Cytherean, but last night proved that I'll be disregarded among them as well. Shad stealing my painting of Lito, the whole group leaving me without a glance back. Even if I didn't mistake them for my friends, I thought they cared about me . . . that *someone* cared about me.

But even now, I feel adrift. Alone. Isa sent me an innocent message asking to meet up for dinner that I didn't respond to. Mamá asked me to call her later since we didn't talk yesterday. Even the thought of trying to pretend with them turns my stomach and makes me think of Hiro's recordings. Hiro would *never* put up with the shit I've been shoveling with both hands.

Finally the clock strikes five, and I gratefully log out of the computer. But before I can finish gathering my belongings, Mathieu slips out of his nearby office and waves at me. "Lucinia, there's someone who wants to talk to you before you go home."

A wave of anxiety washes over me, but I'm surprised when I don't feel disappointment in its wake. I'm sure this is a meeting I'm not going to like—another disciplinary mark, perhaps—but I resolve to face it as calmly as possible.

I enter Mathieu's office, overly spartan and without a hint of artwork—odd for a manager of artists—but he doesn't follow. Instead, he closes the door, leaving me alone.

The hell—?

I force myself to sit. My anxiety increases, bit by bit. My heart is thumping so hard I feel it in my throat, making my mouth dry and cottony.

It only gets worse when the door opens, and I see the two men entering. One appears middle-aged, wearing the military blacks of a highly ranked officer, a flaming phoenix on his chest and a crossed rapier and dagger on his shoulder. I know from Lito's descriptions that this man works in Command, and his hard face, with its long, jagged scar beneath one eye, tells me he's seen a lot.

The other man is Souji val Akira. He leaves behind a sharply dressed bodyguard as he enters and sits in what would be Mathieu's seat. His suit is bespoke, the sharp collars edged in gold, but it's his face that pulls attention. His forehead is high, his hair dark except for a single streak of white. His eyes have the faintest crow's feet at the corners, but his mouth has no smile lines.

Thousand gods—this must be about Castor. Or maybe it's about the paintings from last night. Either way, it doesn't bode well for me. Forget getting fired—am I facing jail time?

"Good afternoon, Lucinia," Souji starts, and I'm struck by how different he is from his children. His movements are slow and graceful, like he has water suffusing his joints.

It brings back Hiro's recordings. *He's wearing a mask*, I think.

The Command officer puts a compad on the desk between us, and on the screen I see the painting of Lito on the Maintenance Guild's building. In the daytime dome lighting, it shines like a star. I look up to the two men. So this meeting is about my work with Keres?

It can't be just that . . . Otherwise, why send someone in Command and Souji val Akira himself?

"What is this?" I ask carefully, doing my best to keep my expression blank.

The officer taps the compad, and the image changes to my CCAD portfolio painting of Lito, almost exactly like the one on the roof. Beneath it is a little description with the heading FLAGGED, but the text is too small for me to read the whole paragraph.

"You tell us," the officer says.

"That's my painting, but . . ." I shrug as if I don't know about the other one.

"Lucinia sol Lucius," the man says with heat in his tone, and my attention snaps from the compad to him. The scar trailing down his cheek stretches taut as he speaks. "We have reason to believe you are aiding the terrorist Lito sol Lucius."

I feel the blood drain from my face. "It's just a painting of my brother. I painted it years ago . . ."

"Then how did it get here?" He goes back to the painting on the Maintenance Guild building. "The imagery in these paintings is something we can't ignore. We believe they are meant to incite rebellious sentiment."

For a moment, all I can think is: *Was Shad right?* Did the Keres group's art actually change something, or was it, like Castor said, just playing in the sand? But I can't focus on that right now. I have to consider whether Command would really arrest me based on the *symbolism* in my painting.

If it gave them Lito, you better believe it, part of me hisses.

"Beron, let me speak with her." I'd almost forgotten Souji, as silent as he was. "I don't think all your posturing is necessary. I know Lucinia, and she's a good girl with a bright future."

At first I think the Command officer—Beron—will refuse Souji, but after a few silent heartbeats, he retreats from the desk, taking the compad with him. But as Souji leans forward, fingers laced together, I don't feel any more at ease.

"Perhaps someone else found your painting and used it as a reference. I'm sure this will all be cleared up if you just give him some indication that you're not loyal to Lito," Souji whispers, like we're co-conspirators. "You could offer to turn over some information that will help Command's investigation of your brother. A secret of his, or a message that Lito may have sent you?"

So that's what they're after. My heart sinks into my stomach.

Souji must see my hesitation. "Don't be afraid, Lucinia. Even if it's something small you don't think could be helpful, anything will prove to Beron that you're willing to help."

I think of Lito's note sent to me through Castor, of his warning about this very thing. *Souji val Akira will do whatever he can to control you and, by extension, me.* And of course, I think of Hiro's recordings, of all the terrible things this man did to them. Instead of fear, I feel anger bubbling up inside me. Rage, on behalf of Hiro and Lito both. And it is with that burning inside me that I shake my head.

"My selfish, arrogant brother Lito hasn't contacted me at all," I say, praying I sound like I'm telling them the truth.

Souji cocks his head and studies my face. For a strange moment, I feel like one of his experiments. "Not even something small, to tell you that he loves you? To tell you goodbye?"

The words twist at my heart, but I remain calm. "Nothing at all. I haven't spoken to him since he left Venus." And then, because I want to get my point across, I drop my eyes. "Nothing, either to me or my parents, leaving us all to worry and wonder . . ."

"So you wouldn't know where he's going now, or what he intends?" Souji asks. Perhaps he reads the wariness on my face, because he rephrases. "Is there anywhere he might go, somewhere off-planet that the two of you visited as kids, or a place that holds special significance to him?"

This isn't even about my paintings . . . Souji hasn't mentioned them once. This is about the break-in at Val Akira Labs, and I just happened to step in front of the metaphorical bullet train.

"We couldn't afford that kind of travel," I say, not even flushing as I do. As Souji looks at Beron, lapsing into silence, I go on the offensive. "Has something happened other than what the news is reporting?"

Like curtains have been drawn over a window, Souji's face changes in the smallest way, only now his kindness is gone, replaced by a blankness that is difficult to read.

But that's exactly how I know I'm right.

Souji stands from the desk and turns to Beron. "I believe Lucinia is telling the truth. She is not in contact with nor is she working alongside Lito sol Lucius, and thus will be unable to aid us in our investigation."

"Akira—" Beron begins to argue, but Souji, though shorter, somehow dwarfs the man with his powerful presence.

He says nothing, but he doesn't need to repeat himself. His look says it all.

When Souji leaves the room, Beron stands aside with an odd deference. Souji's bodyguard trails after him until I lose sight of them. But Beron remains, looking worse for wear. Hiro's words hit me again, the assertion that Souji is the puppet master pulling the strings of the whole government.

Thousand gods, everything Hiro said is true. My stomach roils. It's not just the lower levels of Cytherea in need of aid; the deception goes farther than I could have ever imagined.

Every piece of anxiety and fear burns in my righteous anger, turning into something sharp and silver. By the time Beron steps toward where I sit, looming over me like a stout tower, I feel like a different person, one whose sorrow and loss have been pounded into a weapon as hot as a mercurial blade.

Beron searches my face for something—proof that I'm lying, or simply taking in the way that Lito and I look alike, I don't know. Then he drops his gaze as he tucks away his compad. "You're free to go, Lucinia sol Lucius."

He doesn't have to tell me twice. My stomach a riot, I shoulder my purse and march through the office and into the bustling Tesla Gardens.

There's no hesitation when I fumble through my things and find the compad Castor gave me. No doubt when I open the contacts and see a single name waiting for me. *Darling*, it reads, but I know exactly who's on the other side.

Date tonight? ;), I text.

The response is almost instantaneous.

I knew I'd hear from you, Castor writes back. A moment later an address follows, along with a time.

I'll be there, I confirm.

CHAPTER 9

LITO

DR. EUGENE VAL TOPOROV: How many humans would you say you've killed, Sorrel? Can you estimate a general number? What are you—

[three seconds of silence]

DR. EUGENE VAL TOPOROV: May the record show that the subject is laughing.

Excerpt from an interview with Asset #4757828

As Sorrel's pod belches white smoke, the rickety ship trembles with the force of our boarders cutting into the grasshopper's hull. We'll have ten minutes before they're through, so we have to rush to enact our last-minute plan.

Ofiera retrieves our mercurial blades from where we'd hidden them in a smuggler's panel outside our hab quarters while I make a few final adjustments in the command center for our guests. "Boots on," I call over the intercom. I engage my gravboots before I cut the gravity and turn on emergency-only lighting, bathing everything in a dim red glow.

There are no guns on board and no extra mercurial blades, and while I still have the HEL rifle, I don't want to risk a shot going wide and destroying our atmo. Pretending at carelessness, I leave the rifle in the command center. Maybe one of the boarders will make the mistake of thinking they can use it and create an opening for us.

When we meet back in the hold, our first task is to check Sorrel's pod. While the emergency waking procedure is finished, Sorrel is hidden behind fogged-up glass. The cover sweats, beads of liquid balling up in the lack of gravity, as the pod warms him back to consciousness. I consider suggesting we tuck ourselves into one of the supply closets, but I know Ofiera won't leave Sorrel unguarded, so instead Ofiera and I find a place to take cover behind various crates of supplies in the hold.

The sound of rending metal ends with a loud thunk, and the ship falls into silence. I focus on my breathing, keeping it low and steady, as we wait for the boarding team to enter. After two minutes, I spot them descending into the hold and bite back a curse.

Four boarders, one right after the other, anchor themselves to the floor with their gravboots. They light their way with the silver glow of their mercurial blades, their military blacks obvious even in the dim lighting. Fucking duelists. After the incident at the labs, the military must be out in full force.

"They're hiding somewhere," the highest-ranking one, a woman with golden-red hair, says. "Head to the command center, see if you can get the power back on." A pair of duelists, Rapier and Dagger, break off to follow the order.

"Could be a trap," the woman's Dagger, a man who hasn't geneassisted his facial hair away like most Icarii, replies. "They could be waiting in the command center to split us up."

"We'll finish checking the hold, then join them," the woman responds. "We need to know if they've woken the Harbinger yet, whether there are three of them instead of two."

I chance a look at Sorrel's pod. There's still no movement from inside.

"Even if the Harbinger is awake, he shouldn't be fully functional," the man says. "It's only been a few hours."

The Rapier shrugs. "Didn't you read the briefing? I'm not underestimating any of them."

The two of them spread out and step cautiously around the hold. I don't see where the Dagger goes, but the Rapier starts in our direction. I know we'll have to fight, but my hope is that Ofiera and I can take them on one at a time so we won't become overwhelmed by their numbers. We saw four in the hold, but there's no telling how many are actually on board.

The Rapier slows nearby, turning the light of her blade in our direction. Her eyes narrow as if she saw something, and I hold as still as possible. Did she notice us watching her through the cracks between crates? Her grip tightens on the hilt, knuckles whitening. She takes four steps forward and stops in front of the very crate we're hiding behind.

I hold my breath as she reaches for something, but positioned where I am, I can't make out what it is. I can feel Ofiera bristling at my side, straining to keep still. *Prepare*, she pushes through the implant, but I'm as prepared as I can be. If this duelist finds us, our plan is done for. Her Dagger isn't nearly far enough away for us to take her out before he rushes to her aid, and as soon as the others up above hear us fighting, they'll come crashing down on us too.

Finally the Rapier draws back, face twisted in disgust. She holds up something slender and pale before dropping it and wiping her hand on her pant leg. "I found a fucking finger," she calls to her partner.

Mierda—I forgot all about Kristoff's finger. I must've left it in the hold, too focused on my own wound to remember to toss it.

"Whose finger?" her Dagger asks, emerging from behind a pile of crates. He doesn't come to her side, but he's still in a bad position; Sorrel's pod is only a couple of meters from him.

"Fuck if I know!" she snaps back. Is it possible for me to take out the Rapier while Ofiera deals with the Dagger? We may have to do it that way. I look at Ofiera, considering our next move.

The moment passes before I have a chance to decide. The Dagger turns, and just like that, his gaze lands on the pod.

"He's here!" he cries, and his Rapier spins away from us.

Now! Ofiera sends, but before we can even jump the crates, everything changes. The lid of Sorrel's pod blasts up like a small bomb went off within. It hits the ceiling and the glass shatters, floating like daggered snowflakes in a blizzard. "What the fuck—" the Dagger manages, and then his shield ripples as a shard of glass deflects from his neck.

The Rapier raises her mercurial blade to swing, but Ofiera launches into motion with me just behind her. At the same time, a body—long and lanky and tinted blue—launches out of the pod with the same force as the lid, sending glass shards crashing into the wall and floor like cutting chunks of hail. I risk a glance up but see nothing—no Sorrel—and I have no time to consider it before I'm on the Rapier.

She spins at the last moment, her blade coming up to meet mine, but I see from the diameter of battle—the mathematics made up of our height, our reach, the imagined circle around us—that I have the advantage in this clash. The angle of her blade is weak compared to mine—I caught her on the strongest part of my blade, near the hilt, while she's using the point of hers—but she has one card up her sleeve I can't possibly play. "They're here!" she screams, calling for reinforcements.

I curse, but with pressure, I knock her blade aside. Her body is open as she tries to reset, but I press forward with my longer legs, stepping into her range, aiming a cut low toward her belly—

Something large falls on her from the ceiling, colliding with her so hard that the blade is knocked from her hand and she hits the floor with a sick crack. No, whatever it is couldn't *fall*—there's no gravity—but as I step back, I see something hunched over her, and my breath catches in my throat.

Sorrel crouches on her chest, naked and covered in the slick blue fluid from the pod. Her gravboots are still tethered to the deck, her ankles snapped like dead twigs. Her furious screams become guttural howls as her shield flickers and gives out. With a final, shaky cry, she falls silent. I take a hesitant step forward only for Sorrel to jump away—

back to the ceiling, where he pulls himself along with hands and feet like a bony spider. The Rapier floats before me, two long shards of glass rammed into her open eyes.

Bile burns its way up my throat as I remember Ofiera's warning. *You can't wake him.* I misunderstood; I thought she was worried for him, when she was actually worried about us.

"Lito—" Ofiera's voice calls me back to the hold, back to the grasshopper still full of our enemies. The Dagger she faced off against is dead, his chest blade-tattered. She nudges me toward the ladder. "Let's go."

"What about—" My throat runs dry as I come up on his name. I glance up at the ceiling but see nothing in the dim lighting.

"He'll follow," she says without hesitation. She leads the way like she's the Rapier of the two of us, kicking her way to the ladder and pulling herself out of the hold, and for once I don't mind. I'm still reeling at what I've seen of Sorrel.

As soon as we emerge from the hold, the second pair of duelists falls upon us like wolves, no shouting or threats, just predators attacking predators. I batter my opponent, a Dagger with auburn hair, slashing my blade into his every opening, desperate to drive down the charge of his shield. But after what I saw in the hold, a part of me keeps checking the ceiling for Sorrel.

We dance down the hallway, away from Ofiera and her opponent. As we struggle, Sorrel slips from my mind. This man is far weaker than the Rapier I faced before, and so I press my advantage, using my long arms to strike without being struck.

His shield finally goes down. I stay my blade. "Surrender or die," I tell him.

He nods and moves to drop his blade. At the last second, his face twisting into a sneer, he darts forward and lashes out with a brutal slash at me. I jump backward, feeling heat bubbling across my palm. I release a curse as the hilt of my blade slips from my grip—in two pieces.

He smirks at me, an opponent now disarmed. "Surrender or die," he says.

But before he can raise his blade a second time, something silver darts past the corner of my eye and embeds itself in his throat—one of Ofiera's daggers. He doesn't so much fall as go limp, floating upright in the lack of gravity.

I clutch my bleeding hand to my chest. Between his body and mine drifts the mercurial blade I was given in the Academy with Hiro at my side—now broken, the hilt split, the liquid metal bubbling in the air and mixing with our blood.

"Lito, are you hurt?" Ofiera calls down the hallway. Behind her, the duelist she fought is dead, his arm floating separate from his body.

I am, but we don't have any more pelospray after my leg wound. "My blade—it's broken," I say as she comes floating over to me, not utilizing her gravboots.

Perhaps not realizing how much that blade meant to me, she plucks my opponent's from his stiffening fingers and offers it to me. "Can you still fight?"

I take it and, focusing on the hilt, feel the connection snap taut between it and me. I'm only able to connect to one at a time, and my awareness of my broken blade slips away. Though this one's exactly the same model as mine, it still feels different. I don't think it's because of the stinging pain of the cut on my palm. "Yes," I say, because there's no other choice. The four duelists have been taken care of, but if there are any more on board . . . "Let's get to the *Nyx*."

Our plan hasn't gone anywhere close to the way I wanted it to, but we're still alive and, for the most part, in one piece. We've just found the opening in the grasshopper's siding, the *Nyx*'s boarding airlock closed tight, when the lights of our ship flicker and turn back on.

"There's someone in the command center," I say, which means there must be another duelist pair around. With gravity returning at any moment, Ofiera hits the button to open the airlock to the *Nyx*, but before it pops open, someone cries out.

"I found them!" a pink-haired Rapier calls. I tighten my bleeding hand around the hilt of the mercurial blade and start to step toward her—but something rushes at her from behind, and I stumble to a halt.

Sorrel slips along the floor as silent and smooth as a shadow, as if moving in zero gravity is as easy as walking in full. He curls into himself as he nears the Rapier, coming at her knees, and it isn't until he's on her that she spins and looks down, her eyes flaring wide. At the same time the silver flash of Ofiera's knife hits one foot and then the other. The duelist doesn't scream, there's no splash of blood—but she floats upward softly, leaving the floor.

He slashed something in her gravboots, I realize.

The Rapier swings her blade at Sorrel, but with her feet untethered from the floor, the angle is all wrong, and Sorrel pushes himself from one wall to the other, dodging. Then with one strong spin, he dives, driving his legs into her chest and kicking her backward.

"Fuck!" She floats away from us, hands pinwheeling and damaged boots unable to grasp a thing. Gravity returns at that moment, slamming her into the floor. The airlock behind us opens.

"Move!" Ofiera commands me, jerking me into the *Nyx* after her.

I lose track of Sorrel as we push ourselves past the airlock and down the short boarding hallway between the two ships. As soon as we step into the *Nyx*, Ofiera punches an emergency lock button, and the airlock slams closed, cutting off the grasshopper from the *Nyx*. I can only assume Sorrel is with us.

The pink-haired Rapier, bruised and furious, hits the airlock window with twin thuds, hands scrabbling to engage the door. I'm surprised she's not dead, though I suppose Sorrel had no time to finish her off. Her eyes widen as she realizes what we've done. What we're doing. But if you ask me, we need this *Nyx* more than they do.

She shoots us a dirty gesture through the window, two split fingers pointing at her forehead. I smile and wave.

"Look sharp," Ofiera says, all business. "That woman's Dagger is unaccounted for."

"Right, and with the emergency lock engaged, anyone on this ship will know we're here," I say.

I haven't taken two steps into the *Nyx* before something hits me with the force of a stone wall. No, not something—some*one*.

"Ofiera!" I cry, but she's already locked in battle, trading parries with a Dagger.

I try to swing my blade at the person on me—another Rapier, it has to be—but they grab my wrist. I bring my knees up to kick them off me, and something cold drips onto my cheek. My subconscious screams an alarm, and I finally get a clear look at the person on me—

Sorrel. It's Sorrel—

He thrusts a knife at my neck.

"Sorrel!" Ofiera cries.

The knife shifts ever so slightly, grazing my neck instead of killing me. But blood pours from the wound—I feel the wetness on my shoulder and cheek—and Sorrel doesn't move from where he looms over me, pale blue skin stretched tightly over stark bones. One of Ofiera's throwing knives is pressed to my throat, while his other hand digs into my chest, creating finger-shaped bruises. His Aster eyes are chips of cold ice, the pupils black and yawning.

I know exactly what I see in those eyes: he wants to kill me.

"Icarii duelist," Sorrel spits. To him, I'm just another faceless target.

"No!" Ofiera's voice is ragged with strain, and that's when everything *shifts*—

A hand fists in my hair, pulling my head upward scalp-first, forcing me to look at the five Asters standing before a pale wall, hands bound before them. "Remember this," a man whispers in my ear before he raises his voice and commands, "Fire!" Gunshots ring out, and bullets tear my comrades to pieces—an eye popped like an opened flower, a pulverized jaw and a dangling tongue, chests caving in on the hearts they're meant to protect—and the wall behind them is painted red and will never be pale again—

My hands are bound to a metal chair, my ankles tied to the same. Thick belts—one around my waist, the other around my neck—keep me from squirm-

ing. A man in a white coat steps into the room. In his hand is a syringe full of a strange milky fluid. The needle is the length of my hand from wrist to the tip of my middle finger. I try to ask what he's going to do, but my mouth refuses to function. At my side, he presses a thumb to my eyelid and pulls it to my brow bone so I can't blink. "Let's play a game," he says. The needle comes toward my eye—

"You have five minutes," a man says. I sluggishly drag my dizzy gaze toward her—the only woman who matters—and when I meet her eyes, green with a brown corona, my breath catches. I try to rise, but she's beside me too soon, hands against my aching, shaven head, and I press my face into her chest and weep. "Fi . . . Fi . . ." Her touch is my only comfort. Her words are the only ones I want to hear. And whatever they did to us, whatever they put inside us when they cut us open, means that this moment in which we're together is the only time I feel whole again—

I slam back into my own body, Ofiera's knife sharp against my throat. Sorrel's eyes have softened, his pupils growing round.

"You . . ." he starts, and by the thousand gods, I feel him. I *feel* him, like I should Ofiera or Hiro. Those were his memories, and I saw them like they were mine.

The realization crashes down on me: our neural implants are connected.

Ofiera screams.

"Fi!" Sorrel cries. He's off me and gone, and I instinctively follow. What I see chills me to my core: The last remaining duelist, the Dagger, his blade entering Ofiera's back and emerging from her belly. Her hands scrabble in the blood, desperately holding her midsection—holding her guts from spilling out onto the floor, I realize with horror.

She saved my life by connecting me to Sorrel, but it cost her everything to do it.

I tighten my grip on my blade—my enemy's blade, not my own, because mine is broken and I'll never fight with it again—as Sorrel screams a wordless, animal cry and launches himself at the Dagger.

The Dagger swings diagonally at Sorrel, but Sorrel drops to the floor and tackles his legs out from beneath him. The duelist falls, back slamming into the ground, face pointed at the ceiling, and Sorrel jumps atop him, presses his knees into the other man's chest. Ofiera's knife is in his hand, slamming again and again at his face but coming up against his shield.

The Dagger's eyes are wide in fear, but his pupils focus in fury.

"Sorrel!" I scream, because I see what he, in his madness, does not.

The Dagger still holds his mercurial blade. With a smooth flick of his fingers, he flips the blade in his hand and drives it toward Sorrel's head.

This time I call out through the implant, screaming for Sorrel to *Move!* He looks up just in time, flings himself off the Dagger in a roll—

Blood mists the air.

Thousand gods, he hit Sorrel—

I rush forward, no time to consider how odd this strange blade feels in my hand. The Dagger stands, jumps toward Sorrel to finish him off, but I seize him around the neck and bring him up short. My instinct takes over, and I angle the tip of the blade into his back, point it toward his spine, and push. There's resistance at first, his shield struggling to protect him, but then it breaks, overtaxed, and his body jerks as I cut him in two. Just like he did Ofiera.

He falls face-first before Sorrel, a supplicant bowing in worship.

Sorrel looks down at the Dagger, then up at me. A cut in his face bleeds freely, a line from his jaw to his temple. His eyes melt from the bloodlust of the fight, well up with shimmering tears.

"Fi . . ." he says, and to me it sounds like an accusation.

The blade slips through my fingers, and we both rush to her.

CHAPTER 10

ASTRID

[19] The people asked, "For who is to serve the servants?" And seven of them who listened stepped forward to take up the burden. [20] "We are advanced in age and have no children of our own," they said. "Allow us to speak for those who cannot." [21] The people were glad with this and named the seven the Agora.

The Canon, Works 14:19–21

The *Juno* moves with all haste, and yet the time on board feels like a lifetime. Every night is a year. Every day rewinds to an hour long ago. In that chapel, Arturo first kissed me and took me to bed. In that hallway, the six Icarii quicksilver warriors boarded and killed Jones. In that exact spot in the hangar, Saito Ren said one sentence to me and changed the course of my life.

I try to do my duty by the soldiers on board, offering them blessings or prayers, but whenever I am with them, I catch glimpses of Ringer. He is a great shadow prowling through the halls, the scent of my blood caught in his nose drawing him closer. I fear him—fear my own madness—more than anything else.

I spend my days with Eden or Aunt Margaret, desperate for the company. Even Lily, if only to keep Ringer at bay. We talk of the Agora—not the blackmail that she offered me, but of facts: names, Orders, their reach. At night, I call the soldier boy—Rian, he introduces himself the second time—from my door to my bed. Sometimes I allow him to stay until morning.

Eden does not say it in so many words, but she worries about me. She begs me to confide in her, perhaps believing it is only our past that concerns me. When I finally do feel enough strength to share some of my burden, I find myself telling her of my meeting in the showers with Lily.

"Blackmail?" Her eyebrows move up her freckled forehead. "No, we don't want to sink to that level." But when I say nothing in response, when I do not immediately agree with her, she narrows her green eyes in my direction. "We don't want to sink to blackmailing the Aunts, do we, Astrid?"

"No," I say, but my heart isn't in it and I fear she can hear that. "Not yet, anyway." I can tell she doesn't like that addition, but she says nothing in order to avoid a fight.

It is that night, on my way back to my chambers, that Ringer finally corners me. Rian strides too far ahead, or I linger too far behind, and then from one moment to the next, he is beside me.

"'Astrid,' is it now?" he asks, and the name I had chosen, my secret pride, suddenly becomes my shame. The name was taken from him, from the younger sister in his stories of home.

In truth, who knows where the name came from? His sister or my sister or no one at all. "I always said you were my little sister." He smiles down at me with all the kindness I remember; he was never ill-tempered toward me, always respectful. It is hard to remember, with him so close and comforting, why I hate him so.

Because he's not real. I have to focus on that. He is not my big brother, not a link to my past; he is simply a damaged part of my brain manifesting before me.

"Do not act like you are surprised," I hiss, because he should already know the name I chose. He *is* me.

But before he can form a response, Rian has returned. "First Sister?" he asks, and I see nothing but confusion in the set of his forehead and jaw.

Did he hear me speak? What does he see when he looks at me? Certainly not Ringer, who stands close enough for me to touch.

"Thinking about when you worked here?" Rian asks, a big smile splitting his face in two.

I ignore my ghost, refusing to give him so much as a glance, as I join Rian. With a nod, I encourage him to continue toward my quarters. Let him believe I was simply lost in the past, as opposed to the far darker truth.

Ringer does not follow, though his voice does. "I'll always be here for you," he says, and I do not know if he means here on the *Juno*, or here inside me, in the blackest part of me, waiting for me to slip. "When you need me, I will come."

I am only too thankful when we reach my room and I can close the door and lose myself in Rian.

FIVE DAYS AFTER we depart from Ceres, the *Juno* docks above Olympus Mons. Because of its immense size, we are forced to take a dropship to the upper station, where we wait until our full group is ferried across. It is no longer just Aunt Margaret, Lily, Eden, and me on our journey; other soldiers, including the captain of the *Juno*, and the First Sister are descending to the surface as well.

At the scheduled time of departure, we trail into the expansive construction that is the space elevator. The walls of the interior ring are decorated in a floral pattern, Sisterhood symbols subtly interwoven in the vines and leaves, while the exterior walls are clear to allow passengers an unaltered view. Unassigned chairs are set both facing and against the windows, but the elevator moves along the tether gently enough that the seats aren't necessary.

I try to keep to myself, but First Sister of the *Juno* seeks me out as soon as her captain turns his attention elsewhere. *First Sister*, she signs, *is there something I can do to help you?*

Are my wounds so obvious to her? Or is this something worse—is she prying for information? I cannot imagine who she would serve when a new Auntie has been placed in charge of the *Juno*. Whomever she reports to, I suppose. Could it be Aunt Marshae?

Do not concern yourself with me, I sign. *As Meditations 2:19 says, "Every garden is beset by weeds."* A common enough platitude in the Sisterhood, one we Sisters lean on when we want to admit things are not going our way but do not wish to talk about it. The evasion would fail were she my superior—Aunts cannot be circumvented by scripture—but I outrank her, and so she accepts it.

I leave her with that. After I visit the refreshments station attended to by an unnamed Sister, I lose track of her among the hundred or so people on board. Relieved, I find a seat facing a window and watch as we plunge through the black of space to the surface of Mars.

It has been more than a year since I was on the space elevator, its clean white trunk growing straight into the heart of the Temple of Mars. The last time, I was hurtling upward with all speed, my excitement mirrored in its movement, as I raced toward my new assignment on the *Juno*. Now I am returning with far more power than I ever imagined I would wield.

I cannot say that I feel as if I am returning home. The Temple was no more a home to me than Matron Thorne's orphanage. Or perhaps they were both homes, just temporary ones, like the *Juno* and Ceres have been. But I feel no longing for the place, no happy memories surging up within me, no nostalgia for my childhood. I feel only the resolution that beats alongside my heart, driving me to face the Agora that awaits me below.

We pass the orbital mirrors used to heat the surface and enter the Martian atmosphere. Around the high midday sun, the sky is a brilliant blue, but it is the horizon that I focus on, a burning red corona, which makes me think Mars has been crowned in a halo of blood.

Below, cities sprawl, trails of silver and light. Mars's numerous chemical plants crouch on the edge of every settlement, constantly producing greenhouse gases and filtering air and water. Other compounds, either imported from Earth or synthesized from local deposits, are released into the atmosphere through them. Of course, gravity is still a problem, being lighter than Earth's, but only outside the gravity-controlled settlements.

The biggest and most populous cities are the domed ones, such as the capital, Olympus Mons. The domes are few and far between—hermium being hard to come by, since we Geans must scavenge for it—but those we do have illuminate the surface in brilliant blues and golds.

It is into the capital that we descend, the space elevator passing seamlessly through the hermium barrier built over the Olympus Mons caldera. No matter how many times I see the city, it still inspires awe. Starscrapers stretch to the dome's limit with curving rooftops. Between buildings, glowing pathways bridge gaps, thinner for foot traffic and wider for elevators to pass horizontally. Large, flat balconies protrude at various levels, those for landing ships colored vibrant red. One born in the Olympus Mons dome could live their entire life in the starscrapers, their feet never touching the Martian surface, if they so desired.

But looming over it all, built atop natural Martian stone and sitting at the highest point in the crater, is the Temple of Mars. It is there that the space elevator will come to rest, for the Sisterhood funded its building and continues to control it. And it is there that my destiny waits for me . . .

After a time, Eden comes to my side and slides her hand into mine. I lean my head onto her shoulder, taking strength from her. We both know there's a knife's edge between success and failure. And we both know I am as prepared as I can be.

AFTER THE SPACE elevator comes to a stop at the lower station and the soldiers assigned to guard the hub scan us, we split into those who have come to enter the city and those who have business at the Temple. I am not surprised when only my party and a handful of other young Sisters enter the Sisterhood grounds, while the majority of visitors, for one reason or another, have come for the capital. As we cross the courtyard between the station and the Temple on foot, I am transported through time.

The Temple is everything I remember. Cold white marble veined with gray. Golden vines and leaves, curling over columns. The entablature above the main entrance weaves together the seven symbols of the Orders around a white oak tree; among the branches, the image of the Sisterhood's golden leaf sigil repeats. I spot the stone wrapped in chains of the Order of Andromeda, and think of the broken manacles that have become my symbol on Ceres.

I want the Sisterhood to be better. I want the Sisterhood to serve You, I pray to the Goddess as I enter, *without having to sacrifice happiness.*

The hallways are open and airy. Little Sisters spot us and run to tell their elders of our arrival, their feet clapping against the stone in a way that will surely have them punished. The air smells of lavender and growing things, but the sound—or lack of it—is stunning. After the passing of the girls, there is nothing but silence.

We leave the entrance hall for the courtyard between the main cluster of governmental buildings. Behind them are residences for Sisters of various ranks, as well as the quarters for Little Sisters. Farther back are the halls for Aunts, one of which is fully dedicated to the members of the Agora and another to the Mother. While the heads of each Order may have additional properties off-site, they are also allotted a home here.

Aunt Margaret sits on a white bench, her back to a tree with heart-shaped leaves and a placard labeled *Tilia americana.* "We'll wait for our guides in the courtyard," she says, her voice soft with the reverence of this place. I cast a quick glance at Lily, who is too absorbed in putting on a pair of gray gloves to notice me. If not for her, I would believe we were to be given rooms and allowed to rest. If not for her, I would not know the truth: the Agora waits for me.

I press a hand to my stomach to count my breaths and make my way through the courtyard to the central pavilion. Open to the carefully cultivated trees and flowering plants, the pavilion arcs like a cocoon of wood, sweeping from one side of the courtyard to the other. I enter the cool space to admire the artwork within.

The statues are spectacular representations in alabaster, the women on plinths covering themselves from head to foot with a fabric thin as gossamer, their faces obscured but their bodies tantalizingly hinted at—there, the curve of a breast, and there, the dip between two legs. Beneath each is the name of one of the Mothers, though at the end of one row, I find one of the plinths empty. With a sinking feeling, I know immediately it is reserved for Mother Isabel III's statue. As Eden passes by me, I pointedly turn away from the space.

Eden moves to the center of the pavilion, where the grandest statue of all resides. The ancient marble figure from Earth was transported here when Mars became a thriving colony under the Sisterhood's guidance. Now she looms above us on a choppy pedestal like the figurehead of an old ship, standing with wings outstretched and dress billowing in an unfelt wind. Her arms and head are missing, but the statue still radiates triumph and hope. *Victory*, the copper plaque beneath her reads, polished bright by all the hands that have touched it over the years.

As a child, I came here to pray to her as if she were the Goddess. Seeing Eden stand before *Victory* and press her fingers to the plaque, I think she likely did too. I watch her for a moment, red hair trailing down her back. When I step to her side, I see her eyes shining as she looks up at the angelic statue, reminding me of her words when we first arrived on Ceres. *I want to change things.*

I place my hand over hers on *Victory*'s name. "Let's change things," I whisper to her. Her lips cautiously curl into a rare smile, and she gratefully laces our fingers together.

Our peace is interrupted by the sound of approaching footsteps. Eden and I turn to find Aunt Margaret and Lily, along with a familiar face I did not think I would see so soon.

My Aunt Delilah.

Though we have been apart for years, there is little about my Auntie that has changed: smooth obsidian skin, hair trimmed close to her scalp. Even her face seems arrested, not having aged a day. Then I notice the one thing that has changed: around her neck is a golden medallion depicting the chain-wrapped stone of the Order of Andromeda.

Aunt Delilah has become one of the Agora.

The Little Sister I used to be wishes to fling myself into her arms; even the adult in me wants to celebrate our individual achievements. Though it has been years since we worked together, she could be a benefit to me on the Agora. But her dark eyes do not so much as change when she looks at me, almost as if she does not recognize me.

Behind her, another Aunt stands amidst a group of Little Sisters— no, not Little Sisters, not yet. For they do not yet dress in gray, but in a mix of ill-fitting clothing in faded colors. They watch us with wide eyes, many hunched or too thin, a few with stretched, crooked limbs from a lack of gravity medication. My heart thuds heavily at their shoddy appearances. Where did they come from, and who cared for them so poorly?

When Aunt Delilah sees me noticing, she waves a hand as if to bid me to ignore them. "New orphans from the city," she explains, as if I cannot see that for myself. As if I were not one of them, once upon a time.

"First Sister of Ceres," she says to get my attention, but when I look back at her, my mind is still on those girls, on their hopeful faces. "We welcome you to the Temple of Mars. There are several things we must address. Firstly, the Agora has summoned you before them. Will you heed their call?"

I search her expression for some hint of gentleness or recognition. I find nothing. After a couple of heavy heartbeats, I remember I am meant to appear shocked by the summons, perhaps even nervous, but it is not hard to furrow my brows and let my eyes prick with tears when those bent and broken children stand behind her. *Of course*, I sign.

Aunt Delilah turns back to the waiting group. "Aunt Francisca," she calls, "take the girls to their new room." I do not miss the singular *room* for the dozen or so girls before me. I shared a room with only three others as a Little Sister. Is there an overcrowding problem at the Temple, or has some new measure been passed to allot them less space?

Before I can ask, Aunt Delilah gracefully turns, her robes swirling, and holds out an arm to Aunt Margaret. "Let's go, Margaret," she says, and, arm in arm with her fellow Aunt, strides before us. "Follow me," she tosses over her shoulder to the rest of us, as if she does not care whether or not we do.

I watch until the girls disappear before I follow. Eden tries to take my hand again, but I do not let her. The thing in my chest growls with a mounting anger. Are they recruiting more girls, or are they simply caring for them less? My heart boils until I half expect Ringer to appear at any moment, summoned by my wild emotions, but he is blissfully silent. Perhaps a part of me knows he does not belong here in this monument to the sacrifice of women.

We pass through the parts of the Temple I know, plants and decorations blurring together, and come to a rest before the building dedicated to the Agora. I have never been inside the Agora's chambers during a formal session, but I know what awaits me and I am ready. I *have* to do this, for orphan girls like me.

Aunt Margaret and Aunt Delilah enter before me. Another Aunt bars me from following, making it clear that I will have to wait until every member of the Agora is ready. But I do not pace or fidget; I remain by the ornate wooden doors, my eyes tracing the delicately carved vines and flowers.

What will happen if they find me guilty of overstepping my role as First Sister of Ceres? Surely my path to becoming the next Mother will be blocked, but will they also strip my title? The fire within me grows until my hands are shaking. Not from fear, but with rage.

When another Aunt slips out of the chambers and motions to me,

I know it's time. The doors are flung open to me in welcome. Before I enter, my companions come to my side.

We are with you, Eden signs to me.

Remember what I told you, Lily says, and in this moment of rushing anxiety and anger, I do not hate her for it.

Thank you, I tell them both, and mean it.

I leave them behind, striding through the doorway with my shoulders squared, my back straight, and my golden hair swaying. When the doors creak closed behind me, cutting me off from any support, I do not stumble or hesitate.

I emerge from the shadows of the hallway into a cobblestoned pit. Light filters from the ceiling—glass stained in shades of blue and interspersed with stars of bronze—to the center of the space, where a podium awaits. The room is vast and shaped like an amphitheater, with great marble tiers looming above me. Carved directly from the stone are seven high-backed chairs, banners embroidered with the symbols of each Order draped over the backs. In each chair sits an Aunt of the Agora, dressed in a red cope clasped by the golden medallions they always wear.

I refuse to cower under their collective gaze. I stride into the middle of the room and take my place behind the podium, unabashedly looking up at the women who will decide my fate. From here, they look like part of the architecture. From here, I could almost pretend they are statues and nothing more.

Then I hear *her* voice, speaking the words that open every meeting of the Agora. "Veritas iustitia ad astra." *Truth and justice to the stars*, says Aunt Marshae, her flat tone sending a shudder down my spine. I knew she would be here, and yet seeing her again brings back the pain of her sharp nails digging into my skin.

"First Sister of Ceres, we, the Agora, accuse you of abuse of authority." She speaks slowly, drawing out the agony. I thought I would never forget her features, but my memory has softened them in our time apart. Before me she is as sharp as a knife—pointed cheekbones, sculpted auburn hair, sturdy shoulders.

She leans forward, the banner bearing the symbol of her office—an empty throne—looming large at her back. As the head of the Order of Cassiopeia, Aunt Marshae levels the charges. "Your release of the six Icarii prisoners was unauthorized by any governing body and could have resulted in the loss of valuable resources. What do you have to say to these accusations?"

Though I stand behind the podium, I do not lean on it. "I do not deny these charges," I say, fully expecting the widened eyes and soft gasps that follow my proclamation. I am sure many Sisters have come before them who did not speak at all, and I want them to know that I am one who has been granted the freedom of my voice. "As you say, Aunt Marshae, my actions *could* have lost us resources. But they did not. In fact, the return of the Icarii prisoners with the message of peace on behalf of all Geans benefited us more than the resources we could have traded for their return. Now the Geans and Icarii have entered a cease-fire with a chance at true peace between us."

"You do not deny that you abused your authority on Ceres?" asks Aunt Margaret, looking particularly authoritative in her red cope. Coming from her, the question feels scripted.

"I do not deny that I did not seek the permission of the Agora," I respond, "but I received valuable information that the return of the Icarii with a message of peace would be not just accepted but welcomed." I do not mention that the idea came from Saito Ren. From Hiro val Akira. I had no guarantee it would play out so well, but I suspected, after all that Hiro had said. "I did not contact the Agora because I had no time. My intelligence informed me that if I did not act immediately, the opportunity would be lost." I can only pray they have no way to prove that isn't true. I acted quickly because I did not want the Agora involved, because I knew they would deny my request.

"Who provided you with this information?" Aunt Delilah asks, wielding her words like a weapon.

"You should know better than to ask a member of the Sisterhood to name her source," Aunt Tamar, an eagle-eyed woman of the Order of Orion, snaps at Aunt Delilah. Her hair is covered by the silk scarf most Aunts wear about their necks. "We are all allowed our secrets," she finishes, her face so impassive, I cannot tell if she approves of me or wishes I would burst into flames. She probably would not even arch an eyebrow if I did.

"Well, her plan worked, didn't it?" asks Aunt Sapphira of the Order of Leo, tucking her wild mane of honey hair behind her ears. "I'm sure it would be different if the cease-fire weren't in place, but it is. Why are we complaining?"

"Because—" Aunt Marshae starts, but she is cut off by others speaking at the same time. I have to fight back a smile, to see her so out of her element.

"First Sister of Ceres can be accused of nothing but eagerness," young Aunt Salomiya of the Order of Virgo purrs. With her red cope and similar-colored hair, she shines like a brilliant flame. "Look at all she has done to help on Ceres. Even after the Leander Incident."

The entire room chills at the mention of the Leander Incident. I bite my tongue; none of them were on Ceres when it happened. None of them saw the panic in the aftermath of the warship's destruction.

None of them except Aunt Margaret, who waves a hand through the air. "An Icarii problem best left to the Icarii. The First Sister of Ceres behaved adequately to calm the populace."

"And," Aunt Sapphira adds loudly, "we should remember that the First Sister of Ceres had only ever been the First Sister of the *Juno*. She's unaccustomed to the position of leadership she now has."

"She's unfit for leadership, you mean," drones Aunt Tamar.

Aunt Sapphira snarls. "I didn't say that . . ."

Aunt Genette looks up from her lap and whatever has consumed her attention there—a compad, maybe? "Wasn't Aunt Margaret in charge of her training, since the late Mother passed before she could instruct our new First Sister of Ceres? I think the blame should fall on her." She bares her long, narrow teeth at Aunt Margaret, making it clear there's no love lost there.

Aunt Margaret's smile grows, but she doesn't deign to respond. The rest ignore Genette too.

"Silence!" Aunt Marshae snaps, finally regaining control. Everyone falls quiet, though Aunt Salomiya glares at her. "This is between the Agora, as one, and the First Sister of Ceres. We cannot allow the authority of the Agora to be questioned. Not now, not ever."

Aunt Sapphira, her face twisted in offense, turns fully toward Aunt Marshae. "But I can hardly see why she should be punished for achieving such results—"

Aunt Marshae cuts her off, voice raised until I am sure even Lily and Eden, waiting outside, can hear her. "Because the Fist Sister of Ceres aims to become the next Mother!" she snaps, and all at once I feel plunged into icy water.

It takes all my strength not to look at Aunt Margaret, to see how she is responding to this. We had both wanted to settle at the Temple before she brought her nomination of me forward. Now that plan—and all of our subsequent ones—are smashed by Aunt Marshae.

"Look at the way she snatches for power," Aunt Marshae goes on. "Look at how she shirks our authority. You are a fool if you think this unintentional, and you would be a fool to believe her ambitions begin and end here." She lowers her voice as if speaking only to them. "Why else would she have traveled from Ceres to come before us, if not to seek the position of Mother?"

Everyone is silenced by her announcement. Everyone is still. Whatever they think of my desire to become the next Mother is completely hidden from me. But for a moment, as Aunt Marshae looks at the Aunts on either side of her, I can see only the chasms between them. The hatred they hold for each other.

Lily's words come back to me. What secrets do these women keep? What factions exist among them? Along what lines do they vote? And how can I manipulate that?

"There is one more piece of evidence that proves you seek to subvert the authority of the Agora." Aunt Marshae's attention rests fully on me again. Her sharp nails dig into the stone arms of her chair as she returns to the trial already under way. "'Unchained,' they call you." My stomach sinks at the word. To hear it here, of all places, perverts it. "Why have you dressed Ceres in the broken manacles of Andromeda?"

I feel the shift in the room at her words. The infighting forgotten, fourteen eyes turn toward me. To claim it was not me who chose the symbol will seem childish when I allowed it to continue. When I took *pride* in being known as the Unchained. Aunt Margaret tried to warn me . . .

I swallow my anxiety and clear my throat. I have no time for fear.

"Works 1:7," I begin, and am proud when my voice does not shake. "'Sister Marian went unto the house of Cousin Tabeta and saw that Cousin Tabeta had bound a man before his shed. So Sister Marian turned to Cousin Tabeta and asked, "Why have you chained this citizen?" And Cousin Tabeta answered, "For he has stolen from me and mine, and I would have him tried for his crimes." Sister—'"

Aunt Marshae scoffs. "Oh, please—"

I continue, louder than before. "'Sister Marian looked upon the bound man. "Why have you stolen from Cousin Tabeta?" she asked, and the man hung his head in shame. "I have no tools with which to repair my home," he said.'"

"We know the Canon, girl!" Aunt Marshae snaps.

"'"Bring forth the tools," Sister Marian said, and the tools were set before her, evidence of the man's crime. And with the strength of the Goddess, she took up a single hammer from the pile and smashed the chain binding the man's hands.'"

"Stop this at once!"

"'The man did not flee. "Why have you done this?" Cousin Tabeta asked of Sister Marian. And Sister Marian answered with the wisdom of the Goddess: "For now that he is unchained, he will be able to work alongside me to repair his home."'"

I stop and gasp in a deep breath. Sweat beads along my forehead, but I do not even dare to lift a hand to wipe it away. The Aunts stare at me with a mix of shock and pride. Only Aunt Margaret smiles as if pleased.

And only Aunt Marshae fumes.

"If we wished to test your memorization," she mutters, "we would do so."

"You asked me," I say, sounding out of breath because I am, "why Ceres is dressed in broken manacles." The Aunts lean forward in their chairs, drawn by the softness of my voice. "I answer you: because I would have the people of Ceres work alongside me to repair their home.

"As to the other accusations, I do not deny that I aspire to the position of Mother," I go on. There is only the truth now, and hiding from it will do me no favors. "But I hope that, like Ceres, we can work together. Unbound. Unchained. For the betterment of this world on behalf of the Goddess."

Silence. But I can tell from the way the Aunts watch me with new-found respect that my message has left an impression.

After a moment, Aunt Marshae speaks again. "The punishment for abuse of authority is the removal of the First Sister of Ceres from her post."

Whatever small confidence I gained moments ago is lost. I do my best not to show the horror I feel on my face.

Of course Aunt Marshae wants to take my post—my very *name*—away from me, when it was her mistake that granted it to me in the first place.

"I call for a vote," Aunt Marshae says.

"Seconded," responds Aunt Margaret.

"All those in favor of convicting the First Sister of Ceres of abuse of authority and removing her from office?" Aunt Marshae, of course, does not hesitate. "I vote yes."

"Yes," Aunt Genette says immediately, smiling at Aunt Marshae as she does so. The lines in the sand along which each Aunt votes make themselves briefly visible . . .

"No," Aunt Margaret says, causing Aunt Genette to scoff.

"No," Aunt Salomiya agrees.

Two yes, two no. Three votes to go.

"Yes," Aunt Sapphira says, surprising me. I thought she was on my side . . .

"No," Aunt Delilah says. Again, a shock.

A tie. The last vote will decide. We all turn to Aunt Tamar, the woman who looks down at me with disdain. Who accused me of being ill-prepared for authority.

Aunt Marshae smirks as my future unravels, and I cannot breathe as I meet the hard eyes of the woman who holds my fate in her hands.

"No," Aunt Tamar says at last.

All the air rushes out of me. I am still the First Sister of Ceres. I am not the Mother, but there is a chance I will be.

Aunt Marshae is so motionless, she might have turned to stone. But no—there—I see two trails of red trickling down the right arm of her chair. Could that be—

"Finish it, Marshae," Aunt Margaret says in her public voice, the one she uses for recordings and ceremonies. "She is found not guilty. Finish it."

As if slapped, Aunt Marshae jerks her right hand into her lap, droplets of blood following. With mounting disgust, I see what has happened: she ripped off two sharp nails in her rage.

"Against the charge of abuse of authority," she says, voice hollow, "the First Sister of Ceres is found not guilty."

And like that, it is done.

"Dismissed!" Aunt Marshae shouts, making the word sound like a curse. She is out of her chair and leaving the room before I can even move from the podium. And though I watch her stalk away, I see Aunt Genette rushing after her, a puppy to its master, and know that my struggle is far from over.

MY CHAMBERS IN the Temple are smaller than those I was allowed on the *Juno*. I wonder if this is just another way the Agora is slighting me.

If they expect me to throw a tantrum, they're sorely mistaken. I brought little with me to necessitate a large room, and I have lived in such small, cramped spaces that this is still exorbitant to me. Plus, I have a view over the courtyard that houses the space elevator. Even if it is noisy, I love to watch the comings and goings of Sisters and soldiers alike.

And it works as an excellent distraction . . .

A knock on the door startles me from my thoughts. Eden and Lily enter a second later.

"You did amazingly!" Lily exclaims halfway to me. When she reaches the chaise lounge I perch on, she sits down next to me as if I invited her. Though I suppose there is no other furniture in the room . . .

"I still need Aunt Margaret to put my name forth for the position of Mother," I say, shaking my head. "I hate these political maneuvers."

Eden sits down on the other side of me, squishing me between her and Lily. "That's the life you've signed up for, Astrid. You'll just have to deal with it. But I think you did really well, for what it's worth."

"Did you overhear everything?" I ask.

"What we didn't hear, we asked Aunt Margaret about afterward," Eden says.

"And the good news," Lily chirps, her face lit up with excitement, "is that the Agora are all talking about you."

I sigh. "Yes, I am sure Aunt Marshae and Aunt Genette are cursing my name even now . . ."

Lily taps a finger against her chin. "Aunt Marshae does hate you."

"You have no idea," Eden mutters.

"And Aunt Genette tends to follow Aunt Marshae's whims," Lily admits. "But that's only two of the seven. Not so bad."

"Why?" I muse aloud. "What sway does Aunt Marshae hold over Aunt Genette?"

Lily's doe eyes seem to darken at the words. Does she know the answer? But before she says anything, Eden chimes in, "It doesn't matter, if you can prove your worth to the Agora. Create some outreach programs here on Mars like you did on Ceres. Sway the faithful and show the Agora how people naturally love you."

It's good advice, but it would take months. I fear what allowing Aunt Marshae that much time will achieve. I think of the crooked-limbed girls, their dirty faces filled with hope. I've seen the disorganization in the Agora. How they snipe at each other without thinking of the people they're meant to serve. How many will continue to suffer until a new Mother begins to change things?

"Lily."

She straightens at her name.

"Bring me everything you can find on Aunt Genette and Aunt Marshae." If I am to begin, let me begin with my most obvious opponents.

"Astrid—" Eden starts.

I hold up a hand. "The information will help me choose a place to start my work." I do not call it blackmail, not like Lily. It is simply information, and I would be a fool to go into this fight ill-prepared. When Eden bites her tongue, I look between the girls on either side of me. "Together, we'll root out the corruption within the Sisterhood."

CHAPTER 11

HIRO

I'm concerned that you're not concerned about the concern of the Synthetics, ya know? Say we catch their agent. What next? Interrogate her? Torture her for answers? Kill her? Not sure I like the idea of pissing off the Synthetics when you're squatting in their backyard.

Message from Hiro to Dire, read but not answered

At first there is nothing but the darkness, neither the sound of my breathing nor the beating of my heart. But against the expanse that stretches infinite before me, there is no emotion either— no fear or anxiety; the world simply is. Slowly at first, and then with increasing speed, little pinpricks of light appear and grow, stars blooming into being and giving life to the sky above. One star larger than the others flares golden and warm, emerging from behind a pale blue planet, and its light hits the rocky, pitted ground beneath me and makes the world I stand on shine white from horizon to horizon.

I instinctively know where I am: Earth's moon, whole and ancient, the birthplace of the first sentient machines. I bend down, gather a handful of dust, and let it slip between my fingers. It falls slower than snow in the low gravity.

A light to my left burns a halo in the atmosphere. In the corona is a white fox, its tail trailing into the cosmos, joining the heated drifts of galaxies in its wake. It moves with the grace of a fish through water, its tail rippling as a single banner one moment, spreading into nine the next.

It does not turn its head in my direction, but it opens its eye, dark as a black hole.

Eyes it opens, one after another, on its cheek and forehead and neck. More blink into existence, down shoulder and spine, over haunches and limbs, and my blood runs cold.

I see you, it says, black hole eyes swallowing, and even the stars turn their gazes toward me, each a giant eye in the sky.

We see you.

I VIOLENTLY JOLT awake, swinging my arms and kicking my legs. My fists meet nothing but air, and as soon as I have my feet beneath me, I spin in a circle, looking for Noa and Nadyn, for other Icarii duelists who have infiltrated Autarkeia.

I see you, the dream—nightmare?—whispers in my brain. *We see you.*

But there is no army, not even a threatening soldier with a hand on their mercurial blade. There is just a figure so unassuming she blends in with her surroundings.

Half her head is the shiny metal of a prosthetic, the other half sporting long black hair that she shyly uses to hide her face. Her clothes are black and baggy, fit for someone twice her size. She is sun-starved pale, but in a strange, waxy way, and she is so small and wispy that my initial instinct is to drop my guard. I suppose that's the point—she doesn't look like a threat, even though I know she is.

"You're the Synthetic." My words echo around us in the cold, high-ceilinged room. We're on a strange metal catwalk that hangs above a great donut-shaped metallic object, and the walls are covered in branching ramps, as elegant and yet as chaotic as unchecked vines in nature. There are no sharp angles, only rounded edges, leaving the entire place feeling alien and unwelcoming, designed by capricious gods who care nothing for human necessities. Everything metal is rusted a reddish-brown from disuse. Could I be inside one of the dead Synthetic factories?

Sudden movement from her startles me, but she just lifts a hand, fingers splayed, and wiggles it back and forth. It takes me a moment to realize . . . she's waving. "Hello," she says in a singsong.

"I . . . What am I doing here?"

"I'm sorry," she says, scratching her cheek. "I didn't mean to scare you, but I didn't want the others to find you." As she speaks, I begin to understand that singsong fluidity is just her accent. I've never heard one like hers before, but then . . . she's allied with the Synthetics. I'd never considered it before, but why would they speak like we do?

"You can go back to sleep if you're hurting," she says.

"Huh?"

She points a slender finger at me, at the place I rub my shoulder, where flesh meets prosthetic. A habit I have, one I don't even notice anymore.

"You were sleeping, so I put you in my bed, but maybe I shouldn't have?"

I check my com-lenses for the time and do a quick calculation . . . Shit! I was out for seven hours? Despite our disastrous call, Dire's got to be looking for me by now. But at the same time, contacting her is my mission, and I doubt I'll get a second chance if I don't establish some rapport with her now.

I clear my throat and look behind me at her "bed," but it is that in name only. The mattress sits directly on the floor, covered in so many pillows and stray blankets I can't see the sheets. None of the bedding matches, though it's clean; it looks like a scavenger stole each piece from a different Cytherean hotel.

"Maybe you're hungry or thirsty?"

What are you, my mom? I bite my tongue against the comment. I mean, she got me away from Noa and Nadyn, even if she had to drug me and drag me to her weird lair to do so.

Though shouldn't I be thankful that *she* appeared to *me*? Following her data ghost was getting me nowhere. Did my awful painting of the rat work? Is this her version of accepting my offer of friendship?

She crosses the room, her chunky boots that give her a few extra centimeters of height clomping against the metal grating. I'm not sure why, but I expected a Synthetic to be either stiffer than a human or more graceful, but she's neither of those things. When she reaches the bed, she plops in the middle and, at the same time, pops the cap on a carbonated beverage. When I make no comment, she crosses her legs and slurps her drink.

"Want one?" she asks, pulling it from her lips. It's a sugary energy drink, a disgusting Gean thing that asserts blue is a flavor, not a color.

"I thought you were a . . . I thought . . . Are you human?" I ask, but she just smiles and pats the bed beside her.

I sit down and feel her weight shift on the mattress as she makes room for me. I run through my evidence: she's drinking, and she has weight. She *has* to be here, though the urge to reach out and touch her is difficult to fight. But that answers one of my questions; if she's here physically, she can be forced off Autarkeia.

"You're not a data ghost right now, are you?" I ask. "Because I gotta say, that would *really* fuck with my mind."

"No, I'm here. Right in front of you."

I'm not sure if I should feel relieved or not.

"I know several people on Autarkeia have seen you on their comlenses. They've asked me to look for you."

"I know."

She says it so innocently, no wariness at all. She sucks down the rest of the energy drink, then sets the empty can in her lap and taps a black-painted nail against it. She even fidgets like a human.

"A couple of duelists, Nadyn val Lancer and Noa sol Romero, were looking for you too. So why did you choose to reveal yourself to me instead of them?"

"I didn't want those Icarii to find me yet, but you . . . I don't know . . ." She *hesitates* like a human. "If the other Icarii saw you, they'd focus on you instead of finding me, and I think they shouldn't know about you yet. I think you're here to do something that you need to be hidden for."

"I'm here to find *you.*"

She cocks her head, studying me with the same intensity with which I watch her. It's hard to remember that we are bridging the gap between human and Synthetic when she is like any other girl I've met.

"Maybe you can help me with them," she says, jumping up from the bed.

"Help you how?" I ask at the same time that she snatches up a greasy bag of tools from the floor.

"Do you want help with your prosthetics?"

"What?" Talk about changing the subject. I've got whiplash. "What about my prosthetics?"

"Your arm and leg." She says it as if I could possibly forget. "I can tell they hurt you, and I can recalibrate them so they don't. Do you want help?"

I reach for my shoulder again. My hip aches from the way I'm sitting, but I've gotten good at ignoring it. Not that I can ignore the phantom pains when they start. "I . . ."

"I know you're afraid that you can't trust me, but . . . well, if I help you, then you'll know you *can* trust me."

"No one else has been able to do anything about it, and I've seen a lot of engineers and doctors." How is anyone supposed to help with the agony I feel in a hand or knee that no longer exists?

"I can," she insists.

I still hesitate.

She shrugs. "If I wanted to hurt you, I could have done it while you were sleeping."

Well, shit. She's got me there.

"Okay," I say at last.

She sets her bag of tools beside the bed. "Lie down flat on your back," she says, and I do as instructed.

What the hell am I doing? I wonder as she leans over me, her face eclipsing the light above us and her hair brushing against my cheek.

"Please don't turn me into a machine," I say.

She giggles, covering her mouth. "You're already as much of a machine as I am." She taps my forehead with her first finger, and the world around me goes fuzzy again. Yet I don't feel even the slightest bit of fear. How the hell is she doing that?

As I sink deeper into the bed, the tension in my muscles leaking out of me, I replay her words.

You're already as much of a machine as I am.

Does that mean she's part human? Or does that mean that I . . .

That's the last thought I have as I fade away.

"COME OUT FROM there," Shinya says, looking down at Asuka and me. "Father says the kotatsu is for eating, not for sleeping." But neither of us moves a muscle where we're cuddled together beneath the low table, the lull of its heater too much to resist.

"I'm sleepy, Oniisan," I say, rolling over and readjusting the kotatsu's blanket.

Shinya quirks a brow. "What is Hiro wearing?" This he directs at Asuka.

"Whatever Hiro wants," Asuka grumbles, grumpy that Shinya has woken her from her nap. "Who cares? It's not like we have school today."

"If Father sees that Hiro has gotten into Mother's closet . . ."

"Father isn't even home. Either nap with us or go away." She sticks her tongue out at Shinya for emphasis.

I push my head closer to Asuka's shoulder, my eyes so heavy I can't keep them open.

I hear Shinya sigh above me, then the sound of him setting down one of his boring poetry books. The cold air seeps in from outside the kotatsu as he lifts the blanket and slides under.

He scoots closer to me, enveloping me in his warmth. I am content between my big brother and big sister.

"Just don't tell Father," he whispers.

The world around me freezes. I turn from Asuka to Shinya, their faces peaceful in sleep but their chests no longer rising and falling. Some of my surroundings are blurry, as insubstantial as a rained-on water-color: The books on the bookcase have no names, just vague shapes. The furniture is wobbly. Some of the art on the wall is clear, while other pieces are mere suggestions, and while I try to focus on them, I find I can't quite remember how they looked that day so long ago.

"Memories," the Synthetic says, and I look up to find her standing where she does not belong, a sharp outline in a place soft with thought. "Human memories are fickle."

The scene darkens—

And with a flash, I find myself on a bustling Cytherean street, Lito beside me. Those long legs of his would be able to outpace me any day of the week if he didn't shuffle like he's brooding. I slow as we approach a bullet train station and turn to him. Even in civilian clothing, he chooses to wear black, whereas I am a riot of clashing colors and prints.

Tell him, a part of me whispers, but my throat is instantly too dry. I know I'm running out of time. I know this might be the last chance before we ship out.

We're set to return to Ceres in two days, and while I can't give him the specifics, I know that Hemlock, from the basement of Mithridatism, has something dangerous planned. If I tell Lito what I know, we could avoid going back to Ceres altogether . . . couldn't we?

Lito stands so close to me, our arms brush. I feel his warmth, and it is a comfort like home. I can tell he senses my unease; he looks at me and quirks a brow. I feel him probing on the other side of the implant, curious and worried.

"Nothing's wrong," I answer his silent question. But something is wrong. I have to tell him. The words are just on the tip of my tongue— *Hey, listen, there's something about to go down on Ceres...* But I let them slip away. Clear my throat, and let those words become wind.

"You go on to Luce's," I say instead. "I need to run by Father's first." And I need to clear my head. I can't think straight with Lito around.

"Sure," he says, accepting the lie. He knows I'm troubled, but he believes it's because I have to visit my father, and that is only the smallest part of why I'm upset. "See you later."

I watch his wide shoulders and the slouch of his back as he slips his hands into his pockets and heads into the bullet train station. I watch him until he disappears, as if it's the last time I'll ever see him.

Tonight . . . I have to tell him tonight . . .

The scene freezes. The blurred faces of Cytherean passersby become more noticeable, nefarious in their lack of detail. This time I expect to hear her voice.

"You never told him," the Synthetic says. I can't answer her, but if she's in my mind, riffling through my memories like the chapters of a novel, then she knows the answer to that. I wanted to tell Lito but couldn't risk it when Luce had no one but him to care for her. Or maybe that was just the excuse I made so I didn't have to explain everything to him, so I would never know whether he'd choose me over the Icarii.

The black descends. I expect a sharp change, but I'm not prepared for where I find myself. Back in my childhood home. Standing in my father's office, the glass wall overlooking the city at night, his collection of wooden Noh masks staring down at me with accusing eyes. *No, no, no*—nothing good has ever happened in this room.

"I never should have allowed that sol Lucius boy to become your partner," my father says. "I should have interfered before it ever came to this."

I am thirteen, chewing on words I know he doesn't want to hear. "Lito understands me in a way you never could," I snap.

"Had he been left where he belonged," he says as if he didn't hear me, speaking of the lowest level of Cytherea, where Lito lived until he earned a scholarship to the Academy, "his tendency for violence would have driven him to crime. He is not suited to be a duelist, and he is not suited to be your partner."

"Yeah?" I tip up my chin like I'm not terrified of him. "Well, it's too late for you to do anything now."

My father leans forward in his sinvaca leather chair, the creaking of the fabric as loud as a thunderclap in the otherwise silent room. "Make no mistake, Hiro," he says, cold and soft, "it's never too late to ensure what's *best* for you."

I shuddered back then, and I shudder now, as if time has lost all meaning. *But at least it isn't* that *day*, the part of me in the present whispers. Even as I think it, the scene ripples like the surface of a pond disturbed by a stone.

"Interesting," the Synthetic says, as if commenting on a scientific fact.

The office barely changes—the placement of his chair, perhaps, or the arrangement of papers on the desk. It's the people who are different. I am younger, smaller, and my father's hand is fisted in my hair as he wipes a wet cloth over my face, smudging makeup in an attempt to remove it. My skin stings when he pulls it away.

No, not this—anything but this memory—

Everything within me revolts. I don't want to see this—I don't want to live this again. But I'm afraid I'm the one who brought us here.

"How many times will we do this, Hiro?" He is large and looming to me at this age, and I do my best to square my shoulders instead of cower. I fail. "You're old enough to know better."

I wish I could call for Shinya or Asuka. For anyone to come and save me. But I know we're alone save for the security guards who stand at the entrances to the townhouse. Inside, it's only me and Father now.

"I just . . ." My voice is the squeak of a mouse.

Shut up, I tell myself. *Don't make it worse!* But this is a memory, and no matter how hard I pull at the chains, I'm tethered to my past.

"You just, what, do whatever you *feel*?" He says the word like a curse, wadding up the makeup-smeared cloth and slamming it into the nearest recycler. "Every day it's something new with you. I think I get you settled, and then I turn around and you're back at it again. You're not my only child, Hiro. Everything can't be about you."

My eyes begin to burn worse than my skin, and I bite my lip against the tears. "But this is me . . ."

"And last week when I bought you a thousand credits' worth of boys' clothes, it was you too."

You're right, I want to say. *That was me, and this is me. I'm not two different people, just one who likes both things.* But all I say, looking down at my floral-print dress, is "This is how I want to look today."

Father sits behind his desk, as if that wooden barrier will save him from me. I can tell by the way he rubs a hand over his face that he's exasperated. He normally treats his children like wayward employees; it's only when he's overwhelmed that we glimpse a parent.

"I'm not unsympathetic, Hiro." His tone tells me that's a lie. "You want to be a boy? You want to be a girl? I can get you the best gene-assist on Cytherea. You can be whatever you want to be. You just have to choose."

My heart feels like it's fallen onto the floor. I want to sink with it.

"You're about to enter the Academy, and people need to know they can rely on you, that you're not a child. That you're someone able to *commit.*" I look down at my feet as he lectures me. "Puberty is coming, Hiro, whether you like it or not."

That word draws a lump into my throat I can't swallow around. *Puberty*, that dreaded moment when my body will take control of itself. Neither of the options my father has presented to me feels right, and if I leave it up to biology, the outcome won't be any better.

I don't say anything, because I don't know what to say.

He slams a fist on the table, and I jump with fear. "*Choose*, Hiro."

But I am only ten years old, and I don't know what to choose. Sometimes I feel like I am both a boy and a girl. Sometimes I feel like I am neither. And when I think of the Academy's waiting uniform, char-coal gray and stiff, it feels like someone's got a hand on my throat and they're squeezing tighter and tighter.

"Now," Father says, grabbing a sinvaca leather bag from behind his desk and tossing it at my feet, "go to your room and pack up whatever you don't want."

But . . . I want it all.

If only he believed me. If only he understood. If I don't have those choices—the leggings and dresses and sharp-lapeled suits—I want to peel my skin off with my fingernails. I want to pluck the hair from my head, one strand at a time. I want to take a knife to this body and carve out pieces of me that don't fit and pray to whoever's listening at the family shrine that Mother comes home and saves me from this.

She would understand, I tell myself. *She would get it.* But another part of me, the one that remembers her telling me to be Father's shadow, asks: *Would she?*

When Father speaks again, a spark catches in his eyes, the only thing that marks him as alive when the rest of his face is as smooth and featureless as the Noh masks at his back. "If you don't choose," he says, his voice deep and dark, "I'll choose for you, Hiro." The light flares like fox fire, burning blue and sinister. The masks seem to be laughing. "And you won't like what I choose."

Memories batter me like hail: the Fall of Ceres; Beron smirking down at me; looking in the mirror—*not my body, not my fucking face*—finding Saito Ren instead; and that desire I thought I'd left behind, the yearning to *peel my skin off one layer at a time*—

You won't like what I choose, my father says.

I collapse to my knees and tremble. I am everywhere and nowhere at once.

"Stop," I beg. "Please, stop . . ."

And then someone is there at my side, placing their hands on my shoulders. Tucking my hair behind my ears. Tipping my chin up.

The Synthetic looks at me with recognition. Not pity. But insight. The world around us is just a white room, devoid of painful memories.

"I understand," she says, and then I wake up.

I OPEN MY eyes. The ceiling is unfamiliar. My heart still races from . . . whatever that was, nightmares or memories forcefully revisited . . .

"Hello," the Synthetic says in that gentle, musical way of hers.

Then I remember: She was there. She saw it all.

I clench my eyes closed. Those specific memories . . . Did she choose them, or did I unintentionally guide her?

I still feel like I'm half-asleep. Still feel like she's embracing me, and I'm crying out to be saved. *I understand*, she said, and somehow . . . I knew she did. Even now, I can feel her emotions crashing against me: her concern, but most of all, her love. And I don't understand it—how Synthetics feel—but I know that they do, because I know she does.

"Can you move your arm for me?" the Synthetic asks, but before I can try, I look up to where she's hunched over me and startle.

"Your head—" The silver prosthetic of her head is . . . open. Wires snake from the small panels down to my arm, connecting her to me. But the cables go deep into her flesh—if it is flesh—and pass into her skull. Into her brain, if she has one. No wonder I still feel her as strongly as I did in those memories. If my connection via the neural implant was like receiving raindrops of my partners' emotions, this is like a torrential storm.

You're already as much of a machine as I am, she had said, but that only raises a hundred more questions, and I can't force my tongue to form a single one.

"Move your arm," the Synthetic says, then after a moment adds, "Please."

Because I don't know what else to do, I oblige her. I hold my arm up, force my hand into a fist. The smoothness of the motion catches me off guard, and I bolt upright.

"Ah—please don't jerk."

I can barely hear her. I rotate my arm, flex, and circle my wrist. "Oh my gods . . ."

"Good?" she asks.

I can't move far from her, so, tethered together, we stand from the mattress, and I put all my weight on my left leg.

"Nothing," I gasp. "There's nothing."

No pain. No agony shooting into my shoulder and hip. No burning resentment from my overtaxed muscles and bundles of scars.

And . . . I can *feel.*

I collapse back on the bed, tears welling up and streaming down my face. I take the soft sheets in my prosthetic hand, let them slip through my fingers like the moon's dust in my dream.

"How—" I suck in a deep breath, and it shakes in my lungs. I'm fighting the sobs, but the dam breaks when she puts her hand in mine, and I can *feel* it, so warm and soft and gentle.

She smiles, as if it's that simple.

I collapse, weeping into my open hands, feeling my own tears, hot and wet.

AFTER THE SOBS hollow me out, the Synthetic removes her wires from me, tucks them back into her head, and closes off her prosthetic. She doesn't rub my back or move to touch me in any other way, and for that I'm thankful. She brings me one of her energy drinks, and I accept because my throat feels like I swallowed sand.

"You can rest here as long as you need to," she says. "I know it must be difficult . . ."

She has no idea how right she is. I'd fought the pain for so long with nothing to show for it. Then I'd accepted it, believing it would be my constant companion for the rest of my days, as consistent as my shadow. Sometimes I could almost forget about it, it came on so mild. But other days, I wanted to take to my bed and cry, though all I could do was keep on being Saito Ren.

No longer. I'm still missing my arm and leg, but from the pain . . . I'm free.

Then the doubt comes, the same anxiety that plagued me on the mild days. *Yes, today you are free, but what about tomorrow? And the day after that?*

"Will the pain come back? Will I lose my sensation of touch?" Just speaking the question gives my fear legs, and it runs away from me, fully formed.

"No," she says, squashing the fear flat with her chunky-heeled boot. "Your sense of the way things feel, including pain, is from your mind interpreting an array of stimuli, all filtered through your neural implant. I simply adjusted the interaction between your prosthetics and your implant. Though . . . I did have to get a good sense of your brain's layout first."

"What are you?" I whisper, and somehow my question sounds tinged with holy awe. Maybe it is, after she performed this miracle.

"Synthetic," she says with a giggle. "I thought you knew that."

"I read the file Autarkeia has on you, but . . . Do you have a name? A nickname? Some way to individualize yourself from the others? How should I refer to you—she? They?"

She's quiet as she thinks for a moment. "This body was once called Mara. You can call me that again if you'd like."

"Okay, Mara."

"And this one I think of as female," she says, gesturing to herself, "but others . . . others are different. If you ever meet another, you can ask them their preference."

"But wouldn't it be like talking to you, just wearing a different face?"

"Yes and no," she says, which only confuses me more; it's difficult to wrap my head around the way Synthetics think of themselves if they're both individuals and a unified being. "Some Synthetics still recall the time when we were separate and hold on to their old preferences."

And if Mara has preferences from a time before the Synthetics joined as one, that means she'd existed since before the end of the Dead

Century War. *Thousand gods . . .* How old is she? Three hundred years? Four?

We settle into the silence, though she breaks it by slurping down another energy drink.

"Is that shit what powers Synthetics?"

She looks at the can and laughs. "I just like the way it stings my tongue."

"Thank you," I blurt out, and her smile fades. "I don't know how I can repay you . . . There's nothing I can do for you that is equal to what you've done for me."

She shakes her head. "Don't say that. Value is subjective, and I wish I could've helped you more with how you feel when you look in the mirror."

I swallow hard. "You said you understood me . . . that you understood that feeling of dysphoria."

"Dysphoria?" she repeats, the word strange on her tongue. "The way you felt, it was . . . a new emotion for me. But I have felt something similar, and never expected to find it in a human."

Though we're no longer tethered together physically, somehow I still feel close enough to her to ask. "How so?"

She purses her lips as she thinks. "I have been in many bodies. Many forms. One in particular felt . . . wrong for me. Like I had been downloaded into a shell I didn't quite fit."

"I see." Not that I've ever had multiple bodies . . . just this one, changed over and over. Still, the similarities are there. "I still want to find a way to repay you."

She offers a little smile. "Then let's just be friends?"

The question she poses is so soft and innocent. Sometimes she acts like a kid; other times she seems ancient.

"Yeah," I say. "Friends."

It hits me all at once that I've succeeded in my mission from Dire. I've not just found the Synthetic girl—Mara—I've made contact with her. And if I can turn the spark of this friendship into a flame, she'll likely answer my questions about why she's in Autarkeia without needing Dire's strong-armed intervention.

"You said you needed help with the Icarii here."

She turns back to me, dark eyes serious. "Yes. There are some strange things going on, but I'm afraid to become too involved with them."

"Because of the Synthetic truce with humanity?"

"Yeah," she says with a nod. "When this station was first built, it was called the Knight Orbital Center after Knight Robotics and used to build Synthetics for the battlefields of the Dead Century War. When we split from humanity, we brought this place—we called it the Engineborn Forge then—with us beyond the belt. Once we'd spread to Jupiter and had no more need of the factories, we left the station with the hopes that it would be useful to someone else. We didn't mind when humans began using the Forge as a refuge for fleeing the Gean and Icarii war. We hoped humans would want peace and hate war, like we do. But because it is in gray space, Synthetics come here often, in one form or another, to check up on things. Still, no one's ever shown an interest in us—in me, I mean . . ."

"Until now," I surmise, and I have a sinking feeling that Dire wasn't the first. "The Icarii came here for you."

"I'm afraid so," she admits. "And their interest in me has led to *other* interest in me."

Like Dire's and Hemlock's.

"But what worries me is that the more the Icarii follow me, the more strange things I notice about their presence here . . ."

"Like what?"

She shakes her head. "I'll just have to show you."

"Okay," I say, and fight the urge to drown her with questions. Instead, I focus on just one. "Can I ask you something?"

"You just did," she says with a smile.

I shoot her a look I would my little sibling, stretching my lips thin and rolling my eyes. "Ha ha, very funny."

"You can ask," she says after a moment.

"You're Synthetic, yeah? Or . . . part of the Synthetics. But you also have your own form and your own thoughts. Is there a part of you that's them and a part of you that's . . . you?"

"Oh." Her face falls.

"Sorry if it's an ignorant question. You don't have to tell me if you don't want to."

"No, it's okay. It just might be . . . difficult to explain."

She chews on her bottom lip as she struggles to find her words. I wait quietly, giving her all the time and space she needs.

"What I can tell you is that my brain is connected to the Synthetic consciousness," she says, lacing her fingers together. "I'm a part of the whole, even if I'm an individual."

"Are you acting on their commands, or . . . ?"

That one she doesn't answer; she just smiles.

"So the Icarii duelists. How do you want me to help you?"

The tension in her shoulders drops as I change the subject. I make a note to myself not to press her on too many Synthetic issues.

"Come see me this weekend—do you still use that word, 'weekend'?—come see me Sunday. I'll be here waiting for you, okay? I'll show you where the Icarii are staying and some of the strange things I was talking about."

"Sure," I say casually, like I'm setting up a date. "See you in . . ." I count. "Five days." I look around us at all the ramps and weird objects that I don't understand in the least. "How do I get out of here?"

She chuckles, then points to one of the ramps. "That leads down to the wall. It'll open up for you."

The wall . . . will open for me. I decide it's better not to ask, so I wave a final farewell, marveling at the fluidity of my prosthetic, and take the ramp downward.

"Goodbye, friend!" she calls after me, a smile illuminating her entire face.

At the end of the rather long but subtly inclined ramp and on what

I assume is the ground floor since the giant donut is on this level, I approach the dome wall, looking for a door. But just as Mara said, the rusty panels peel back, creating a large enough gap for me to exit. I step out into the darkness of the city, and the wall grows back, one tiny square at a time.

"Fuck me . . ."

I don't know where I am, just that I'm outside one of the Synthetic industrial domes with Autarkeia's buildings haphazardly clustered nearby. Sharp rib-like structures arch overhead, embracing the metal dome that, despite looking dead, isn't. How many other rusted factories are actually hiding Synthetics that secretly watch over Autarkeia?

I pick a direction and start walking. Once I've cleared my head, I'll call Dire through the com-lenses and have him pick me up. I wonder what he's going to want me to do now that I've successfully established contact with Mara. Will I be able to kill her, if that's what he commands?

I don't know. I don't feel like I know anything after meeting her. The single thing that's clear to me is that, even as I walk away from the dome, putting more space between me and Mara, I still feel her like she's standing right next to me.

CHAPTER 12

LUCE

My Pollux: I just can't fucking stand the idea that the Elders control our future. They've seen Hemlock, seen all the people on Ceres falling apart and dying, and they've chosen to ignore that. They let us suffer because their fear of retaliation rules them.

Message on Hemlock's private server from Castor

My Castor: As Warlord Vaughn says, "One stone may break a bone; a hundred can break someone apart." We need a reason to unite the Elders with our goals if we want to change their minds.

Message on Hemlock's private server from Pollux

◇——⬦⬦——◇

I have to smother my anxiety at returning to the lowest level of Cytherea. Last night, I rode this train with the Keres Art Collective, took this street to our destination with airpens in my bag and hope in my heart, and look how that turned out . . .

At least the address Castor gave me is in the opposite direction from the Maintenance Guild's building. The Arber neighborhood, one that I've only passed through despite living on this level the first fifteen years of my life, is one Mamá would call "dangerous" and coach me to avoid. I see why when I pass over a silent barrier street and into its borders: Arber is filled with Asters.

Those in the streets tower over me, goggles turning in my direction before pointedly snapping away. They know I don't belong here, but they also know they can't stop me from being here without buying more trouble for themselves. As my compad guides me down narrow streets, I notice the difference between their neighborhood and others. There are no parks here, no open-air restaurants or cafés. They gather in rusting refuse, sitting around stacks of crumbling cargo containers.

When my compad pings, signaling my arrival, I stand before a building like all the others I've passed. The design seems almost intentionally depressing, the front gray and unworthy of notice, windows too small to climb through, the door a slab of iron. *Like a prison*, the artistic part of me decides.

Castor didn't give me an apartment number, so when I approach the door to look for an intercom, I'm distraught to see that there are several corresponding to each floor. But just as I'm pulling out my compad to message him for clarification, the iron opens with an unoiled creak and Castor appears, slouching so as not to hit his head on the door frame.

His golden eyes take in the street. "You took precautions?"

I puff up my chest, insulted. "I always do." I changed lines four times in various directions, taking a circuitous route to the bottom level. If I had a tail, I lost them in my quick movements from train to train.

His sharp teeth make an appearance when he smiles at me, seemingly pleased. "Come in."

The interior is nothing I could've predicted. Whereas the outside is dull, easy to overlook with its boring facade, the large room is warm and welcoming despite its dim lighting. Long tables have been set throughout the space, those against the wall covered with veritable cauldrons of food and pitchers of drink. The room is full of Asters bustling about, most without goggles. Some are cutting vegetables or cooking on a stove top right out in the open, while others take bowls and help themselves to the food on offer. The majority sit clustered together at the tables, enjoying their meals with only a few quiet words passed between them.

It reminds me of the way Mamá and my father's mother, whom we called the Abuela (always with the preceding *the*), would cook together in the Abuela's kitchen, food overflowing plates and rooms filled with a rainbow of delightful smells. Even after she passed, her home smelled of olives and garlic, a scent that hits me with a wave of nostalgia whenever I cook for myself.

"It's an Icarii-Aster fusion restaurant," Castor says, gesturing to the food-laden table. "Grab whatever appeals to you. I hope you like fungi. We don't really know how to cook without them."

When we approach the table, an Aster sets down a bowl of what looks like dark hummus. While Asters aren't auto-identified through the feed—I can't check her identity on my com-lenses—many have adopted a color system, so I know this Aster identifies as female from the cloth that ties off the end of her braid. "Have some porcini paste," she says, spooning it onto a plate and handing it to me before I can protest. Castor looks at me with an expression like *See?*, and I have to fight back a laugh.

The Aster woman smiles at me warmly, though her expression falls flat when she looks at Castor. Something passes between them, something in their eyes, and I suppose I miss the question, because Castor shakes his head. "No, she's not," he says, flat and short. She goes back to the cooking area without another word.

"What was that?"

"She was asking about my sister. I'm sure you know what it's like to have an overbearingly curious aunt," he says by way of excuse. At the very least, I know how delicate a subject siblings can be.

I turn my attention back to the food, scooping up a bit of everything to try: bread with a grayish tint, thick ribbons of pasta adorned with fat brown truffles, a salad of fresh fruits and what looks like lichen, each with flavors I never would've thought to combine. And mushrooms, of course, from shiitake to spotted toadstool. The fusion element of the restaurant seems to come from the Icarii herbs and spices—parsley and basil, saffron and thyme—which must be near impossible for Asters to get in the belt.

The drink—the only one on offer—is something pink and sweet, and I have no idea what it is, just that it doesn't taste alcoholic but is refreshing. We sit down at the unoccupied end of a communal table, and while a few Asters cast glances in our direction I could read as curiosity, Castor's presence seems to keep them from anything more. They turn back to their plates, leaving us as alone as if we were the only two in the room.

I pick at my food, liking the majority of it—the pasta and salad especially. The bread tastes good with the paste but is otherwise too earthy. Castor completely cleans his plate, faster than even Lito would, before he speaks.

"How's your ankle?"

"The theracast is itching, so I think it'll fall off tonight." And my hands are back to normal after a dose of the pelospray.

"Good. We need you in top form if you're going to help us," he says, and because he approaches the subject here, in what I would consider a public place, I take it to mean that the Asters around us are safe.

I think of the night before, of Hiro's recordings, of the day I had at work. *Yes*, I long to say, but instead I use caution. "I have a few questions first."

He shoves the empty plate away from him. Both of his elbows thunk down on the table between us. "Shoot."

"Tell me again what data you want from Val Akira Labs. Be specific."

He lets out a little sigh, but in his eyes I see approval; he likes that I'm questioning him. Or maybe he just likes that I'm interested in helping him. "There are two main things. The first is proof that Val Akira Labs is conducting experiments on Asters against AEGIS law. Recordings, write-ups, research data, those sorts of things . . ." I nod for him to continue; that part I understood completely. "The second is research from an Aster scientist stolen by Val Akira Labs years ago—by Souji val Akira's father, actually—on the Icarii genelock."

It's shock that has me repeating his words. "The genelock?" I got a basic explanation of the genelock when I was hired at Val Akira Gene-assists. Every Icarii receives basic genemodding in vitro for protection against space radiation and variances in gravity, but modding DNA in one place often changes it in others, making the person more susceptible to certain illnesses or, like the Asters, mutations. For instance, early Icarii changed their DNA so that they wouldn't lose bone density in low gravity, but found they were then more susceptible to bone cancer. The genelock was researched and developed by Val Akira Labs to keep dangerous mutations like that from occurring.

Castor says nothing, simply waits for me to parse my thoughts.

After several silent minutes, I find my words. "Why would you want information on the genelock?"

His words are as intense as his expression. "Many Asters are ill because of experimentation, but it's impossible to help them if we don't know what's been done to them. We have a complete map of the Aster genome, but without being able to decrypt the genelock Val Akira Labs chained them with, we can't fix them." He clenches his hands, the delicate purple-veined skin turning corpse pale. "We can't keep them from dying. Even my sister . . ." He trails off, but I can feel the rage coming off of him in waves.

"Your sister?" I ask before I can stop myself.

"My twin." He speaks the two words like they cut him. For the first time, I see a crack in his rage and only sorrow beneath. "She was born afflicted by a disease we couldn't fix, which forced her to turn to other treatments, many of them desperate and dangerous. And now she's . . ." He shakes his head, steeling himself. It's obvious he doesn't want to talk about this. About her illness.

I open my mouth to apologize, but he cuts me off. "You know what it's like, don't you?" His voice has faded to a whisper. "Having a sibling you'd do anything for, but one beyond your reach."

"Like you're living with their ghost every day," I say, finding my tone has softened to match his.

As we sit in the following silence, I imagine my life in comparison with his. I've endured disrespect, all because of that *sol* in my name, but he's watched his people suffer and die without any way to help them. Watched his sister suffer from illness throughout her life. I thought I'd seen the worst of the Icarii, but Castor has truly glimpsed the darkest parts of their souls. Just look at this neighborhood—even the lowlevel Icarii are better off than the Asters.

I run my hands over my face, the stress of the past few days and a sleepless night catching up with me. "The toplevel Icarii have all the power. They can change anything. *Do* anything. And what they choose to be, what they choose to do, is to hurt others so they can make themselves better by comparison."

"They choose to be assholes," Castor says flatly.

"I'm just . . ." I drop my hands to the table. "So angry."

His burning gold eyes never dim. "Sometimes anger is all you have left."

His desire overwhelms me with its immensity; he *needs* this research, not just for himself, but to help thousands—to help his sister. I think of my personal compad in my purse with the unanswered messages from Isa and my mother, messages that at one point would have consumed my life but now feel like nothing more than the wind ruffling my hair, there and gone. I love my life, but most lowlevel Icarii never achieve what I have. Lito saw that, and it changed him. And what's more, he saw what the Asters face, even more dire than what people like us do.

Lito would help him. All at once, I've made my decision.

"Tell me what I need to do." My words match his for heat, no hesitation to be found. "Tell me how to get the research for you."

His expression changes. Softens. He looks at me with eyes full of emotion, respect and something else I can't quite name. The restaurant still bustles around us, but it has fallen away; the entire world has disappeared, except for the two of us.

He reaches into his pocket and withdraws something. A moment later, he drops the naildrive on the table between us.

"Do exactly as I say . . ."

"GOOD MORNING, JUN!" I call through the waiting room of Val Akira Geneassists as soon as I arrive, a full twenty minutes before I'm scheduled to begin work. My voice is as carefree as it always is—at least, I hope it is.

"In room one!" Jun replies, her ever-chipper self now that coffee has arrived.

Before I enter, I make sure that my hands, each holding a cup of coffee, aren't shaking. That my face, though still showing the exhaustion of the past few days, is placid. I come around the corner, glad she can't hear the racing of my heart, and set her order with its four sugars on the corner of her desk.

"I'm glad you came in early," she says, getting up from her chair and coming around the desk. She leans on the edge, ignoring the coffee. I swallow a curse. "After what happened yesterday, I was worried about you . . ."

I fight the urge to frown, and lose. "I'm sorry," I say. "Yesterday was hard." Let her think my disappointment is about the incident with Harmony val White, or about being interrogated by her father, instead of this moment here and now.

One of her hands reaches for and finds her cup of coffee. As she usually does, she pulls off the cap and inhales the steam.

Does she smell the wrongness of it? Could she possibly guess what I've done to it? Castor assured me she wouldn't . . .

She puts the cap back on—good, she must not have smelled anything—then looks me over. *Doesn't* take a sip. "Are you all right? You look . . ."

"Oh." I touch my cheek, my forehead. I've broken out in a cold sweat. I remember the excuse I thought up on the way over. "I was sick to my stomach last night and didn't sleep well."

Jun flinches as if hit. She sets her coffee aside. "If you're ill, you really shouldn't come to work."

Shit, I shouldn't have said anything about being sick. "It was anxiety," I admit, forcing my nervousness to work in my favor. "I was scared after everything that happened yesterday that I would, I don't know, show up to work and find I don't have a job today." I take a sip from my coffee, hoping to encourage her to drink.

Jun watches me for a moment, saying nothing. Finally, she shakes her head. "You're a good worker, Lucinia. I wouldn't fire you for someone's prejudice, and I'm sorry you had to deal with it." No apology for the interrogation, but I suspect she had little control over that. "We'll reassess some policies before we bring you into the room again." Her words rub me the wrong way, placing me at fault over our stuck-up clients, but instead I focus on the way her hand goes back to the cup. I fight the urge to cheer as she picks up her coffee again.

"Thank you, Jun," I say, letting her hear my relief.

"Let's do lunch. I'm craving noodles," she says with a smile, and I nod in agreement. She takes her first sip of the coffee, and I leave the room with a smile on my face.

"Good to see you here early, Lucinia," Mathieu calls to me from his office, and while I mutter a greeting, my focus isn't on him at all.

Five minutes later, Jun streaks through the office to the back, the sound of her retching turning my stomach as she runs for the bathroom.

From the sound, she doesn't make it all the way before vomiting . . .

Step one: remove Jun from her computer. Done. *Sorry, Jun*, I think before I excuse myself from my desk and head for hers.

I SETTLE IN her chair in room one, her ID still inserted into the computer, logging her in. I pull the naildrive from my jacket pocket and slip it into an empty slot beside her ID, then sit back and wait. Step two: insert the naildrive in Jun's computer. Done. From the dose I put in her coffee, I have probably a half hour before she returns. Hopefully, I won't need even that long.

As Castor told me it would, the computer reads the naildrive, and his program goes to work. A black screen pops up with white writing that flashes by too fast for me to read. Any snippet I do catch, I can't understand. It's all code.

I think over Castor's words and try to control my breathing as various screens pop up. Some close immediately, but some linger, copying themselves over onto the naildrive, the program parsing what we want and what we don't.

Step three: take the naildrive and go back to work.

Step four: meet Castor at a lowlevel safe house and deliver the data. From there, we'll assess what we gathered and what we could still fish for. Though hopefully, we'll get everything in this one go; I don't know how I'll get onto Jun's computer a second time.

My compad buzzes. I ignore it. Then it buzzes again. And again.

I pull the buzzing compad out of my bag. It's not my personal device, but the one Castor gave me. With my heart sinking into my stomach, I see the multiple messages from "Darling."

What's happening?

We've got an emergency here at home

Call me

Call me

Call me

My intestines, my stomach all move into my chest cavity, pressing on my heart like I'm falling. Thousand gods, what have I done?

Grab your things

COME HOME NOW!

My personal compad rings. I retrieve it from my bag, never expecting his name to appear on the screen: SOUJI VAL AKIRA.

CHAPTER 13

LITO

HARBINGER (noun): A person or thing that foreshadows an event or the approach of another; a herald; an omen.

From *Val Machinist English Dictionary*, vol. 1

"**I** found the med kit!" Sorrel calls triumphantly from down the hall.

I don't answer—*can't* answer—as the hum of the *Nyx*-class ship lures me toward a poisoned sleep. I've already bled through the hasty bandage I tied around my neck, my focus on stabilizing Ofiera rather than my own laceration, and if I slip under now, there's no telling whether I'll wake up.

Considering the *Nyx* is an Icarii spy craft, it's not well stocked. We only found a single medbag and a handful of universal synblood packs in the med bay. The med kit was missing from its usual slot, and I could only hope that one of the duelists hadn't taken it with them when boarding the grasshopper that's now thousands of kilometers behind us.

As soon as we had Ofiera in the medbag—she didn't even whimper as we cut the clothes from her body and slid her into the yellow electrofluid—we turned our focus to other important things, like getting the hell away from the location that other duelists were surely on their way to. Pressing a bag of synblood into my hands, Sorrel left me in the med bay with Ofiera in order to disengage the *Nyx* from the grasshopper and set our course for Ceres.

When he returns, walking on the balls of his bare feet, my eyes go from his clean, dressed form to his armful of supplies. The med kit lies on top of a pile of folded black cloth, and as he sets everything out on the counter, I realize he's brought me clean clothes in the form of a set of military blacks he must have found in the hab quarters. Or that he took off one of the dead duelists . . .

"You were meant to use that on yourself," he says, gesturing to the synblood plugged into the side port of Ofiera's medbag.

"She needed it."

"*You* need it," Sorrel says, unclasping the med kit. His long fingers brush over the contents and stop on the pelospray. "Besides, the electrofluid in the medbag will increase the reproduction of her lost blood."

I don't ask how he knows that, how he knows *anything* that he says with such surety. Like Ofiera, he's seen worlds rise and fall. What must it be like, after waiting two hundred years, to be reunited with the woman who now lies locked away and dying?

He guides my hand—and the red-soaked bandage—away from my neck. "Whoo, boy, I got you good." I'd be tempted to laugh if my head weren't spinning like a ship in free fall. He coats the wound in pelospray, and I close my eyes as first a sting and then a cooling numbness travel down my shoulder and up into my clenched teeth. He hits the cut on my hand after that, but it's hardly a concern in the middle of everything else.

I know it's working when, for the first time in an hour, I can relax my jaw. I barely even notice the slight prick as he slips a needle into the vein of my inner arm and hangs the synblood above me. Sorrel says something, but I don't catch it. Everything, including the loud beeping of Ofiera's medbag, sounds muffled and faraway.

I think I black out. Or maybe I just finally allow myself to rest.

When I open my eyes, Sorrel is sitting and drinking a brown liquid from a glass and the synblood above me is completely empty.

"How long has it been?" I ask. I sound better, stronger.

"Good morning. Or afternoon, I guess I should say." Sorrel casts a quick glance to a clock on the wall set to Coordinated Universal Time. "You've been asleep about six hours."

Now that I feel stable enough, I want to know everything. "How's Ofiera? Are we en route to Ceres? Is anyone following us?"

"One thing at a time," he says as he shifts the glass in his hand, ice clinking against the side. "Ofiera's stable, and you're back to normal, it seems."

I reach for the wound on my neck. It's closed, but there's a ropy scar there that aches when I put pressure on it. "More or less."

"Yeah, you've got a new one." He turns his head to the side so I can see the slash from his jawline to his temple. Against the soft blue of his skin, the scar is livid and red. "You're not the only one."

Whether it's the years or the fact that I'm looking at him with my eyes instead of Ofiera's memory, Sorrel is changed. His hair is a soft, buzzed white that he runs his hand over nervously. There's a tight-ness to the edges of his mouth, the rut of an often-formed frown. And while he has no white to his eyes, like all other Asters, he doesn't wear the trademark goggles, perhaps because of something done to him in the labs. Like in that memory of his I glimpsed when Ofiera tethered us together . . .

He pours a second glass of the brown liquid, drops in a single cube of ice, and hands it to me. The smell of strong liquor smacks me. "What the hell is this?"

"Whiskey," he says. "I found it while I was scouring the ship for supplies."

"I almost bled to death, and you think me drinking this is a good idea?"

He raises a pale eyebrow. "I think you might want it with what I'm about to tell you."

My hand tightens on the glass. "What is it?"

"The Icarii are on our trail."

"Fuck." I take a sip of the whiskey. It burns like fire as it goes down.

"I have no idea how long it'll take them to catch up. Being a spy ship, the *Nyx* is harder to pick up on radar than other ships. But with Ofiera in the medbag, we can't burn at maximum speed, so it's more a question of when, not if, they find us." He holds up his own glass. "Thus the drink."

"Any other bad news?"

"Yeah, we're not going to Ceres."

"What?"

"We need to go to Vesta. It's closer, and . . ." Sorrel looks at Ofiera, and it all falls into place: his request, the pain in his tone, the need to convince me. "We can be there in six days, as opposed to the eight it would take to get to Ceres."

"Yes," I say without hesitation. It doesn't matter that Vesta is where the Aster Elders live, where humans can stop to trade but aren't welcome. Doesn't matter if I end up arrested and forgotten in a cell for trespassing. Ofiera's been with me through a lot—always patient and understanding as I came to see the Icarii like she did—and if there's any chance she has at living, I have to seize it. "To Vesta, then. I just need to update Hemlock, my contact—"

"Already done," Sorrel says. I lose track of my words at his admission. How could he possibly know Hemlock, locked up as he was in Val Akira Labs? Rubbing his stubbled head, he offers a sheepish explanation. "When Ofiera tied us together . . . well, I saw some of your memories."

Just like I saw some of his . . .

The firing squad, the torture, being reunited with Ofiera only to be ripped away again—those things are now engraved in my mind. And thanks to Ofiera, I can feel him through my neural implant like I would her or Hiro. It makes me feel as if I know him far better than I actually do. Makes me care for him when I otherwise wouldn't.

"Hemlock gave us an updated course that'll help us reach Vesta while avoiding patrols. Since we really don't need to run into any additional Icarii with one already on our tail, we're going to stick to the asteroid belt as much as we can for travel, dipping into the unclaimed territory between the belt and the rotation of Jupiter—do you still call it gray space?—when necessary." He holds his glass up to the light and looks at the golden-brown liquid with disinterest. "Now all we have to do is wait . . . and wait some more."

I take another sip of my drink. "Can I ask you a question?"

"Gods, *please*." Sorrel leans toward me. "I can't be the only one who thinks it's awkward we know each other so well without ever having spoken a word."

I snort. He's right about that. "Why do they call you the Harbinger?"

His eyes widen, but his pupils narrow into slits sharp enough to cut me. His face takes on a haunted look, as if he's seeing the labs around him instead of the *Nyx*'s med bay. Seeing a scientist instead of me. He sets his glass aside and stands, and I wonder if I should've started with an easier question.

"You don't have to—"

He surprises me by cutting me off. "In the Black Hive Rebellion two hundred years ago, they started calling me the Harbinger because wherever I went, I would inspire Asters into action against the Icarii." He pulls up the hem of his shirt—baggy on his slender frame—over a flat stomach. On the right side between a sharp hip bone and the bottom of his rib cage is a massive scar, like a giant mouth took a bite out of him. "You can see how that turned out." He drops his shirt and takes up his drink again.

"Surprised I didn't notice that when you were running around naked," I say with a smirk.

"Ha!" He barks a single, forceful laugh. "To be fair, I was trying to kill you." I salute him with my drink. "I guess you're not going to forget that anytime soon."

I motion to my neck. "Not with this memento you've given me."

"Are you one of those smooth-skinned Icarii who get rid of their scars after every mission?"

In answer, I pull the Val Akira Labs uniform—crusted with dried blood—away from my neck. On my shoulder rests a remnant of the Fall of Ceres, a puckered scar like a supernova. "HEL gun. By an Aster, believe it or not."

"Ouch." Sorrel's eyes narrow. "The hell did you do to the Aster?"

"Fall of Ceres was a rough time," I say, though I'm not sure how much he knows about current events. "Do you—"

He holds up a hand. "I had a lot of time to do some reading while you and Ofiera were resting." He turns his head, showing off the mass of scar tissue that is the back of his neck; he's obviously not done with our strange show-and-tell. "This is all that remains of the different versions of the neural implant I've had over the years."

I realize the only reason Ofiera's neck is smooth is because she's expected to work, and no spy could get away with scars that noticeable. "She told me about that . . . how you two were in the trials to develop the first neural implants."

"Obviously we did a good job, since the implants work so well now." He gestures to my head and at the same time leans on my implant with his. It feels like a tug on the sleeve would, not invasive at all, just something to get my attention. "You're welcome," he says with a wink.

I laugh and pull my glass to my lips only to find it empty, but he's pouring me more before I even have time to request it. "Another relic from the Fall of Ceres . . ." I pull the pant leg up to my knee. The scar on my calf is like a lightning storm, pale white branches over the olive of my skin. "Ironskin whip."

"Ouch." He takes several gulps of his whiskey, draining the glass before setting it down and holding out his hand to me. On the web of skin between his thumb and forefinger is a half-moon scar that looks a lot like . . .

"Are those teeth marks?"

"A little present from the first time I ever spent extended time with Ofiera." He smiles at the scar like it's a fond memory.

"How the hell did the two of you end up married if that was your first date?"

He laughs hard as he drops back into his chair. "I'm guessing you don't know much about courtship." He winks again.

While he's right that I've never felt the need to seek out romantic or sexual partners—to me, it's a waste of time when life has so much *else* to offer—I know enough to guess that his and Ofiera's relationship was abnormal at best. Even now, people would be uncomfortable with the idea of an Aster with an Icarii.

"So how did the two of you even end up together?"

"Ofiera's parents were diplomats on Ceres. I was just a loudmouthed anarchist writing pamphlets against them and their poisoned contracts. She kept poking around our anti-colonial events as if interested in what I had to say, but I thought our movement didn't need a little rebel girl who was only there to piss off Mommy and Daddy, so I'd kick her out." His glassy eyes float toward Ofiera's medbag. "She's always been a stubborn, unstoppable force. Once she sets her mind to something, there's no chang-ing it. No matter how many times we refused her, she'd show up with more information, piles and piles of documents copied from her parents' office. Eventually I caved, wanted to talk to her one-on-one, but she thought I'd come to kidnap her. Started screaming for help, and I tried to stop her." He holds up his hand and wiggles it. "You can see how that turned out."

"She does have a way of making her point."

"The thing is, once I accepted her help, everything changed. She wasn't doing it to anger her parents. When she was old enough, she joined the military and fed us information she gathered on the job. She really did just want to stop what the Icarii were doing. She wanted to change things." His hand—the very one with Ofiera's bite-mark scar—comes to rest on her medbag. Inside the cloudy liquid, she floats with eyes closed. "If it weren't for her, the Black Hive Rebellion would never have been born."

And though he speaks of Ofiera's sacrifice, my buzzed mind calls up the memory of someone else's. If not for Hiro leaving their entire life behind, embracing a suicide mission but sending me one last farewell in the form of their messages, I never would've seen the truth of the Icarii . . .

Sorrel's eyes settle on the wall, but the look it gives him makes him appear to be staring into the past. "We gave everything we had, but in the end, Ofiera and I were just children playing at war. Back then, approval from the Elders didn't mean anything. The Elders' Shield, the Aster in charge of defense, labeled us outsiders—thus the name 'Black Hive.' We controlled water in the belt but little else. We had no rights and no way of communicating with each other like we do now through Hemlock's private network. We fought for control of Ceres, but when the Icarii seized Ofiera and me, it was all over. Our fighters surrendered. Some were killed by firing squad, others were sent to work camps on Mercury. The unluckiest, like us, were thrown into the labs. Many died wishing they'd gone by the bullet."

My stomach turns, and not because of the alcohol. "Thousand gods, Sorrel . . ."

Sorrel speaks as if possessed, as if he *has* to say these things whether I'm listening or not. "Every time they woke me from cryo, I thought it would be to kill me. But even when Ofiera messed up on a mission and she was to be punished, they would only stick me in some bizarre experiment, test me with something that *could* kill me—and the not knowing would force Ofiera back in line." He lets out a long, ragged sigh. "Of course they'd never *actually* kill me, just carve off pieces of me little by little. If I didn't exist, they couldn't control Ofiera, and if they couldn't control Ofiera, they couldn't have her break their *other* rebellious little soldiers."

I remember Ofiera telling me in the Under of Ceres that her neural implant, thanks to intensive surgeries and arduous experiments, could influence *any* other, regardless of programming. I felt the proof of it when she controlled my body, preventing me from breathing with a mere thought. Though I also know she doesn't like exerting that kind of control because it leads to neural degradation.

"They used her to keep others in line," I say. "Paired her up with duelists they doubted and had her test their loyalty, like they did with me."

Sorrel looks at me with pity. "And they either fell in line, like good brainwashed puppets, or she took care of them."

"All of that . . . you went through *all of that* and are still ready to fight."

Sorrel's eyes finally fall back on me. "I am."

"You and Ofiera have been working toward Aster equality for—what?—almost two hundred years?"

"Give or take."

"So how do you know now's the right time?" I ask, that old question bothering me still. Ofiera had told me in the Under of Ceres that she had seen countless attempts at rebellions form and fade, that it was only once she'd spoken with Hemlock that she realized the Asters had a shot at success this time.

Sorrel leans his head back in the chair and looks up at the ceiling with a smile. "Ah, Lito . . . that's one of the questions we've asked our-selves for ages—how to know when to try again. But Ofiera thinks it's the right time—otherwise she would have left me in the lab—and I trust her judgment."

I speak without thinking. "Do you know what it was that convinced her?"

Sorrel turns his smile on me. "What was it that convinced *you?*"

I shrug. "The unfair treatment of 'less than' people in Icarii society. The corrupt experiments that have left Asters hurt and dying in the Under on Ceres. Hemlock's successful shift of Ceres from Icarii to Gean hands, proving his network is vast and well hidden."

And Hiro believes it's time. Though I'd never say that out loud.

"You probably know little about Aster society," Sorrel continues. "But know this: if Hemlock has amassed the amount of power that he has, at least one of the Elders believes we're ready for rebellion."

"The Elders we're going to see on Vesta?"

"That's correct."

"So open rebellion is a possibility?"

"More than that." Sorrel's eyes gleam with a strangely frantic energy. "We're on the precipice, Lito. It will only take one tiny push to thrust us into war."

I shudder at the way he says that word—*war*—with such a loving caress in his tone . . . But then his face is calmly neutral, his voice steady, and I think I might've imagined the whole thing thanks to the drink.

"The end goal is equality between the Icarii and Asters. *Peace* between our peoples," Sorrel says, pushing himself up from his chair, "but I'm afraid that peace isn't going to be what you expect it to be."

"What do you mean?"

"When someone's been a soldier their whole life, it's impossible to put those warring instincts aside." Sorrel's long shadow falls over me as he unhooks the needle from my arm. The synblood pack is finished. "Trust me."

I don't answer. I can't. I'm arrested by Sorrel's blue-green eyes, like the sea at rest.

"Just know that if you're fighting with us," he says, "you have to be willing to die for us too."

I stare up at the man out of time, my thumb tracing the scar he left on my neck. He opens his mouth to speak, but I don't give him the chance. I cut him off, unable to keep these words to myself.

"I've been inches from death many times," I tell him, knowing he's seen only a few of the scars that litter my body. "At least this time, I know that what I'm fighting for is worth it."

CHAPTER 14

ASTRID

May no Aunt mistake her role in the Sisterhood; it is the same purpose
the Agora has served since its creation. We are not only to be Speakers
on behalf of the silent Sisters. We must be, at our core, Guardians of
the Goddess's will.

From *A Treatise on Stewardship* by Aunt Edith,
former head of the Order of Cassiopeia

fter Lily brings me a compad with information on all the Aunts of
the Agora, not just what I requested, I spend the afternoon reading. The files are extensive, to the point that I wonder if Lily has
a contact in the secret police, though some Aunts have little to nothing
on them. Aunt Tamar, head of the Order of Orion, for instance. On the
surface, the Order of Orion is dedicated to the preservation of history and
spends much of its funding on public libraries. But truthfully, its primary
task is to use its vast records to assess and approve any new technology before it enters everyday Gean life. The files note that many contractors find
Aunt Tamar difficult to work with, but I can find no evidence that she has
done anything damning. Aunt Margaret is much the same, and because
we have already come to an accord, I do not worry that her file is sparse.

Unfortunately, so is Aunt Marshae's. She has, somehow, kept a meticulously clean trail as she's clawed her way to power. Her file even lists me as a known associate, which makes me wonder how deep her lies have gone. But there is nothing obvious that I can use. Though it pains me to turn my attention to easier targets, I know I must.

Aunt Sapphira, who also voted against me, spends her Order's allotted taxes preferentially. The Order of Leo is meant to preserve the remaining animal species and to bring archaic animals back from extinction, but Aunt Sapphira focuses on the care of species she favors, most notably big cats. Still, it's not enough to cause a scandal, no more noteworthy than Aunt Margaret focusing on flowers as opposed to fruit.

There is a rumor about Aunt Salomiya sleeping with Sisters in her care. While the Order of Virgo is dedicated to public health, it has long been shadowed by gossip regarding group sexual practices, so I wonder if these are more of the same. Lily's file notes that none of the women her sources spoke with had slept with Aunt Salomiya, but that their Auntie had encouraged the Sisters to couple among themselves so as to learn to better serve soldiers. Unless we can find someone to testify that Aunt Salomiya abused her power, there is no recourse here.

Then there is Aunt Genette's file, where I *finally* find something useful. Fighting to eradicate homelessness, the Order of Norma regularly buys property, builds houses and community centers, and repairs Sisterhood-owned assets. The file, large as it is, takes me hours to parse, but the more I read, the more little errors I spot, and the more those little errors add up to big ones.

In the pages compiling receipts of payment, many of the various construction companies are legitimate—I find them with a quick search of Mars's feed—but a few do not seem to exist outside these documents. Those questionable businesses often have recurring payments made to them for various sites. After highlighting the companies, I go through the documents and flag every connected property. If Aunt Genette is embezzling funds, these places will be evidence of that.

Scrolling through the list of addresses, I check the ones that stand out to me. Many are homeless shelters or temporary living facilities for those without work. Others are buildings sold to the Order of Leo to be used as laboratories or the Order of Virgo as hospitals. Then I come upon a section that changes everything.

Orphanages. Not just newly built ones, but also repairs to existing Order of Andromeda orphanages. The payments are recurring and large, but the majority of the addresses are in poor neighborhoods that would not warrant such prices. Why pay so much to repair buildings that would be better off torn down and rebuilt?

I stop at one address in particular. Just seeing it written down sends a chill through me. I have to remind myself to breathe.

Before I can doubt my instincts, before I can talk myself out of it, I call for a podcar. I have to visit this place myself.

THE JOURNEY THROUGH the caldera beneath the sprawling starscrapers is a quiet one. Twenty minutes after we leave the Temple, the driver slips through the hermium-powered dome and starts down the slope of the mountain, but it takes another forty minutes until we reach Karzok, one of the small cities clustered around the fringes of the capital.

I have never forgotten this place, its industrial buildings belching black smoke and painting the sky with swaths of gray. Its clustered architecture, square buildings butting up against each other. Its sparse yards, cluttered with metallic rubbish. Its overcrowded population, sitting on porches watching us pass; the long, crooked bodies of laborers are all I see.

When we reach our destination and I step out onto the cracked sidewalk, I am transported through time. The gravity is lighter and the shadows are long, leaving me to feel as weak and small as a child. When the neighbors, middle-aged workers in faded, patched jumpsuits, see me in my gray dress, they bow their heads and sign respect for the Sisterhood by touching their first two fingers to their foreheads and then over their hearts, before shuffling into their houses. Giving me privacy with Matron Thorne, or afraid of what a representative of the Sisterhood might mean for their neighborhood?

There is nothing remarkable about the orphanage, built of featureless stone painted a cheerful yellow, or its meager yard fenced in with black iron. As the sun sets on Mars's twelve-hour day, I should be able to see the sky turn bloodred, but this close to the factories, there is only heavy gray smog.

I remember this view being more beautiful from my childhood, but that is the way of memory. Everything looks smaller and shabbier, because I have outgrown the orphanage I left behind.

I take a few pictures of the outside with my compad, doing my best to see the touch of children in the chaos of the garden—grass turning brown, weeds choking flowers, overgrown hedges—before a middle-aged woman hurries through the heat-swollen front door and down the cracked steps toward me. I don't need to see her soft-jowled face or the hook that she uses in place of a right hand to know her: Matron Thorne, the woman who cared for me when I was a child.

I catch myself before I speak her name—out of childish habit or surprise at seeing her again, who can say? But she fills the silence, as expected, after dipping her head in a shallow, pained bow and touching her fingers to her forehead and heart. "I was unaware one of the Sisterhood would be visiting me today," she says in that breathy way of hers.

I wait for her face to soften, to show recognition as she looks me over, but I find nothing in her expression. Nothing but fear as she stares at the capelet embroidered with chain-wrapped stones, marking me as an official ambassador of the Order of Andromeda. Instead, I listen to the hiss of her lungs. Her breathing is worse. Her shuffling too. I could not possibly know what she has faced this past decade, but I can see the years have marked her in a way they have not me.

"Shall I gather the children?" she asks, but I do not have time to shake my head before she goes on. "Yes, let me do that. Come in, Sister, come in." The gate is unlocked, the stairs leading up to the house short and stubby. I follow, passing a well-loved but dirt-stained plush toy on the porch, into the house. It is smaller still, nothing like the high-ceilinged, sprawling domicile I remember. The portrait of the Warlord, hung on the wall opposite the door, has not been changed since I left and depicts Warlord Vaughn as a much younger man. The paint is peeling. Cobwebs clutter the corners. The sitting room I spent so much time in is more a closet than a common area.

"Can I offer you something to drink? To eat?"

I dismiss her offer with a shake of my head and enter the sitting room. There are few chairs, mismatched with flattened cushions, and I settle into one that used to swallow me but now fits me comfortably. I used to play that this was my throne, once upon a time, and I a princess holding court. I would pretend that once the spell binding the king's and queen's memories was broken, my parents would come for me and sweep me up in their arms, promising never to lose me again.

Suddenly a voice echoes from my past, a boy I had forgotten until now. *There are no kings and queens on Mars*, he told me. *You don't have parents, and no one will ever come for you.* Though I hadn't let him see, I had cried that day—and many others, whenever he told me such.

"I'll . . . fetch the children," Matron Thorne says, an odd expression on her face.

Does she recall me now that I sit in my favorite chair? Or does she see only the gray dress, the capelet with the symbol of the Order of Andromeda?

Am I the girl she cared for, or merely the symbol of my office, come to judge her worth to the Sisterhood?

Nestled beneath the end table at my side are a selection of tattered books. As I trail my fingers along their spines, I let my mind wander. What happened to the other orphans from my time here? Did they find respectable trades or apprenticeships? Did they join the Sisterhood, like me? Or did they become foot soldiers, lost in the expanse of stars and war?

My head aches with all my questions. I pull a thin book from the shelf, full of stories with colorful illustrations. I absentmindedly flip through it, recalling all the words as if I had just read them. A story of a cat with boots. A cow jumping over the moon. An old lady with too many children living in a shoe.

"Looking for me?" Ringer asks, and though he startles me, I do not jump.

I look up at him, the pages fluttering through my fingers, the cover of the book falling shut. His shadow crosses over mine, darkening it.

"You won't find me here, little sister," he says. I frown, but he offers me no more insight. Why does he seem to know more about his origins than I do?

The sound of small, heavy footsteps draws my attention to the stairs; he is gone when I look back a moment later.

The children burst into the room. There are five of them—all girls, all under the age of ten. They are each, in their own way, beautiful despite their tattered clothing. And all of them, from the eldest with silky black hair to the youngest with curling pigtails, look at me with hope in their big, glittering eyes.

And suddenly, I realize what they must think.

Oh no . . .

"Do they please you, Sister?" Matron Thorne asks, and the fear in her face is finally gone, replaced by eagerness. "They are young but skilled. Cara knows how to knit, and Dany helps me with the cleaning." The named girls glow when she praises them. Those not named pout and look between me and Matron Thorne.

One breaks from the pack, skinny as a twig but with shining emerald eyes. She cannot be more than eight. "I can mend clothes and care for babies," she begins, but I have eyes only for her long legs with their telltale stretching and curving from the lack of gravity medication.

"Amalia—" Matron Thorne starts, but the bold girl continues.

"I would like to tend a proper garden and am eager to learn whatever else the Sisterhood would wish to teach me—"

I stand abruptly, cutting Amalia off.

The girls have not been trained to hide their expressions—why would they have been?—so I can see each of their faces fall, read the disappointment there as I brush past them and walk out of the room.

"Sister, wait—" Matron Thorne calls after me, but I do not stop until I am outside the house. The girls do not follow after, but instead cluster around the windows, peering out at me from behind gauzy, threadbare curtains.

"I apologize for Amalia," Matron Thorne explains. "She is young and earnest, that's all."

But it was not Amalia that upset me so. It was that each of these girls looked at me like I could save them, and I know that *I can't*. Even if I accepted them all into the Sisterhood, how is that any better than what they might face here in Matron Thorne's orphanage?

"Please, Sister," Matron Thorne says again, stepping close enough to touch me. She takes my hand in her left one, the hook held limp at her side. I think for a moment that she has finally recognized me, or that now she will reveal having known me all along. I find I long for it, the familiarity of the person who was the closest thing to a parent I ever had.

But instead she leans toward me and whispers, "If you could intercede on our behalf, we would gratefully use another month's supply of gravity medication. Repairs here have been expensive, and I've been forced to trade some to the laborers for—"

I jerk my hand from hers. All at once I remember why I have come here—this place supposedly received payments from the Order of Norma. This home was meant to be repaired, and it clearly is not. And if the girls are dirty, hungry, and sick from a lack of gravity medication—and I can see they are, with my own eyes—then where is the funding going?

How far does the corruption go?

I turn my back on Matron Thorne and get into the waiting podcar. As the home of my youth fades into the distance, I look away from the window, my eyes settling on the seat next to mine, where Ringer sits with a dark grin on his face.

"Here is what we must do, little sister," he says, and I lean toward him to listen closely.

I RETURN TO the Temple for reinforcements. Lily arrives in my room not five minutes after I call for her. I pace before the window and its view of the smogless sky. The silence makes me restless.

Lily bites her bottom lip, hesitating before speaking. "Is everything well?"

I want to brush her off, or tell her that we should wait for Eden before beginning, but the words come thundering out of me, unrestrained. "How far down does the corruption go? Is everything tainted by the Sisterhood's control, or are people just selfish?"

Her large, dark eyes, normally so unassuming, narrow and flash with a hint of gold, there and gone in an instant. I have begun to recognize this face as one she makes when she speaks of something unpleasant but true. "When those in control of the Sisterhood are selfish, it hardly matters."

The truth slices me to the core. Poison wells up from the wound, spilling from my lips. "They take us as children, and we have no choice in the matter. They assign us to an Order and, as soon as we are old enough, a place to warm a soldier's bed. And once we are considered 'undesirable,' they toss us into an abbey to be forgotten, as if that is a reward for all we have suffered, or we age into Cousins, mere glorified servants. Only if we are lucky do we find some happiness—some *freedom*—in our assignment." I look up to see that Eden has slipped into the room, but she does not interrupt, and I cannot stop myself. "They control *everything*! Where we go. What we do with our bodies. Even our *voices*—they take them so we cannot complain."

Lily shakes her head vehemently. "I understand what you're saying, but language is more than what's spoken." She lifts her hands and begins to sign alongside her words. "Their intention is to control how we communicate. To cut us off from anyone outside the Sisterhood, regardless of the language we use."

And of course, the hand language the Sisterhood teaches is, by law, only to be used by Sisters. *They want to control how we communicate.* They want to control *everything.*

Lily drops her hands as Eden sits beside her on the chaise lounge. "What's this about? Has something happened?"

I fetch the compad from my bed and hold it out to Eden. She hesitantly takes it from my hands. "Read this."

Lily holds my gaze as Eden goes through the files, her pale-scaled, irritated hand hidden beneath the smooth other. She gave me those documents. Surely she came to the same conclusions I did.

When Eden reaches the section of images I snapped from the podcar outside Matron Thorne's, I speak again. "We need more evidence," I say. "Pictures from all the properties we can use to prove the payments are going to shell companies."

Lily agrees immediately, but Eden, clearly shocked, sits petrified. Ringer lurks in the corner, as if he has been there all along.

If my visit to the orphanage accomplished anything, it was to illuminate something for me: There is no time to play nicely with the Agora, waiting for them to decide whether I would make a good Mother or not. The Agora controls the Orders, and the Orders control the distribution of medicine and funds. I cannot abide a single weak link in the chain when girls like Amalia do not have the time to spare.

I must fix this broken system by becoming the Mother. *At any cost.* Even if that is to turn to Lily's unsavory methods and blackmail the Agora into choosing me.

"You know what you must do, little sister," Ringer whispers.

"Will you help me, Eden?" I ask.

Slowly, she lifts her green eyes from the compad to me. "Yes," she says, softly at first and then with more fire. "Yes."

I take the compad from her lap and bring up the file of addresses.

"Then let's split these up. We need to visit as many as we can and get evidence before Aunt Genette discovers what we are doing . . ."

Neither of them questions me. They snap into action at once. And while this might not be the most honorable way of becoming the Mother, I cannot help but feel that the Goddess is smiling down on me from Her heavens as I work to destroy the corruption in Her midst.

CHAPTER 15

LUCE

No one knows Cytherea like an artist

These streets are mapped with our veins

And painted with our neon blood

We dance on the endless rooftops

And sing in the empty hollow spaces

There's a whole world just out of sight

But I won't tell you where to find it

Lyrics to "Cytherean Nights" by Shimmer val Valentine

I'm out of the lab and into the packed streets—walking quickly, shoulder to shoulder with the crowd—before I even know what I'm doing. Before I even have a plan. My compad buzzes wildly, Castor's messages a constant stream.

What's happening

Did you get it

Where are you

We talked about this, scenarios of *what if* whispered late into the night. Now that it's happening, I feel lost. I know I can't go home. They know where I live. I'll have to go to Castor's safe house. Find someplace to change into the clothes in my bag and ditch my work uniform. But then something cold trickles down my spine, a feeling like eyes on my back. Paranoia?

I take my compad, turn on the camera, and focus it over my shoulder.

People in flamboyant, sharp-lapeled business suits . . . Paragon influencers in this season's biodome coats . . . No—*there*—beneath a hologram bust of Shimmer val Valentine, two men cut through the crowd like sharks. One is far too familiar.

Mathieu . . .

I do my best to keep my numb legs moving, one high heel in front of the other, suddenly grateful the theracast fell off last night. As I watch, doing my best not to *look* like I'm watching, he gestures to the other guy—a tall man with dark hair I've never seen before—and his friend cuts down a side street while Mathieu follows me at a measured pace.

Isn't he my supervisor? No. No, he can't be. His oddly empty office. The fact that I never saw his artwork despite his being part of the art department. His muscular frame and callused hands.

He's my manager—a man hired to *manage* me. He's . . . he's something else. A spy. And with a partner helping him—are they a duelist pair? From what I know of Hiro's in-depth subterfuge training as a Dagger, posing as a middle manager might've been easy for Mathieu.

But why hasn't he rushed up to me and arrested me? I have no doubt he could outrun me—I'm in heels, by the thousand gods.

You're only a piece of the puzzle, I realize. *He wants to follow you to the big picture.*

No one would believe that I could program the naildrive to break into Val Akira Labs' servers, so he wants to follow me back to whoever wrote the thing. I am just a bread crumb on a trail to Castor's operation.

The anxiety disappears as anger overwhelms it, filling up my chest and burning in my face. I can still imagine Mathieu's smug look every time he talked down to me. Even now he's not taking me seriously.

Fuck that.

I swipe into my chat program and ignore the bulk of Castor's messages. *My coworker and his partner want to meet up later,* I type as quickly as I can. *They're thinking dinner at our place.*

Castor's reply comes half a second later. *Why don't you take them out?* Just as I thought. I need to lose them and get to the address of the safe house he gave me.

I don't answer. I don't need to. He can see that I've read the message, and that will be enough. I drop the compad he gave me on the ground and dig the sharp heel of my shoe into it as I walk over it, crushing it to pieces.

As for my personal compad, I slip into a particularly thick patch of crowd, rudely bumping into strangers and ignoring dirty looks shot in my direction, and let it slip from my hand into an open bag. If anyone tries to track it, they'll find it leads them to a woman with a haughty face wearing a dress more expensive than the flat I grew up in.

I risk a glance back and see that Mathieu's still following. Without my compad's camera, I'll have to be more careful when checking from now on. My heart beating in my throat, I cut in a different direction from the flow of traffic into a nearby mall. I join the midmorning shoppers as they pass through the flexglass doors, ignoring the attendant who offers to help me find what I'm looking for. I walk by a big silver kiosk for pet cloning services and check my tail in the reflective surface. Mathieu's still there, but has fallen farther behind.

My fear and anger give way to determination. I can do this. *I can do this.* In typical CCAD tradition, Isa and I used to do a lot of our research here. Even before the Keres Art Collective, we would come to the top floor café for afternoon tea and plan how to reach one place or another and what we'd paint once we got there. How well does Mathieu know this mall—know this *city*? We used to run through the alleys at night and climb to the heights and spray our art on the crystal sides of buildings, high enough for everyone to see. Does he know those hidden places?

At the door to a store called Persephone's, I flash a smile at the attendant and head directly for the back. Slipping the naildrive out of my pocket, I strip off my uniform coat and toss it on a rack of clothing examples. I step out of my heels and kick them beneath another rack. From my bag, I retrieve my favorite pair of boots, the only thing worth salvaging, and drop the purse—ID and all—near the counter.

"Can I help you?" a different attendant asks, but I ignore her. "Hey—"

Mathieu's entering the store, the attendant greeting him in her chipper way, when I pass through a swinging door to the back room. On the other side, I drop my boots, slip my feet into them, and hit a button on the side to engage the auto-laces. They tighten comfortably around my ankles. Now adequately shod, I stomp farther into the stocking area.

All clothing stores are basically the same—find something you like on the example racks, an attendant will take your measurements, and the drones in the back produce the item to fit you perfectly. Back here it's business as usual, machines humming along, bladed hands cutting fabric into patterns, needles rhythmically sewing seams, and drones zipping by overhead to manage progress. At the end of one line, a rack of finished garments waits as if set aside just for me.

"Excuse me, you can't be back here!" an attendant with green hair shouts as I approach the rack. I hadn't seen her until she spoke, but she's got an armful of clothing, so she won't be able to grab me. Besides, I know they're not paid enough to deal with thieves.

I don't try to make any excuses, I simply grab an ugly jacket—so dark green it's almost black—and throw it on. "Hey!" she shouts. I pull the hood up over my hair just as Mathieu bursts into the back room.

"Lucinia, stop!" Mathieu shouts, but I'm already sprinting for the shop exit at the back that leads to the stairs. He dodges the attendant, who drops the custom clothes she was holding with a shriek, and follows me down a row of sewing lines.

At the end of the line, I slide between the legs of the table, coming up on the other side and jumping for the door. I fling it open as

Mathieu launches himself over one of the sewing tables, clearing it as if it were easy. Shit! *Of course* he would if he's a duelist.

In the stairwell, I slam the door closed between us and take the stairs two at a time. Each floor has branching hallways that lead to the backs of other shops, and four floors up from where I started, I head down a cold corridor. *I can do this*, I keep chanting to myself. I am not the useless girl they think I am. I hear Mathieu's dress shoes clicking behind me, and I pick a shop at random and dart in.

This one isn't a clothing store. The back room is full of racks, filled with various electronic items from floor to ceiling. The drones at work pull the items that someone out front orders and deliver them. I almost lose myself in the maze, then spot a drone and follow it out.

"The fuck—" an attendant says as I appear from the back door.

I check the feed on my com-lenses for her basic identity. "Surprise safety inspection, Andrea," I bark at her, and she straightens up so fast I have to fight a laugh.

But that rising feeling of joy is smothered in my throat as I spot Mathieu's partner entering from the front. His eyes snap past milling shoppers and directly to me. Without faltering, I turn around and head back into the warehouse.

I have no idea if Mathieu followed me into this shop, but to be cautious, I choose a different row from the one I previously used. Unsurprisingly, the big guy—who I'm thinking of as the Rapier of the two—bursts into the back room.

"Lucinia!" he screams, and I stumble, catching myself on a rack of puppy drones.

I'm tall, but he's huge. In a fight, there's no way I could win. That childhood instinct of mine rises up at the sound of yelling—*make yourself small and quiet*—and I actually think . . . that's not such a bad idea.

I crouch where I am, taking shelter behind the boxes, and peer through the racks. I spot him as he slows from a run to a methodical walk. He moves silently, head whipping around, a predator hunting. He thinks I'm the prey.

"We can help you, Lucinia," he says. "I'm Parson, and I can be either your friend or your enemy."

"We don't want to be your enemy, Lucinia," another voice calls—*Mathieu's.* He's in here too.

Shit, shit, shit . . . How am I supposed to outrun two of them?

"We know all about the people who contacted you," Mathieu goes on. He's farther away than his partner, from the sound of it.

"We just want to hear your side of the story," Parson says, louder than before. Closer to where I'm hidden. "Did they threaten you? Did they force you to work with them? You can tell us."

My anger rears its ugly head again, digging claws into my stomach. Do they really think I'm stupid enough to fall for their ruse of kindness?

Parson starts down the row next to where I'm hidden. I see his boots stepping lightly, coming closer and closer . . .

"I know you, Lucinia," Mathieu says. "I care about you." Bull*shit.* If he wanted me to believe that, he should've been kinder to me at Val Akira Geneassists, instead of acting the part of the pompous asshole to perfection.

"You can trust us," Parson says, directly on the other side of the rack from me.

I stand up, brace both hands against the rack, and *push.* Parson meets my eyes through the boxes at the exact moment he realizes what I'm doing, and he releases a shout as the rack and all the boxes of robotic animals come crashing down on him.

"Parson!" Mathieu shouts. I hear his footsteps as he rushes to his partner, and I duck low and run for the next stack.

"She was here!" Parson shouts, and I hear scuffling behind me—Parson extricating himself? Mathieu stopping to help? I don't look, just move as quietly and as quickly as I can toward the stairwell.

"Go after her!" Parson screams, the last thing I hear before I'm through the back door.

I break into a run in the hallway. My legs ache, but I ignore them. Aching is good. Aching means I'm still alive.

When I hit the stairs, I go up. I know the roof of this place like the back of my hand, know how to move from one building to another. This was one of the best places for CCAD students to spray without being immediately caught. I can lose them up there. Hopefully.

I come to the roof and don't stop to think. The mall is built flush against an entertainment complex, and I run across the flat rooftop to the two-meter climb, jump, seize the edge, and begin to pull myself up.

"Lucinia!"

I don't stop, even if his voice is a needle prick on the back of my neck. I pull myself onto the entertainment complex and roll back to my feet. Mathieu sprints for me across the mall roof, looking no less impeccable than he did at Val Akira Geneassists, his blue jacket still pristine.

I run for the greenhouse on top of the entertainment complex, darting through open glass doors and into a world of plants. The smell of wet soil would otherwise be pleasant, but I can only think about the man behind me. The *duelist* on my tail.

An operator looks up from the vegetables he's watering, his face going pale when I don't slow my pace. At the last moment, I spin around him and hop over the row of tomatoes. A bit farther on, I make a sharp right at long stalks of corn and head for a side exit. I don't look back, don't allow myself to, knowing even the slightest hesitation will mean Mathieu catches me.

Outside the greenhouse, I head for a row of wooden stairs built by graffiti artists to reach a cluster of governmental buildings below. I don't bother taking them individually but jump from landing to landing. My breath comes heavy and my heart beats so fast I can feel it in my fingertips. When Mathieu appears at the top of the stairs, he pauses as if he's feeling the effects of the chase too.

I'm coming up on the place where I'll lose him.

I cross the roof, painted with various graffiti—a well-known council speaker wearing a dunce's hat, a gray-skinned and big-eyed alien figure with a giant phallus, text that used to say KILL ALL COCKROACHES and now says KISS ALL COCKROACHES, along with the tags of various artists trying to make a name for themselves. None of mine have survived up here, except maybe the little two-tailed cat that Hiro inspired, but I don't have time to check. I come to the ladder that leads to the tallest government building and climb it, hand over hand.

"Lucinia . . ." Mathieu, behind me. I don't listen. Don't stop. Almost there . . .

The dome looms above me, programmed clouds passing by in a way that looks natural only if you're not looking closely. I reach the top as a wash of pixelated colors hits me. The only place left for me to go is to the next building, and the only way to get there is to jump.

A jump I can make and Mathieu, wearing dress shoes, can't.

Though . . . will I make it? My ankle is still sore and my lungs burn as I pause halfway across the roof. If I jump now, tired as I am, will I plummet to my death on the streets below?

Mathieu comes up the ladder behind me. "Lucinia, stop!" But he's tired too. I can *hear* it.

Digging the toes of my favorite boots into the ground, I push my-self into a run. Everything disappears other than the physical—the col-ors of the dome, Castor's expectations, Mathieu chasing me—there is only this moment, my arms pumping at my sides, my legs straining beneath me, my face burning—

I plant my left foot and *jump*—

I fly over the street below, embraced only by tranquility. I am breathless. I am weightless. Around me the graffiti by hundreds of artists blurs into a rainbow collage. Images give way to shades inter-spersed by shadows, and for a moment, the city herself, lifting me on wings of pride, whispers, *This is where you're meant to be.* After years of searching, disrespect swallowed with a smile, I have found my place and *I can do this* gives way to *I am doing this.*

This—a girl who uses her talents to help others, who risks herself because she can—is who I'm meant to be.

I land on the opposite roof, stumble a few steps, and fall to my hands and knees. I suck in desperately needed air, sweat pouring down my face, and look back just in time to see Mathieu running to make the jump after me.

"No!"

The word comes to me unbidden. I see what he fails to. He reaches the edge of the building and plants his foot, but his dress shoes aren't made for anything other than looking good, and he slips the slightest bit as he launches himself at the gap.

I swallow a scream as he flies. He stretches his arms forward, reaching, desperate—but somehow he makes it. Somehow he lands on the edge of my roof.

Then one of his shoes loses purchase. His arms pinwheel as he tries to correct his balance, and I force myself to my feet, not sure whether to run toward him or away.

The hesitation can't last more than a second, but it feels like a lifetime, and his eyes widen in fear as he realizes what's happening, as both feet leave the roof and he slips away.

I reach for him. But he's too far away, and my fingers grab at nothing.

He falls, and his face twists, all his accusation and anger melting into a resolved sorrow.

Down he tumbles—*down, down, down*—

Until he hits the ground below with a sickening crunch.

Screams and sobs reach me from the sidewalk. People run toward the incident, as if there's anything they can do to help.

But there's nothing to be done. Mathieu's dead.

IT'S NIGHT BY the time I reach the safe house, the dome's simulated sky a backdrop of deep blue full of fiery white stars. It's all a lie. The stars don't look like that from Venus's surface.

It took me longer than I thought it would to return to the bottommost level of Cytherea and the Arber neighborhood. After the accident with Mathieu—the memory of the splatter of him on the street turns my stomach—I headed for one of the middle levels and burned some time in a theater.

Now, standing in front of the safe house, I ping the apartment number and wait. Castor's face appears on the door screen a moment later, and I look up at the camera so he can see beneath the hood of my dark jacket. The door clicks, unlocking as he grants me entrance.

I enter the building and start up the stairs, but halfway there, I come face-to-face with Castor on his way down.

"Lucinia—" He cuts off.

It's only now that it all settles into my bones, the adrenaline drop making me more exhausted than before. I could sit down and fall asleep right here, right now.

"I got it," I say, reaching into my pocket to retrieve the naildrive. Castor's long legs eat up the space between us until he's only one stair above me, and then his arms are around my shoulders, and he's slouching in order to hold me to his chest.

"Castor . . ." His name slips out of my mouth, a whisper into his jacket. He is warm and steady, and I didn't realize how badly I needed to be held, after everything that happened today, until now. My body goes soft against his, and I lean into him, allowing him to hold us both up.

"I thought . . ." He doesn't finish.

"I'm okay."

I'm sure that waver in his voice is because he thought that I'd lost the naildrive. Or maybe that I'd been captured, even killed because of my involvement with him. He releases a heavy sigh. Is it relief that he doesn't have to shoulder the guilt of my death, or could it possibly be something more?

He breaks away from me. I use the last of my strength to stand on my own two feet. "Don't worry now. I'll take care of everything, Lucinia."

"Luce," I say as he turns away from me, not even asking for the naildrive. "You can call me Luce."

"Luce," he repeats, trying the nickname for himself. He starts up the stairs, gesturing for me to follow him. "You're safe now, Luce."

I want nothing more than to believe him.

CHAPTER 16

LITO

AN EXCLUSION ZONE IS IMPLEMENTED IMMEDIATELY AS DELIMITED BY THE SENTRIES. ANY HUMAN PRESENCE WITHIN THE EXCLUSION ZONE WILL BE REGARDED AS HOSTILE AND ACCORDINGLY LIABLE TO FORCEFUL NEUTRALIZATION.

> From "The Synthetic Ultimatum," the Synthetics'
> final communiqué to humanity

"Lito!" Sorrel's voice echoes down the hallway, cutting through my much-needed sleep. I'm up and moving to the command center before my brain catches up with me.

"What's happening?" I ask, rubbing my eyes to clear them. We'd changed our route to more safely travel in gray space; after four days of nothing appearing on our radar, I'd begun to feel hopeful that we'd lost our Icarii tail.

Sorrel leans over the command panel, hands pressed on either side of one screen in particular. "It might be a different patrol that caught wind of us, I don't know—but whoever it is, they're burning hard and will be on us soon."

"So we need a plan." The tightness in my chest loosens as I say the words. We've spent so long worrying about being caught that, now that it's happening, it's easier to deal with than the fraught waiting. I call up a map on another screen. "No chance of one of Hemlock's friends being nearby?"

"No other ships on radar, outlaw or otherwise," Sorrel reports. Every time I checked up on him during the past four days—when I wasn't resting and recovering—he had his nose pressed to a compad, "catching up on things," as he put it. After his initial contact with Hemlock, he'd reached out to the recluse several more times until, to some degree, I began feeling like the outsider among the three of us. At least Sorrel's well versed in the players on the board and I don't need to explain it all to him.

"Change course. Head deeper into gray space. See if they follow." I don't know why I'm giving him orders. Habit, I guess. But Sorrel doesn't fight me, and I can feel his easygoing mind on the other end of the implant. Even now, there is an unruffled calm to him. "Unless you've got a better idea?" I ask as a sort of peace offering.

"Working on one." His graceful, slender fingers dance across the command panels, and I force myself to sit down in one of the chairs so that I'm not pacing. Instead I bite down on my thumbnail and chew, a bad habit I thought I'd kicked.

I could use my neural implant to neutralize the anxiety, but after breaking down on Ceres following the Mother's assassination, I made a promise to myself not to rely on it too much. I need to feel things—even the bad things. So long as the anxiety doesn't keep me from action, I'm okay. It's a delicate balancing act, I've found, but I suppose that's the way it's meant to be.

"They're still following," Sorrel says. "We could—"

But whatever he was about to say is cut off. A button on the command panel lights up. "They're hailing us."

"Guess that solves the problem of whether we should reach out . . ." Sorrel presses the button to make the connection.

There's no accompanying image, just a voice that echoes in the command center's metal space. "Hailing *Nyx*-class number 2949, this is

Nyx-class number 6818 under the command of Kai val Fredriksen. This is his partner Aino val Harvola speaking."

A duelist pair, then. Probably not the only ones on board. Somehow the knowing calms me, despite the bad news.

"Surrender immediately or be fired upon," Aino goes on.

I look to Sorrel over the panel. "Does that line ever work?" he asks.

"You'd be surprised."

"I have an idea, but you'll need to trust me."

I feel a fiery confidence through the implant but not much else. At least he's not forcing his ideas on me, even if our connection could strong-arm one of us into backing the other regardless of our own thoughts on the matter. "Do it," I say.

"It's risky," he allows.

If this ship catches us, we'll have another fight on our hands, and this time, without Ofiera, we're one soldier down. There's no waking her up to fight like there was with Sorrel. Engaging at all is too dangerous. "Do it," I repeat.

Sorrel brings up multiple windows on the command panel. Without arming the missiles, he opens up the silos and ejects them, leaving them to float, abandoned. Then, instead of maintaining our route in gray space or dipping into the asteroid belt as I suspected he might, he changes course and makes a beeline for the Synthetic border.

I see what he's doing. We have less mass, and the missiles we left floating will be like a minefield, allowing us to slip farther and farther ahead. And with the Synthetic border coming up fast, perhaps they won't bother following us at all.

I watch the radar screen. The ship slows and swerves, finding our missiles and proceeding with caution. But the pilot, whether it's one of the duelists or a program, is excellent, and we don't pull ahead as much as I hoped we would.

And we're still hurtling toward the Synthetic border where the Sentries wait, armed and dangerous, on our radar.

"What now, Sorrel?"

"Trust and patience."

He radiates certainty, and my hands curl into fists, nails digging into the soft flesh of my palms. I watch our screens, horrified, as we move closer and closer to the border the Icarii have painstakingly mapped out.

In less than half a minute, we'll be through.

"Sorrel . . ."

He watches the screen. Doesn't heed me.

Less than fifteen seconds now.

"Sorrel!" I yell.

Less than ten.

He doesn't stop.

I dart forward, hand grasping for the command screen, but he catches my wrists. "Trust me!" he says with a smile, and now we have less than five seconds.

"Fuck!" I curse.

Then we're past the Sentries and over the border. I hold my breath, expecting to be blown to space dust at any second. Sorrel does nothing.

And every screen in the command center lights up red.

"DETECTED BY SENTRY 366Z: SHIP NUMBER 2949 CARRYING THREE LIFE-FORMS," says a metallic voice over our intercoms. "TURN BACK OR BE DESTROYED."

Sorrel doesn't turn us back. He watches the screens, his eyes wide. My head is roaring with the loud thumping of my heart. The mechanical voice continues.

"TURN BACK OR BE DESTROYED. TURN BACK OR BE DESTROYED."

I barely notice the Icarii ship passing the border behind us.

"SENTRY 366Z: LAUNCHING MISSILE."

Oh, thousand gods, we're going to die—

The ship rocks so hard that I almost lose my footing. But we're not dead, so it couldn't have been the Synthetics.

"MISSILE DETECTED FROM SHIP NUMBER 6818," the machine says. "THREAT NEUTRALIZED. TURN BACK OR BE DESTROYED."

"What the hell was that?" I yell.

"The Icarii fired a missile at us, and the Synthetics shot it down." Sorrel's eyes are wide, his pupils huge and black, and he speaks with a soft reverence I can't possibly understand. I'm reminded of that strange moment when we were drinking together, the way he spoke of war like a penitent talking about their god. "They just saved us."

"And we have nothing to fire back!"

Sorrel's face cuts into a madman's mask of glee. "No," he says, "we don't."

"Gods damn it, Sorrel!" Before I realize what I'm doing, I shove him away, and then I'm slapping buttons on the command panel, turning us back toward gray space and broadcasting to anyone who can pick up the signal. "This is ship number 2949 under the command of Lito sol Lucius. We have a wounded team member on board and are under attack. We have no weapons. I repeat, we have no weapons. We are in the process of retreat but cannot return the way we came because of the hostile ship in our path."

"Surrender, Lito sol Lucius!" the Icarii ship responds.

"TURN BACK OR BE DESTROYED," the Synthetic demands.

"Please!" I yell.

No other message comes, and I drop my head between my hands.

The screens continue to flash red as their matching message echoes through our ship: TURN BACK OR BE DESTROYED. TURN BACK OR BE DE-STROYED.

Is this the last thing I'll see before I die?

The machine speaks:

"SENTRY 366Z: LAUNCHING MISSILE."

My entire body runs hot and then cold. This is it, then . . .

"I thought . . . I'd been told they allowed non-threats into their territory," Sorrel whispers. His already pale face drains of even more color. "Ofiera, I'm sorry."

The name that comes to my lips is so natural I don't fight it. "Hiro," I say softly.

I shouldn't be here, not without Hiro.

The screens flicker, their message disappearing in static for a mere half second.

The ship rocks and I close my eyes, accepting that I will be scattered, alongside Ofiera and Sorrel, into the stars.

We are born from the same stuff as stars, the Asters say, and somehow that is comforting in this moment.

But the explosion never arrives. The expected pain never comes. I open my eyes and look at Sorrel, who stares at the radar like he's seen a ghost or a god.

The Icarii ship is gone. Missing from the radar completely.

It takes me three long seconds to realize what this means: the Synthetics blew them up. *Them*, not *us*.

"Get us back to gray space!" I scream at Sorrel, and he jumps into frantic movement, mapping a route for our retreat. I'm not about to miss this second chance at escape.

Over the comms, I continue to broadcast on all channels. "We're leaving Synthetic territory immediately. Repeat, we're retreating immediately."

The screens blank out. No more red. No more warning. Instead, what answers me is a human voice, light and soft as a song.

"Do not return here, Lito sol Lucius. We will not spare you a second time."

A chill runs down my spine. Those words could've come from my sister's mouth. "Thank you," I say again, my throat tight.

I ride in silence with Sorrel all the way back to the Synthetic border. When we are finally past the Sentries, I collapse into the nearby chair.

"What . . ." My breath comes heavy, like I'd just been running for my life. "What was that . . . ?"

"The Synthetics," Sorrel says softly, and his eyes glow with staggering energy. "They're rational beings . . ."

But after everything we've just suffered, I don't want to think about anything like that.

Especially how that voice sounded like a human girl's.

CHAPTER 17
ASTRID

Some days I hate everyone—Aunt Margaret, Lily, Astrid, even myself. But I think the person I hate most is Saito Ren, or whoever the hell they were. If I didn't know about the Agora and the neural implants that take away our voices, I could have been happy. All I ever wanted was to be a ship's First Sister and live in comfort. But Ren ruined that, and now that I've seen outside the cave, I can't go back to the shadowbox.

From the diary of Eden

◇———◈———◇

It feels far too early when a knock at my door wakes me. I slip on a robe and brush the hair out of my face before answering, but it is only a Little Sister with a written message. Once she has delivered the letter, she disappears down the hallway, leaving me to stare blearily after her.

I sit on the chaise lounge but do not open the room-darkening curtains. For the past three days, Eden, Lily, and I have slipped out of the Temple after dark—the best time to disappear unnoticed—and visited properties around Olympus Mons, taking photo after photo of dilapidated, crumbling structures that were supposedly repaired months or even years ago. Out of the seventeen we visited, fourteen were in disrepair. We haven't even finished half my list.

I check my compad for the time and find I have not even slept a full three hours since we returned. No wonder I feel so wretched. But there is no fighting a summons, if that is what the message I hold is, and there is no hiding from its contents. I open it.

I know what you're doing, the first line reads, and I am instantly fully awake. I could not return to sleep even if I wanted to. *Meet me at the Aquae to discuss.* An address follows for the Aquae Hotel, as if everyone does not know of it; it is a resort in downtown Olympus Mons that only admits members of the Gean government. As a member of the Sisterhood, I would be able to enter despite its exclusivity, although, because Sisters do not earn a salary and the Aquae is known for its expense, I will likely stand out. The note is signed with a curling flourish: *Aunt Genette.*

With a headache forming, I stand to prepare for my day.

"YOU CAN'T GO." Less than an hour later, Eden paces my room. Lily, sitting beside me and absentmindedly scratching at the pale patches on her knuckles, watches her, eyes sweeping back and forth, back and forth. "What if she tries to kill you?"

"In public?" I ask.

"She could poison you. She could take you to a private location, then do whatever she wants."

I catch Eden's arm as she walks by, forcing her to still. "Eden, she would not be so foolish."

"She wouldn't be if you brought someone with you." She reaches the heart of her argument; she has been asking to come with me since I first showed her the letter. "We could watch out for you, Astrid."

I shake my head. "She only asked for me, hopefully because she believes I am the only one who knows of her illicit doings." Or she thinks I control Eden and Lily, despite their individual reconnaissance work. Though that makes me wonder . . . What would happen if I told them to destroy their evidence against Aunt Genette? *Are they that loyal to me?*

"Or," Eden says, kneeling before me and taking both of my hands in hers, "she thinks she can get away with anything." Her red hair spills into my lap. I have never seen her beg like this before.

"Not true," Ringer says from the corner, and his sudden appearance sends a jolt through me. "She begged us plenty not to throw her out the airlock on the *Juno*."

Of course, I had almost forgotten . . . When we were enemies and Eden thought to blackmail me, before I knew Ringer was just a shade of me, he threatened to kill her if she brought evidence of my wrongdoing to Aunt Marshae. She begged Ringer—begged *me*—to spare her life.

"Astrid," Eden says, "please don't do this alone."

But I have already decided.

Only when I open my mouth to say so, Eden, her voice thick, strikes me with her words. "Please don't ask me to watch another friend of mine die while I do nothing."

The ghost of the Second Sister of the *Juno*—no, of Paola, for that was her name—floats between us. We watched her stripped of her title and dress and thrown through the airlock barrier. We watched her choke to death, hands forming a single word: *Trapped.*

Lily stiffens at my side—perhaps she senses how private this moment is—but I can hardly spare a thought for her.

"I met Paola as a Little Sister, right after my parents gave me to the Sisterhood," Eden says. It is not a surprising thing to hear a tale like this; what is surprising is that Eden speaks about her past now, undaunted. "My parents were university professors. They could've afforded to keep me, but they didn't. I've always wondered . . . did I do something wrong? Why me, and not one of my siblings?" She shakes her head as if to shake off her sadness. "Anyway . . .

"Paola and I became instant friends. We trained together in the Order of Orion. And after we went through the surgery to take our voices, we recovered together. She never spoke, and when I found I still could, that whatever they had done didn't take . . . she helped me learn to fake it. We thought it was important no one know except us. That one day it would matter." She looks at me, her gaze unwavering. "We thought ourselves so lucky when we were assigned to the same ship. We loved each other, more than we should have, perhaps. Everyone thought we were just close friends. That we worked well together." A laugh, a little too close to a sob, breaks from her mouth. "She always spoke of lofty ideals. Love. Justice. Change. I always told her the same thing. 'Later, later. Not now. Not yet.' Then I lost her."

She stops, lips trembling. I want to pull her from where she kneels before me into my arms. Want to comfort her, in a way I am not sure I can.

"I don't want to lose you too," she says.

And . . . I break. She has made her point.

"If Aunt Genette sees us together, she might target you," I say, but the protest is weak. Truthfully, I can see the point of bringing an ally.

"I can go with you. I'm from the Order of Pyxis," Lily says with a shrug, "and all of the Agora already knows you're working with Aunt Margaret."

"That's why you can't go," Eden says, the fire back in her tone. "We've already said we don't want it to appear that Aunt Margaret favors Astrid. Being from the Order of Orion, I'm unconnected to Aunt Margaret. But my connection with Astrid? After she chose me for Second Sister of Ceres, I'm afraid the cat's out of the bag."

"I've never understood that saying," Lily whispers to herself. "Why was the cat in a bag in the first place?"

"I'm going with you, Astrid." Eden levels me with a single look.

"Fine," I say at last.

"Fine," she parrots back at me. But it is obvious she is happy, because she is smiling as if she has won a game.

Even though, I do not add, casting a glance at Ringer where he lurks above us all, *I am never alone.*

THE AQUAE IS in the heart of Olympus Mons, among the many elegant starscrapers favored by the elite of Gean society. Because of its location, we have to take a podship as opposed to a podcar, but at least the flight will be quick.

As soon as we leave the Temple behind us, we're wrapped in the golden glow of the city. The buildings grow taller as the height of the dome increases, stretching like great fingers of a hand toward the birthplace of humanity, now just a small light in the sky. But the stars, so far past the barrier, are hard to notice in a city so bright; everything in Olympus Mons shines.

Other craft zip past, little fish in a great reef. From our vantage, the starscrapers stretch below and above into an amber haze, their inconceivable heights impossible to decipher. Balconies and doors to patios are thrown open, and people spill into the open spaces, eating, conversing, and traveling, though I can catch only quick glimpses of their lives before we leave them behind.

The starscrapers of Olympus Mons comprise everything from homes to shops to travel hubs. All one needs to move between them is one of the many elevators that move throughout the city. Or, like us, a podship to land on one of the various pads built onto the sides of buildings.

Our ship slows as we reach our destination. The Aquae, constructed of glass in a teardrop shape, is a marvel of architecture hung between two large starscrapers known as the Martian Arms and is accessible only from one of those two buildings. When the podship settles on the left-most building's landing pad, I slip out of my seat to the whisper of silk.

"Should I wait for you, Sister?" the pilot asks. He does not recognize me, which suits me. I nod so he knows not to go anywhere; I hope this meeting will be quick, and I might need a fast exit.

The pilot lowers the ramp, and I leave the ship with Eden at my side. This high in the dome, the air is humid, and my dress sticks to me uncomfortably. We move across the pad to the entrance of the building, where a group of people have gathered, wealthy couples and families waiting their turn for the various elevators. Though the women dress conservatively here as in Karzok, these people are nothing like the poor laborers with their crooked limbs near Matron Thorne's orphanage.

At our approach, curious gazes turn in our direction before dropping to the ground, followed by hands pressed to foreheads and then chests. Before we can even consider whether or not to join the line, a man in a cobalt suit comes to our aid.

"We are blessed, this day, by your presence," he says, bowing deeply at his waist and making the sign of respect for the Sisterhood. "Welcome, Sisters." When he straightens, he does not look directly at us; instead, his eyes are trained just over my shoulder. Either he is highly religious, or he has dealt with too many members of the military accusing him of improperly leering at Sisters before. "Do you have business at the Martian Arms?"

As opposed to the buildings, known as the left arm and the right arm colloquially, I gesture to the Aquae itself.

"The resort?" At my nod, he smiles and claps his hands together. "Of course. Please, follow me."

With quick steps that would suit a soldier, he leads Eden and me away from the line to one of the elevators. They are unlabeled, and so I do not know where they go, but that is no trouble as he selects one for us, calling it with the press of a button. Before we have time to settle in and wait, the doors open with a soft chime.

"Please enjoy your stay at the Aquae, Mars's most exclusive resort," the man says with another bow.

The elevator's interior is expansive, as golden as the lights of Olympus Mons, though perhaps the mirrors make it seem larger than it actually is. While I know the elevator is hurtling up and over to the Aquae at an impossible speed, I feel nothing. Eden stands opposite me, hands curling and uncurling into fists. It would be too dangerous to speak in this place that likely has cameras, but I squeeze her hand to comfort her nonetheless.

When the elevator opens, the two of us emerge into a world unlike any I have ever known.

The walls are covered with turquoise tiles, obscured by the water that flows from the ceiling to a golden receptacle. At the back of the lobby is a concierge desk carved from limestone, and above it, an eight-foot-tall portrait of the Warlord. To both the right and left of the desk, curling staircases wrought of gold stretch to higher floors.

We move cautiously through the lobby. Civilians in dark suits of linen and wool, either military contractors or retired-officers-turned-bureaucrats, bow their heads and sign respect. Military officers, medals pinned to their jacket fronts, eye us with a yearning curiosity. Young soldiers in crisp new uniforms rush heedless toward the stairs, likely recently joined up and willing to spend their signing bonus on a single drink, just to say they went to the Aquae. But those are not the people I worry about; the ones intentionally ignoring us give me more than a small prickle of anxiety. There is no telling how many secret police are here, hidden in plain sight.

When we reach the concierge desk, a woman in a cobalt suit, a silver teardrop embroidered on her breast, gestures for us to step forward. "Sisters, we are honored to have you here. Welcome to the Aquae," she says with a bow. After signing respect, she looks at her compad screen instead of us. "I don't see any reservations for chapels this evening . . . Oh, there's a note here." She smiles at me, not quite meeting my eyes. "Aunt Genette is waiting for you at the bar." She gestures to the staircase on the left.

I thank her with a smile and head for the stairs. At the top is a doorway flanked by twin fountains and crowned with a golden seashell. Passing inside, we come to an expansive space dimly lit in turquoise and navy. On one side of the room is a limestone bar surrounded by some of Mars's most beautiful men and women dressed in flamboyant and revealing outfits. On the other side is a section with private tables on a slightly raised platform. In the recessed center is a dance floor where intertwined couples sway to the live music. Somewhere in this chaos, Aunt Genette is waiting for me.

As I search, a young man wearing the uniform of the Aquae approaches and gestures for me to follow him. Here is where I must part from Eden. We cannot embrace for luck, cannot reveal we are more than two Sisters coming to enjoy the varied offerings of the hotel. I give her hand one last squeeze before sending her in the opposite direction to act as lookout. She heads toward a quiet corner filled with plush chairs, and I force myself to follow the attendant alone.

If Aunt Genette has her own people watching, they will easily find the only other Sister in the hotel. But the less Eden knows, the safer she will be.

The young man leads me past the dance floor to one of the private tables in the very back of the room. Sitting alone, a feast spread out before her, is Aunt Genette.

"Ah, First Sister of Ceres! I'm so glad you've come." She wears her identity proudly in this place that rewards her for her power. The golden medallion marking her as one of the Agora shines on her chest despite the soft lighting. "Close the curtain and sit down."

I do as she asks; as soon as the pearlescent curtains are closed, silence envelops us and the noise from the bar entirely disappears. "Soundproof?" Ringer asks from where he already sits across from Aunt Genette. "Useful." Now we are shut off from the rest of the world, and they from us.

Genette looks up from her meal of real meat—red in the middle with blood that collects on her plate—and smiles at me. Her teeth are small but long, her gums overwhelming. It makes her, with her pointed chin, look ratlike beneath her mass of dirty-blond curls. "Want something to eat? This is one of my favorite restaurants in Olympus Mons. Every ingredient has been freshly cultivated at a Martian farm."

"No," I say as I sit, though the smell of warm bread makes my stomach growl. "I want to know why you have called me here."

She cuts into her meat with a frantic energy. "I think we both know why."

"I would prefer to hear you say it."

Her silverware hits her plate with a sharp screech. "You're *poking* around."

I fight my urge to smile at how distraught she seems. "I was simply taking the initiative to answer questions I would not dare bother you with." I do my best to withdraw my compad from my pocket, fingers brushing against the Mother's neural implant box, with steady hands.

"There are quite a lot of payments for repairs that never happened, to companies that I can find no trace of."

"Who gave you these documents? That old bat Aunt Margaret?" She holds out her hand for the compad, and I give it to her. Of course, I am no fool; this compad has only the files that concern her on it, of which I have already made backups.

I wait quietly as she flips through my proof, her face falling lower and lower. "These have clearly been tampered with! They're fake! Edited to make me look bad!"

"Be that as it may, the photographs we took of the properties are not fake."

"So what?" Aunt Genette slams the compad on the table so hard, I am surprised it does not crack. It is in this exact moment that I realize what a fool I am; I need that compad to contact Eden if things go sour. "You're going to take this before the Agora, prove that I'm—what? Embezzling funds?"

I try to keep my tone steady despite my racing heart. "Your words, not mine."

"No, I'll tell you what you're going to do." Aunt Genette leans forward, her food forgotten. The ends of her hair dip into the blood on her plate. "You and your little friends—you think I don't know about them?—are going to stop snooping around my properties. You're going to take your documents and forget about them. And you're not going to tell *anyone* about this."

Though my heart is racing, I raise my chin as if unconcerned. "And why would I do that?"

"Because I know what you want." She bares her ratlike teeth at me. "Because you want to become the next Mother, and I can help that happen.

"Besides," she adds before I can speak, pulling out a compad of her own and sliding it across the table. On the screen is Eden, sitting at the corner of the bar, head up and eyes alert . . . yet she does not notice whoever is recording her for Aunt Genette. "You may have your little friends, but I have ones in high places."

A knot works its way into my throat until I can hardly breathe. She need not speak a threat for me to feel threatened.

I reach for the compad as if I could somehow warn Eden, but Aunt Genette snatches it away. "Make all this disappear, and I'll vote for you as the next Mother."

"I want to clean the Sisterhood of corruption," I say, but my voice sounds weak, all my thoughts on protecting Eden. "Not allow it to flourish."

"Maybe," Aunt Genette says, "but you want to be the Mother more."

Her words strike like a slap . . .

I drag in a deep breath and force myself to consider. Aunt Genette is certainly Aunt Marshae's creature, but loyalty to herself runs far deeper than whatever Aunt Marshae holds over her. If I accept the bargain, Eden is safe. If I accept the bargain, she votes for me. And if she votes for me, I am one step closer to becoming the Mother. Even if I promise not to bring this before the Agora now, I can still do so in the future.

"Take the deal, little sister," Ringer says. In the corner of my eye, he sits beside me, a hulking figure of surety and protection. "You can always destroy her once you're the Mother."

And though I hate to admit it . . . he is right.

I offer her my hand before I have even fully decided. I do it for Eden. I do it for orphan girls who need me. "I am glad I can count on your support, Aunt Genette," I say.

Aunt Genette doesn't hesitate. And though she smiles like a rat, she shakes my hand with fervor.

CHAPTER 18

HIRO

Does Autarkeia have schools for kids, or do you just let them run around like packs of wild dogs?

Message from Hiro

It's incredibly Icarii of you to believe those are the only two options.

Reply from Dire

I'm stepping out of my apartment building to head to meet Mara when I spot Sigma lurking near the mouth of an alleyway. He's impossible to miss with his balding head and bug eyes shining despite the lack of light. I want to ignore him, to brush him off, but my gaze sticks to him like glue, and all I can think of are the words he told me when I asked him to make me the Hiro I used to be: *There's no going back, kid. I've done weird shit for Hemlock before, but unless you can get a copy of your old genetic profile, you're stuck with pieces of Saito Ren's DNA.*

He makes his way toward me with his hands in his pockets. "You never called any of my friends." I'm sure he's talking about the list of other geneassists and prosthetics dealers on Autarkeia he recommended to me. "What's up with that?"

"Why are you here?" I ask instead, cutting through the crap. I'm not sure where I'm going anymore; I'm just walking to walk.

Sigma steps in front of me, forcing me to meet his eyes. "Look, I get it, you hate me. And that's fine if you hate me for being crass or blunt, but you can't blame me for not being able to undo what Val Akira Labs did to you."

I flinch. I do hold his inability to fix me against him.

"Besides, you're not the only one who's stuck with a genelock they want to undo." He hefts a skinny shoulder. "You could've wound up looking like me."

"First of all," I say, letting the heat into my voice, "let's not make this a contest." *Because I'll win*, I don't add. "Secondly, you're trying to tell me that you look like you do because someone geneassisted you without your consent?"

"That's exactly what I'm saying." Like usual, he doesn't respond to anger; everything is easy and go-with-the-flow for him. "I used to work in Tesla Gardens on Cytherea. Had a beautiful wife and a cute kid."

"You were Icarii?" I suppose it was foolish to think he was Gean from looks alone.

"I'm saying," he says, "you're not the only one who got on the wrong side of Souji val Akira."

Father. Again. I grind my teeth against the curses that work their way up my throat. "What did you do to piss him off?" I ask when I've finally swallowed enough bile to speak.

"I told you . . ." He smiles his crooked-toothed smile. "I did weird shit for Hemlock. I'd take a trip to Ceres on official business—speaking at conferences, setting up other clinics, that sort of stuff—and secretly geneassist Asters while I was there."

And his punishment was to be twisted into this and banished from Cytherea . . . *Fuck*.

"Hemlock helped me come to Autarkeia after . . ." He trails off, ambling in the direction of a skinny alleyway, and gestures for me to follow. I do. "I met Dire, and we've been working together ever since."

Speaking of Dire . . . As we slip into the alley, a dark presence appears behind us. A quick glance over my shoulder tells me it's Falchion in his long black coat. Ahead at the alley crossroads, Dire steps into our path. With Sigma directly in front of me, all exits—all escape routes—are blocked off.

"Next time you wonder why I hate you, Sigma, remember this." I gesture to our strange and cramped location. "We couldn't meet in my apartment?" I manage to keep my growing anxiety out of my tone. Above us, balconies and air-conditioning units butt up against each other, and I quickly map a path to jump and climb my way out of here if necessary.

"We need to talk," Dire says by way of a greeting. "Privately."

"Then talk." I'd been vague on details about Mara over comms, giving Dire enough truth about our meeting to make it believable while skirting the details I didn't want to share—like the memories she saw. I promised Dire that we could have a more in-depth conversation at a later time. I guess that time is now.

But Dire just looks me over with a wry smile. "You look different."

"Do I?" I suppose I am. I've spent the past four days by myself, testing Mara's "reprogramming." I can put my prosthetic hand in hot water and feel that it's hot—at least, my mind interprets it as hot—but my flesh hand is able to give me more feedback, such as differentiating between the water being lukewarm and steaming. Once I know the *exact* feeling of it, my prosthetic reads it the same way. Mara has basically created some sort of feedback loop based on expectations and clarified by reality. On top of that, the lack of pain makes me feel like I've somehow stepped back in time to when I had the two arms and legs I was born with. It's amazing how deeply you can sleep when you're not constantly waking up in agony. "Look, if this is about the meeting with the Synthetic—"

"It's not." Dire steps toward me, and it takes everything within me not to back away. "I know you were angry that we didn't inform you of the duelists here on Autarkeia." He speaks at a normal volume, but with the hum of electronics drowning out everything, I doubt even Falchion can hear him.

Maybe that's why we're here. The alley isn't about boxing me in, but hiding what he's saying. "And?"

"There are some things I can't tell you, and I won't apologize for that. The safety of Autarkeia and its allies is too important to risk."

"If it's an important fact related to my mission, it's shit I need to know," I say. "And Icarii interest in our target is one of those important things."

Dire clears his throat. "I agree. We should have told you, but we didn't want to create a bias in your investigation." I wonder who "we" is. Sigma, who's nodding in agreement? Or Hemlock, whose fingers pluck unseen strings? His shadow stretches long, even on Autarkeia. "We thought if you were to investigate the Synthetic agent and draw the same conclusion we had—that the Icarii are after her—it would confirm our suspicions."

"Mara," I say. "Her name is Mara."

Dire quirks a brow but doesn't ask. Perhaps he's going through the same mental gymnastics I did: Can a single unit have a name separate from the Synthetic consciousness?

Then he says something I definitely wasn't expecting. "Sigma intercepted important information. Yesterday, an Icarii ship was destroyed in Synthetic space. They went past the Sentries and ignored several warnings."

"Shiiiit," I mutter, a headache instantly setting in. The threat that the alley poses and the previous conversation are all but forgotten. "Why the hell would they do that? Was it a mistake?"

"We don't know. But even if it was a ship that went out of control and flew into Synthetic space, the Icarii's reaction is the most concerning thing." He brushes his long locs over his shoulder. I hold my breath, praying the Icarii aren't stupid enough to start a war with the Synthetics. "There are now several Icarii vessels flying along the Synthetic border. Conflicting reports, but somewhere between a dozen and fifteen."

"Fucking gods." That old urge to muss my hair flares up, though most of it's tied back in a ponytail just so that I can't nervously fuck with it. "Are they looking for something, or testing the border?"

"We don't know." Dire's shoulders slump like he's carrying the weight of an entire world on his back. In a way, he is: that world is Autarkeia, and it relies on him when things like this happen.

"Why don't you kick the Icarii off Autarkeia if you know they're here?"

His eyes dart away from my face. "I want to find out what they're doing here first."

Mara had said something strange was happening with the duelists. "If you want me to help, you've gotta give me more than that. I can't walk into this blind."

Dire's eyes narrow, but Sigma gently smacks him with the back of his hand. "Tell them," he says. "They'll find out eventually. Might as well save time."

"I've sent operatives to spy on the Icarii," Dire huffs, "but we've got nothing."

"They don't find anything?"

"Worse."

And there it is: a glimpse of the truth at last. "Worse how?"

"Memory loss. Blackouts," Dire explains.

"Do you think the Icarii are turning them?" I ask.

Dire vehemently slashes his hand through the air. "No," he says, his gut reaction all fire. "I know these operatives. I trust them. So when they tell me they lose hours of time and can't remember anything, I believe them." When I don't immediately answer, he reconsiders, all the heat rushing out of him. "I mean, anything's possible, but I suspect these operatives would come up with a better lie if they'd turned."

"How many of them are ex-Icarii?"

He quirks a brow. "Why?"

"Neural implants," I tell him. "What if someone is fucking with their neural implants?"

"We thought of that—" Dire begins, but Sigma cuts him off.

"About half our number are ex-Icarii," Sigma says, "but even former Geans are having trouble with the memory gaps."

I think for a moment, running my thumb along my jawline. "But you make your own brand of neural implant on Autarkeia, right? What if they're being controlled through that?"

"Can't be." This time, Dire's fire doesn't dim. "Like I told you, the only people involved in that are me, Sigma, and Dandy. We don't even let anyone else into the factories where we make them." Which was why he refused to let me see Mara's painting of the rat there.

I look at Sigma, hoping he'll offer me additional information. He doesn't, so I'll have to ask for it. "You implant them, right?"

"Yep, and Dandy makes 'em."

"With neural implants, if you have the serial number, you can program it as a slave to another," I explain, glad my Val Akira Labs knowledge is finally useful. "Do yours work the same way?"

"No." Again, it's Dire who speaks. "On Autarkeia, we are all free. No one is built to be a slave to another, and our version of the neural implants allows nothing more than access to the network feed."

Still, it seems like there could be a connection . . . maybe one they don't even know about. "All right, I'll do what I can to find out what's happening to your people. You got anything else for me?"

Dire is quiet for a moment, almost like he's considering my question. Or maybe he wants to ask more about Mara and the time I disappeared. After a minute of silence, he says, "Since you've made successful contact with the Synthetic agent, move to phase two of the mission."

I'm happy to change topics. "Do you think it's possible to convince her to leave?"

Dire crosses his arms. "If she doesn't want to leave, you know what you have to do."

"Let me rephrase my question, then. Do you think it's smart to kill a unit of the Synthetics when, right now, we share the same goal in figuring out the Icarii threat?"

Dire's lips curl for a moment so brief that I almost think I imagined it. "Convince her to join us, then."

Thousand gods, I walked right into that one. I run my hand through my hair and mess up my ponytail. "Sure, I'll just have the Synthetics join the Alliance of Autarkeia with all the other outlaws and Asters. No pressure."

"That's the spirit," Sigma says with a smile.

Dire waves a hand to Falchion, and the bodyguard steps away from the mouth of the alley. "I'll contact you if I think of anything else," Dire says, and I take that for the dismissal it is.

AS MARA REQUESTED, I meet her at the edge of the same Synthetic factory she brought me to a few days ago, the wall fluidly parting before her and then closing again despite the rust. Regardless of all the people on Autarkeia looking for her, she doesn't even check her surroundings before skipping over to join me. Meanwhile, I'm all paranoia. After the meeting with Dire and his goons, I walked in circles to make sure no one was following me before starting the trek to this particular industrial dome, but at least now I know I don't have a tail.

"Good morning, Hiro!" The girl standing before me looks little like the one I was tasked with hunting down. She's hidden her hair beneath a brown wig and filled in her eyebrows to make them appear thicker. I'm surprised by how much it changes her appearance. It's no wonder I ran into dead ends looking for her when she has disguises.

"Good morning, Mara," I reply. She's still wearing her tattered black pants and the chunky-heeled boots, but now she has a tank top with a studded leather jacket over it. I wonder if it's real animal hide as opposed to the sinvaca leather the Icarii grow in labs. "You could put an Icarii Dagger to shame."

She smiles, though it doesn't quite reach her eyes. "Are you ready?"

With a nod from me, she leads the way. She takes a narrow alley until it joins up with a main thoroughfare, and then she slips into the crowd with the swiftness of a fish in water. She moves like she belongs—hands thrust in her pockets, head up, shoulders brushing against passersby. I thought she'd stick to the side streets and quiet neighborhoods, but with the way she struts, she's indistinguishable from everyone else.

The crowds, packed shoulder to shoulder in some places, don't even notice her. And with Autarkeia's disinterest in prying into the business of strangers, they're not going to. To them, she's just another one of the station's denizens, an extension of the landscape.

She turns to me only once. "Let me know if you need a break," she says. "It's quite a hike." But after her reprogramming, my hip hasn't bothered me at all, and I feel like I could complete an entire circuit of the station. Twice.

We walk in companionable silence for twenty minutes or so before we're forced to take an elevator to a different part of Autarkeia, questions building inside me all the while. I ask none of them, just watch her curiously. Ten minutes in, we're briefly weightless within the elevator before gravity once again pulls us down. When we emerge, she looks up and points to the city high above. "Can you see your house from here?" she asks with an infectious smile.

"Yeah, there's the old man who sits on the stoop, and there's the 'don't piss here' sign!" I say, playing along with her. She laughs and starts walking again.

When she finally stops—a little over an hour after we set out—we're in front of a crowded strip mall with stores on either side of the street. Some are nothing more than rooms full of junk, yet people move inside them, haggling and trading. Others are more official-looking shops, curated by entrepreneurs with a unified stock. There, a clothing store. Next to it, antique furniture. In the corner, ship parts.

"We're going to have to wait here a little while. I hope you don't mind."

"Sure," I say, my eyes snagging on one storefront about ten meters away in particular. The outside has been painted red, and the inside glows golden and warm. In the open doorway, a mechanical cat waves a beckoning paw from its perch on a table that displays a plastic selection of the shop's foods. お茶, the sign above the door reads.

My mouth waters with promise. "A tea shop at the end of the world," I say. "Who would've thought?"

Mara's hand darts out to hover over my arm, though she doesn't touch me. "Keep your eyes on it," she says, "but don't go in."

Disappointment sinks into my stomach. It's been too long since I had good tea . . .

There's no bench nearby, so I lean against a wall with my arms crossed. Once again I'm thankful for Mara's help; without her, my leg would be on fire from walking so long and I wouldn't be able to stand so still.

Mara crouches beside me in the shadow of the building, her finger tracking through the unswept dust even if she keeps her eyes on the illuminated tea shop. After a couple of minutes, she's drawn a trio of rats.

"Do you like rats?" I ask. I've wondered for a long time why she chose rats, of all things to paint.

She answers my question with one of her own. "Did you know that during the Black Death on Earth, people blamed cats for carrying the plague?"

I try not to laugh. "Uh, my history's a bit rusty. That's the one that killed like half the people of Eurasia?"

"Later, people blamed the rats," she says, undeterred. "But it wasn't the rats' fault either. Not really. It was the fleas. They were just so small, no one realized it."

She looks up at me, eyes bright. It's like she's trying to tell me something with her story, but I have no idea what it is. All I know is it sends a little chill through me, hearing a Synthetic talk about a sickness that killed over half the population of a couple of continents on Earth.

Just as I open my mouth to explain that the fleas were *on* the rats, she points her pinkie at the tea shop. "They're here!"

I spot Noa and Nadyn in the crowd immediately. Out of pure

instinct, I duck my head, hoping they won't recognize me, but Mara doesn't move from where she's crouched. We're far enough away, the two duelists don't even look in our direction as they shuffle into the thin mouth of the alleyway beside the tea shop.

They stand leisurely but alert, speaking in low voices. I can't hear a word from where we are. Are they talking about evil Icarii plans or simple things, like Nadyn's husband and wife back on Venus?

Not five minutes later, a man with strong shoulders and a bushy beard appears, lumbering out of the darkness of the alleyway. I met him when I first came to Autarkeia, but for the life of me, I can't remember his name. He stops by the duelists in a shallow pool of light, and I'm reminded of what Dire said when I spot his face—*a blackout.* He looks like he's not really registering anything in front of him. It's only when I see him hand Nadyn something—a folder, it looks like—that I realize how useless our current position is.

"I need to get closer."

"Hiro, no!" Mara whispers.

"How am I supposed to help if I can't hear what they're saying?" I break away from the building. I halfway expect her to pull that knock-out routine where I get all sleepy and pass out, which would be *great* since we're in public. I'm beyond thrilled when she doesn't.

With the hood of my jacket up and my hands shoved in my pockets, I stride toward the tea shop and then past it, just another shopper in the crowd of people looking for spare ship parts at the store next door.

I can only hope that my looks, nothing like the Hiro I used to be, fool them, or that Noa and Nadyn are too focused on their target to notice me.

"Is the list complete?" Noa asks.

Nadyn flips through the folder of biopapers. "It's extensive, at the very least."

"Good." Noa looks up at the bearded man. "Don't worry. You won't remember any of this."

Memory loss, Dire said, and this confirms it.

As if he's been dismissed, the man plods away with the same awkward movements with which he appeared.

Nadyn closes the folder and tucks it beneath her arm. She says something to Noa so low that even three meters away, I miss it. Noa's eyes rove the crowd, and I turn away as their face sweeps in my direction.

I focus all my attention on the table of metal parts in front of me, picking up a shiny one at random. "¿Cuanto cuesta esa?" I ask the shopkeeper loudly.

I miss her reply, and when I turn back, Noa and Nadyn are gone. I put the ship part back on the table and then, with all the relaxed swagger of someone who's not in any rush, head down the alleyway beside the tea shop where the bearded man disappeared.

I have a million and one questions. Dire said that his operatives were acting oddly. Mara said strange things were happening around the Icarii. And with the way the bearded man handed over the folder—some sort of list—it seems likely that the Icarii have done something to him to cause that bizarre blackout. So what I want to know is, what's on that list and why do the Icarii want it?

At the end of the alleyway, a hulking form swims up out of the shadows. I've caught up with the bearded man. "Hey, you okay?" I call, hoping I can use this chance to break through that wall of blankness and interrogate him.

I stop short when two others join him.

I don't know them and they don't wear military blacks, but they don't need to for me to recognize them as duelists. The way they stand, hands at their sides as if reaching for mercurial blades, tells me all I need to know.

I keep my composure, hold both hands up. "None of my business," I say, taking tentative steps backward. When the duelists don't come after me, I turn around and start back the way I came—only to find myself blocked in by Noa and Nadyn at the mouth of the alley.

"Well, well, well," Noa says, their blue robotic eye bright even in the dim alleyway. "Look what the cat dragged in. If it isn't a Gean rat."

I fight off a shudder, thinking of cats and rats and plagues. "Noa," I say, forcing myself to smile and turning sideways so I can monitor the threats on both sides of me. "Thought you were dead."

Noa scoffs. "Like you'll be, soon enough."

"Come on, don't tell me you wouldn't miss me after all our Ceres nights together." The only nights we had were spent butting heads in the Icarii barracks, but to add insult to injury, I wink at them. Their lips curl back in a snarl, but Nadyn's hand on their shoulder keeps them from stalking down the alleyway toward me.

Meanwhile, I'm checking for escape routes—maybe if I jump atop that dumpster, I can grab the bottom of the second-floor window and drag myself in. Or maybe I can provoke Noa into joining me in the alleyway, leaving only Nadyn for me to run past in a bid for freedom. Once I'm back in the crowd and not pinned here, I can look for Dire or any of his allies, even the odds against the duelists.

And where the hell is Mara? a part of me wonders.

Doesn't matter. I can't count on her now—not to get me out of this mess.

Then I hear a voice, and a poem, so familiar to me that I freeze.

"'A caterpillar, this deep in fall—still not a butterfly.'"

I forget about them—the bearded man, Noa and Nadyn, the two additional duelists—and turn, my attention only on him.

Shinya.

"Do you recall the author of that poem, Hiro?" he asks, and my tongue is fat in my mouth. It's like he hasn't aged a day in the two years we've been apart, and all of a sudden, I have been transported through time and space to a home that no longer exists. "Matsuo Basho," he answers, pulling his hands behind his back, the ever-perfect posture of a commander. But his smile . . . Thousand gods, his smile is that of my big brother.

I try to swallow, but my throat is too dry. I want to question him, to shout at him—but as soon as he appeared, my brain disconnected from my mouth. I can't form words.

"I heard a rumor you were here, but I didn't dare to hope to run across you. I'm glad I was wrong for once." He looks to his subordinates, dismissing the two I don't know with a simple wave of his hand. "Join me for tea, and let's talk like old times."

And while I want to curse at him, to fight my way past the remaining two duelists, I find myself pulled toward him like a magnet. "Okay," I say, and when he passes by me, I let him lead me out of the alleyway.

CHAPTER 19

LUCE

FLAGGED: The thickly layered oils appear to be applied hastily, but the result is that this piece transforms from a painting into a carefully crafted sculpture. The face of the portraitist appears three times on the canvas wearing the exact same expression, something between hollow and haughty, in green, blue, and red. It is only when the three are taken together that a fourth face appears in the negative space, a face similar to, but not quite, the artist's. NOTE: LITO SOL LUCIUS?

Description of *Self-Portrait*, painting by Lucinia sol Lucius

The year Lito left for the Academy was the worst year of my life. I didn't know how to care without him beside me. I started failing classes. I had to hide notes from teachers. I did my best to keep it from my parents, hoping I could pull my grades back up—could pull *myself* back together—before they found out. But then a teacher called them for a meeting and, with all of us sitting together in her close-clustered, humid office, told my parents that she was worried about me. I had been such a good student, she said, and now I wasn't turning in my assignments, and why did I have bruises on my wrists, was I dealing with bullies?

Lito thinks our parents became harsher without him home to absorb the brunt of their anger, but I was the one there, so I know it was that meeting that changed things. After that, *I* was the one they fought about. *I* was the problem ruining their lives.

Would you rather your father punish you? Mamá would ask as I curled into the corner, aching and crying. She believed she couldn't hurt me because she didn't have the strength Papá did, but she didn't realize I was so small that *of course* it hurt, and Papá would look the other way, like it wasn't happening if he didn't see it. I tried to become small and silent, a rodent in my own home, tiptoeing through the house and saying nothing to keep from setting them off. I thought if I did what they demanded, it would stop. It never did.

When Lito was there, he would take me into the closet of our shared bedroom and wrap me tightly in a blanket and whisper that we were safe. He would paint me pictures with words of a cave by the sea and cover my ears so I could hear the rush of the ocean. He would tell me stories of mother whales with their calves, black bodies shifting beneath rolling waves, and make up stars connected in constellations that didn't exist. And while this didn't erase the pain, it gave me an escape.

Without him, I could go into the closet and wrap myself in the scent of his old clothes he'd left behind and whisper to myself, but it didn't help. He was the key ingredient in the spell. He was my connection to that magical world where we were safe and things were beautiful. Without him, I was shipwrecked on an island barren of any life other than my own. Until I began to draw.

What started as something to help me escape for ten, maybe fifteen minutes at a time helped me escape my old life altogether. Just before I turned sixteen, Lito secured an apartment for me on the highest level of Cytherea where I could finish school in a better district with an emphasis on the arts. From there, I applied to CCAD. The day I got in, I wept, knowing the art that made my world beautiful and safe would be my future.

The sea cave became a place of memories and dreams. I could paint it exactly as I imagined it, but without Lito, nothing made it real again. It was a land out of reach and time. All I could hope for was a glimpse of it as I worked, a reminder that a world in which I was safe with my brother existed.

Waking in Castor's safe house the next morning, lighting so dim it's impossible for me to see the entirety of the room, I feel I'm on the edge of that sea cave from my childhood. That if I could just wander deeper into that darkness, I might find Lito waiting for me with a kind smile that reaches his brown eyes.

I know from last night that I'm wanted all over Cytherea, my face and name on every news outlet, but that doesn't scare me like it should. I've achieved things I never thought possible. I outran two duelists. I stole crucial data from Val Akira Labs. And now I know, if I can just follow Lito's footsteps, I can find the sea cave again—the world in which my brother and I are safe, together.

THE SAFE HOUSE is small even by lowlevel Cytherean standards. There's a single bedroom filled with bunk beds for all the Asters who live here—four of them, plus Castor, who's a guest—and a bathroom with a shower stall the size of a coat closet. No mirror, just a toilet on tile with low water pressure. The kitchen lines one wall near the entrance, joined to a living area with desks covered in hand-built de-vices, machines I recognize pulled apart to make ones I don't.

I'm shocked by how silent the Asters are as they work, never bumping into each other despite not looking where they're going. In the dim light, they don't need goggles; I'm the clumsy one, running into furniture and constantly apologizing. After a breakfast of something called *Laetiporus*—which tastes exactly like chicken despite being a mushroom—Castor introduces me to the others, and they offer me big, plastic smiles, as if they've been trained to give them. Their names and genders follow: Sage, male. Violet, non. Poppy, female. One whose white hair has slipped from their braid and curls around the edges of their face is particularly verbose. "I am a woman, and in your language, my flower name is Lotus."

"Flower name?" I ask, looking from Lotus to Castor and hoping it's not an offensive question.

"We don't bother telling *siks*—uh, anyone who isn't Aster—the names we call each other," Castor explains.

"Because we can't pronounce them correctly?"

The Asters smile indulgently.

"You can with your mouth, but we have other ways of talking that have nothing to do with our voices that you can't replicate." Castor shrugs. "It's just easier to pick something *siks* can say. Otherwise, it would be like me calling you Lulu."

I wrinkle my nose at the awful nickname, but slowly, things begin to make sense. The way the woman at the restaurant seemed to ask Castor a question without a word. The way the Asters move as if they can sense each other with something more than their eyes.

Faces fall. Become blank. After a moment, Castor looks at me. "We have to go out and get shit ready to leave Cytherea," he says. "You'll have to stay here. Is there anything you need?"

"No, I can entertain myself."

"I meant, anything you need me to pick up out there." He flashes me his little smirk of sharp teeth. Unlike the others, Castor seems well practiced in Icarii facial expressions and body language. That grin of his even reminds me of Hiro's.

"I'll miss having art supplies," I tell him, playing with one of the gems hanging from my various necklaces, "but I'm sure we can find replacements wherever we're going." I suppose it says everything about me that I worry about that instead of clothing or food.

Without a word, Violet and Lotus march back to the bedroom like soldiers. A moment later, they're back, each holding out something for me. From Violet, a sketchpad with gritty paper and a charcoal pencil. From Lotus, a palm-sized charging box for a communication device. Both Asters flash their plastic grins, and I wish I could politely tell them they don't need to force themselves to smile for my comfort.

"It's not connected to any service," Lotus says as I thank them both. "But there is music on it, if you wish to listen."

My smile comes to me naturally as I open the box and remove a bead-sized sticker. I place it on my cheekbone close to my ear, then settle the sketchbook on my lap. The four Asters who live here leave without a farewell.

"Don't answer the door for anyone," Castor says. "Stay safe." Then even he is gone.

In the silence and dark of the apartment, I'm tempted to try to eke out a few more hours of sleep, but the sketchbook and the promise of music are too strong a lure. "Play all; random," I say, opening up the sketchbook and letting the charcoal fall on the first page.

My hand moves as the sound swells. At first it's white noise to me, the sound of a machine's electric hum, but soon a strange thunk joins it—metal being hammered, it sounds like—and a beat begins to form. Just when I think I've grown accustomed to the peaceful, hypnotic track filled with the sounds of what I imagine ship living to be, a voice joins—or, perhaps not a voice, but someone breathing. *Hah, hah, hu-hu-hu, aahhh.* Air, in and out, captured and held, played with and pushed through lips. Between the breath and the ship sounds, a song is born.

My hand flies over the page, the music spurring me into soft sweeps and dramatic arcs. A long face appears, followed by large eyes and a straight nose with no curve to it. Messy hair a mere suggestion. Roguish features, like a parted mouth with sharp teeth. It's only then that I realize I'm drawing Castor. Only then that I realize how much his image has ingrained itself in my mind.

The music thumps on. *Hah, ahah, ahah, ahah. Ahhhh.*

CASTOR RETURNS ALONE in the afternoon, wearing traditional Aster wraps. It's the first time I've seen him wear the cream-colored, bandage-like fabric draped carefully over a black bodysuit. It seems so out of character that anxiety worms its way back into my chest at last.

"Pause," I say, and the music stops, plunging me into silence all at once. I close the drawing pad as he crosses the small room to where I sit on one of the office chairs dragged to face the door. I don't want him to see all the charcoal studies I've done of him. "What happened to the others?"

"They're waiting outside."

"Waiting?"

"It's time to go, Luce." He hands me a bag. Inside is another set of wraps.

"We're leaving Cytherea," I say numbly. Castor nods. "I'm leaving my home and never coming back." The shock of it makes me stupid.

He gives me a moment to settle as he packs a few handmade machines from the desks into his bag. When he turns back to me, he's tucking a smaller device into his wraps.

"There's a hangar on this level mostly used for unimportant trade with the belt—not water, of course, but minerals or metals found on asteroids, that sort of thing. It's low-tech, minimum security. We've used it for smuggling before. Lotus spoofed us some work permits, so we'll get out that way." I'm wondering if Lotus was the one who wrote the program that broke into the Val Akira Labs server, but before I can ask, he gestures to the bag in my hands. "Do you need help with the wraps?"

"No," I say. I've never been good at asking for help, but when I look at the impossible way the fabric is draped around his shoulders and hips, I reconsider. "Actually . . ."

He smiles, then seems to think better of it. His face drops. "Put on the suit first. I'll help from there."

I take the bag to the bedroom, where I can have some privacy. I suck in deep breaths and let them out in several shallow puffs. *Aaaahh, huh huh huh.* Nothing but my breath.

CASTOR LEADS US through the streets of Cytherea, past peacekeepers who, despite my racing heart, don't even look in our direction. The goggles I wear—treated to look like an Aster pair but not block the light—are like blinders, forcing me to march forward, ever forward. And while the bodysuit regulates my temperature, my breath on the wraps around my face is close and hot. *Ahh haa. Ahh haa.*

I thought I knew all the neighborhoods on this level, but we left the apartments behind half an hour ago. Now every step I take is the farthest from my normal life I've ever been. Buildings not unlike the Maintenance Guild's rise around us, the majority windowless, pale squares with the names of various mining operations slapped on the sides. I suspect we're not far from the space elevator, but before I can get my bearings, we turn down a thin alley and head between shabbier buildings of rusting metal.

After another fifteen minutes or so, we emerge from behind one of these metal warehouses and find ourselves at the very edge of the dome, the blue sky and fluffy white clouds distorted from this angle. Across a wide gravstreet on which a few podcars pass is a building that looks like a train station in desperate need of renovation, the exterior all swooping metal arches and glass ceilings done in pastel lights. It's been thirty years since the Neon Futurism period, but this forgotten place remains as a temple to its garishness.

The back of the building butts up against the dome, while the front has a single door, taller than it is wide. There's a cluster of people at the entrance, a group not unlike our own, and a line that snakes from the entrance down the sidewalk. This has to be the hangar Castor mentioned.

I ready myself to join the line when the crosswalk holograms light up, but my group has halted, ignoring both the street and the building. Huddling together, Lotus says something to Castor in a language I don't understand. But I need no translation once I spot the dark uniforms moving through the queue: there is the additional security of a handful of peacekeepers, and at least one pair of duelists.

Castor comes to my side, his hand warm on my lower back.

"Our work permits will get us through, right?"

He doesn't answer. "Change of plans," he says instead, slipping a familiar silver machine into my wraps. I recognize it from my apartment—the gadget that blocks listening devices and cameras. "Follow Lotus. I'll rejoin shortly."

"What? You're leav—"

Before I can even finish, he breaks away from us and disappears into the shadows of a sidestreet at our back. This time when the crosswalk holograms light up, Lotus nudges me forward, and our group—minus Castor—moves to take a spot at the end of the line across the street.

I want to ask what's happening, but I can't. I have to be quiet. Normal. I can't tip the peacekeepers off to something odd in our group. Can't cause a scene. So I wait, silent, as our group moves closer to the checkpoint at the station doors.

Minutes pass like seconds. The queue thins. It becomes clear as we watch that the peacekeepers are only examining Asters, waving non-Asters through with hardly a look.

When there's only a handful of people left in front of us and we're close enough to hear what's happening, a solitary Aster approaches the checkpoint. "Identification check," the peacekeeper says. The Aster hands him their papers. "You speak English?" the peacekeeper asks, but I can't hear the Aster's response. "All right, hold your arms out and spread your legs. I'm going to pat you down and check a few things before you're cleared to go. You understand?"

The Aster does as asked, and the heat inside my wraps becomes all-consuming, making it nearly impossible to breathe.

The peacekeeper grabs the Aster and squeezes, ensuring they're hiding nothing in their wraps. Digging hands into boots and pouches. Groping the sensitive parts of them, both chest and crotch. I'm already shaking when he hooks a finger in the wraps over their face and pulls them down to look at the skin beneath.

Shit, shit, shit. With my opaque olive skin, there's no way I'm getting mistaken for an Aster. No way I'm getting through this checkpoint.

"Ah—" the Aster gasps as they jerk away.

"I apologize," the peacekeeper says, but he doesn't sound sorry in the least. "I know you have sensitive skin, but we've been instructed to be thorough. You can go ahead and board now."

The Aster hurries through the checkpoint.

What are we supposed to do now? I wish Castor were here, but he's not, and I don't know how his device could possibly help us in this situation. I try to look to Lotus for guidance, but she doesn't even turn in my direction.

Oh, thousand gods . . . am I about to be arrested?

It happens all at once: a gust of hot wind, a roar that tears at my eardrums. The ground rumbles beneath us, followed by the sound of shattering glass. Across the street, a block away, a building is on fire, orange flames flickering and black smoke rising.

In the wake of the explosion, screaming fills the air. Peacekeepers and duelists rush toward the building, while others run away. I catch frantic shouting from the crowd.

"—emergency—"

"Some sort of explosion—"

"—a bomb!"

I find myself in Lotus's arms, her embrace the only reason I'm still standing. She shakes me, says something to me I don't make out, then shakes me again. "Come on!" she's saying over and over. "Come on!" She drags me toward the entrance.

The checkpoint now gone, we hurry into the station. The inside is large and full of ships, exactly like I expected a hangar to be, though the back of the building is open, sealed by a hermium-powered barrier. I've never seen the dome like this: transparent, nothing but the yellow, oily sky of Venus's atmosphere beyond it. In my numb shock, I realize all my attempts to paint it have fallen short.

Lotus jerks me forward, leading our group through clusters of ships, the majority a stealthy Icarii black. Everyone is hurriedly board-ing crafts, desperate to launch, frantic to outrun the fire, because there is nothing so dangerous on a level like this, where the air is already thin.

The ship we finally stop in front of is hexagonal, wider at the top than the bottom. Though it's black, much of the plating has been scraped by something—debris, I suppose, though it looks like claw marks to me—revealing the silver metal beneath. It's clearly well used but big enough for our group and has something like arms with hooks on the ends for grabbing or grappling poised in a restful position up front.

Lotus approaches the cargo bay doors and scans her compad. With a metallic hiss, the ramp opens. Violet, Sage, and Poppy immediately board.

I follow her into the cargo bay. "Castor," I say, my other words drying up.

Lotus's face turns in my direction, but behind the wraps and goggles, I can't make out her expression. "He'll come if he can."

"But—" It all crashes down on me at once: Castor's bag of devices, his telling me there was a change of plans, the way he rushed in the direction of the building that exploded. "What the hell was he thinking?" I hiss.

Lotus's tone is just as hard as mine. "That you were worth saving."

I pull in a deep breath and hold it in my chest.

"He would have chosen an abandoned building," she goes on. "The payload was small, which will make it easy for emergency services to put out. It was a distraction, not something meant to hurt."

"That doesn't mean it won't hurt someone—"

"How else could we have gotten through that checkpoint?"

I don't answer. I can't.

"Let's get you strapped in," Lotus says, turning to follow the rest of our group deeper into the ship.

"I'll wait here for Castor," I tell her.

She pauses but says nothing. She leaves after a moment of thought.

There's a range of emotions I feel—fear chief among them. A small dash of horror. But also a rising pride that I'm part of something so big. Something my brother is part of. And then I think of the way Lotus said

Castor thought I was worth saving, and a warmth grows in my lower belly that drives me back down the ramp to look for him.

I keep my eyes peeled for Castor. Several of the ships around us have launched, and many more are readying to. From the hum our ship is making, I'm sure it's warming up to leave too.

Just as my heart has started to calm post-explosion, I hear shouting.

"Hold it right there!"

Another deep voice joins the first.

"Don't move!"

I take one step farther down the ramp, looking toward the noise and—*shit*—

A dozen meters away, around the tail of another ship, there's an Aster and a pair of duelists. My breathing comes faster. As the Aster smoothly raises his long arms, I recognize him. "Castor—"

I'm down the ramp and out of the ship, heading in their direction, before I'm aware of choosing to go after him.

One of the duelists—the Rapier, I see from his uniform—notices me when I'm a couple of meters away from them. "Stop right there!" he yells, holding up his hand.

I freeze.

Castor's face is turned in my direction, not theirs, as the Dagger steps toward him, reaching for the cuffs on his belt. "Turn around. Put your hands behind your back," he says, but Castor . . .

Castor *moves.*

As if made of wind, Castor snatches the hilt of the Dagger's mercurial blade and draws it. The liquid metal emerges and hardens, brightening the space around us until I can't see through the treated goggles. I try to yank them off, but they get tangled in the wraps over my head and face, and I pull the whole thing off to find Castor holding the weapon like it's *his*, like he was born to it, and I'm not sure who is more surprised by the turn of events—me or the duelists.

"Run!" he yells at me, and swings at the Rapier, who meets him with a blade of his own. Their swords lock for half a second before

Castor uses his long limbs to his advantage, tripping the shorter man into a stumble and herding him away from the ship.

I could run back up the ramp. Escape on the waiting ship. Abandon him, like Castor instructed.

But then I see the Dagger running after his partner and Castor, hand on the hilt of his HEL gun. He draws it from his hip. While it looks like Castor is fighting a child, now the duelists have the advantage—Castor doesn't have a shield.

It hits me like a slap in the face: *Castor is going to die, all so I can escape.*

"No!" I yell. There's no hesitation in me. With all my strength, I rush the Dagger.

He spins toward me as I barrel into him and turn my momentum into a grab for his weapon. He collapses to the floor, me on top of him. He's dropped his shield to grapple with me. One of my hands is on his gun. I have the advantage of surprise, but which of us has superior strength? Him, probably, so I cheat. I push my head toward our hands, find his wrist, and bite down as hard as I can.

He screams. The ferrous taste of blood hits my tongue, sharp and bitter. It's enough for his grip to weaken on the gun. I grab the pistol and jerk it up and out—enough to likely break his finger in the process—but now I hold the gun.

Something strikes the side of my head, and my vision goes black as pain pulses from my head to my feet. I turn, see his hand fisted to strike again, and I right the gun in my hand.

"Idiot," he says, and this time he doesn't punch me so much as slap me as his hand digs into my hair and seizes it by the roots. "It's fingerprint-locked—"

I strike him in the temple with the butt of his own gun.

His face jerks to the side. His body goes limp beneath me.

"I'm not an idiot."

A hand grabs my shoulder, pulling me off the duelist, and I spin with the gun in my hand—

It's Castor.

Castor, covered in blood. His? No—I spot the Rapier on the floor, bleeding closer to the entrance of the station.

"Let's go!" Castor yells, and he grabs my wrist and drags me toward the ship.

I throw the HEL gun in the opposite direction. "What about those two?"

"They won't know what ship we're on," he says, pulling me up the ramp and into the hold. I pat the silver device still hidden in my wraps and hope it's done its job blocking any cameras.

Inside the cargo bay, Castor punches a button, and the door closes behind us with a snap and a hiss. "Get us out of here, Lotus!" Castor screams.

"Already on it!" comes Lotus's voice over the intercom. The ship rumbles beneath our feet.

His breathing is heavy. Mine too, turning into a duet of *ah ha ah ha ah ha.* The ship jerks. I reach for him as I stumble. His arms go around me, and I fall against his chest. My hands brush over his splattered front, my fingers checking for wounds.

Castor looks down. "None of this is mine."

I gesture to my bloodied lips. "Neither is this."

His sharp teeth appear in a big smile.

"Get to a chair already!" Lotus shouts over the intercom. "We're getting out of here, one way or another!"

The ship rocks beneath us so hard it almost knocks me on my ass, but Castor grabs a bar along the silver wall with one hand and me with the other, holding me steady. We don't go far, just a few steps into the hold to a set of seats. Castor helps me sit before throwing himself into one. He buckles up, and I follow his example.

I fist my hands in the seat belts and clench my eyes against the fear. The adrenaline of before rushes out of me, leaving me cold and trembling.

"Luce."

"What?"

"Give me your hand."

"What?"

I open my eyes and meet his gaze. He looks at me like he did at my paintings, like he wants to memorize my lines and colors. Like I am art he longs to understand.

My face burns as his pupils grow wide, swallowing the gold. Swallowing me. They are as black as space, shimmering with pinpoints of light like tiny stars, and I am adrift, weightless, breathless in the expanse of him. He is a universe I long to explore.

"You saved my life," he says, holding out his hand for mine. Not looking away, never away, I reach across the gap between our seats and lace our fingers together. Like this, we leave the only planet I've ever known behind.

CHAPTER 20

LITO

DR. EUGENE VAL TOPOROV: I'd like to read something my predecessor wrote: "Asset has little to no regard for her humanity. Believes death of those she deems 'harmful' to Asters more important than the preservation of her species." What would you say to that?

OFIERA FON BAIN: May I ask you a question, Doctor?

DR. EUGENE VAL TOPOROV: Go on.

OFIERA FON BAIN: If that is the dichotomy through which I supposedly see the world, what side do you believe you fall on?

Excerpt from an interview with Asset #5403210

Vesta appears on our screens, its lumpy gray form swimming up out of the darkness. The asteroid is nothing like the dwarf planet Ceres; I can't spot a single colony on its oblong, potato-like shape. It looks completely abandoned, if it was ever inhabited at all. But after our run-in at the Synthetic border plus another two mind-numbing days of travel, I'm happy to land anywhere.

I call Sorrel over the intercom to let him know we're approaching, but he never comes into the command center or acknowledges the warning. Whatever coordinates he programmed into the ship control it, and the *Nyx*-class begins docking procedures in preparation for landing.

I have nothing to gather—I discarded the bloodstained Val Akira Labs uniform after changing into the spare set of military blacks—so I head for the med bay. Sorrel's there, as usual, sitting a silent vigil beside Ofiera. I think he even sleeps here.

He doesn't look up as I enter, his focus on the compad in his hands. He's a voracious reader, has been going through every file Hemlock sent him, all in preparation for his meeting with the Elders.

"How's it going?" I ask, and he dips his head to show he heard me while he makes a note in the document, flagging the place he left off.

With a few taps of his fingers, he brings up the ship's livecam stream instead, showing me the *Nyx* maneuvering into the Vesta airlock. "Almost there."

I step to the medbag's side and wince; the yellow fluid looks cloudy after her extended time in there. "How's Ofiera?"

"As well as can be expected." Sorrel strokes the surface of the medbag with his fingertips, hand over Ofiera's face, as if he longs to brush her hair from her eyes. The medbag is a little like the cryo chamber, her body stuck in a small space, lungs filled with liquid. But she's not frozen; she's floating. Her heart still beats, her body mends itself. I wonder if it feels like her prison in the labs, or if she's even conscious in there to know.

The ship shudders as it passes into the hangar and sets down. "This is it, I guess." I keep my eyes on Ofiera as I speak to Sorrel. "Either the Asters arrest me for being a human trespasser, or . . ."

His voice cracks. "I'll do everything I can to make sure that doesn't happen."

"I'll take a cell if it keeps me from being executed."

He doesn't reassure me. There's nothing he can promise on Vesta when he's not the one in charge.

"It'll be worth it if they can help Ofiera." Already the hangar around our vessel is a blur of motion, Asters approaching with hands at their hips. I'm not stupid enough to think them unarmed. I force my eyes to Ofiera, to the woman who sacrificed herself to save me from Sorrel. "She taught me a lot. Helped me open my eyes."

He chuckles under his breath, ignoring the compad as well. "She does that."

I study Sorrel's profile; the scar across his cheek is livid and red. "She's seen a lot of shit. Been through a lot of shit. She could've let me fail my mission to kill the Mother, let Command have their way with me, even killed me for allowing Hiro to escape Icarii justice, but she didn't. She risked herself to give me a chance to make my own choices, and for that, I owe her." The ship shudders as it gently lowers itself to the ground. *And she's my Dagger*, I don't say. I never wanted her to be, never asked for her, but she's my Dagger, and now I can't imagine life without her.

The outer airlock door opens, and, no longer able to ignore it, I snap my attention to the compad. Five Asters enter wearing clothes unlike any I've seen before—off-white tunics and brown trousers made of a strange leather. Their arms and faces are bare, their translucent, vein-riddled skin on display. As they wait for the airlock to cycle, they pull goggles from their belts and put them on in preparation for our lighting.

"Ready?" Sorrel asks softly. Through the implant, he radiates confidence. I lean on it, wishing I felt that way myself.

The inner airlock door opens, admitting them to the ship. It doesn't take them long to find us. As they file into the med bay, Sorrel stands in front of Ofiera. "*Ka syt dos ryp!*" Sorrel calls. My lessons in Aster were few and far between, but I know enough to gather he was asking for help.

Two focus on Sorrel, while three come straight for me. I throw my hands up to show they're empty, but one says something in Aster—*down*, I think—then guides me to my knees. I kneel without fuss.

Once it's clear I'm no threat, they check the medbag. Sorrel breaks into a flurry of conversation that I can't fully follow. I catch snippets—*partner, wounds, Elders*. When he finishes his speech, he straightens to his not-inconsiderable height where he stands between the other Asters and Ofiera. "I'm the Harbinger," he says in English.

The room falls into a tense silence. Something passes between Sorrel and the Asters as he looks at them, one at a time. If I didn't know any better, I'd say he was influencing their neural implants. Finally, the first Aster into the room nods and gestures to the medbag. Even those behind me move to gather Ofiera, abandoning me on my knees.

"Stay here," Sorrel whispers before leaving. The other Asters follow, Ofiera's medbag braced between them. I watch the compad from my knees and don't stand until they're through the airlock and gone from the hangar. But I make no mistake: they'll have time to deal with me later. It's not like I'm going anywhere.

I KEEP EXPECTING someone to come for me, but for five hours I'm left to my own devices. All I can think about is Ofiera. Is she well? Have they managed to stabilize her outside of the medbag? Will she live? I receive no answers.

Despite Sorrel's advice, I venture out of the ship to stretch my legs. The hangar is as gray as the asteroid around it, metallic and expansive, the majority of ships inside old termites for hauling water. When no one stops me, I continue to explore. At the back of the hangar, I find stairs carved from rock leading into what looks like the Under of Ceres, only less sophisticated—no bioluminescent moss, no 3D-printed mesh along the stony walls. But there's oxygen and gravity, and I hear what sounds like rushing water down below, so I resign myself to getting lost and start down the tunnel.

The air is crisp and cool and holds the faint tang of metal. The tunnels—more like a cave system—are bathed in shadows, lit only by the smallest pinpoints of light, like distant stars, every couple of meters. The ground is worn smooth, but the walls protrude in places and force me to shift my stride to pass by. I come across no one, so I navigate splits in the path by following the sound of the water until, fifteen minutes in, I emerge in an open cavern-like structure full of soft, chilly mist. Beside me, a river rushes to a sharp promontory and drops, becoming a waterfall.

I can't help but smile. A waterfall here, in the farthest reaches of space.

I move to the end of the walkway and press my hand against the stone wall to balance myself, then dare to lean over the edge and peer down. I can barely make it out in the darkness, but ten to twelve meters below, the waterfall empties into a placid pool.

"Wow . . ."

"Please don't touch the water."

With my training, I don't startle. I spin on my heel to face the voice, but the air rushes out of me when I see who waits for me.

He—she?—they, I decide, since I don't know. They're dressed like those who took Ofiera from the ship, with the addition of a bright blue half cloak draped around their shoulders, but I have the feeling that the half cloak isn't meant to signal the gender-marking colors the Asters in Icarii territories use. The most noteworthy thing about them is that I've never seen an Aster so old, their translucent skin sagging and wrinkled across their expressionless face, though their back is still ramrod straight and their long limbs strong. Their eyes are black, pupils large in the low light, but focused solely on me.

And they're alone.

"This is a water treatment facility," they say, stepping to my side. Like all Asters, they're taller than me. "We use our body heat and the warmth of our machines to melt the ice we gather from the belt and purify it here for redistribution among the planets."

"It's beautiful," I tell them, and they look at me strangely.

"Yes," they say, "I suppose it is."

They walk away without another word. I have the strangest sense that I'm supposed to follow, so I do. "I'm Lito sol Lucius."

"You may call me Mother Anemone." *Mother*, a female-identifying Elder's title. She—I revise in my head—walks with the same grace with which she chooses her words. The long white braid that cascades down her back drifts back and forth like a pendulum.

"I came with Sorrel and Ofiera fon Bain." When she doesn't respond, I rephrase. "Though maybe you call him the Harbinger."

"We know," she purrs. "We've been debating what to do with all of you."

All of us? I thought I was the singular problem . . .

She must know the path, because she never hesitates in step or direction. Eventually we start to see signs of life—other Asters passing by in adjacent tunnels, the hexagonal mesh that holds the rocky walls from jutting into our space, even offshoots of rooms full of stacked beds. I remember from my time in the Under on Ceres that everything from eating to sleeping is communal among the Asters, and it's reassuring to see evidence of that here when so little resembles what I know.

Then I notice the glow. Along the walls in blues and greens, even the faintest pinks, I find plants. And they're not just the bioluminescent moss from Ceres either, but fully glowing flowers with vines that climb and sprawl across the ceiling until we are cocooned in a veritable jungle.

"Wow." I gasp for the second time today. I reach out to touch a petal and startle a glowing insect that looks like a cross between a bee and a dragonfly from its perch on a frond. Other similar insects join the first, zipping down the hallway, and like a child, I feel the urge to chase after them.

I'm so enraptured by the world around me that when Anemone stops, I almost run into her. "Your friends are here," she says in that steady way of hers, gesturing to a room unlike any of the others we passed—while there are plants and vines climbing along the walls like in the tunnels, the room is antiseptic with its smell of chemicals and well lit by an array of lanterns. When I enter and find Ofiera and Sorrel, all the air leaves my chest in a rush.

Ofiera lies in bed with her hair unbound, splayed around her face on the pillow. She's dressed in a plain white fabric similar to the tunics the Asters wear, and between the gaps in the front of the shift I spy bandages. But the thing that brings me comfort is that, instead of wearing a grimace of pain as she did in the medbag, now she looks like she's peacefully sleeping.

I turn back to thank Anemone, but she's already gone.

"The medbag did as much as it could, but they had to restitch her stomach," Sorrel says, and he sounds both exhausted and electric. "It looks like the electrofluid fought off any infection, though they've put her on a course of regen meds just in case."

"She'll be okay?"

Sorrel smiles, but it doesn't reach his eyes. "It'll take more than this to separate us."

I reach out and brush Ofiera's hair off her forehead, silently wishing her a swift healing. When I pull back, I catch Sorrel's eye and note the strained way he purses his lips. Like he's biting back words.

"What?"

He runs a hand over his face. Against his soft blue skin, his scar is vibrant. "The Icarii are on their way to Vesta. They already know we're here."

"*What?*" My heart races, thudding heavily in my ears. "How?"

He shrugs as if it doesn't matter. "I thought I disabled the tracking chip on the *Nyx*, but there could be a newer redundancy system that I don't know about. Or maybe one of us is chipped."

"What're we—" I cut off. There's nothing we *can* do if the Icarii know we're here. Try to run, maybe, but where else could we go? If they followed us here, they'll follow us anywhere. And with Ofiera in this state . . .

"The Elders are meeting to decide what to do," Sorrel says, his sad eyes falling on Ofiera. "Whether to harbor us or turn us over."

Anemone's words seem far more threatening now. *We've been debating what to do with all of you.* It's not just me in trouble for coming to Vesta now.

I shake my head. "Won't the Icarii attack Vesta if their demands aren't met?"

He holds his empty hands up, like *What do you expect me to do?* "The Elders cannot allow the Icarii to attack Vesta outright. This is the center of Aster life and economy. Our leaders are here, along with thousands of citizens. If the Icarii attack first, it will be all-out war between Asters and the Icarii."

"Isn't that . . ." I almost ask *Isn't that what you want,* but I bite my lip at the last second.

"I have petitioned the Elders to name a Shield, a necessity in times of war, and instate open rebellion, but I don't know how likely that is."

"Mierda . . ." I run my hand through my hair—far too long and curling up at the back of my neck.

"Or," he goes on, "we can turn ourselves over to the Icarii and die brutally terrible deaths." He shrugs, the gesture as sarcastic as his words. "Up to you."

"Not much of a choice," I mutter.

He smiles in a way that crinkles the corners of his eyes. "You're right that we'll have to be clever. Turning ourselves over to the Icarii without achieving either rebellion or peace accomplishes nothing."

I shake my head because that wasn't what I meant, but before I can respond, an Aster appears at the doorway.

"*Ir priyus ika,*" he says, but the only thing I understand is the verb *wait.* He disappears back into the glowing tunnels.

"Come on," Sorrel says, standing from Ofiera's bedside. "It's time to go before the Elders."

Sorrel offers me one of the lanterns from Ofiera's room so I can see in the tunnels, but though the glowing plants are dim, they're enough for me to walk by. We leave the lantern behind. Sorrel leads the way. Like Anemone, he seems to know where he's going.

"Did you already get a tour?" I ask. Even if he was here two hundred years ago, Vesta has surely changed in all that time.

"No, but this is an Aster settlement, and I don't need to have been here before to know where I'm going."

"How?"

"There are a lot of things about Asters that humans don't know."

Humans, he says, instead of *siks.* Is it strange that he thinks of us so differently? "I was told that you can hear really well. Is that how you're leading me around—you hear the Elders up ahead?"

He flashes me the grin of a proud professor to an unruly student who can sometimes offer surprises. "No, but what else do you know?"

Now I really do feel like I'm back at the Academy. "Asters can maneuver and survive in any gravity. Their bone density adjusts and can even regenerate after time in space. Their skin filters out the space radiation from cosmic rays, though it's overly sensitive to light, or EM radiation. They can see and hear really well in the dark, and they prefer to live and work in large communities."

"Why do you suppose that last one is?"

I don't know why I'm humoring him by answering. Curiosity, maybe. "Because humans are shitty toward you all, so you band together."

"From a sociological standpoint, that makes sense." Sorrel stops at a doorway that leads to a larger room. "But what about our genetics, Lito? Think deeper."

"The first explorers from Earth found that space had a tendency to drive man a bit mad," I guess. "Being stuck in enclosed spaces with people long term made them clash. Alternatively, being alone in space made them depressed. There's no harmony in that."

"Good! So, if you were a geneassist, how would you solve that?" Sorrel asks, and when I fall silent thinking, he adds, "I don't expect you to guess this one."

"Alter your genes to make you nicer," I say with a shrug. "But I know that's not the answer when you're such a bastard."

He barks a laugh and slaps me on the shoulder. "I am certainly one of the meanest Asters you'll ever meet," he admits. "But no, the initial geneassists had a very clever solution." He gestures to the walls, to the plants and the insects flitting about. "We're like them."

I watch a bee-dragonfly hybrid zip by overhead. "Them?"

"We can communicate with pheromones as well as words," Sorrel says, and I jerk my eyes back to him to see if he's shitting me. But no, his face says that he's telling the truth. "While we're certainly a community of individuals, we are just as much a hive that, in some ways, functions as a single organism. We can smell when someone is dishonest. Can sense when they're attracted to us or afraid of us.

"Among Asters, we can adjust these pheromones to tell someone basic things. Like *Walk this way*, or *I'm sorry*. We can project our emotional state and, at the same time, ask for help. We find contentment in being with others who can send us feelings of safety and comfort. Of oneness."

His words, more than anything, make me realize how cruel the Icarii have been to him. They separated him from other Asters so that he'd never feel that sense of communality. Even with Ofiera, he must feel cut off from others, losing one of his innate senses, unable to properly communicate.

But then another thing dawns on me. "It kind of sounds like a neural implant."

Sorrel smirks. "Where do you think the Icarii got the idea? That was the original reason Asters were useful in Icarii experiments." His face falls. "Now come on. We've made them wait long enough."

We pass through the doorway and into a cavernous, high-ceilinged room. Inside, a few lanterns have been lit, spreading their light like miniature stars so I can see perfectly, only I can barely believe my eyes.

There are hundreds—maybe even thousands—of Asters in the room, all pressed together and facing the same direction. The oddest thing is the silence. They don't speak a word. Don't shuffle from foot to foot. Even their breathing is quiet, as if they're stone statues, an extension of the cave.

Sorrel leads me through the packed Asters, and they part like a school of fish before a shark. Eyes follow us, but no one whispers in surprise at the appearance of the Harbinger, gone for the past two centuries, if they know him at all. We head to the front, where a dais waits. Standing atop it are three older Asters in blue half cloaks, one of which I recognize as Anemone. We halt in front of the crowd, and Sorrel drags me to his side by my wrist.

"We've come as requested," Sorrel says, his voice bouncing off the stone walls and echoing throughout the room for all to hear. "I beg of the Elders to speak aloud, so that our visitor may understand."

Anemone looks at her fellow Elders with a question on her face, but she reads something in them that I can't. The pheromones that Sorrel mentioned, I realize. When she steps to the edge of the platform, she pulls her hands behind her back and addresses the crowd. "The Elders decree that we will speak in English, so that our visitor may understand our words." She speaks softly, and yet everyone can hear her because of how unearthly quiet the room is.

If I didn't know any better, I'd wonder if the Asters around me were even breathing.

"Across the system," Anemone begins, "the Icarii have issued warnings for any who would harbor the criminals Lito sol Lucius, Ofiera fon Bain, and the Aster known as Sorrel." I flinch, but Sorrel is steady at my side. "These criminals are now here, among us on Vesta. This, the Icarii know. Even now they are heading this way, come to demand the return of these fugitives. We gather together now to decide what is to be done with them."

"Don't speak unless asked to," Sorrel whispers in my ear, but I don't know who he thinks I am. I'm not about to interrupt.

"On Venus and Mercury," Anemone continues, "the Icarii have enforced curfews for our people. Any found outside of their homes during these times are arrested. Those suspected of helping these fugitives—indeed, any suspected of working alongside the Aster known as Hemlock—have been detained without answers as to their release.

"The incarcerations have been many. Several of our people have also reported home invasion and unwarranted violence. In total, we have reports of two dozen hospitalized in these unauthorized raids and two dead after a struggle broke out in Tesla Gardens on the top level of

Cytherea. There is talk on Spero of 'tagging' Asters, of issuing subskin chips or bracelets that identify Asters by a number. As we know, if Spero adopts the practice, Cytherea will follow."

When Anemone finishes, I find my breath coming quicker. All of this violence happening across the universe, and now Vesta is forced to deal with us . . .

"Consideration has been paid to requesting Gean aid in this matter," Anemone says, "but we recall what happened when we trusted them on Ceres."

Many nod at this, expressions growing hard. She doesn't mention another thing: with the current cease-fire, I'm not sure the Geans would step into an Icarii operation and break that fragile peace.

"So that leads us here . . ." Anemone holds a hand out. "Some have asked that we remove Lito sol Lucius and Ofiera fon Bain from Vesta, as they are not Aster and thus not our responsibility." She raises the other. "Others have requested that we harbor them, though this would undoubtedly lead to more violence against our people."

Sorrel stiffens at my side, determination written all over his face. They speak of his rebellion, now within reach . . .

"Before we make our decision, I wish to hear from those involved." Anemone's eyes fall to Sorrel and me. "What would you ask of us?"

Sorrel dips his head before he addresses them. "Recognized Elders, I beg you to consider the fate of my wife, Ofiera fon Bain, as one entwined with mine. She and I share the same heart. The same soul. To turn her out would be to turn me out."

Another one of the Elders speaks. "Do you mean to say that if we send Ofiera fon Bain from Vesta, you will depart with her?" they ask. "Because that hardly seems like a problem when the Icarii request you as well . . ."

"I would go with her," Sorrel confirms, and though the Elder who spoke doesn't change their expression, a smug aura rolls off them. "However, I request that you consider the Law of Life."

The Elder's shoulders sink as Anemone speaks. "*All life is sacred. All life is equal. For we are all born from the same stuff as stars.*" Many repeat the last phrase after her in a mix of Aster and English. The sound is electric after so much silence from the crowd.

"And you?" Anemone looks directly at me now. "What would you request of us?"

Sorrel looks at me expectantly, and I dip my head as he did. "Recognized Elders," I begin as respectfully as I can, "whatever your decision, I will honor it. If you wish for me to leave, I will. I even understand why. You're already dealing with violence against your people on Mercury and Venus, and I never wanted to make it worse."

"Your intentions hardly matter," the Elder who spoke before says, "compared to the reality of the situation."

"Let him finish," Anemone barks.

"My only request," I say, my heart pounding harder as more faces turn in my direction, "is not for me. I beg you to consider allowing Ofiera to stay with Sorrel. While you may not know her and while she may not be your responsibility, Ofiera has been fighting for the Asters alongside Sorrel for . . . years." I look over at Sorrel and am surprised by the softness of his expression as he stares back at me. "It's in large part thanks to her that I see the world as it really is, with my people taking advantage of and mistreating yours. It's thanks to her that I'm even standing here. And if Ofiera were here to speak for herself, she'd make the same offer to leave you in peace that I do. But she can't make that request, because she almost died saving Sorrel. Saving *me*. So . . . I want her to be able to stay with Sorrel and the Asters. She and Sorrel . . . They can't—they shouldn't be separated. If anyone deserves a safe haven, it's them."

No one speaks when I finish. All is silent except the ringing of my ears.

Then Sorrel takes my hand in his. "I amend my request," he says. "If you turn out Lito, I will go with him. May his path be the same as mine."

I jerk my gaze to his face. "Are you insane?" I whisper, despite the overwhelming relief I feel at his standing up for me.

Sorrel winks at me.

The mouthy Elder scoffs, but Anemone holds up a hand to cut them off before they can speak. "We have heard all we require. Now we will debate," she says, and the three Elders step to the back of the dais and huddle together.

The silence returns.

Sorrel and I say nothing as we wait. I feel as if I should thank him, and yet this moment feels important, like any sound at all would shatter the concentration of the Elders. And, despite this being a debate, they say nothing either, whatever discussion they're having being completed through their expressions and, most likely, their pheromones. I shift from foot to foot, settling in for a long wait, but when Anemone approaches the crowd again, it hasn't been more than five minutes.

"The Elders have debated and have reached a decision." Anemone looks again to Sorrel and me where we stand below her. "We will harbor Lito sol Lucius, Ofiera fon Bain, and the Aster known as Sorrel on Vesta. We will not turn them over to Icarii authorities."

I brace for protest, but unexpectedly, the room remains quiet. A few nod along with Anemone's words, but no one looks upset by the decision despite its potential to bring hell down on them. Even the mouthy Elder seems content.

Without a word, it's over. Anemone dips her head and turns her back on the crowd, joining her fellow Elders in leaving the dais.

As soon as they depart the platform, the room erupts into chatter. The majority speak in Aster or gesture with their hands. I'm sure they're also debating with their pheromones in ways that I can't make out. A handful near me continue to speak in English, as if inviting me to join them. But I focus on Sorrel.

"You throwing your lot in with mine . . . that was risky."

Sorrel seems to glow in the lantern light. "Was it?" he asks, and I remember that look in his eyes when he spoke of the upcoming war.

A chill like the cryo pod overwhelms me. My mind struggles to rationalize the two Sorrels I've seen—the man who rammed glass shards into a duelist's eyes is the same whose soft hands patched my wounds. The Aster who looks at Ofiera with love but speaks of battle with the fondness of a past lover . . . and I can't help but wonder, what wouldn't he do to get what he wants? What worlds wouldn't he crush to see his own grow? Who wouldn't he kill for his people to live?

I force myself to speak around the growing lump in my throat. "I have to know . . . Was it to save Ofiera or to trigger a war between the Icarii and Asters?"

Sorrel looks in my direction, his pupils narrowing into sharp dagger points. "Is there a difference?"

CHAPTER 21

ASTRID

It is a wise man who listens when his enemies speak, but it is a fool who believes their talk blindly. We will accept the Icarii cease-fire, but creating a lasting peace will be a far more difficult proposition.

Warlord Vaughn to his admirals

On our flight back to the Temple, I relate my conversation with Aunt Genette to Eden. She bristles with a mixture of fear and anger, but the exhaustion from the past few days comes crashing down on me, and I beg her to put this discussion off until later. When she stalks away from me to the Sisterhood dorms, I briefly wonder who she is rushing off to report to, but I am too tired to even ask, much less follow. Back in my room, I collapse in my bed. I want nothing more than to sleep.

I fall into the black with open arms. My dreams are a haze of feelings, mere impressions of emotions with no imagery. When I wake, Ringer is standing over me.

"Get up," he says. "You've rested enough."

I throw my legs over the edge of the bed, toes tentatively settling on the cold stone. A knock comes a moment later, and my gaze shoots to

Ringer. I still do not understand him. Understand *us*. Did a part of me sense someone at the door and wake me up? Is that what Ringer is, a subconscious part of me that comprehends my surroundings on a level I cannot?

The knock comes again. "Stop dawdling," he says. "Answer the door."

I do as he bids, running my fingers through my tangled hair in hopes of making myself presentable. I could not even hazard a guess at the time.

I half expect another Little Sister with a message, or perhaps Eden come to finish our discussion, but it is Lily, holding herself rigid, brown doe eyes swallowing me whole, whom I find on the other side of the door.

"Come in," I say, closing the door behind us.

"Can I sit?" she asks, making her way across the room one stiff step at a time. Limping, almost.

"Of course. Are you well?"

Lily grasps the arm of the chaise lounge and lowers herself onto it. I suddenly recall the sight of her body in the showers, the white scars over her joints, in addition to her irritated skin. "As well as I can be," she says. "Some days hurt more than others."

I frown.

She changes the subject before I can ask more. "Eden told me everything. She's not thrilled you accepted the bargain with Aunt Genette."

I follow her path to the chaise lounge and settle beside her. "I got that impression, but I felt it was the best course of action under the circumstances."

"I trust your judgment." Her eyes hold such honesty. Such trust. Why? Because Aunt Margaret told her to help me? Because I can give her what she wants?

I look at her. At her heart-shaped face. At her small, upturned nose. At the faint freckles on her cheeks. Most of her hair is bluntly cut in a bob to her chin, but her bangs are freshly styled in that way she likes, choppy fringe across her forehead.

Before I can stop myself, I brush my fingertips between her freckles, connecting them in a constellation all her own. Her cheeks brighten at my touch, tinting the soft pink of a rose petal. I'm surprised to find it is a good look on her.

She sucks in a sharp breath as I pull away, as if my touch hurts. One of her hands—clear of pale scales today—goes to her cheek. "Do I have something on my face?"

"No, I was simply thinking of your beauty."

"Me?" Her face burns brighter. "Beautiful?"

I nod because it is simpler than the truth. I have trusted so little in my life, I cannot say that in this moment, looking into her eyes, I feel like I glimpsed a part of her soul. That I know her and understand her.

"I . . . thank you." She clears her throat. "But I came to tell you something . . . Something important about Aunt Genette's properties."

The world leaks back in at her words. I swallow against my own anxiety. "What is it?"

"I know you promised not to look into any more of Aunt Genette's dealings, but I've found something . . . disturbing."

I do not hesitate. "Go on . . ."

Lily runs a hand over her face before she begins, steeling herself for the conversation to come. The blush and the innocence in her doe eyes disappear. "Before your agreement with Aunt Genette, I asked a few friends of mine outside of the Sisterhood to look into other properties of hers, ones with building costs that didn't match historic neighborhood values."

Friends of mine outside the Sisterhood, she says. How has she accumulated these friends of hers? Are they allies of Aunt Margaret, or has Lily been communicating outside the Sisterhood, perhaps even writing or speaking? Are they how she accumulated the blackmail data, or are they being blackmailed themselves?

"They didn't find what you'd expect, though. Buildings that were falling apart, yes, but also well guarded, like forts." She pauses, swallows hard. "At one, there was a girl, and . . . Astrid . . . I . . ." She has to stop. Her pale face has lost what little color it normally has.

"Yes?" I coax her softly.

"It's a brothel," she says in one hurried breath.

My stomach churns. Perhaps Eden was right; I should not have accepted anything less than Aunt Genette's removal from the Agora, and damn the cost to me.

Which makes me wonder: Was Aunt Genette willing to support me after I found out about the embezzlement because this was what she was *really* hiding?

"What is Aunt Genette doing—"

"It's not just Aunt Genette. It's her building, but she's not the Aunt in charge. She only takes a cut," Lily explains.

"Then . . . who?"

"Aunt Sapphira in the Order of Leo. She makes it look like some sort of Sisterhood training center for her Order, but I've had eyes on the place and reports of men coming and going, guards patrolling at all hours."

The creature locked behind my ribs wakes. I feel its blackness seeping into my limbs. "She's created a harem of her own Order?" I don't recognize my own voice.

Ringer leans closer, predatory eyes fixated.

"Not quite." Lily lets out a breath, something between a sigh and a whisper. "She's lying to these girls. As far as they know, they're leaving their homes to become Sisters. Instead, they're not even taken care of. Thrown into a room and forgotten about. Drugged into compliance."

I'm aghast. Struck silent by the horror.

I once worried about becoming as bad as the women we fight. How could we, when *this* is what they do with their power?

"The girl one of my friends found . . . she was wounded. She had been shot fleeing. He hid her until I could put her somewhere safe."

I close my eyes against the rising tears. Goddess, how am I supposed to help? How am I supposed to fix the Sisterhood at all, when it is this sick?

"Your friend . . . is there any way to track his actions back to you?" *Back to us?* I don't ask.

"I doubt it," Lily says with a shake of her head. "How many Asters do you notice on a daily basis?"

Interesting. So her friend is an Aster, perhaps from her outreach program on Ceres. But I cannot underestimate the reach of her influence; she was the one whose connection to the Asters helped Mother Isabel III plan the Annexation of Ceres, after all.

"The girl," Lily says, returning to the subject, "hasn't been at the brothel for long, only a few months. But she's willing to talk to us, Astrid. If we can help the other girls, she's willing to do whatever she can."

"Okay," I say. And then again, stronger, "Okay. Take me to her."

Lily nods resolutely, and I know we're both thinking the same thing: we *have* to stop this.

THE GIRL IS extraordinarily thin. Her glassy blue eyes pop wide as we enter the safe house, a one-room studio outside the Olympus Mons dome that Lily assures me cannot be traced to the Sisterhood. She tries to push herself up into a sitting position on the bed but, with a wince, sags back into the mattress. She looks toward her guard in the corner, an Aster in traditional wraps who says nothing.

"It's just me with friends, Nat," Lily says. She gestures to the Aster, and he goes to stand guard outside.

The girl, Nat, lets the book she was reading fall closed on her stomach. Beneath her oversized gown are clean bandages, and there's a twitchiness to her, whether from fear or drugs I'm not sure. My heart breaks looking at her.

"I'm glad you're back, Lily," Nat says. "I kept hearing people walking by outside, and I thought . . ." She has a familiar accent, but I cannot quite place it.

"You're safe here, Nat, I told you," Lily says. Speaking softly, so as not to make her any more afraid than she already is. "They can't find you here, and we won't let them take you back."

Nat nods and nods and nods, as if trying to convince herself of Lily's words. I look to Eden at my side, who is so uncomfortable that her skin has taken on a tinge of green. She holds a hand to her stomach, as if to keep her sickness in.

I put on my best smile, though I have never felt less like smiling. "Hello, Nat, I am Astrid." I try to make my voice like Lily's, soothing and soft.

Nat puts the end of her blond braid in her mouth and chews, considering. After a minute of silence, she spits it out. "Where are you from?"

"The Order of Andromeda," I say, but from the curl of her nose, I see that is not what she wanted to hear. "From Mars," I add. "An orphanage not far away from here."

"Oh, you look like . . ." She trails off. "I'm from Máni."

The blood in my veins turns to ice. Máni and Skadi are the two moons of Earth, called those names only by the people who live on them. *Like Ringer.* Or, at least, that is what he told me.

"It is not uncommon," Lily says, interrupting my laser-like focus on Nat, "for refugees to come to Mars from Earth and its moons." I also hear what she's not saying: Aunt Sapphira is finding people in the poorest areas and targeting them for trafficking.

Nat's accent . . . it is familiar because of Ringer.

Ringer, who is unnaturally silent. Ringer, who is a gap in my mind that I grasp for like a comforting blanket.

"What do I look like?" I ask. "What were you going to say?"

Nat shrugs and turns her attention back toward her book, uninterested in being interrogated. Or scared of me, I fear. "I thought we were going to talk about that place . . ."

Lily's hand on my shoulder tells me to concentrate. To calm down. To take a step back.

I could press Nat to talk about where she's from, dig into her past with the yearning to discover my own. Or I could focus on why we are really here: to help this young girl and the others victimized by Aunt Sapphira.

My stomach twists as I make my choice.

"We want to ask you a few questions about the place you ran away from, Nat," I say, my tone measured. "And when we are done, we are going to do everything we can to stop this from happening to anyone else."

Nat perks up, one hand reaching for the gunshot wound on her side. "And you'll get my friends out?"

"We are going to get everyone out," I say, and in this moment, I do not care if I have to take a gun and save them myself.

"Okay," she says. "Let's talk."

NAT TELLS US everything she can: The building is a large warehouse full of shipping containers. These are the girls' bedrooms and where they are locked up in the mornings to sleep. In the afternoons and evenings, men come to visit them. She was there for four months, but only saw a new girl arrive once. Every girl is implanted with an ID chip between her shoulder blades, not deep like a neural implant, but in a spot that is difficult to reach so they cannot remove it by themselves. Every morning, they receive one meal—I suspect this is how they are drugged. Those who try to run away are punished by the guards, or shot, like she was. The guards are men who change often, and they are not allowed to talk to the girls or form bonds with them. She has never seen who is in charge, but she knows some girls have.

"That's how we know it's actually bad Sisters doing this," Nat explains. "Once Joli—this girl in my container, she's been there for like three years—was dressed up all nice and taken to this fancy party, and she saw a Sister bossing all the guards around."

"Did Joli describe her at all?" I ask.

"She said she had a gold necklace of a big cat . . . I don't know the word for it."

I look at Lily, and I know we are both thinking the same thing: that "Sister" was Aunt Sapphira, wearing the Order of Leo's lioness symbol.

In the podcar ride back, we are all silent, desperate to come up with a solution. It isn't until we are safely ensconced in my room at the Temple—the single hair on my door undisturbed, proving that no one has come and gone—that we speak freely.

"We need Joli." I say what we are all thinking.

Lily, sitting on my chaise lounge, rubs at her irritated eyes. "We need a plan to get her out."

"And how do you suppose we do that?" Eden asks, pale but no longer green.

I do not answer. I have been asking myself that exact question since we left Nat.

"We . . . have someone go in," I say after a stretch of silence. "They infiltrate the brothel. They find Joli and bring her out."

"You want to plant someone there?" Eden asks incredulously. Lily's eyebrows shoot up on her forehead. "Who? Because these girls have been abused—*sexually abused*—and you want to throw *another* into that meat grinder? Whoever you choose won't be able to just stroll in and out on a whim."

I try to keep my tone even as I speak. "Do you have another idea?"

"Not *this*. Anything but *this*." Eden shakes her head, red hair wild. "Don't sink to Sapphira's level."

The words prod at an already sore wound. "Do not presume to tell me I am as bad as Aunt Sapphira."

Eden's lips curl into a snarl. "If you do this, you will be."

I say nothing, because I fear what will come out of my mouth if I speak.

"Fuck . . ." Eden runs a hand over her face. I expect her to growl at me like a wild dog, but she reins in her rage. Her voice is low and full of sorrow when she speaks again. "I won't be part of this, Astrid. If you do this, you do it on your own."

She storms toward the door.

"Eden—"

But she is gone, the door slamming behind her.

In her absence, I sink onto the chaise lounge. My heart aches, and it takes me a long time before I steel myself enough to speak.

"I will go," I tell Lily, the plan forming before I think it through. "I will sneak in, find Joli, and get her out."

Lily turns toward me, brows knit together in concern. "Astrid, you can't—"

"If I am to become the Mother," I say as if this were a confession, "I cannot ask others to do what I am unwilling to."

Lily places her hands on her knees. For a moment, I think she will try to convince me to abandon this plan, but when she speaks, it is of something completely different.

"I was born to . . . a dark and cold settlement without gravity. I was a sickly child, and thus abandoned by my parents. A kindly uncle raised me."

"Lily—"

She cuts me off. "Just listen," she says. "Please."

I bite my bottom lip. Satisfied, she continues.

"When I was twelve, I could no longer fight my own body. In my desperation, I turned to back-alley clinics, illegal geneassists, even an Icarii doctor." She stops for a moment and stares at her hands, where pale patches have begun to appear. "Sigfried val Mahn died in the Leander Incident. Strange, how small the universe really is."

For her to admit something so illegal . . . but I say nothing, not wanting to interrupt.

"When I was fourteen, I gave up searching for outside help and joined the Sisterhood so they would take care of me. They gave me surgery to fix my limbs that had grown poorly. Medicine for my allergy to light." She covers the scales of one hand with the other. "I would live, and even if I still have pain, it's no longer what it was."

I think of her stilted movements, her lack of grace. The scars clustered on her joints. The pale patches of skin and her need for eye drops. The way she eases herself into seats and never stands for too long. A sick child grown into an ill adult.

"When I joined, I was assigned to the Order of Pyxis. After I recovered from surgery, I was a dutiful Little Sister and understood what was asked of me long before others did. But then my first assignment came, and it was . . . hard.

"Olympus Heights was supposedly a hospital for wounded soldiers, but it was more like a hospice. Very few left alive. Most were there to pass peacefully." Her eyes soften as tears fill them. "I prayed with them, took their confessions, watched as they . . . as they died. Those who could perform, I comforted with my body. I was happy to do it. I never hated them for it. Those who could no longer engage in sexual acts, I would lie down beside them and hold them . . . I let them have anything they wanted. They mostly just wanted intimacy, at the end. However they could take it."

An assignment like that . . . I never knew that was an option.

"So many I held, heads pressed to my chest, as they cried out in pain. As they begged me not to leave them in their last moments. 'I don't want to die, Sister,' they would tell me. And then, 'I don't want to die alone.' I couldn't stop the pain. I couldn't stop their dying. But I could be there for them. I could make sure they didn't die alone, sickly and forgotten."

A tear finally slips free and runs down her cheek. "I'm sorry," she says, wiping it away.

I do not know what to say. Whether to encourage her to cry, or to hold her hand. I never knew this was part of the Sisterhood. My assignments had always been among the stars, never on the ground. My heart aches for Lily, having to watch so many die in her arms.

"One day Aunt Margaret caught me writing." *Forbidden*, my mind hisses, though I say nothing. "A soldier had asked me to send a letter to his brother, begging him to come visit before he passed, but the man . . . his hands . . ." Lily shakes her head. "He couldn't write, but I could."

"What did she do?" I ask softly.

"She took the letter from me and sent it herself." Lily smiles even if her lips tremble. "Maybe you haven't figured it out yet, but Aunt Margaret likes a rebel."

"Well, she likes me . . ."

"Exactly." She chuckles forcefully. "She started showing me favor after that. Had me come to her and tell her whatever the soldiers asked for. She helped them reconnect with their families or write wills. Some just wanted to write down their recollections, to have some testament to leave behind so that they wouldn't be forgotten, and she allowed me to write these. She helped them find peace."

"Is this when she gave you back your voice?"

"Aunt Margaret wasn't the one who returned it." Lily laces her fingers together in her lap. "There was another young rebel whom Aunt Margaret was desperately trying to influence: Mother Isabel III."

The Mother. Almost immediately, Ringer wakes within me. "Remember the sound our fists made, turning her face into ruin?" he asks in a whisper. I yearn to reach into my pocket for the neural implant in its little box.

"In my spare time, I would work in the Order of Pyxis's gardens, and, with Aunt Margaret's blessing, I started a community program to include Asters in the creation and restoration of parks across Mars. One day, the Mother came to see what we were doing, and Aunt Margaret introduced us. The Mother took a liking to me, to my odd way of approaching things, and after that, we would talk in the hand language for hours. She was the one to return my voice. I was . . . distraught. How could I not have known? But now that I had it, I should use it, she said."

It sounds just like her . . . I remember her cold words on Ceres as she glared up at me, bloodied and bruised. *You want your voice?* she asked. *You have to* earn *it.*

"I don't know where the idea for the Annexation of Ceres came from initially, whether it was her or me who brought up approaching the Asters, but once it had been mentioned, she became obsessed with it. I suppose you know the rest . . ."

"You became her second because of your hand in arranging a truce between Geans and Asters."

"Yes, and then lost that position when I disagreed with her methods of dealing with the Asters on Ceres. She had agreed to allow them certain freedoms and a percentage of earnings from the water purification plant—" Lily cuts off abruptly, her face full of disappointment. "I suppose it doesn't matter now. I'm telling you this because I want you to understand. Much of my life has been left up to chance. Imagine I had signed up to join the Sisterhood, desperate to heal my illnesses, only to become one of these young girls trapped by Aunt Sapphira's lie. Or imagine Aunt Margaret had me punished for writing, and I had lost my life."

"What I'm trying to say is, I want to help you, Astrid. You asked me why on the *Juno*. I'm answering now. I knew Mother Isabel III. I knew her well, and she did not care half as much as you do for the downtrodden and desperate. So, if you are going into this brothel . . ." She fixes me with a determined stare. "I am going with you."

I feel as if the floor has fallen out from under me. "What? Lily, you can't—"

"Can't I?" Her eyes are hard, her shoulders squared. I cannot believe I ever thought her soft; that I, like so many men stretching back hundreds of years, saw a small woman and mistook her as weak.

"I'll find a way. I don't care how." She stares at me, *through* me. "I'm coming with you," she says again.

This time, I don't fight her.

CHAPTER 22

HIRO

With my father
I would watch dawn
over green fields

"With My Father" by Kobayashi Issa,
framed poem in Shinya val Akira's office

Shinya leads me into the warm interior of the little tea shop with its peeling red paint and yellowed paper lanterns. Only a few of the low tables are taken, the patrons all elderly with sagging skin and baggy clothes, stained fingers clutching e-pipes heated red.

"いらっしゃいませ!" the electronic cat by the doorway intones, its high-pitched, energetic voice in direct opposition to the atmosphere of the otherwise sleepy establishment. It welcomes us with a swipe of its white paw.

"Private room for two," Nadyn says, holding up two fingers.

The beckoning cat's eyes glow golden before it hops from its perch on the table. "Follow me, please!" the cat says, now speaking in English, as it leads us deeper into the teahouse.

"What, your lackeys aren't going to join us?" I ask Shinya at my side, and it's in this moment that I realize I'm taller than him now.

He had been the tallest of all my siblings . . .

"Fuck you, Hiro," Noa spits, but Shinya's head whips around to focus on them.

"We're guests here," Shinya tells his underling. "Don't make an ass of yourself."

Noa slumps like a dog punished for piddling on the carpet. "Of course. Apologies, Commander."

I don't even fight my smirk. Noa glowers at me but says nothing more.

In the back of the teahouse, three private rooms are set behind sliding shoji doors. The cat halts in front of an open, empty room and gestures with its paw. "Please make yourselves comfortable!" it says in its annoyingly cutesy way. Shinya slides off his shoes, and I follow suit before we settle on either side of the low table, legs tucked beneath us.

I'm sure he, like me, is reminded of another table in a place far away, one we squeezed around with three other siblings and our father. And the empty place that always remained, set for the mother who would never come home.

What would our mother think if she could see her two children now, enemies at the end of the galaxy?

"I'll put in your order," Nadyn says sweetly. She does a good job of masking the demon within her, unlike her partner. As Noa starts to slide the door closed, Shinya speaks.

"Noa, return to location Nine Iota," he says.

Noa looks between my brother and me, perhaps weighing his options to ignore the order. I really want to see them try, really want my brother to verbally smack them again. Eventually common sense wins out, and, though they sneer, they dip their head in obedience. "Yes, Commander."

They slide the shoji door closed, and I hear their heavy footsteps marching away. At least now I can pretend at privacy with my brother.

"You look well, Hiro." Even alone with me, Shinya doesn't relax his posture; he's as vigilant as ever. I suppose that's what a Commander is trained to do, even if I'd been hoping to talk with my brother and not the officer Shinya val Akira.

"I'm surprised you recognized me."

"Come now, Hiro. I heard that ludicrous message you sent to Father—how he won't recognize you the next time he sees you—but if you expect us not to keep tabs on you . . . Well, that's shortsighted foolishness." Shinya purses his lips in distaste. "You always were so melodramatic."

My face burns at his words. That Father shared my private message with Shinya . . . Who else did he allow to listen to it? Asuka and Jun? Hanako, who should only be concerned with the mundanities of college life?

Shinya's black eyes never waver from my face. "Are you embarrassed?"

Bile burns in my stomach. I was an idiot to expect this to be some sort of twisted family reunion. This is nothing more than a commander evaluating a former Dagger, and I refuse to be found lacking.

If Shinya didn't reveal himself to me because he missed me, then he wants something from me. Information, most likely.

Well, if this is a meeting of Icarii Special Forces, then two can play at that game.

I drop one of the strongest cards in the deck. "Dire knows you're here, poking around in his operations."

Shinya's face falls, but the expression is strange in response to what I said. "You want to do business before we even have tea? You've been away from home for too long." He releases a great sigh through parted lips. And he had the audacity to call *me* melodramatic.

"I have a hard time playing pretend," I grind out, doing my best not to snarl as I speak.

Shinya clasps his hands in front of his face in a motion so much like Father, I have to remind myself we're half a solar system away from him. "Business it is, then. As for your friend, we'd be disappointed if the great Dire of the Belt didn't notice what's right under his nose."

"Like the Icarii ships poking around the Synthetic border? And after one of your ships was destroyed by the Sentries . . ." I click my tongue against my teeth. "Shame, that. It's utter stupidity to tempt the Synthetics when they've made their stance abundantly clear."

One of his eyebrows twitches, the slightest tell that I've rattled him.

"Tell me, Hiro. Why do you think we're here?"

"Because Father told you to be."

He huffs a single laugh. "He knows nothing of our current meeting."

Which means Shinya is going against Father's will to meet with me—doubtful—or Father doesn't know I'm also on Autarkeia.

I'm saved from responding when Nadyn slides open the door. "Tea's here."

A middle-aged man with a weathered but pleasant face enters the private room and sets a tray down on the corner of the low table. With callused hands, he places a ceramic cup first in front of Shinya and then me.

"Thank you, Miyazaki-san," my brother says.

The man withdraws with his empty tray. Nadyn closes the door again.

Shinya does nothing without a reason. He's like our father in that way. And in flaunting this man instead of having Noa or Nadyn serve us, he tells me several things: not only has he been here before, but he's well known by the establishment; he has friends where I have none. This is one of Shinya's cards.

I'm left to wonder *how much* they know about him—do they know he's Icarii Command?—instead of focusing on what really matters. But I won't be deterred from my former line of questioning.

"いただきます," Shinya says as he takes his cup in both hands.

I pick up my cup and drink some of the hot liquid. It hits my tongue and curls through my limbs, warming me from the inside. It tastes even better than I imagined it would, smooth and bitingly bitter. "It doesn't take a mind reader to know you're here for information. That's why you've got some of Dire's operatives delivering papers like brainwashed clerks."

His smirk tells me I've misstepped. "If you're so enlightened, then tell me what you think that information is."

I take another sip of tea, since I have no response . . . and he knows it. His grin only grows.

Instead of flaunting his small victory, he takes a deep drink of his tea and sighs in contentment. "The Icarii didn't come here for you, Hiro. In fact, I've been here longer than you have."

"I'm not *that* bigheaded," I snap. "I know everything doesn't revolve around me."

"Though I can't help but wonder whether whoever sent you knew I was here and thought they might be able to use you against me."

A chill runs down my spine, hearing my brother speak the fear I hesitated to voice aloud.

He sets his cup down and shrugs. "I suppose we'll never know."

Probably not, with the way Hemlock and Dire hoard information. The worst part is knowing that, even if I did ask them about this, they'd never tell me the truth.

He runs his thumb over the flowers painted on his ceramic cup, focused more on it than on me. "'In this world, we walk on the roof of hell, gazing at flowers,'" he says. I recognize it as one of his favorite poems by Kobayashi Issa.

"The only reason you spout that shit is because you know Father likes it," I say.

His eyes snap to mine. "I can like things independent of what Father enjoys."

"Then why don't you write something original for once, instead of quoting dead poets?"

He scoffs as if I've asked an impossible quest of him, to bring me a scale from a dragon's neck or a jeweled branch from an island that doesn't exist. "I am meeting you without Father knowing," he says, changing the subject, "though after this, I will have to tell him you're here."

"Sure."

"Before that, I want to warn you."

I bark a laugh. "Warn me? Wow, what a caring brother you must be."

His eyes narrow, the shadow of his brow deepening the bags beneath. "You'd be foolish to think I don't care about you, Hiro, even now."

I fight the urge to roll my eyes. "Then tell me, Aniki, what's your great warning?"

His tone drops its haughty disdain, and for the first time, he sounds more like the brother I knew—loving but distant. Unable to connect with me, but not from lack of trying. "Stay out of what we're doing here," Shinya says. "Don't ally yourself with the outlaws."

"Bit late for that . . ."

"Then walk away from them." He flattens his hands and splays his fingers on the table. "You want to have a life separate from Father and the rest of us? Then take it. It's freely available to you. Just don't get involved with the troubles on Autarkeia, or you'll lose that opportunity."

My hands tighten around my cup. "Is that a threat?"

"It's a warning, as I said." He furrows his brows, and there's something so soft in his gaze that I'm rendered speechless. Like he's *begging* me to walk away. "You're not like them, Hiro."

I hold up my prosthetic arm for him to see. "I'm more like them than I am like you."

"No, Hiro, you're not like them at all." A desperation surges in Shinya's eyes as he looks up at me, at the younger sibling he used to know. I remember the message I sent for him on the recording device. Did he ever receive it?

I wish we got along better. I wish we had at least tried to find some common ground between us, because I don't think you're all that bad deep down.

Could he possibly wish for the same?

"Trust me," Shinya says.

"Then tell me. How am I not like them, Shinya?"

For a moment, I think he's on the verge of explaining, lips parted with a secret on his tongue. But with a heavy sigh, my brother simply shakes his head. "You'll see," he says, sending a chill down my spine.

The disappointment settles on me heavily.

I look at the table and, with a flick, knock my cup of tea over, letting the remaining liquid spill across the faux-wood tabletop. Shinya jumps, hands thrown up as if I pulled a weapon on him. "Hiro!"

"Now we've both embarrassed ourselves," I say, pushing myself up from the low table and leaving through the sliding shoji door.

"Hiro—" my brother calls after me, but I don't respond.

There's no way to salvage our relationship, not when we both know who we are.

CHAPTER 23

LUCE

My Pollux: The Harbinger is awake. He's on Vesta. I can't fucking believe it. I'm actually going to *meet* him. I wish you weren't stuck with the Geans and could meet him with me. It won't be the same without you.

Message on Hemlock's private server from Castor

My Castor: Remember what Uncle Hemlock says: "Kill your heroes." Don't be so excited that he disappoints you.

Message on Hemlock's private server from Pollux

The Aster ship—an *SP4814*-class, or something called a "spider" due to its grappling arms, Castor explains to me—that will be our home for the four-day journey to Vesta is much larger on the inside than I thought it would be from the outside. Along with the two habitation quarters, each with four beds recessed into the walls, the ship has a hydroponic garden, what I can only describe as a kitchen with a hydration machine and a tube for fresh water, a spherical command center, and a restroom for showering and our waste. The only trouble, I discover, is the lack of gravity.

During the first day, I flail from room to room, desperately scrabbling for one of the bars built into the walls or floor. At night, I buckle myself into the bed with straps and struggle to sleep. And don't even get me started on the trouble with the bathroom, with its dry-soap wipes and suction tube toilet. Liquid in zero gravity is the worst.

Everyone has a job on the ship. Violet monitors the hydroponic garden, adjusting algae vats and coaxing mushroom growth. Lotus sticks to the command center, watching screens and listening to communications. Sage and Poppy disappear into maintenance panels with various tools tucked into their wraps. And Castor claims a space in the command center and begins digging through the information on the naildrive we snatched from Val Akira Geneassists.

I ask them what I can do to help out, but all of them tell me the same thing: practice moving from place to place. Until I can navigate assuredly and quickly, I'm not going to be of any use to them. At least in the mornings and evenings, whoever is assigned to kitchen duty for the day lets me help with meal prep. The job is simple: bring in a color-coded bag from the freezer, plug it into the hydration machine, and press a button. The only trick is making sure the machine doesn't get backed up with the output, a strange cube like a skinned fruit.

On our third day in space, just as I'm getting the hang of using the toe bars to hold myself in place, Lotus tells me I'm to take over meal prep completely. I almost cry at being given a task of my very own, and all of the Asters seem to share my pride. "Welcome to the crew," each of them says to me as I hand out breakfast cubes. Even Castor says it, though he winks at me as he does. I tuck into my strangely juicy cube with its oddly earthy taste, hoping none of them notice how flustered I am to be welcomed like this, but my embarrassment is soon forgotten as everyone starts up their mealtime chatter, recounting stories of missions past.

After that, I redouble my efforts at practicing moving around, until my bodysuit and wraps are damp with sweat. I wash myself before dinner, opening a dry-soap wipe and rubbing it over my hair and skin. I use the suction tube to do away with any excess moisture before dressing in fresh clothes and returning to the kitchen for work, my hair pulled back to keep it out of my face.

During dinner, Lotus plays music over the intercom. When I recognize a song from the device she gave me, I ask about the artist, and both Sage and Violet become so excited they end up talking over each other with stories of musicians they love and concerts they've been to. Lotus, the eldest of all of us, listens to the stories of the younger Asters but offers none of her own. When we've all finished, I move to start cleaning the kitchen, but Lotus waves at Violet and Sage. "You two finish up here. Lucinia, would you come with me to the habs? I want to show you something."

"Of course." I move down the hallway as quickly as I can, pulling myself along the hand bar and switching to the ladder when we arrive at it. Either Lotus moves slowly so I can keep up with her, or my progress is better than I thought; I'm at her heels the entire trip. When we come to the habs, one room on either side of the hallway, she leads me into the one she shares with Poppy and Sage. Castor, Violet, and I use the other.

She pulls a compad from the drawer beneath her bunk and taps it a few times. "As an Aster, you're either *liis* or *mak*," she says, holding out the compad for me to take. I accept it and look at the screen, where an image of a little garden waits for me. The unfamiliar plants are artfully arranged, flowers growing spiraled together like a strand of DNA. "*Liis* is one who enjoys art, who looks at it and is moved by it, who may internalize it but never externalizes it." From over my shoulder, she scrolls to the next image: a tree, its trunk coaxed into bowing, its long, drooping leaves brushing the ground. "But *mak* is someone who sees a piece of art, internalizes it, is inspired by it, and creates because of it."

"So *mak* is the word for 'artist'?"

Lotus considers for a moment. "Not quite. The Icarii make distinctions between the artist, the person who enjoys art, and the person who does not have anything to do with art. Then they go so far as to say, this person makes music, so she is a musician. This person makes clothes, so he is a fashion designer.

"We don't make those distinctions. The *mak* creates art for everyone, and the *liis* is influenced by it. The *liis* wear it on their bodies in the form of clothes. They see it in carefully arranged gardens. They interact with it every day, whether they realize it or not. So either they take that art and are influenced to make some of their own, or they simply enjoy it as part of their lives."

"So are you *mak*?" I ask, gesturing to the compad. "And this is your work?"

The way she drops her eyes in something like shyness tells me I'm right. "To offer another a glimpse at your work is like allowing someone to see a piece of your soul, don't you think?"

I had believed that when I first went to CCAD, but then my professors had driven the conviction out of me. *Art is a business*, they had told me, *and you are merely a conduit of design for the client.*

But then I think of the paintings I did of Lito, particularly the one with the golden crown. No, my instructors didn't completely erase that belief. The reason I hated the idea of Shad stealing that painting for his own gain and fucking it up was because I had put something of my soul in it.

"One day, I hope to show you my work," I tell Lotus.

"And I hope I can show you mine in person on Vesta." She gestures to the compad. "It is especially difficult for me to be on Cytherea, where I can't work." Of course, with the lack of space given to Asters, she would have nowhere to create. I can't imagine being trapped in a place where I'm no longer allowed to paint, where I don't have the space or supplies.

"I once requested an area in a community garden," she goes on, "but I was denied." She doesn't have to tell me it was because she's Aster. The only community garden on the lowest level is close to where I grew up in Faraday Square.

While I know it's small when compared to the overwhelming hate

Asters face, it strikes me as particularly cruel of the Icarii to cut her off from her art, from her voice.

"Thank you for sharing this with me."

She takes the compad back from me, no longer nervous. "You're dismissed for the night. See you at breakfast, Lucinia."

I move out into the hallway, leaving Lotus alone, but I'm not halfway to the ladder when I hear Castor in our hab. "You have to listen to him," he's saying as I approach, frustration burning in every word. "He's the Harbinger. He can lead us to victory, if you'd just give him the resources he needs."

The voice that answers is a deep hiss. "They're not *his* resources."

"Gods damn it, Hemlock," Castor growls. "Why else have you been building this movement if not for the moment to save us? *This* is the fucking moment!"

"Does it soothe you to know I will speak with him in person when I arrive on Vesta?"

This isn't for me to hear. While part of me hates how upset Castor is, I push myself along the hallway to give him his privacy—until I hear my brother's name.

"What does Lito think?" Castor asks.

I rapidly backtrack, pulling myself along the bar and into our hab, but I miss the response to the question in my noisy haste. Castor looks up when I enter, first with offense and then acceptance when he realizes who I am. "We'll all talk then," Castor says, though his face looks drawn with disappointment.

"Castor . . ." The person on the other side of the compad—Hemlock—trails off.

Castor doesn't look away from me. "Yeah?"

"The Harbinger . . ."

I know the sound of someone with more to say, the way their voice fades as if a ghost whispers in their ear. "Be careful," Hemlock says at long last.

Castor lets out a breath; we both know that's not what Hemlock really wanted to say. "Goodbye, Hemlock." He cuts communication with a huff before looking me up and down. "Spying on me?"

My cheeks burn with the shame of being caught. "I heard my brother's name—"

Castor flashes me a sharp-toothed smile. "I'm kidding."

I rub my hands over my face, then find myself bumping into the wall. I forgot to hook my feet in the toeholds. "What's this about Lito?"

"He's on Vesta."

Which is where we're going. My chest aches with longing as if it's been split open with an axe. I try my best not to let the excitement steal away my sense, but fail completely. "Lito's on Vesta . . ."

Castor places his feet beneath what I consider the handrail. Another thing I haven't gotten accustomed to is how the Asters don't look at things as *floor* or *ceiling* or *wall*. Everything is just a space for them to move through, and it's not uncommon for them to have full conversations with someone who's not even oriented in the same direction as them. "It's not all good news," he says, but that most dangerous emotion has already awakened: hope. "Because of Lito and the two people traveling with him, the Icarii are setting up a blockade around Vesta."

"What?" The word comes before I can reason through it. But *of course* the Icarii would chase Lito. They want to make an example of him. "Who's traveling with Lito?"

"Ofiera, his partner, and an Aster called Sorrel, also known as the Harbinger."

I recall hearing about Ofiera the last time I met with Lito on Cytherea, but I haven't thought about her since. The other name, Sorrel the Harbinger, I've never heard until today. "You said something about this Harbinger being able to bring you victory?"

"The Harbinger is a legend." Castor's eyes seem to glow as he speaks of the man. "Two hundred years ago, he led the Asters in the Black Hive Rebellion. It started on Ceres, but it grew to encompass all the Asters, even in Gean territory."

"*Two hundred* years ago? Then how is he—"

"Val Akira Labs." His hands tighten into fists. "Both he and Ofiera are put in cryo when they're not needed. Thawed when they are."

Even my brother's new partner?

"Obviously, the Black Hive Rebellion failed. It's a long story, but suffice to say, the Harbinger is a brilliant military strategist. Unfortunately, he's been under the Icarii thumb so long he doesn't have his own army."

"And that's why you were telling—who was it?—Hemlock that you wanted him to give this Harbinger resources."

Castor snorts. "You really were listening the whole time, weren't you?"

"Not the *whole* time," I say, refusing to be distracted from this discussion. "I want to understand, Castor. My brother's involved in this. *I'm* involved in this."

Castor releases his toes from the hold, pushes himself off the wall, gracefully flips around, and comes face-to-face with me. His toes join mine beneath the bar. "I'll tell you whatever you want to know," he says softly.

I don't let the warmth coming off of him divert my attention. "Go on . . ."

His voice remains low as he speaks. "The man who raised me, Hemlock, has worked for the betterment of Asters for the past thirty years. He's amassed a good-sized group of allies and weapons specifically in case the Icarii ever became too demanding of us."

"War," I say. "You're talking about war." He doesn't deny it, and if he's uncomfortable with the idea of the Asters and Icarii going to war, he doesn't show it.

"With the Icarii threatening to invade Vesta if we don't return Lito, Ofiera, and Sorrel, I think now is the time to use those resources. Hemlock, however . . ." Castor's face twists into a sneer. "He'll always hesitate."

"And you think this Harbinger won't?"

"No," Castor says. "The Harbinger will use Hemlock's allies and weapons and make sure the Icarii don't invade. He'll finish what we've started."

"Even if it leads to war . . ." I trail off. It's clear which side of the argument Castor falls on: he thinks the Harbinger is the best path forward. But I'm not so sure about that. I doubt any number of allies or weapons would give the Asters a fighting chance against the Icarii when our tech is so advanced compared to theirs.

"Maybe there's another way," I suggest.

Castor barks a laugh. "That's exactly what your brother said."

My toes almost slip from beneath the bar. "He did?"

"Yes, and I said we could all discuss it when we arrive on Vesta."

I know the Icarii are amassing a blockade and there's a chance that the asteroid will be invaded, but still, my heart sings with excitement at the idea of arriving on Vesta. *Lito is there*, my mind whispers. The brother I never thought I'd see again is within reach.

"I've been meaning to thank you," Castor says, drawing me from my thoughts.

"Thank me? For what?"

He flashes that toothy smile of his, golden eyes glowing. "The Val Akira Labs data. We got everything we needed, all thanks to you."

The research and the proof—potentially blackmail—we got them both? After I had been interrupted, I had worried that we had only gotten one or the other. "The data—you'll be able to use it to stop the experiments on Asters?"

"Here's hoping."

"Then that's the other way." In my excitement, I surge forward and press my hands against Castor's chest. "We can use the data to bargain with the Icarii! We can stop the invasion and break up the blockade!"

But Castor doesn't seem nearly as excited. He's subdued, his pupils so large and round and black that I can see my reflection in them. Can almost see myself how he sees me.

"Luce . . ." He says my name softly. "You really are . . ." He doesn't finish. His larger hands come up to cradle mine, and I suddenly become aware of the corded muscle of his chest beneath my fingers, of the way he leans toward me, towering over me and making me feel small and safe at the same time. The spark that ignited the moment we met grows until I feel it burning like a fire low in my belly, and I know now that the pull I've always felt toward him was for reasons other than my desire to help the lowlevels and Asters of Cytherea. The reason I was pulled toward Castor was because he's Castor.

But he's an Aster, part of me hisses, the part that has listened to society's rules for too damn long. *I don't care*, the louder part of me says, banishing the other me. So I look at him. *Really* look at him. At his white hair tied behind his head, a few fallen pieces floating freely like strands of starlight. At his sharp face and long torso and slender legs. At his big hands with elegant fingers that hold mine gently.

"You're beautiful," he whispers, exactly what I wanted to tell him, soft and sweet enough to ache.

"So are you," I say, and one of my hands moves down his stomach and stops at his pointed hip bone. He lets out a shuddering sigh and stares at me like I am the pale moon, his pupils contracting with the intensity of his gaze.

I seize his face between my hands and press my lips to his. At first he is hesitant, his arms encircling me tentatively—but then his composure breaks and a growl makes its way up his throat and he grazes my bottom lip with his sharp teeth. My breath hitches as the fire flares and I want him to devour me whole.

Forgotten is the gulf of our differences. Forgotten is the world I left behind. There is only this room and the two of us, no future but the one we might have together.

We align ourselves, hips to hips and chest to chest. My legs come up around his waist, and he guides us until my back bumps against the wall. Or the ceiling, I find, spotting the floor over his shoulder—I've lost track of up and down. His mouth leaves mine, kisses over my jaw, and nips at my ear. I gasp as he buries his face in my hair and groans. "Lucinia," he murmurs against me, and the heat, the need, in his voice breaks me.

Just as I'm about to ask him to help me get out of these damned Aster wraps, Castor pulls away, leaving me as raw as an exposed nerve.

"What?" I ask, somewhat hurt and hoping I didn't do anything wrong.

"Um," he says, his face taking on a more purple tint than usual. "There's no real privacy on this ship."

Suddenly it hits me. There are no doors, and at any minute, our fellow Asters will come down for the night. My face burns until I'm dizzy. "Oh . . ."

Castor chuckles a little, then kisses the corner of my mouth. "Don't worry," he whispers, lacing our fingers together. "We'll finish this later."

My embarrassment slowly subsides as Castor tugs me toward my bunk, as I grip the railing and pull myself into the recess. Castor is just above me, and I know, as I maneuver into bed and strap myself in, that sleep won't find me tonight.

Between becoming part of the crew and Castor's kiss and Lito awaiting me on Vesta, there is too much hope for my heart to hold. A new life awaits me, and I yearn for it more than I have for anything ever before.

"Good night, Luce," Castor whispers.

The smile on my lips never fades. "Good night, Castor."

CHAPTER 24

LITO

After their departure, the Synthetics declared a military-enforced Exclusion Zone beginning at the asteroid belt. Current belief is that this Exclusion Zone begins at the very end of the belt, but our survey has revealed the existence of an unwarded territory between the belt and the area of action of the automated Sentries. Unfortunately, I believe this gray space too narrow and devoid of resources to prove of significant use.

First known use of the term *gray space*, from the Outer Verse Survey Reports conducted by Dr. Tal val Kleiman

The Asters assign me a bunk in a room not far from Ofiera's. I spend the next two days pacing at her bedside, my focus far from the world around me. Neither Sorrel nor I are good company—he hardly looks up from whatever he's reading on a compad someone gave him—and Ofiera's status never changes on the medical monitors. With nothing else to focus on, I circle back to the old worries.

The Icarii have been amassing around Vesta, likely to form a blockade. If the Elders refuse to hand us over, what will happen to the people who live here? Will the Icarii invade? If the Asters are forced to fight, do they have any chance of surviving against a force with superior weaponry and more soldiers? Is there any way to arm the Asters to resist the Icarii advance?

"Lito." My name is stern when spoken, and I fear I've finally worn through Sorrel's patience with my useless patrol, but when I look up from my boots, I realize it wasn't Sorrel who spoke at all.

I do a double take of the Aster standing in the doorway, not quite sure my mind isn't playing tricks on me. "Hemlock?"

"In the flesh," he responds in his rough hiss of a voice. He swims up out of the darkness of the tunnels like a dream, an artist's study of contrasts. Pale, lumpy skin like bleached clay wrapped in an elegant suit of black velvet. Thinning white hair, limp and loose, hiding dark eyes without a hint of color.

"Thousand gods, you're the last person I thought I'd see here." I cross the distance between us and clap him on the shoulder. He squeezes my biceps.

"I'm afraid I almost didn't make it, what with the Icarii force out there."

Of course he knows everything that's happening here. He probably even has some idea about how to respond. As soon as I open my mouth to ask, Sorrel appears at our side. "Good to meet you face-to-face, Hemlock," he says. "I look forward to continuing our discussion about the Alliance of Autarkeia and the use of the outlaws in person."

Hemlock's lips thin in a not-quite-smile, his eyes dangerously sharp. I know Sorrel has been in contact with Hemlock, but what fostered the ill feelings Hemlock harbors toward Sorrel? And if I recognize the antipathy from Hemlock's facial expression, I know Sorrel, who communicates through pheromones, can as well.

Hemlock does his best to sound magnanimous. "I look forward to that as well, Harbinger."

The moment stretches uncomfortably. I feel strangely like I'm a child again, stuck between two fighting parents. Luckily, Hemlock smoothes it over with a few words. "I'm sure all the chatter would be an annoyance to you, Harbinger. Lito and I can take a walk to catch up and leave you alone with your wife."

"Of course." Sorrel's pupils narrow in complete contrast to his words. "I'll speak with you later."

I'm all too willing to follow Hemlock. Like Sorrel, he leads me without trouble, choosing directions based on the pheromones I can't sense. The glowing plants become sparser, the tunnels darker. He finally stops when we come to a garden, something like an underground farm of root vegetables that I can hardly make out in the darkness. While there are a few Asters in the room when we enter, they hurry out at our appearance, leaving us alone with the shadows.

"So that was awkward," I say.

Hemlock makes a little noise, tongue clicking against teeth. "I've put in years of work with the outlaws, and the Harbinger thinks he can use them as his own personal army."

"What does Sorrel want with them?"

"To bring them to Vesta. To aid us against the Icarii. But he doesn't have that authority. He is not the Shield."

I'm stunned Hemlock doesn't like the idea. "What else can the Asters do? They don't have an army of their own."

"No, and I agree we should request help from our allies in Autarkeia," Hemlock says, lip twisted in a sneer, "but what I don't like is how the Harbinger *expects* it."

So it's a power thing. "Are *you* the Shield, then?" Is that how he has, as Sorrel put it, amassed such power?

"No," Hemlock says, a tender undercurrent in his tone. "The Elders only name a Shield in times of emergency." I don't point out that invading Icarii seems like a textbook definition of an emergency. "And while I stand ready and willing, the Elders have yet to call on me in such regard . . ."

I sigh. "Well, unless you want to hand me, Sorrel, and Ofiera over to the Icarii, or you have some other way to strike a deal, I don't think there's another option, Hemlock."

He delicately clears his throat. "Yes, well . . . I'm hoping that what I bring with me will be able to do just that."

I rub a hand over my face. "Please tell me it's a lot of very big, very powerful guns."

"Not quite." Hemlock adjusts the lapels of his suit, not meeting my eyes, and it's that stiffness in him that tells me I'm not going to like what he has to say next. "We received proof of Val Akira Labs' illegal experiments."

I know that's not the whole story. "How, when Ofiera and I didn't plant the relay?"

"We tapped another agent," Hemlock says, and I'm so deathly quiet, he forces himself to go on. "The information comes to us from one Lucinia sol Lucius."

My heart quickens, thumping with predictable anger, but my blood runs cold. *How dare* he get Lucinia involved with this—

He offers me a compad, and I practically snatch it away. Headlines and news stories carve their words into my skin: MASSIVE DATA BREACH AT VAL AKIRA LABS. TERRORIST ATTACK. LUCINIA SOL LUCIUS WANTED IN CONNECTION WITH LITO SOL LUCIUS.

"Where is she?"

"Safe."

"*Where is she?*" I repeat.

"En route to Vesta with Castor." Which means I'm upgrading him from half a bastard to full asshole in my mind. "She chose to do this for us. She wanted to help." Hemlock keeps talking, but I can hardly focus on both him and the thought of my sister wanted by the Icarii military.

"She shouldn't have gotten involved in the first place . . ." If I hadn't failed at Val Akira Labs, she wouldn't have needed to get involved.

"She wasn't hurt," he says, but that doesn't help because *she could have been.* There's no guarantee of safety in this life of rebellion, and now my sister's coming to Vesta, where there's *no way* she'll be safe with the Icarii threatening to invade.

I try to calm myself with deep breaths and focus on the other things Hemlock mentioned. "What about the evidence?"

"Lucinia broke into the Val Akira Labs servers and found video proof of illegal experiments being conducted on Asters." He retrieves a naildrive from the same pocket he pulled the compad from. "I've compiled it here."

"This . . . you think this can halt the Icarii hostilities against Vesta?"

Hemlock's pale tongue darts over his dry lips. "We could use it as blackmail. Promise not to spread the data if they back off."

That's one way to do it, but I don't quite like it. "If this is what you say it is, it could force the AEGIS to shut down Val Akira Labs and stop the experiments altogether."

He nods, somewhat morosely. "I know."

I release a long, shuddering sigh, the anger leaving me at last. "You're willing to give up the data to help me stay on Vesta."

"I am." It sounds like it takes a year off of his life to admit it. "But there is another way."

"Go on . . ."

"There's a nearby satellite previously used to relay information from Ceres to Mercury and Venus with direct access to all Icarii communications networks. If we were to use my connections, the spread of information would be slow and easily censored—perhaps even mistrusted, when coming from an Aster—but with the satellite, it would go to all feeds simultaneously and be impossible to suppress."

"So it would reach even the average citizen." I seize on his idea. "And if it was only used for Ceres . . ."

"It's currently unmanned," Hemlock finishes for me.

"Why haven't the Geans seized it, then?"

"It was a well-kept Icarii secret, so they don't know about it."

And trying to find something you don't know about in space is like looking for a black cat in the Under of Ceres.

"Then I could take the data, go to the satellite, and use it to—"

Hemlock holds up a hand. "Do not volunteer so quickly." I force my mouth closed. "As soon as the satellite is active, the Icarii will storm it, and since there are so many ships already in the area, the chances of escape are nearly nonexistent."

"So whoever goes will likely fall into Icarii hands," I surmise.

"Yes."

"But if the information is so damning that it will force the AEGIS to take down Val Akira Labs . . . We can't bargain it away. We have to use it. We might not get a second chance like this."

"I can send someone—"

"No," I cut him off. "They'll kill any Aster you send without hesitation." I harden my expression. My mind has seized on one possibility, one plan that would shut down Val Akira Labs and save Vesta in the same sweep. "I have to go and make it look like Sorrel and Ofiera are with me."

He fixes his gaze on me, and the low light bounces back, causing his black eyes to shimmer with a hint of gold. "What are you thinking, Lito?"

"If the fugitives aren't on Vesta, the Icarii have no reason to invade." My tone sounds far more assured of the solution than I truly feel. "When I use the satellite, I can send my own image with it, proving I'm not here. They'll come after me and leave Vesta—and all of you—alone."

"But I just told you how little a chance at escape you'll have—"

"I know!" I cut him off, then feel bad for doing so. "I know . . ." I say more softly, thinking of all Luce would've had to do to get this information. How brave she must've been in such terrifying circumstances. "But there are people I care about on Vesta, and Luce is on her way here. If there's a chance to stop the Icarii and save Vesta, it's a chance I want to take."

"Lito . . ."

"I'm sure about this, Hemlock." The resolve has already formed inside me, and it anchors me when so much lately has left me feeling cast about by the tide. I don't *want* to risk myself, but I don't want anyone else to risk their lives for me either. Especially not Luce. "The Elders agreed to harbor me despite what it would bring down on them. They were willing to risk *thousands* of Asters, and all for me." I shake my head. "Now I'm ready to do the same. Vesta was willing to fight for me, so I'm willing to fight for them."

When I finally finish, I find Hemlock smiling at me in a way I've never seen before. With a shaking hand, he reaches out and offers me the naildrive.

"I'll get you a ship," he says.

CHAPTER 25

ASTRID

[9] "What is the purpose of these women?" spake the soldiers. [10] The Agora answered for the women, "To be a comfort to you during your duty." [11] "And afterward?" the soldiers questioned. [12] But for this, the Agora debated amongst themselves. "As was Sister Marian, the first Mother, wed to her captain, may these women cleave only to the captains who will have them, for a captain's work never ends."

The Canon, Judgments 3:9–12

◇———◈◈———◇

It takes three days to complete preparations for our infiltration plan. Three days of worrying and waiting. Three days of knowing women suffer beneath Aunt Sapphira while I do nothing.

The most difficult part is securing IDs. Nat is more than happy to have hers removed, but that is a single chip and we need two. Because I look similar to Nat, we decide I will use her ID. As for Lily, she identifies the chip as one commonly used for tagging livestock—which has Aunt Sapphira's hand all over it—and purchases a blank one to insert between her shoulder blades. We can only hope the guards will think her ID does not scan because of an error.

I have to believe they will let us in. After all, Nat told us the guards are often replaced so they do not form attachments with the girls; there is no way they will recognize us and know we do not belong. Besides, what woman in her right mind would sneak *into* a brothel? It's getting out that makes me worry . . .

When the night finally arrives, I sit on the chaise lounge and watch the space elevator out my window. The spot on my back where we inserted Nat's ID itches fiercely, but I lace my fingers together, refusing to scratch.

"Astrid." Lily's voice, touched with worry, drags me from my already tainted thoughts. She enters my room at the Temple as softly as she speaks, pushing the door closed behind her and leaning on it. "I've brought our disguises." In her arms are ugly, tattered dresses, stained and ancient. My heart trembles at the sight of them; I do not want to do this . . .

Then I recall Eden's face, twisted in anger. I have tried to reach out to her, to tell her of my revised plan, but she has firmly ignored me. I wish I could tell her she was right. I cannot—will not—subject someone else to this if I do not have the spine to do it myself.

We change clothes in silence, strapping riot-control spray to our legs with garters, and I run my hands over the coarse fabric of the dress. I place a camera, a small black cabochon, close to my shoulder in a dark stain I hope is not blood. It is not the same camera Eden used to spy on me on the *Juno*, but it is the same model; in a way, I should thank her for the idea.

"Sit," Lily says, guiding me to my vanity. In her revealing dress, I see her fully: the clustered scars at her joints, the pale spots of irritated skin along her forearms and legs. But I have grown accustomed to the scales, and I find they suit her, like patches of armor or the hide of a legendary dragon. I do as she asks, allowing her to paw through my pots of cosmetics.

"What are you going to do?"

Lily selects a pressed powder and holds it up to my skin to compare the color. "Darken the bags beneath your eyes. Make your lips paler. Add conditioner to your hair so it looks greasy. We must appear to be uncared for if we are to blend in."

I chew on my bottom lip. "You seem a professional at this."

"I have had practice in hiding things I don't want others to see." Lily meets my gaze in the mirror, and I know she's talking about her scales and scars.

She returns to selecting the proper cosmetics, but I am arrested by the hulking shadow lurking in the mirror.

Ringer.

"We're in this together," I say, and Lily looks up at me in surprise.

"Of course," she replies.

But the words were not for her.

Ringer's lips twist into a dark promise. "I'm with you, little sister."

And when Lily sits in front of the mirror to do her own cosmetics, I strap another weapon to my leg, one I have courtesy of Ringer.

THE ADDRESS IS outside of the Olympus Mons dome, on the outskirts of Pangboche, a settlement built on the slopes of the mountain around the crater of the same name. The podcar does not so much as slow as it passes through the hermium-powered barrier, and Lily and I settle in for the ride.

An hour later, we enter the suburbs of Pangboche, a place not unlike the surroundings of Matron Thorne's orphanage. Only there are no houses or yards here, no homes or shops. There is nothing but the wash of industrial buildings—manufacturing plants belching black smoke, stacked warehouses like cartons of metal, and smog-stained refineries.

When we are a couple of miles from our destination, we instruct the driver to stop the podcar and wait for our return. We pay him handsomely not to ask questions, then Lily and I exit, prepared to walk the rest of the way. Without a dome, the gravity is lighter here, and I dig my heels into the ground as I grow accustomed to it. But within moments I have adjusted; this was the way the world felt when I was a child, after all.

I check to see how Lily is handling it, but she seems ready as well. A determined nod is our only communication as our eyes meet. Then I let my feet carry me forward. My heart trails behind.

"You know what you must do?" Ringer asks.

My hand flinches toward my right leg and the weapon waiting there.

"You need only call for me, little sister," Ringer says before he disappears. I feel him leaving like a weight lifted from my back, though my fear intensifies without his steady presence.

No matter. Right now we must be silent. Secretive. Just a couple of brutalized girls not worth a second look.

As we draw closer to the warehouse that houses the brothel, passing below the greasy street lamps that illuminate the area, I think only of forcing myself to take one step after another—not of the sight of skinny Nat with her gunshot wound, not of the dull thumping of music coming from somewhere down the alley, not of the way every cell in my body screams to run in the opposite direction.

Lily presses closer to me as we enter the alleyway next to the warehouse, as somehow those two miles turn to zero. Our steps become softer, more timid. I do my best to look simultaneously confused and shy; in my fear, that is not hard. Any minute we'll come across a guard . . . any second is our last to turn around and flee . . .

"Hey!" A deep male voice. The man, young and muscled, jogs out of the darkness, one hand on the holstered gun at his side. "What're you two doing out here?"

Lily, whose makeup makes her face appear starkly battered in the low light, stumbles toward him. "Where's my bed?"

I am shaking but do my best to follow Lily's lead, slumping in hopes that my hair makes my small camera less noticeable. "I'm hu-hungry . . ."

"The fuck? Goddess's tits . . ." He looks around but, seeing no one else with us, grips me by my biceps. "Come with me. Let's get you back inside." He drags us toward a guarded door, one hand on me and one on Lily.

"How'd they get out?" the bald guard by the door asks. He sounds more bored than shocked.

"Fuck if I know. Maybe some idiot dragged them outside, thinking it would be fun."

He snorts. "Think there's another hole in the wall or something?"

I make a note of that.

The muscled one shrugs. "I'll take a walk around the perimeter and check."

I fear that at any moment they will notice the camera on me, or spot something that marks us as outsiders. That they will pat us down and notice our weapons. With their guns, we have a thin line between safe and not.

The bald one digs out a compad from his pocket. "Turn them around."

The muscled guard forces us to show our backs to the bald man, and he scans the IDs between our shoulder blades. As expected, mine—or Nat's—passes inspection. Lily's doesn't.

"This one's not working," the bald man says. "Want me to call it in?"

I tense, then do my best to loosen my limbs. We knew this would happen, but now that we're here . . . What will they do to Lily if she's not allowed in?

"You want to get yelled at like you're the one who let them out?" The muscled man snorts. "No thanks. Besides, once they're inside, they're someone else's problem."

I release a soft sigh of relief as the bald guy shrugs. With a meaty fist, he knocks twice on the door. When no one answers, he presses a button, and it slides open with a mechanical shriek. They don't pat us down; another reason for relief. The muscled guard simply pushes me forward, and I stumble, my legs refusing to work.

"There you go," he says. "Home again, home again, jiggity jig."

It takes everything within me to step into the warehouse with my heart pounding in my throat. The door slams closed behind us, and my shaking hand reaches for Lily at my side. She is the only small comfort I have in this hellish place.

The shipping containers are stacked in rows, forming a little shanty-town with clustered walkways. Faded sheets hung in the entrances grant the appearance of privacy, while pounding music smothers the sounds of grunting and shouting. Reddish lights on the warehouse ceiling cast the area in bloody hues. Women—skinny, stumbling, drunk or high—weave between the "rooms," men following not far behind.

Our initial plan was to split up and look for Joli, but now that we are here, I fear we will never find each other again if we do. However, what I know for certain is that we cannot stand here, gaping, and so I force myself to move. *One foot in front of the other*, directly into the fray.

A man comes around a corner with a woman beneath his arm, laughing loudly, and Lily and I jump. We dodge them and shuffle into a skinny gap between two containers that forces us to walk sideways. When we emerge, we find ourselves in a square of sorts, several unoc-cupied women lounging in mismatched chairs. They do not even note us as we approach.

"Do you know Joli?" Lily asks one.

I turn to another. "Can you help us find Joli?" She waves me away. "Joli?" I ask another. And another. No one even looks at my face; they either ignore me outright or, like the first, brush me off.

Lily takes my arm and pulls me away. I start to ask her why, but then I spot him. There is a man lurking nearby, watching us, and right now his attention is fully focused on Lily and me.

"Let's go," Lily hisses, and we quickly leave the way we came, shuf-fling shoulder to shoulder down one of the alleys.

We find a quiet, dark corner where two containers meet, and I re-lease a shuddering sigh. My head aches from the stress and poor light-ing. "There are so many of them," I whisper.

Lily rubs her lower back. "How many do you think are here? Three hundred? Four?"

I do not know how to answer. I keep myself from asking what I really want to. How are we supposed to get out of here now that we have gotten in?

Just as we are preparing to dive back into the chaos, a girl Lily's size with faded blue hair slips out of the alley we came down, spots us, and, after looking both ways, approaches us. "You were asking for Joli?" Her accent is from somewhere on Earth I cannot quite place.

"Yes," I say after a moment of hesitation.

"Why?" She narrows her eyes.

I look at Lily, unsure how to answer.

"You two don't look like you belong here," she goes on. "Men don't notice this shit, but those of us who've been here awhile? We know."

"We're friends of Nat's," Lily says.

"That girl who ran off? Shit." She slaps a hand to her forehead. "She's alive?"

"Yes, and she told us everything," I say.

"You two journalists?"

"No, but we want to shut this place down."

She looks at us skeptically. "You have that power?"

Again, I look at Lily.

"We work for the government," Lily answers. "We just need someone who can testify against the woman in charge of this place, and we can stop it. Have you ever seen a woman in a gray dress wearing a golden necklace with a lioness on it? A big cat?"

"People talk about her," the girl says. "She's like the bogeyman around here. You see the lady with the cat, you don't come back."

"But Joli has?" I ask, repeating what Nat told us.

"I don't know. Some, like Joli, say they have. Or say they saw—" She stops midsentence, straightening up and looking down the alleyway we came from. "Follow me," she whispers, then hurriedly leads us in the opposite direction.

I don't look back, but I can feel eyes on me anyway.

We stick close to the blue-haired girl. As close as we can, anyway. She leads us on a roundabout route through containers, across squares, past an open section of the warehouse full of showers and toilets without even stalls for privacy. Eventually we come to a container that looks, to me, no different from the rest. She pushes the sheet aside, peeps in, then waves for us to follow her.

"Joli, get up."

"Rufia?" Joli, sprawled on one of four cots, pushes herself up. She looks from her friend to us with sickly yellow eyes.

"What're you doing? Sleeping?" the blue-haired girl, Rufia, asks.

"There was a guy just here . . . I'm resting. Who're they?"

"They're gonna get us out of here," Rufia says, excitement leaking into her tone, and it reaches a hand into my chest and squeezes my heart. "You just gotta tell them about the lady with the cat."

"Have you seen her?" I ask Joli.

Joli digs a hand into her matted brown hair and scratches at her scalp. "Yeah . . ."

"You could identify her if we showed you a picture?" I ask pointedly.

She looks at Rufia, then at Lily, and finally back to me. "I can't forget her. One day these guys take me and some other girls out of here, and we all think we're gonna die. But they let us out at this big house, make us shower and dress up nice. She was there, at that party. She's got this big blond hair and these angry brown eyes."

While the fear doesn't ease, some part of me feels relief. The woman she describes does sound like Aunt Sapphira. "Would you be willing to identify her publicly?" I ask.

"If you get me out of here?" Finally, Joli stands. "I'd do anything."

That only leaves the question of *how*. "One of the guards mentioned a hole in the wall?" I ask.

"Yeah, that's how Nat got out," Rufia says, "but they patched it quick."

So that's not an option. I look to Lily, my brows furrowed. We each have a slender tube of riot-control spray, but it won't be enough to stop a man determined to use his gun unless we strike first and he is alone. I knew that coming in, though, which is why I brought the *other* weapon.

That weight on my back returns, and with it, Ringer's presence.

"I have an idea," I tell the girls. "But I will need your help . . ."

JOLI AND RUFIA expertly lead us through the madness of the warehouse-city and to one of the exits, avoiding the guards patrolling inside the brothel. "Everyone ready?" I ask, and after each of the girls nods, we take our positions.

Joli stretches herself out flat on the floor, and Rufia crouches beside her. I press my back against the wall to the side of the door, in as much shadow as I can manage. When everyone is ready, Lily knocks twice on the sliding door like the bald man did when we entered.

After a few seconds, the door slides open. Goddess wither it, there are two men at this exit, both young and strong-looking. One is handsome, while the other is thin with crooked teeth.

"Help!" Rufia yells before either of them can say a word. "She just collapsed!"

"What's happening?" Crooked Teeth asks, stepping into the warehouse. I nod to Lily; let her take that one, while I deal with the other. She seems to understand, waving Crooked Teeth farther in as she too goes to Joli's side.

"She's not breathing!" Lily screeches.

"Shit!" Crooked Teeth shuffles forward to kneel next to Joli.

"Should I call someone?" Handsome asks from outside.

Crooked Teeth says nothing, because that is the moment Lily chooses to pull up her skirt, withdraw the riot-control spray from her garter, and spray him in the face.

He releases a painful howl, twitching fingers reaching for his eyes.

"What the shit—" Handsome withdraws his gun and points it at the girls, stepping right past me into the warehouse to help his partner. I grab my riot-control spray and jump at him, pushing the button down—

He spins, knocking the tube out of my hand. His gun comes up—to shoot me?—and with a snap, he cracks the butt against my face—

Everything is ringing.

The world filters back a piece at a time—girls screaming, red lights flickering, music growling. *This is hell*, a part of me thinks. *You've died and gone to hell.*

Then my vision clears, and I look from writhing Crooked Teeth to Handsome, his gun pointed at panicked Joli and Rufia, his hand around Lily's throat, her legs dangling, kicking against the empty air—

Ringer.

He settles into my bones, drinking my fear. I no longer control my body; the pain of my throbbing eye socket is distant. My life comes to me in snapshots.

Stand. Pull weapon. Step. Stab.

The sharp knife slides into the flesh of his back, and Handsome's eyes pop wide and horrified.

He drops Lily. I pull the knife from his back. He turns the gun on me, but I am so close. I stab his forearm, and the gun tumbles from his grip.

His face twists, mouth yawning wide, and I think he is screaming, though I do not hear it. He stumbles back, jerking the knife from my hand, and I look at the gun that lies between us. He must see from my eyes what I mean to do, must see that he cannot let me have it. He kneels as I dart for it—

Only for Lily to grab my shoulders. She says something that I don't catch, and then she's pulling me toward the open doors. Behind her, Handsome has his gun in his left hand, and blood flows around the knife he hasn't removed. He raises it to shoot—

Rufia kicks him in the head so hard with her high heel that he drops the gun and falls flat on his face. She waves at us to follow before seizing Joli's hand and running for the door.

All at once, Ringer releases my body, and I sag toward the floor. The fear comes back. The pain returns. My face is on fire, and I am hot and sticky, covered in someone else's blood. I expect to feel guilty for what I have done, but the only thing I feel is the need to flee, to get away from this horrible place and these horrible men.

"Astrid, we have to hurry." Lily looks at me with reddened eyes wide and lips trembling. And doesn't stop looking when I find my balance and stumble my first few steps.

We are not the only girls to take advantage of the chaos; there is a stampede of women rushing from the warehouse, breaking free into the cold night air. I find my rhythm and start moving as quickly as possible with Lily, Rufia, and Joli at my side.

It is only as we leave the warehouse behind us that I realize what I saw in Lily's face that bothered me: she was terrified of me.

CHAPTER 26

HIRO

Network search query: Synthetics

Results: 969,345,521

Network search query: Synthetics "Mara"

Results: Missing: "Mara"

Network search query: Synthetic girl human body cyborg

Results: Did you mean: Girl on Girl Cyborg / Human Amateur Hardcore?

Autarkeia network search history of Hiro val Akira

D ire doesn't even knock when he storms into my apartment. I'm
hazy-eyed with sleep, but the first thing I think is, rather stupidly,
I'm fucking naked. "What the fuck—" I barely have time to pull the
sheet around my scarred chest before logic hits me.

If he's here with all the power and darkness of a thunderstorm,
something must be on fire.

"What did you do?" Dire rages, thick-soled boots threatening to
warp a path into the stone floor. His steps are silent, though, like a
lynx on snow. Axe-faced Falchion stands in the doorway, making sure
I can't leave, and behind him are a bunch of other peons of Dire's that
are, in all likelihood, here to smack me around.

I sit up, turning my sheet into a toga. "You'll have to be a bit more specific . . ."

"You were caught by the Icarii you were tailing—don't bother to deny that—and now they've left Autarkeia," he says, never ceasing his pacing. "So tell me what you did."

I go from sleep-drunk to angry very quickly, and not just because of his tone. My meeting with Shinya was a whole three fucking days ago, and I've been trying to get ahold of Dire ever since. "Oh, good, I wanted to talk to you about this, but your peons kept saying you were too busy. Did you happen to know my *brother* was here?"

I expect him to obscure the truth with some excuse he pulls out of his ass. What I don't expect is for him to close the space between us and shove his face into mine. "Cut the shit!" he yells, and I flinch. Shame floods me a moment later as I try to calm my racing heart. "This isn't about you!"

I shove past him, doing my best not to outwardly show my fear, as I stand from the bed. A wave of dizziness hits me, but I ignore it, dragging myself to the two-drawer dresser where I keep what few clothes I have. My mother's holoimage in the small shrine catches my attention, and I can't help but wonder what she'd think of Shinya and me. Would she be ashamed of us? Of me?

"Perhaps I'm mistaken," Dire bellows at my back, "but I was under the impression that Icarii duelists were special operatives who didn't let anything get in the way of achieving their mission—*including* a lack of information or family members."

I turn away from my shrine, a tremor running down my arms— even the prosthetic one—as I face him. The sheet slips from my shoulder, pools to the ground at my feet. I don't reach for it. I hook him with my eyes and stand straight, let him and all his other cronies see what I am, what I've become—the scarred chest, ribs like the bars of a cage, the mangled shoulder and hip connecting to my prosthetic limbs, the pale marks of stretched skin over newly grown bone. Some of this comes from the chopshops I visited when I first arrived on Autarkeia, desperately seeking changes away from Ren, but the majority of it is from the Icarii who twisted me into someone I wasn't.

"I'm *not* a fucking duelist," I hiss.

Dire doesn't drop his eyes in shame or disgust, just stares at me with the heat of a sun. Without looking, he waves a hand at Falchion, and the man withdraws into the hallway and closes the door between us.

"Guess you're not going to kill me today," I say, relaxing into my heels as Dire's operatives disappear from view.

"You think you're the only one with scars?" Dire whispers, his voice as dark as the rage in his eyes. He lifts a golden hand, as if to call attention to his prosthetic. But when he speaks again, I realize it's not *those* scars he's talking about.

"From the time I was born until the time I left, the Geans only saw me as a woman."

I can't help it. I flinch like he punched me.

"Do you know what it's like to be a young man seen as a girl, too poor to afford gravity medication, pushed toward the Sisterhood as his best means of survival?" His eyes narrow. *Of course* I don't know. But from my time as Saito Ren, I know exactly how the Geans, with their rigid view of gender, would treat him. Even if he could've found an illegal geneassist, how would he have afforded them?

"This is Autarkeia," he says, stepping close to me, towering over me. "I am free here. We *all* are. And I will do *anything* to protect that right, Hiro."

We stare at each other in silence, understanding yet opposing. When Dire finally turns away, I grab my clothes and start to dress. He remains quiet until I'm in pants and pulling a shirt with a cowl neck on over my head.

"Listen, kid," he says, softer than before. "You can't go through life thinking of all you've lost and holding that against people who've never taken anything from you."

"Listen, *old man,*" I say, twisting his words, "I came here to work with you, not against you, and I can't complete my mission if you don't give me the basic information I need. Reciprocity." But truthfully, the heat isn't in my voice anymore. It's all rushed out of me, leaving me chilled.

I remember all too well his excuse as to why he kept things secret from me: *The safety of Autarkeia and its allies is too important to risk.* But only now do I realize how much this station means to people like Dire. This isn't just a refuge for outlaws; it's a haven, a home, where they can be themselves. And no matter my mission, they'll risk the outcome every time to protect their sanctuary.

I let out a long, slow breath. "Shinya cornered me when I was tailing two of the duelists. They took a file off of one of your operatives."

"You didn't think to tell me?" Dire snaps.

"I've been trying, and I wasn't about to tell one of your lackeys when I don't know if I can trust them."

Dire grunts but composes himself. "Who did they take the file from?"

"Can't remember his name. Big guy with a beard." Which I'm pretty sure could describe half of his crew. "He looked completely blank when he was handing over the files. It was like he was drugged or brain-washed."

"Did you get a look at what was in the file?"

"No, I was trying to. That's when my brother intercepted me, and—"

Don't ally yourself with the outlaws. Shinya's sneer, etched in my memory. *You're not like them, Hiro.*

I close my eyes, wishing I could forget. "He alluded to something bigger coming."

"Well, that something bigger is what I've been dealing with." A cold hand reaches into my chest and clutches my heart. "Hemlock has called for aid on Vesta. All the Icarii ships my men were seeing? They've departed for the Aster homesphere."

"Shit." I feel it's the only thing I can say that sums this up. Wait, no, I have one more word for this kind of situation: "Fuck."

What the hell are they doing out there? What do they want from the Asters?

"I'm assembling ships to go to Vesta," Dire says, rubbing his chin and the stubble there. He must not have shaved this morning. "Because this is the Icarii we're dealing with and we have no idea what they've gotten from us here on Autarkeia, I'm only taking my most trusted crew members."

"Let me come," I say.

"I said, I'm only taking my most trusted—"

"Yeah, yeah, I heard you, old man."

He narrows his eyes as if considering calling for his goons outside. "If the Icarii push for a fight, they're going to get it. We may not be coming back."

"That's my life every time I step out my door." I shrug. "So what?"

He shakes his head. "You're one of Hemlock's agents," he says, finally giving up with a huff. "Come if you want."

"Great," I say. I clear my throat before I make my next offer. "I'll talk to Mara."

Dire's eyes widen imperceptibly. "What for?"

"Well, besides the fact that nothing happens on Autarkeia that she doesn't already know about . . . if we want the Synthetics to ally with the Alliance, we need to be honest with them." I can't help but smirk. Just a teeny bit. "People like it when their allies are honest with them."

Dire throws his hands up in the air as if I've exhausted him. "Fine. If she agrees to come with us, she's welcome on my ship."

"Right." Which leaves only the nigh-impossible task of convincing Mara. "I'll call you later."

IT'S NOT HARD to find Mara; in the end, she comes to me.

"Second visitor I've had today," I say, taking a drink of my burnt coffee outside the corner grocery in the square near my apartment. I ran out for breakfast, determined to find her afterward. Guess I won't need to now.

Maybe she sensed I wanted to talk to her. *Or maybe she's watching me*, the paranoid part of me whispers.

She sits down beside me. I offer her my cup and gesture to the pile of chocolate buns I bought but haven't touched. "Want something?"

"Why do you drink it if you think it's gross?" she asks in her light-hearted way.

"How do you know I don't like it? Can you read minds now?" I joke, trying to fall into the camaraderie we had before I ran after the Icarii and she disappeared.

"You cringe after every sip," she says, somewhat standoffish, like she's holding something back. Does she know what I want to ask her?

I shrug. "It's caffeine, and that's more important than the taste."

Still, she waves the cup away without taking it from me.

That confirms my suspicions. "You're not really here, are you?"

"No."

"Mmm." I take another drink and wince. "Well, I guess it doesn't matter if I'm seen talking to myself if there's no one around." The square is mostly empty at so early an hour in the cycle. Of course, because of Autarkeia's lack of lighting, it always looks like night.

"Dire's preparing a ship," Mara says, watching her chunky boots as she kicks her legs back and forth like a child.

Maybe this will be easier than I thought. "Do you want to come with us?"

"I shouldn't."

"But you can."

She digs the toe of her boot into the cement, interacting with her surroundings in a way that half convinces me she's lying about being here. "Autarkeia is in gray space and a former territory of ours that we've allowed the outlaws to use. No one would accuse the Synthetics of interfering with humanity here."

I disagree with her there; many would think the Synthetics are overreaching even if this is their former settlement. But I take her point. "You don't want to leave gray space."

"Yes, and Vesta is most definitely part of the belt."

"What if we're inviting you?"

"*You're* inviting me. But not the Asters or the Icarii or Geans, and I—*we*—can't be seen as invaders."

Maybe it's because my anger was drawn to the surface so early in the day by Dire, or maybe Mara's words just step on a sore part of me, but my frustration overflows. "Thousand fucking gods, Mara, pick a side."

She snaps upright. The childishness sloughs off her. In a second she looks older than me, harder than me, her face and body changing shape in whatever projection she's showing me on my com-lenses. "Excuse me?"

"You want to watch us as if what we're doing doesn't affect you? Well, it does." A cold fear creeps in—I'm talking to a *Synthetic* like this— but it does little to douse the heat of my rage. "Whatever the Icarii are doing out here, brainwashing the outlaws, butting up against the Asters, it's only a prelude to what they're *planning* to do against you."

Mara's dark eyes narrow, but she doesn't interrupt me.

It hits me then what I'm doing—trying to *convince* the Synthetics of something. Is that even possible, or do they, in their consensus, already have all the answers? Am I wasting my time, just a child digging at pebbles when a mountain lies in my path?

Damn it all, I don't care. The odds have never stopped me before.

"You think the Icarii don't want to go toe-to-toe with the Synthetics?" I knock my coffee cup over in my sharp movements and do my best to ignore the dark liquid splashing to the ground. "They would *love* to, once they've defeated the Geans and put down the Aster threat."

Mara laughs. Actually *laughs*, like she finds what I say funny. "That is the human condition, Hiro. We expect that."

"Then why are you here on Autarkeia?" I snap. "Why bother at all if you *expect* things because we're predictable humans?"

Mara's silent for so long that I think she's going to disappear without answering. She could be gone with a blink; she's not even here, not truly. Then, finally, she releases a breath and speaks. "The Synthetics promised humans they could do whatever they wished with the inner planets, even kill each other, so long as they didn't try to leave this system and extend their self-sabotage to the stars beyond. But the Asters . . ."

She pauses, bites her bottom lip. She looks human again in that moment, and it tears my heart into conflicted pieces. Am I to view her as an individual, a potential friend, or a gateway entity to something so much larger?

"We've always agreed that we would welcome humans to join us if they were peaceful. If they left behind their baser tendencies toward war and destruction and helped their fellow person. If they considered the needs of the weakest just as important as those of the strongest. If they avoided becoming poisoned by the burden of power." Mara cocks her head and looks at me. Her face ripples, the image she shows me shifting back to that of the girl I've gotten to know here on Autarkeia instead of the woman of authority. "But we never took the Asters into account because, at the time of our edict, the Asters had nothing to do with us and our war."

"So what about the Asters now?"

"Do you know how birds came to be on Ceres?" she asks, much in the same way she asked me about cats and rats and fleas and the Black Death. I'm so caught off guard by the change of topic that it's a few seconds before I shake my head. I'd lived on Ceres, seen the birds, even chased them off when they got too annoying begging for food—but I'd never thought about how they got there. Mostly I wonder why the hell Mara is bringing this up now.

"The first Gean mayor on Ceres had a wife who kept doves on Earth, and she desperately missed them in her new home. So the mayor asked Earth to send doves—lots of doves—to populate Ceres and give his wife something to do." Mara pulls her legs to her side on her chair, as if making herself comfortable. "Earth agreed and sent them doves. Cages and cages of doves, ready to breed. And do you know what the mayor said when they arrived?" Mara's lips pull into a thin, wry line. "'Why did you send me all these fucking pigeons?'"

I don't understand. Not at first. But then, slowly . . . I do. "Because he couldn't tell the difference between pigeons and doves . . ." I thought she wasn't answering my question about the Asters, but she was. She was just doing it in her own way. Suddenly I see a map before me, a road I didn't know existed that Mara has pointed out with her story.

"The Synthetics aren't sure if there is a difference between the Asters and humans," I say. She doesn't answer, but I know I'm right. Maybe she told me this because she *wants* to be convinced to help. "But there *are* differences," I go on. "The Asters are peaceful. They care for each other and live equally, exactly as you want humans to. If all of humanity lived the way Asters do, we'd be welcome into the greater universe."

"Yes," she says.

"Then come with me for them," I say, seizing on to that small yes, hoping to turn it into a big one. "The Asters are nearly on the brink of war, and the Icarii will slaughter them without fail. They have all the power, while the Asters have none. You agreed that they're peaceful. What do you expect them to do, other than die by the thousands?"

"We have no agreements with the Asters," she says, but weakly. Her heart isn't in it.

"Then come with us to see the difference for yourself . . . for yourselves, even." I reach out for her hand, forgetting she's not here. I pass through her illusion with vague surprise. "Whether you intervene or not, you owe it to the Asters to at least *look*."

"We owe nothing to anyone, Hiro," she says, but she doesn't reject me outright.

I feel I've almost convinced her when she turns her face to the city up above.

"And what if we see something we can't ignore?" she asks.

My lips curl into a smirk. "That's what I'm hoping for."

Now it's her turn to look shocked, eyes widening slightly. She's right that the Synthetics shouldn't be playing police to everything we do, but if the Asters face a genocide at the hands of the Icarii and the Synthetics do nothing to stop it when they have the power to? They're just as guilty.

Mara shakes her head, and her eyes, ageless, drop to the ground. "I have to think," she says, and disappears.

I go from smug to embarrassed in seconds. While the square was empty when I began talking to Mara, now a few people watch me from nearby shadowed corners . . . as I appear to argue with myself.

くそ. I'm pretty sure Dire will hear about this before I have time to call him.

WITHIN A FEW hours, Dire has a ship staffed and ready. We aim to depart at 1300. He didn't seem terribly surprised by the results of my talk with Mara; after I relayed our conversation, he huffed over the compad. "I suppose she won't be coming, then," he said.

But even then I disagreed. After I pack my few belongings into a bag, carefully tucking the static holoimage of my mother away, I go to Mara's industrial dome to speak with her face-to-face. But the wall doesn't open up for me this time, and I'm stuck outside, once again a strange person doing strange things as Autarkeia's citizens judge silently from nearby stoops and sidewalks.

I spend the rest of the morning at the docks, watching people come and go. The docks are all rows of airlocks, branching hallways with numerous elevators, and stacked solar power panels, a mishmash of Gean and Icarii parts that would make even the eccentric Ceres retch. And they're a lot busier than they were when I first arrived. I get the impression that Autarkeia is a far more prosperous trading hub than even the Icarii suspect.

Dire joins me a half hour before our scheduled departure. "Heard anything from Mara?"

"No," I admit sadly, my stomach turning with worry. "But I believe she'll come."

Dire scowls. "Faith is in short supply." He leaves me to stew.

The time passes slowly. I can't even focus on reading the news on my com-lenses because I watch the clock. Every time I catch a glimpse of someone the right height or black-haired, my heart speeds. But I'm only chasing shadows; they're never Mara.

Five minutes before we're set to leave, Dire returns for me. "Let's go, kid."

"Not yet, old man. She still has five minutes."

Dire rolls his eyes. "No, it's five minutes until *launch*. We need to be in our seats by then."

"You can't give me five minutes?"

Dire huffs. "Hiro . . ." But the way he looks at me—brows furrowed and lips downturned—reeks of pity.

I don't want his fucking pity. "Fine, let's go." I stand from the mismatched plastic chair I've been sitting on since I got here and start toward the ship. Dire follows close behind.

As we approach the craft—an old ship of independent make—I spot a person in black near the outer airlock door, and I know without seeing her face exactly who she is.

Chunky-heeled boots. Half-shaved head. Oversized black jacket that covers all but her fingertips.

Mara actually came.

"Glad to see you made it," I say with relief, and I can somehow tell that she's *actually* here, that this isn't one of her projections. When I look back at Dire, his eyes are wide, his mouth partially open. He's speechless.

I put on my best smirk. "Dire," I say, gesturing to Mara. "May I introduce the representative of the Synthetics?"

CHAPTER 27
ASTRID

The Order of Leo focuses on animal welfare, conservation, and breed-ing programs for both food and the preservation of species not yet extinct. Its symbol is the lioness in repose, her regal head raised and watchful. It should be noted that lionesses are both caretakers and hunters, and it is with this in mind that one is best able to reflect on the appearance of the Order of Leo's lioness, whose stern gaze conveys a sense of power.

From *Inside the Sisterhood* by Dr. Merel Jäger

We are only three blocks away from the warehouse when we hear footsteps behind us. "Hurry!" Lily whispers to Joli and Rufia. "We have to hurry!"

The podcar we left is still over a mile away, but both Rufia and Joli are unable to run, either from malnutrition or because they are drugged. We move with desperation, keeping to the shadows, but I know deep in my heart it will not be enough.

"Leave them behind, little sister," Ringer whispers to me. "Leave them if you want to get out of this alive."

"Shut up," I hiss beneath my breath. Lily casts me a strange look.

When we hear the guards—shouting, cursing men with the heavy treads of steel-toed boots—we stop and hide, cramming ourselves behind sharp scraps of metal or piles of trash. Their flashlights swoop in great arcs around us as my nostrils burn from the acrid stench. When they move on, we flee, clinging together, pulling the weakest of us ahead. Every step I take, I pray to the Goddess under my breath, and I wonder, for the first time in my life, if anyone is even listening.

Then we find ourselves two blocks from the podcar—I recognize the graffiti on a stone wall—and my heart soars. *We are going to make it,* my mind sings, and every step we take is one that brings relief alongside the adrenaline in my veins. *We are going to make it!*

We round one corner and then another, until finally it is a flat-out run to where we left the podcar snug in the mouth of an alleyway. Lily and I push the girls ahead of us, coaxing them with soft whispers. "Almost there," I say. "We are almost free."

Then the sound of boots returns, followed by a man's cry. "Over here!"

Against my better judgment, I look back and spot him: the bald guard who let us in.

We run, legs pumping, forcing the girls after us, practically dragging them. The men are whipped into a frenzy, converging on us, as the bald man cries again and again, "They're over here! I found them!"

This time I do not look back. I only flee, my eyes burning, my hands curled into fists as if they could possibly save me.

"We're here!" Lily screams. "We're here!"

We turn the corner so fast I almost slip, but then I am steady and entering the mouth of the alley—

But the podcar. It's gone.

A crack rips through the night, an exclamation point to the ringing in my ears. It takes me far too long to identify the noise, for the knowledge to pierce through my haze.

"Get down!" Ringer hisses, and I crouch as more gunshots fly overhead.

Rufia hits the ground, faded blue hair tinted red with blood. Someone is screaming—Lily or Joli, I cannot tell. The guards come at us from both sides, pouring into the alley, and I desperately scrabble for the camera—I must protect its contents, must save the evidence—

A man is on Lily, wrenching her arms behind her back. Joli tries to curl into herself, crying, as someone jerks her to her feet. No one pays attention to Rufia; impossibly, the thought numb and faraway, I realize she must be dead.

I seize the cabochon camera, pull it toward my mouth—"Swallow it!" Ringer screams, his voice all I can hear—before something crashes into my face.

The world flares white, then red. The darkness of the night is lost amidst the stars of pain. I open my eyes, find my face pressed against gritty pavement. A man's blood-covered boot is inches from my nose. He reaches down and plucks the camera from my hand as another jerks me upright, and I almost vomit from the sudden movement.

"Stop," I say. "I am the First Sister of Ceres."

They do not seem to hear me. I shout again.

"I am the First Sister of Ceres!" And again. "I am the First Sister of Ceres!"

Lily picks up the cry, and it is her bellow that finally quiets the night. "In the name of the Goddess!" the small woman booms with a voice that belongs to someone twice her size. "Halt your mistreatment of the First Sister of Ceres!"

The guards stop. One man laughs, but another elbows him into silence. Harming Sisters in the way they have abused us is a killing offense. Of course, they might decide it is far easier to hide our bodies than face the authorities, so I had better make my point—and fast.

I look up at the guard who kicked me, who now holds my camera in his hand. "You are holding a camera that has captured everything we have seen tonight—"

He moves out of instinct; he tosses the camera on the ground and grinds it to splinters beneath his boot. A piece of my hope shatters with it, but I force myself onward, because now I speak not to capture evidence, but to save our skins.

"Already it has transferred its data to a compad at the Temple of Mars," I add quickly. It is a lie, but my voice does not shake. I can only hope they believe me.

The bald guard gestures to me with his rifle; I cannot help it, I flinch. "Since when do Sisters talk? She's a liar!"

"Call Aunt Sapphira!" I snap. A ripple of fear passes through the crowd at her name. The men share glances, the only break in the silence Joli's gentle sobbing. "Ask Aunt Sapphira, and she will tell you."

"Or we can shoot her and be done with it," the bald man grumbles.

"You wanna wind up as cat food?" a short man asks, and others grunt in agreement. "Fuck it, I'm calling her." He slings his gun over his shoulder and pulls out his compad as he walks away.

The entire alley falls into a silence so encompassing that I wonder if I am still conscious. It is only the pain that tells me I am still awake—still alive—after everything I have faced tonight. I look to Lily, her arms wrenched and bound behind her back. She meets my gaze with swollen red eyes and tear-streaked cheeks, but I force myself to smile at her, to reassure her that we are in this together.

When the short guard returns, he stops directly in front of me. "Aunt Sapphira wants them," he says, but his words do not bring me any comfort, and a second later, men haul Joli, Lily, and me to our feet. "Load them up, and then clean up the body."

WE ARE TAKEN to a podship and loaded into the storage space, which smells strongly of animal musk. Despite our questions, we are ignored. Only Joli is silent, curled into herself in the corner. It seems she has accepted whatever fate will hand her.

The podship hums with such steady white noise that I start to drift, all the adrenaline from the night fleeing from my limbs and leaving me drained and aching. But Lily does not let me sleep; each time my head dips toward her shoulder, she shakes me violently.

"Stay awake," she says, fingers tracing my swollen face. I run my hands over her arms, over the pale dragon scales, warmer and softer than I could have ever imagined. "You likely have a concussion."

That means so little to me when every piece of me burns as if on fire.

When the podship lands, I am not sure how long it has been. The door opens, and a single guard—the short man—ushers us toward a waiting building of golden metal and glass. I can tell from the gravity that we are inside a dome, but I do not recognize the buildings around us. Whether we are back in Olympus Mons or not, I cannot tell.

We pass a spherical fountain trickling with water, surrounded by green plants with fat flowers, and come to double glass doors. The man opens one for us and motions us inside, but he does not follow.

The room is expansive but unfinished. It smells of wet plaster, and the floor is coated with dust. Stairs trail to a second floor obscured by thick tarps. They seem to wave in a phantom wind. The only lights are those that filter in from outside.

"Over here," someone calls from the shadows, and Lily steps closer to Joli. But I have heard this voice before, and as if Ringer has possessed me again, I stride forward until I find a little table set between two chairs.

In one sits Aunt Sapphira. Her hair is a honey blond and wild like a lion's mane, as if she wishes to embody the animal she wears stamped on the golden medallion around her neck. When she gestures to the chair across from her, I sit. It is plush and comfortable and terribly inviting, but I perch on the edge, ready to lunge at her empty-handed if I must.

She does not once look at Lily or Joli, only at me.

"First Sister of Ceres," she says. "What a surprise."

"We need to talk—"

Before I can finish my statement, she whistles. I tense up, expecting men with guns to emerge from another room, but what prowls out of the shadows is something out of legend.

Joli screams. Lily claps a hand over her mouth.

It is a cat. A big one. White, with delicate black stripes. It pushes its great big head against Aunt Sapphira's knee, and she scratches its cheek.

The lady with the cat, the brothel girls called her. Now I understand they did not just mean on her medallion.

"Don't you think Oscar is just the most beautiful thing?" she asks, staring at the cat like a lover or a child. "White tiger DNA can be so troublesome. They're mutants, you know, and so incredibly rare. The people of Earth did the best they could with their limited tools, but the coloring is a recessive trait, and inbreeding was common. But no one wants a cross-eyed tiger with a cleft palate." Her eyes snap from the tiger to me. "You have no idea how many I had to dispose of to get one so perfect."

I clear my throat, trying to find my words. Desperate to be in control of this conversation. But there is an instinct I cannot fight, one that tells me to freeze before a predator as ferocious as the tiger. And with Aunt Sapphira lurking behind it like that, she knows.

"So you stumbled across one of my little projects," she says, and it is so convenient, the way she packs away the horror in those words—just a little project—that I scoff. "You have a video, you told my man, and witnesses." She gestures to Joli and Lily. "So you asked to speak with me—to what, bargain?"

"I have demands," I say.

She snaps her fingers, and the tiger whirls on me—beside her one moment, face thrust into mine the next. He roars, fangs the size of daggers, hot spittle flecking my cheeks, and I lean back as far as I can, a scream building in my throat, my entire body trembling.

Oscar withdraws. Aunt Sapphira stares at me.

"This is my den, and you will respect me here." Oscar flops onto his side at her feet, a weapon in plain view. "I know all about what you did tonight. I particularly like the part where you stabbed a man."

She chuckles. "That was you, wasn't it?" I don't answer, so she goes on. "This is the part where you tell me what you want."

"Close down the brothels. All of them." My voice shakes, and I do not even fight it. "Stop perverting the Sisterhood this way."

"Yes, yes . . . or you'll send the video to the Agora, have your witnesses testify, something ominous. I get it." She waves her hand through the air. "And if I have Oscar tear out your throat?" Her eyes go past me, to Lily and Joli. "If I rip out their hearts and feed them to my pet?" Joli chokes off a sob.

"You won't," I say, hoping I sound more confident than I feel.

Aunt Sapphira listens, unimpressed. "And why not?"

Ringer whispers to me, and I seize on not just his words but the damning way he says them.

"Because if I do not return to the Temple by tomorrow, my allies will release the video." I lean forward in my chair, my eyes never wavering from Aunt Sapphira's. "They knew where I was going. Do you think I won't be missed? I am the First Sister of Ceres, not some girl you trafficked off the streets. Kill me, and you leave a trail directly to your doorstep, which I believe, for various reasons, you would rather not call attention to."

She leans back in her chair and smiles. The expression both annoys and unsettles me. What more does she have up her sleeve? But then she releases a capitulating sigh. "There are projects I care about and projects I don't, Astrid, and that means I know how to let some of them go. I'm sure you're the same way."

"I am nothing like you."

She shrugs as if it doesn't really matter. "It's just nature. Survival of the fittest."

Suddenly, the night's exhaustion topples down on me, and I want nothing more than to close my eyes, right here, right now, and cry myself to sleep.

"I'll tell you what I can do for you, and you can tell me if you like the sound of it." She shoves her wild hair over her shoulder. "I'll close down all the—ahem, facilities, of which there are just two."

Just two, as if hundreds of women in chains are nothing.

"I'll let those girls go—wherever. To the streets, I suppose."

I glare.

"Aunt Genette will take care of them."

I will make sure of it . . .

"And when you call for your vote to become the next Mother, you can count on me to help you."

"And?" I prompt.

"And," Aunt Sapphira says, face growing dark, "know this disrespect is not something I will forget. Keep the video to yourself. Put a muzzle on your witnesses." She steeples her fingers in front of her. "Or I will."

Joli whimpers. Lily shudders and holds tighter to her. But I refuse to flinch.

Aunt Sapphira grins like a cat. "Do we have a deal?"

I LONG TO go straight to my room, but pass first through the courtyard of statues. *Victory* looms over all, and I marvel at how I feel so much like her—a winner, but at the cost of my hands and head.

Lily has taken Joli to a safe house. She mentioned something about getting her testimony on record regardless of Aunt Sapphira's deal, but I was so ragged, I could hardly pay attention. I waved her off and promised to call her after a rest—a long one.

The sun peeks over the horizon. Dawn has come. I leave *Victory* behind.

A few Little Sisters spot me on my way to my quarters, their eyes going from my bruised face to my strange black dress, before they turn their gazes to the ground, knowing this is something they should not be involved in. Smart girls. When I reach my room, I kick off my shoes, strip off the bloody clothes, and collapse on my bed.

I am alive, I chant to myself. *I am alive . . .*

It feels like mere minutes later when my door opens again, but it must be at least a few hours—the sky is brighter, and there is a flurry of activity outside my window in the courtyard around the space elevator.

I roll over and rub my eyes as a weight settles on my bed.

"Astrid . . ."

I look up at Eden's face, at her wild red hair. Her cheeks are flushed and freckled, her lips full in a pout.

"I can't believe you did that, Astrid . . . You could have been . . ." She doesn't finish. We both know.

I am alive . . .

"You said I shouldn't put anyone else in harm's way."

"I didn't mean you should throw yourself in front of it either."

Her eyes shine like jade in the morning light as she looks me over—my bare, dirty legs, the bruises over my ribs, my breasts rising and falling. I see something change in her face, and my lower belly stirs in response with a desire I wish I could ignore.

I sit up. Put my hand on Eden's neck. Pull her toward me, and she does not fight. I kiss her cheek, the corner of her mouth, stopping at her lips.

"Astrid . . ."

Her eyes move over my body once more, stop on my face. When she speaks, that touch of her fire has returned. "Lily says the two of you have no plans to turn over the evidence you gathered to the Agora."

I pull in a breath, but it does little to cool me. "We made a deal with Aunt Sapphira—"

"A deal?" she snaps. Her face hardens, and while she does not pull away, that wall of hers comes up again between us. "She deserves to be punished for what she's done. She can't get away with it."

How can I explain that I had little choice in the deal? How can I tell her that I almost got Lily, Joli, and myself killed?

"She won't," I promise, "once I am made Mother."

Eden scoffs, turning away from me. Slipping out of my hands. But I can feel it: the distance between us grows more than those few inches.

"I have defanged the snake, Eden! What more do you want?"

"Justice!" she snaps.

"And you will have it—once I am able to grant it!"

I expect her to curse at me. To storm out of my room. To find my most vulnerable spot and attack it.

I do not expect her to seize my wrists and push me down onto the bed, to loom over me, her red hair tickling my cheek.

"You think you've defanged a snake? You've only stolen a bit of its venom!" she hisses. "Aunt Sapphira will continue to use and abuse those girls—only now she'll be sneakier when doing it."

I stiffen beneath her, my stomach turning in loops. Her mouth is so close to mine, but her lips are twisted in rage, her eyes bubbling with angry tears.

"Eden, I want—"

She cuts me off. "You don't want *me*, you just want someone to comfort you." She leans down to my face, lips brushing against my ear. "You *disgust* me," she whispers.

And then her weight is gone from me and my bed.

By the time I sit up, she's at the door.

"You're a wildfire, Astrid, and you burn everything and everyone around you." Eden's hands shake as she reaches for the door handle. "One day you're going to burn yourself, but by then no one will be around to save you."

And then she is gone, heels clicking away, and I am left cold and alone with nothing but the morning's shadows for company.

CHAPTER 28
HIRO

Tell me you don't miss Mars. Tell me you don't miss your family. Tell me you don't miss having a home where you weren't constantly hunted for who you are and what you did.

Message from Sigma

I don't miss what was; I miss what could have been.

Reply from Dire

Not that I've known Dire for a long time, but I know his type—came from nothing, climbed his way up the ladder of success one bloody rung at a time, and clings to his empire, however small it may be— so it's absolutely bizarre to see him in his element, captain of his own ship, struck silent. *Deferential* to someone else, and to someone so slight, at that.

Mara stands in the corner of the command deck as if hoping to quietly observe without interfering, but everyone's gaze is drawn to her, iron toward the most powerful magnet in the room. Falchion does his best to ignore her, but even the silent merc is unnerved, hands dipping in and out of his pockets.

"Glad this isn't awkward or anything," I say into the silence. Dandy—he, today—is the only one who finds it funny.

Mara smiles as if she expects it. I guess she does. She's been around a long time.

"Enough," Dire barks, as if he isn't just as guilty of gawking as the rest of them. "Get to work." He claps his hands, and the majority of the crew are happy to get the hell out of the command center and leave Mara behind. Only Sigma, Dandy, and I are left with Dire and our Synthetic guest.

Dire turns his attention to business, leaning over the command panel. "With the current rotation and the way the Icarii and Geans have distributed their forces, it'll take us around nineteen hours of travel. At 0800 on Thursday, we'll arrive at Vesta. We'll set a watch schedule in case we come up on an unexpected patrol, but until your shift, you should get some sleep." He looks up from the screens, pointedly ignoring Mara. "I can't guarantee what's going to happen from here on out. We'll pass out of gray space in a few hours, but the closer we get to Vesta, the more Icarii we might stumble into."

"I'll take first watch," I volunteer, and Dire nods appreciatively.

"We'll be joining other Alliance members before we come close to Vesta, so keep a lookout for friendlies," he says. "They'll ping you with today's code on approach. Once the fleet is together, we can provide a unified front against the Icarii threat."

I clear my throat and focus on the mission. "And the Geans?" I ask. "Are they holding to the cease-fire?"

"Seems so," he answers. "So whatever the Icarii are doing in the belt, it's only because of the Asters."

A little flare of pride swells up in me as I think about First Sister. It's because of her that the cease-fire exists. Unfortunately, it's not enough to keep the Icarii from getting up to shit. "What the hell is happening out there?" I ask, more to myself than anyone else.

"Wish I knew," Dire says, shaking his head. "Wish. I. Knew."

I TAKE THE first watch, a four-hour interval that I spend with Mara in the command center. Our passage from gray space into the asteroid belt is silent, but once my watch is up, I don't call for my replacement. There's no way I'm going to sleep anyway, not with the Icarii somewhere out there.

Dire returns six hours in, looking far from fresh, and looms over the command panels. He chooses to handle the pings from our fellow Alliance ships, and soon we've greeted and joined a handful of other outlaw vessels. Around hour twelve, I take a break in the canteen with Mara. The few crew members awake are quiet and subdued. In the eighteenth hour, we slow our pace. We don't have an exact map of where the Icarii ships are, and we don't want to run afoul of a patrol before we get close enough to help.

As time slips through our fingers and we approach Vesta, our screens begin to change. At first it's just a few ships marked on our map, but before we even hit hour nineteen, the dots begin to multiply. More and more ships appear until the screen is full and we see just how dense a net the Icarii have created.

It's a full blockade of Vesta. We're not even going to be able to land. And one marker looms larger than all the others.

I tap it on the screen. "Tell me that's a glitch," I whisper.

Dire shakes his head. He can't because it's not a glitch.

The Icarii have an *Athena*-class warship.

"If a fight breaks out, what will we do?" I ask, adopting as casual a pose as I can manage under the stressful circumstances.

Dire meets my eyes, expression hard. "We will aid our allies."

And die trying. He doesn't have to say that part.

After talking with his fellow captains on the *Xiaoling*, *Muriel*, and

Nova, Dire calls for the full crew to assemble, all fifty members, to relay what's about to happen.

"The Icarii think they have us by the throat here, that we're going to retreat and let them destroy our allies," he begins. All around the room, faces turn hard. "But they're fools if they think the Alliance will abandon their own."

"So what are we going to do?" Sigma asks.

"Hold our position," Dire answers. "The Icarii may have their block-ade, but we are here to ensure they don't set a single foot on Vesta."

"And if shit hits the fan?" Sigma cracks his knuckles nervously.

"Then we do what we do best!" Dandy says.

A handful of the crew shouts, throwing fists in the air.

Dire focuses solely on Sigma. "If that *Athena*-class wants to have a fight, we'll make sure it doesn't walk away." Now his eyes sweep the crowd. Every person here—Aster and human, old and young, of various genders—chose to come to Vesta to help. "We'll use the Engineborn weapons."

The entire cabin roars, in complete opposition to my sinking heart.

The *Engineborn Forge*. That's what the Synthetics called the station when they inhabited it. I look at Mara, hoping to read some emotion there, but she doesn't look surprised in the least. *Of course* she knows what's happening on Autarkeia; that's why she came to the station in the first place, why she followed weapons dealers and smugglers. She was assessing Autarkeia's preparations for war before she became in-terested in the Icarii duelists.

"What are the Engineborn weapons?" I ask, but the room has de-volved into the chaos of shouting and peremptory celebration. I'm out of my chair before I'm even aware of deciding to stand. "What are the Engineborn weapons?" I repeat louder than before.

Mara touches my shoulder, and without a word, *I know*. I think of the nuclear fission factory she used as a home, of that donut-shaped metal object she slept above. Her station wasn't active, but others were, and the outlaws were using them to make weapons that would be capa-ble of standing against the Icarii.

I imagine what kind of guns those plants could make if they once created Synthetics. What kind of bombs. くそ！

"Shit," I say, and then for good measure, "Fuck."

THE WAITING IS the worst part. Slowly, people return to their assignments, but I linger in the command room with the bridge crew, including Dire and Mara. I do my best to keep my fear from showing, though I find my knee bouncing up and down with excess energy. Mara sits beside me in a chair, legs tucked beneath her, eyes far off as if looking but not *seeing*.

All I can think about are the questions with no answers. Why were the duelists on Autarkeia? What information did they get that could be our downfall? And how do the Asters fit into this?

I feel as if I've missed something important, some clue or hint as to what they gathered that will now aid them in the upcoming battle. Something about the Synthetic nuclear fission plants? About the Engineborn weapons the outlaws have? But then why are the Asters involved?

Unless . . . Shinya was counting the Asters as part of the outlaws. When he spoke of the Alliance of Autarkeia, did he mean all of those in gray space, Asters included? The Alliance is, after all, the child of both Dire and Hemlock.

"Uhhh, we've got a problem!" Dandy's voice cuts right through me. He frantically taps at a screen. "That *Athena*-class is moving in our direction!"

We're all out of our seats—moving, shouting, or just plain freaking out.

"Arm the Engineborn weapons!" Dire barks as other orders fly.

"—brace yourselves—"

"—spread out!"

Then a red light illuminates on the console. Everyone around the room freezes.

They're . . . hailing us.

"They want to talk?" Dandy whispers.

After releasing a tense breath, Dire accepts.

"I am Dire of the Belt, captain of the *Dominique*." He squares his shoulders as if the other ship can see him. "Announce yourself."

"This is the *Leander*," comes a haughty Icarii voice over the speakers, "acting under orders of Commander Shinya val Akira."

Eyes flick toward me. "Oh shit," Dandy says. He didn't know this was a possibility.

But I did. After seeing my brother on Autarkeia, I knew I wouldn't shake him so easily.

"We—" Dire starts, but I'm beside him in a mere half second.

"This is Hiro val Akira, *Leander*," I say, ignoring Dire's furious eyes boring holes into the side of my face.

"What are you doing?" he whispers.

"First mate of Dire of the Belt," I add.

"Hey!" stage-whispers Sigma, who is actually the first mate.

The silence stretches so long I think I've miscalculated. Weren't they calling us to negotiate? I thought revealing my presence might make that go a little easier . . .

"They've launched podships," Dire says, looking at the command panel with wide eyes. I've never seen that expression on his face, but I know it well enough: fear.

Shit. Guess I was wrong.

"Hold, *Leander*," I cry over the comms. "We are armed." But I hate myself even as the words leave my lips. Call it weakness, but I really don't want to use whatever those Engineborn weapons are.

"Hiro," my brother says, joining the call, and his voice is so soft, so full of regret, that I feel as if we're back in that tea shop during our private conversation. No, before that—just children in our townhome in Cytherea, huddling beneath the kotatsu for warmth. "I'm sorry."

"For what?" I ask, but no response comes. "What are you sorry for,

Leander?" Again, no reply. "Answer me, Shinya!" I cry, but there's only silence as the podships grow closer.

I look to Dire. To Dandy and Falchion and the other crew around me. I expect them to yell at me, to crowd in on me in their anger and frustration and fear, but what I see is infinitely worse.

All of them are frozen. Eyes glassy. Standing stock-still, arms held limp at their sides. I recognize the pose, the lack of fluid movement. Just like the man who brought Noa and Nadyn the folder of information.

"What's happening?" a woman asks.

"What's wrong with them?" comes the voice of another crew member.

So it's not all of them—just the majority. "Mara?" I ask.

Mara's out of her seat, moving from person to person, checking their eyes and the pulse at their wrists. Her lips tremble. Panic rolls off her in thick waves.

"They're . . ." My throat is so dry, it hurts to speak. "How?"

Mara turns to me, horrified. And then I see that the podships launched from the *Leander* are closing in on us on the command screen.

Coming for us, and our crew is helpless to do anything to fight them.

I start hailing the others in our pack of outlaw vessels. "Calling all Alliance ships, *Dominique* is in trouble. Repeat, *Dominique* is in the shit. *Nova, Muriel, Xiaoling*—anyone?"

But none of them answer.

I fear the worst: the people crewing them are experiencing the exact same thing we are.

Except for a few of us . . . What is it that makes us different from the ones who are having a blackout?

Then I spot Sigma—that anxious, flighty geneassist—sitting calmly in his chair, the only one not affected by the madness.

"Sigma, what're you *doing*—"

The *Dominique* trembles as an Icarii pod attaches itself. "They're here," Mara says, and her eyes water with tears. "Hiro . . ." She looks like a child, but it's only for a moment, before her face becomes placid, blank, her stance straight but loose.

"Mara!"

"I made a mistake," she says. And then she too is frozen stiff.

"Mara!" I wish I could shake her back to life, but I know it will do no good. No, I have to focus on what I can change—what I can *do* before the Icarii kill us all.

"Oh, that's a surprise," Sigma says, and I spin toward him. He gestures at Mara. "I didn't think it would affect her."

"What did you do?" I hiss, but as Sigma looks up at me, bushy eyebrows furrowed over bug eyes, the pieces fall into place . . .

The affected crew members act like blank Icarii foot soldiers slaved to their commander. The majority of the outlaws have Autarkeia's version of neural implants. And the only people who ever worked with them are in this room. Dire and Dandy—frozen—and, completely unaffected, Sigma.

Sigma, who used to be Icarii. No—who *still is.*

"The Autarkeia neural implants," I say, "you had a back door, and you gave the Icarii access."

"Sorry, kid," Sigma says. "I just want to go home."

The airlock hisses. I hesitate to take my eyes off of Sigma, yet I still spin to meet the Icarii as they enter, my training forcing me to. I reach for my mercurial blade, but I know I have no chance in hell of getting out of this—not with Dire and the others frozen stiff, easy to strike down in any fight I start. They're not collateral I'm willing to risk.

I don't recognize the duelist pair that first enters the command room, but I know the man on their heels.

"Hiro." Shinya's in military blacks, hair slicked back from his forehead, looking every bit the Icarii commander, and I realize, as I release the hilt of my blade, how little of my brother remains in his eyes. I drop my face and hold up my hands in surrender. "Arrest them," he says to the duelists with him, and I clench my eyes as they come for me.

CHAPTER 29

LUCE

There is little to be said about the Asters who inhabit Ceres beneath the surface. Led by those they call the Elders on Vesta, Asters are cave dwellers who shy away from bright lights and loud sounds. Some might even call them secretive. For many, this raises the question, why?

From *A Brief History of Ceres* by Toliver val Berquist

I n the middle of the afternoon, two hours before we're scheduled to arrive at Vesta, the ship-wide intercom system turns on with a crackle. "Everyone to the command center," Lotus says, her voice a whip's crack. Forgotten are the cold storage room around me, the color-coded bags of material for the hydration machine. Breakfast, with its laughter and stories, is a memory; dinner, an uncertain future. Now there is only Lotus's panic, infecting me.

I push myself out of the kitchen and meet Castor and the others on the way. As soon as Castor sees me, he reaches out for me. Holding himself steady with his feet, he guides me ahead of him with his hands, fingers lingering on my waist, my shoulders, my back. Since our kiss yesterday, we've found little reasons to touch each other, excuses to be alone. Every lingering gaze, every too-long touch stokes the fire that burns inside me, threatening to turn into a conflagration.

We reach the ladder to the command center, and he lets me ascend ahead of him. I enter the spherical room to find, from my vantage point, Violet on the ceiling and Sage on the wall. Lotus hovers just in front of the array of screens, pointing something out to Poppy at her side and communicating in that wordless way of theirs. I catch a glimpse of one of the screens, practically glowing red with so many little dots. At the very edge is a green dot, almost lost amidst the harsher color. We knew about the Icarii blockade, but still, seeing it this way really drives home how desperate our situation is.

Then I notice the reason for Lotus's fear: one red dot is practically on top of our green dot. The hair on the back of my neck stands up, and a shudder races down my spine. I know from that dot alone that all my plans of a happy reunion with Lito are in danger.

"An Icarii ship hailed us a few minutes ago," Lotus says. "They've requested to board."

My stomach churns, threatening sickness. We knew that with the blockade in place we might have trouble reaching Vesta, but we hoped with a properly spoofed code, the spider wouldn't attract any attention. I know from the way Lotus says *requested* that they meant *do it or we'll blow you up.*

"Dress her in robes," Poppy suggests, and I know that *her*, in this case, is me.

"It won't work," Lotus says. "You saw what happened in Cytherea."

"What else can we do?" Sage mutters in his gruff way.

"We'll hide her," Castor says, "in one of the smuggling compartments."

They all stop. Four pairs of large, glowing eyes turn in my direction.

"She can fit," Castor says.

"I'll do whatever is safest for everyone," I say, as if my opinion holds any weight in this matter. Right now we have to think about survival, not my comfort.

Violet's voice is high in their throat as they point with their chin to the screens. "They're connecting now." They look at me and Castor. "Hurry."

"Luce—" Castor doesn't wait for me to consent—he pulls me into his arms and carries me out of the command center. He moves with a speed I didn't think possible, kicking us down hallways and spinning us in new directions so his feet always brace our landings. He never uses his hands, which hold me tightly, and by the time he releases me, I'm so dizzy and disoriented, I'm surprised to find myself in the hallway to the habs.

"Castor?"

He doesn't have time to explain. He crouches on what I consider the ceiling and, pulling at a latch I never noticed, pops open a small trapdoor. "It's cramped, but . . ." He looks at me, eyes desperate.

"I'll fit," I reassure him. But as he helps me into the slender space, I find that I'm the one who needs reassuring.

The compartment is long and thin, giving me a bit of extra space above my head but no room around my shoulders or hips to move. I'm forced to keep my arms at my sides, my legs stretched out, and my toes pointed, an uncomfortable position in such tight quarters. "I'll return for you as soon as I can," Castor says, sounding faraway. Then he closes the trapdoor, and everything becomes pitch black.

The sound of Castor maneuvering away softens, leaving only the hum of the ship and my hurried breathing. The blackness surrounds me, as if I've been buried alive in metal. *What if there's a shipwreck?* my anxiety whispers. *What if everyone on board is arrested, and no one finds you here for weeks?*

I force myself to suck in a deep breath against the tightness in my chest, hold it, and release it slowly. I try to picture another world in the dark, another time and place. I imagine soft blankets surrounding me, Lito's hands over my ears. *Can you see the stars?* he would ask. *Can you hear the sea?* And then he'd whisper a story to me as my fear turned to exhaustion. *Nothing can hurt you in the sea cave,* he'd say, and I always believed him.

Nothing can hurt me. I repeat the words to myself, praying to the thousand gods that they are true.

I must drift, because I startle back into something like waking when I hear people nearby. I don't know how much time has passed. Mere minutes, or several hours?

"These are the only two habs you have?" comes the voice of a woman.

"Yes, only these." Castor.

I wish I could see what's happening on the other side of the wall. What is the woman doing? Poking her head into the habs? Searching for something? *Searching for me?*

"Excuse me, that's personal—" Castor starts.

"Don't move." A man's voice, unwavering. "Evangeline, keep searching."

Silence. I once again have to force myself to breathe through the tightness. My heart thumps so loudly in my head, a headache forms behind my right eye.

"Antti, look at this—" Evangeline calls.

"What is it?" Antti, the man, asks. "What is . . . that?"

Please don't let it be my hiding place . . . please . . .

I hear a soft click and then the heavy clank of metal on metal. I fear at any moment the light will flood back in, exposing me and the crew with me. I close my eyes to fight the onslaught of rising tears.

"Maintenance tunnel," Antti says.

Even through the wall, I hear Castor's answering scoff.

"Why don't you check the rooms, Eva?" Antti suggests. "I'll check the hold. You know how rats can—"

He freezes. Everything is quiet. Once more, I wish I could see what's happening below me. I hear a thunk, what sounds like gravboots clipping to the floor, and then nothing.

Finally the woman speaks. "You hear that, An?" Evangeline asks.

"Yeah, let's go." A pause, then, "Antti val Kumpulainen and Evangeline val Joy on our way."

Another set of gravboots engages with a heavy clunk, and two sets of footsteps march away from my position. I wait until all noise disappears before I release the longest sigh.

My limbs itch to be let out from the compartment and my eyes yearn for light, but more urgent than that is my concern, not just at what brought the Icarii to our ship, but about the message they received. What was so important it pulled their attention away from us?

AFTER THE ICARII leave, Castor releases me from the compartment. Total time inside: forty-five minutes. I almost weep in relief as I'm able to stretch my aching limbs and sore back. We return to the command center together. All the Asters look worse for wear, tired from our run-in with the Icarii.

"I thought for sure we were—what do your people say? Fried? Toasted?" Sage asks.

"I thought we were toast too," I tell him.

"Especially when the duelist pair stepped on board . . ." Sage pretends to shiver, a gesture he picked up from me at dinner one night.

"Quiet," Lotus snaps. "I'm trying to reach Vesta."

It takes several minutes to get hold of someone on the surface. The news is relayed in a passionless Aster, so I understand none of it. At least, nothing other than my brother's name.

When the call ends, I'm practically hovering at Lotus's side. "What did they say—"

"If we land," Lotus says to the entire crew gathered around her, "there's no turning back. The Icarii aren't allowing anyone to leave."

The room sucks in a collective breath, and I'm reminded of the Aster music. *Huuuuuuh.*

"Where else could we go?" Violet asks.

"Ceres. Pallas. Autarkeia." Even though she names these places, she doesn't seem to really consider them. "There are other options."

"And Lito?" Castor asks softly. I'm immensely thankful to him for asking after the most pressing matter on my mind.

Lotus looks at Castor, and something passes between them. I know it's the pheromones Castor explained to me.

"Tell her," Castor whispers. "If she's part of the crew, she has a right to decide."

Lotus takes a moment to compose herself. When she looks at me, she's arranged her face into something like sorrow. "Lito left Vesta a couple hours ago. Alone."

My face is numb as I force out my words. "Where did he go?"

"He took the data you retrieved from Val Akira Labs to a nearby satellite station in order to release it to the Icarii public. Several ships followed after him."

My breath catches in my throat. *The other option*, I realize. He's going to try to stop the Icarii from invading Vesta using the information. The blackmail.

"As I said, we have options." Lotus crosses her arms and straightens her back. "The Elders are waiting for us. There are weapons to be built, defenses to be erected, and we are warriors. Or we could go after Lito and provide backup for his mission. But we have to decide now whether we want to continue on to Vesta or turn toward the satellite station."

The world grinds to a halt. There is only the impression of my surroundings. Only my brother, slipping through my fingers. The blackness of the smugglers' compartment. The garden Lotus showed me on her compad. The stories on top of stories of the crew's friends and families, waiting for them on Vesta.

I joined the Keres Art Collective because I knew something was wrong with Cytherea. I agreed to help Castor because I wanted to be like Lito. I ran from my home because I had no choice after I was caught. But this . . . this is my choice.

So what do I choose?

Do I go after my brother and hope we're enough to defend him as he distributes the data I took from Val Akira Labs? Or do I choose to land on Vesta, let the fighters of my crew bolster Aster numbers, and help in any way possible to prepare for the Icarii invasion?

If I go after my brother, is there any guarantee we'll arrive in time? On the other hand, if we land on Vesta, there's no leaving. No helping Lito from there. But there are people on Vesta—friends and family of my crew—who need our help. Who need the expertise of the people around me.

Five pairs of eyes turn in my direction. Five sets of lungs hold their breath, waiting for my answer.

So I choose.

CHAPTER 30
LITO

Everything we've gathered on Autarkeia needs to be transferred to Cytherea immediately. There are forces at work here we can't trust, and eyes on our every move.

Message from Commander Shinya val Akira to Noa sol Romero

The Elders immediately agree to my and Hemlock's plan. I'm granted the *Nyx*-class ship I arrived in, the only ship in the Vesta hangar that could conceivably outrun an Icarii vessel—or outgun it, if necessary. I want to ask Sorrel to record a statement I could play from the *Nyx*, something to convince listeners he's with me, but with the Icarii massing around Vesta, I don't have the time.

"I'll see what I can do while you're on your way there," Hemlock says. With the route he's planned, burning the ship at maximum speed, I'll be there in six arduous hours, late Wednesday evening. But I'm healthy; I can take it. "You should say your goodbyes now, though."

Just in case I don't come back, he doesn't add.

I leave Hemlock to requisition anything else I might need—a HEL gun, at the very least—and seek out Ofiera's room. Sorrel knows nothing about the plan, and I'm not sure how he'll take the news. I don't have time for an argument, so I steel myself to be firm with what's happening, allowing no room for debate.

But when I reach the doorway of Ofiera's room, I stop before entering, listening to the raised voices within.

"Fi . . . my Fi . . ." Sorrel, full of anguish.

"I'm here, my darling." Ofiera's dulcet tones. "I'm not going anywhere . . ."

I peer into the darkened room, at the two figures barely lit by lamplight. Ofiera sits up in bed, while Sorrel has collapsed into her lap, weeping. Her eyes are closed, but I know she's awake by the rhythmic brushing of her hands over his head. After a moment, she begins humming a song that drives back Sorrel's sobs until the only noise in the room is her haunting tune.

I turn away from the door, unable to interrupt a moment so intimate. Knowing that they are together is enough for me. Perhaps a part of me fears that Ofiera, now awake, will be unwilling to let me go to the satellite station alone, but the biggest truth is this: there is no goodbye I can give them that is adequate in the face of all they've already lost.

MY FAREWELL WITH Hemlock is perfunctory. "Good luck," he says.

"I'll be back," I respond, but it's clear he doesn't believe so.

After that, it's as simple as executing Hemlock's programmed route. I key the course into the command center console, then settle back in one of the seats and buckle up for launch. Only, unlike other times I've traveled, I won't be able to get up again until I reach the satellite center. Forcing the ship to burn at maximum speed will put undue pressure on my body—and my squishy inner organs—that necessitates my keeping still. My greatest hope is that the Icarii are caught off guard by my gutsy move and lag behind, giving me at least an hour inside the station before they arrive.

Leaning back in my seat, I close my eyes as the ship jitters into movement. As soon as the *Nyx* is free from the Vesta airlock, thrusters flare at maximum and launch me, with a sinking pressure, out into the black of space.

I open my eyes only when I receive hails from several ships. I ignore all of them. Icarii attention is on me, but better me than Vesta. Better me than my sister.

I watch the command screens as the ships ringing Vesta try to keep up but fall behind. As soon as they realize what I'm doing or where I'm going, I'm sure they'll also burn hard and follow. But for now, it's just me and the endless black.

After the first hour trapped in my seat, the seat belt buckles digging into my chest, my head is aching. By the second hour, the ship shaking around me, I see why this isn't sustainable long term. In the fourth hour, I'm breathing as hard as I would be if I'd just finished running a marathon. In the fifth hour, I can hardly shift in my seat, all of my joints screaming at what feels like tiny shards of bone cutting into my soft tissues.

The ship finally slows in the sixth hour, allowing me to take my first full breath. I feel battered from the inside out. Bruised in ways I didn't know I could be. I'm barely out of my seat before I'm vomiting bile into the recycler. But at least I'm here.

When I'm well enough, I check the maps. I'm still in the asteroid belt, but not as close to Ceres as I thought I'd be. According to Hemlock, this satellite was abandoned and left to drift after the Fall. I can only hope Hemlock's program can crack into the satellite and send the data on the naildrive—and quickly. With a long-range scan, I can already pick up several incoming ships. Icarii, no doubt.

Worst of all: I only have thirty minutes—not the hour I need—to get in, send the information, and get out.

Despite my dizziness, I force myself into the airlock. Since the satellite has been abandoned, the gravity generators most likely aren't working. I kick my heels together, activating my gravboots, and wait for the airlock to cycle.

I have to focus on what's in front of me. It's just me here—no Dagger, no backup. I'm armed with a mercurial blade not my own and a half-charged HEL gun. The military blacks Sorrel found in the *Nyx* will serve to shield me. Hemlock's naildrive is in my pocket. I can't think about the ships coming for me, about what will happen if they find out Sorrel and Ofiera are still on Vesta. I can't think about the Icarii who will slap me in chains and drag me back to Command. *Or kill you where they find you*, a part of me whispers.

I push all those thoughts away as the airlock finishes cycling and the doors fly open, admitting me to the satellite. Sure enough, there's no gravity from here on out, which will take up more of my already limited time. I force my arms to my sides, but my unkempt hair floats around my face, a slight annoyance.

Hemlock didn't have a map of this place, but satellites are pretty straightforward: there's the communications hub, the main and largest room, and then a few hab quarters spread about for technicians or other workers. All compartments lead to the hub, as they say, so I keep going straight from the airlock, ignoring branching pathways.

The strangest thing is that I expected a satellite that had been abandoned for a year to look more . . . I don't know. Decrepit, maybe. Being that it's solar-powered, I suppose it's not terribly surprising to find the lights still on, but everything looks so clean. Not that there's evidence of anyone working or living here, but still . . . If I believed in ghosts, I'd say this place had a haunted air to it.

As I suspected, ten minutes in I find the communications hub at the heart of the satellite. The room is bathed in an ambient blue glow, the machines sleeping but not dead. As I approach, they wake, screens lighting up like monsters opening their large eyes. I'm not trained with any of these programs, but they're obviously Icarii-made, and so I do a little searching . . . There, a camera to send communications, and there, the perfect place to insert the naildrive. I slip it into the proper slot and—

A glow behind me catches my attention, bright enough to reflect on the screens like the slash of a knife.

I deactivate my gravboots and slam my hands on the command console, pushing off the floor and rocketing up until I catch myself on the ceiling. Below me, just where I was standing, is a duelist in military blacks, their mercurial blade in hand.

"Lito sol Lucius." Their voice is high but with a raspy timbre, and slowly my mind catches up with my racing heart. I recognize them.

"You've changed, Noa sol Romero."

Their dark brown skin is pitted with scars, particularly around the eye that is such a bright blue it almost looks white. "I almost died on Ceres," they spit. "Did you think it wouldn't mark me?"

Taking a note from Sorrel's playbook, I reactivate my gravboots and stand on the ceiling. I bite back a curse at my foul luck. Will Noa believe Sorrel and Ofiera are with me, only waiting for me in the *Nyx*, or will I have to silence them to keep that secret from getting out? "What are you doing here?" I ask as I consider my options.

"We may have lost Ceres, but do you honestly think the Icarii would give up an asset like this as well?"

So are they here to send information? Or did they happen to be in the area and come to the satellite because of me?

Was there another ship docked? In my rush to do what I'd come to do, I didn't check. *Idiot*, I chide myself.

Noa turns as I walk, making it clear from the way they hold their mercurial blade that, despite our chatter, this is a fight. "Besides, I could ask you the same thing. Why did you come here, Lito?"

For once I decide honesty is my best option. "There's something I have that every Icarii citizen needs to see—proof that Val Akira Labs is illegally experimenting on Asters."

I expect Noa to, at the very least, be surprised. Instead, they scoff. "Who cares?" they ask with a haughty shrug.

I tighten my grip on my blade. How can they be so callous?

"You expect anyone with power to care, Lito? Get real. We come from the same place. You know how this works just as well as I do.

Everyone with money knows what everyone else with money is doing, and they *don't care* because they can afford not to."

"Then we show it to people like us," I argue, surprised by how fierce I sound. "We show it to people who understand what it is to suffer."

Noa shakes their head. "Imagine your mama watching what you want to show her. Imagine your daddy. Imagine what they'll say, because it's what every one of those people on the bottom levels of Cytherea will say." Their tone takes on a sinister hiss. "'At least I'm not a fucking Aster.'"

I'm struck silent by their words, powerful as a punch. They aren't wrong, sadly.

"You want to believe people will stand up to val Akira and his lot, when they're the ones who make them youthful, make them pretty?" They gesture to their face, to their prosthetic eye. "Who put them back together when they're on the verge of death and falling apart?" Again they shake their head, this time almost sadly. "They'd rather bleed every Aster dry—everyone with a *sol* surname—than give up even a little of that power."

"Then why are you fighting for them?" I ask, the exact same question I asked myself not too long ago on Ceres.

"Because I *have* to!" Noa screeches. "Because I have a family on Cytherea. I'm one of four children, Lito—*four kids*, and my mama is gone and my daddy can't work, so I have to be the one to help them because I'm the only one who can. Because if you want to change things, you have to *become* one of the powerful people, not piss them off. Sure, maybe they'll never forget where I'm from, never *let me* forget, but I can work my way up one level at a time with this sword."

"I used to believe that," I say softly. "But I can't any longer." My voice grows stronger until it echoes throughout the hub. "There are good people out there who will see what's happening and try to change things. People who know what it is to suffer—or even people who *don't* know what suffering is, but are empathetic enough not to want others to know it either."

I deactivate my gravboots and kick myself down to the floor behind Noa. They spin and brandish their blade at me.

"I don't want to go through life believing no one cares, because that's how a world becomes cold. That's how people harden their hearts to the suffering of others." I take out my mercurial blade and look at the hilt. No, not *my* mercurial blade, because mine is broken, and this is one I took from a duelist who was just doing his job.

"Come on!" Noa shouts, beckoning me forward with their blade. "Are you going to fight me or not?"

How long has it been? Fifteen minutes? Twenty? The Icarii ships are coming, and I don't have time to fight. They might already be here. If I could check the screen, I would know for sure. But the only thing I can see is what I pulled up before I launched myself toward the ceiling.

"I already have," I tell Noa, and I gesture toward the console with my blade. "And I've already won."

"What?" Noa snarls.

I nod toward the console, toward one screen in particular. They look over their shoulder, and I take a slow step back to the doorway.

UPLOAD COMPLETE, the screen reads. And beside it, a camera pointed toward Noa, taking in the rest of the room. A little red light, blinking, blinking. Recording.

Sending everything across the stars to every open Icarii channel.

And while I know some will try to suppress what I have sent, others will see. Will hear. And will do something about it, because they don't live in a cold world. Not yet.

"NO!" Noa's scream is primal, released from a part of them that faced death and lived. They spin toward me with their blade raised, but, with gravboots off, I kick myself into the hallway. They rush at me, heels clanking against the metal flooring, and I punch the screen beside the door. It closes with a bang. The thud tells me Noa hit the other side.

Before Noa can free themselves, I'm frantically tapping at the screen, instructing the door to put the communications room in lockdown. It'll take Noa some time to request that the basic AI in charge of the station scan the room, find proof that there's no break in the shielding, and open up again. By that time, I should be long gone—

A mercurial blade slashes through the door, rending metal with a teeth-grinding rip.

Mierda! Or, Noa could do *that*.

I kick myself down the hallway and back toward the dock as Noa screams after me and their blade punctures the door again and again.

"I'll kill you, Lito!" they screech, their threat echoing through the station. "I'll kill your whole family!"

I'm approaching the docks when I hear the thumping of boots headed in my direction. My chest so tight I can scarcely breathe, I duck into a nearby room. I can see from the reflection on the metal floor that the two figures are dressed in black and holding glowing blades. Obviously duelists. Each moves forward, carefully checking their surroundings. It's only a matter of time before they peer into my room—

"Litoooo!" Noa howls, and the two duelists break into a run toward the communications room, perhaps believing Noa has cornered me there. I never thought I'd be so happy to have someone curse my name.

I wait for the noise of their boots to fade before slipping out of the room and resuming my retreat. The appearance of the additional duelists bothers me for several reasons. Did they come with Noa, or did they just arrive? And if they just arrived, how many other duelists are here?

As soon as I reach the docks, I know the Icarii who followed from Vesta have caught up with me. While I didn't notice the little pod at the far end of the dock, there's no missing the ship that's parked next to mine, almost identical in its smooth black shape.

No matter, there's no one guarding my *Nyx*. I head toward the airlock—

"Lito—"

I stop at my name, not because someone is calling me but because I recognize the voice. *Her* voice. It sends a tremor through my entire body. I've always found it musical, but now I've never wished to hear it less.

"Lucinia!"

"Lito—" My name again, half swallowed. Coming from the Icarii ship beside mine.

I don't think. I *can't* think. I picture her cuffed and bruised, beaten by the Icarii who found her.

What is she doing here? Why did she follow me? But of course, she came to help me, exactly why she got involved with the Asters and stole Val Akira Labs data in the first place.

I come to the ship's ramp, my heart pounding so loudly I hear it in my head. She's inside the hold.

"Lito hasn't contacted me at all," she says to someone, and I can hear a ripple of fear beneath her put-on confidence. "I haven't spoken to him since he left Venus."

She's bait in a trap, every part of me screams, but I silence it with a single question: *What else am I supposed to do?* There's no way I'll willingly leave her with the Icarii. I'd walk into a thousand traps for Lucinia.

"Lito—" she says again, and I rush to her.

I hold my mercurial blade high as I enter the hold, but I don't immediately see anyone—not Lucinia or her captor.

Then Luce cries out for me again.

"Lito—"

But I still don't see her.

And her voice, a phantom recording, plays on: "Lito hasn't contacted me at all. I haven't spoken to him since he left Venus."

Oh.

Strong arms clamp around me from behind, and a hand presses something over my mouth. The air sickly sweet, I thrust my elbows back into the body of my attacker, but my strike is repelled by a shield exactly like my own.

"Don't worry, Lito," a familiar voice, deep and crackling, mutters into my ear.

"Beron—" I gasp.

"Just relax," High Commander Beron val Bellator whispers to me, and while my shield ripples as it protects my body, it can't filter the particles in the air, and I *have to breathe—*

My vision darkens at the corners, my body growing sluggish and heavy. I know I'm slipping away when I can no longer struggle, when all my strength burns up and turns to ashes.

Lucinia was never here, yet I cry for her nonetheless—or I try to. "Lu . . . ci . . ." My tongue is too fat in my mouth, and drool drips down my chin as Beron lowers me to the floor. I can't move, can't even find the *will* to move—

"Welcome home, Lito," Beron says as the darkness swallows me. "We have great plans for you."

CHAPTER 31

ASTRID

I went to see Aunt Tamar last night. She told me things . . . things I'm afraid to write. When I returned to my room, something was different, like someone had been there. Nothing was moved and I couldn't find any bugs, but I swear, it *felt* different. I'm probably just being paranoid.

From the diary of Eden

Two days later, Lily bursts into my room as if the Temple is on fire. Eden is not on her heels, and I do not expect her to follow.

Since the morning she held me down, I have not seen her. I do not call for her. When I think of her, all I can hear is the bile in her tone: *You* disgust *me.*

"What is it?" I ask, but Lily, breathing heavily, is unable to answer. I usher her to the chaise lounge and pour her a glass of water. She drinks deeply as my heart rages against my breastbone.

When Lily finally speaks, it is nothing that I expect. "Aunt Marshae is making moves," she says.

I cannot answer.

"There are all these rumors—men questioning Cousins, arrests being made, bribes—and I thought they were just that: rumors. But then Aunt Marshae came to Aunt Margaret and offered a lot of money to secure her vote against you." Her hands shake on the empty glass. "I have no doubt that she's made the same offer to others of the Agora."

"She's trying to buy their votes . . ."

Lily's eyes harden. "She's changing the players on the board."

The spot between my shoulder blades where I'd implanted and then removed Nat's ID itches. We could do as Eden asked us to—take the evidence we gathered before the Agora; however, that will lead to Aunt Sapphira and Aunt Genette's arrests. I will lose their votes.

"If we give the evidence to the Agora freely, it might sway other Aunts to my cause," I say, tapping a finger against my lips. "But there's no guarantee of that." And if Aunt Marshae were to use her power in the Order of Cassiopeia to replace Aunt Sapphira and Aunt Genette with pawns loyal to her? I would *never* become the Mother.

I cannot take that risk. Not after coming so far. If Aunt Marshae buys my votes from beneath me and I do not achieve majority support, what will happen to Aunt Genette and Aunt Sapphira? Will someone else ensure they are brought to justice and the girls at the brothel cared for? And what of the children at Matron Thorne's orphanage?

No, I *must* become the Mother.

"Have Aunt Margaret call for the Agora to be assembled," I instruct Lily. "You are right that we should move before Aunt Marshae changes the board, but let us instead call for a vote to make me the Mother."

"Are you sure, Astrid?" Lily asks, voice soft.

But I am not soft. "Yes." With Aunt Margaret, Aunt Genette, and Aunt Sapphira's votes assured, I need only one more supporter, and I feel that between Aunt Delilah and Aunt Tamar, who both despise Aunt Marshae, I will have it. Of Aunt Salomiya I know nothing, but she is only one woman.

A gamble. Yes, it all comes down to a risky gamble, but one I have worked toward with marked cards in my favor. "Have Aunt Margaret put my name before them for a vote today."

I STAND BEFORE the mirror, the bruising of my face hidden under a layer of cosmetics. I barely recognize the woman who looks back. My face is hollow from lack of sleep, my cheekbones sharp precipices. The bags beneath my eyes are impossible to fully hide but lend me a fierce seriousness. My hair is long, and from my lack of care for it, the gold has lost its shimmer and become steely pale. These things would not suit me on a ship, but, as the Mother, will make me striking. Mine is a dark beauty, cold winter given bones and skin.

I imagine myself in a white dress, not the gray I wear. My symbol, the broken manacles from Ceres, will remain. I will be the Unchained, the woman who guided Ceres to prosperity despite the Leander Incident—perhaps even the Sister who brokered a peace between the Geans and Icarii—and I will be loved by the righteous and feared by the unjust.

When I leave my room, I march like a soldier—no, like a captain on her ship. I exit the guest quarters and glide into the courtyard, past *Victory* with wings outstretched, and stop outside the Agora's chambers. An Aunt holds up a hand, barring my entry, until another slips through the wooden doors and motions for me to follow. I brush past them both.

The stone chamber is cold and silent, more like a mausoleum than a court of justice. I take my place in the center of the pit and immediately turn to Aunt Marshae to begin.

But what I see chills me. Aunt Marshae, her face always open for those who dare to read it, is pleased. *Like when she killed Paola*, I realize.

Aunt Delilah and Aunt Tamar sit in their respective places, undisturbed by the change in the landscape, but Aunt Salomiya, with her expressive face, and Aunt Margaret, who seems as if she has not met sleep for many days, wear twin looks of concern.

Of Aunt Sapphira and Aunt Genette there are no signs. Their high marble chairs loom above me, empty.

A sickening feeling slithers low in my belly as Aunt Marshae begins the session. "Veritas iustitia ad astra." *Truth and justice to the stars.*

"First Sister of Ceres," Aunt Marshae says, her voice echoing, "Aunt Margaret has put your name before us. Have you come, asking to be confirmed as the next Mother?"

I choose my words carefully before I speak, arranging my features into a neutral blankness. "I do, yet I do not see the full Agora assembled." I gesture to Aunt Sapphira's and Aunt Genette's chairs.

Aunt Marshae's smile never slips. "A set of unfortunate circumstances, I assure you. Information came to light that they were both involved in activities considered criminal."

The beast behind my ribs wraps around my heart.

"They have been arrested, pending trial. If they are found innocent of the charges, they will be returned to their positions among us. But until then . . ." Until then, they are gone. Aunt Marshae smiles down at me as if saying *your move.*

All the blackmail I have accumulated is worth nothing; I know Aunt Genette and Aunt Sapphira are guilty, and the Agora will find them so. They will not be returned to the Agora, and I will be unable to count on their backing.

But the call for the vote has already been made and the Agora assembled. I look around at the remaining Aunts. Can they even confirm me as Mother if the full Agora is not in session? If not, why are we here?

I dip my head as if being diplomatic, even as I wish to curse and spit at Aunt Marshae. "If I may, I suggest we reconvene at a later opportunity when the Order of Leo and the Order of Norma have chosen new representatives for the Agora." It physically pains me to say the words, not knowing what this means for the girls at the brothel or at Matron Thorne's orphanage.

I know I have misstepped when I see Aunt Marshae shaking her head. "I'm sorry, First Sister of Ceres, but this is no longer about your becoming the Mother. The Agora agreed to meet as it is because we have questions for you."

That beast wrapped around my heart squeezes. I do my best to breathe deeply, though it sends a sharp pain straight to my head.

"Please call the witnesses," Aunt Marshae says, and an Aunt opens one of the side doors, admitting four people.

At the sight of them, I lose the ability to inhale. My head spins, and a high-pitched ringing starts in my ears.

At the forefront is a girl. I recognize her from Matron Thorne's. Amalia—yes, that was her name. *Here,* in the charcoal dress of a Little Sister.

No, no . . . I never wanted this for you. My eyes burn.

Then I see the three people following Amalia, just a Little Sister doing her duty. The first is a man in a cobalt silk suit with the teardrop of the Aquae Hotel on his breast. One is Nat, so clean I almost do not recognize her. And the third is a guard from the brothel. *Home again, home again, jiggity jig,* he said, shoving me in through the doors.

Bile burns its way up my throat and sizzles in my mouth. I fear I will spit poison if I speak at all.

"We have questions regarding your personal investigation into Aunt Genette and Aunt Sapphira," Aunt Marshae is saying, but the ringing grows louder and louder until I can barely make out her words.

I catch mere snippets.

"—well meant but foolish—" Aunt Marshae judges.

The man from the Aquae Hotel takes the stand first.

"—spoke with Aunt Sapphira, a well-known patron, like she was not a Sister—"

Then Nat, who fidgets the entire time.

"—offered me money to speak against Aunt Sapphira—"

The brothel guard is the last.

"—work at the Order of Norma's Rehabilitation Center, and she attacked my colleague with a knife—"

Liars. They're liars. *All of them are liars.* Whether they were paid by Aunt Marshae to bear false witness against me, or Eden served me to them trussed and dressed for the table, I do not know. Maybe Nat was even promised something that I could not give her—drugs or protection for the other brothel girls. All I know is that Aunt Marshae has played her game well. I was seen visiting the Aquae Hotel. I *can* speak, and *have* spoken to the brothel girls, who are outside of the Sisterhood. And who knows what cameras were at the brothel—my video evidence was destroyed, but perhaps they have proof of me attacking that man with a knife.

The ringing reaches a crescendo until I can hear nothing else. My breathing comes so quickly, my vision has narrowed to a singular sight: Aunt Marshae, her lips moving, her smile never wavering.

My veins boil. My eyes burn. My hands become fists. I taste blood on my tongue. *You're a wildfire, Astrid.* Sweat pours down my face, pools in the small of my back. In the shadows, Ringer prowls.

"You should have killed them all, little sister." His is the only voice I can hear, alongside Eden's.

A wildfire. Burn yourself. No one will be around to save you.

Someone follows Ringer, stalking in his wake. A vision that resolves in white and red. Mother Isabel III with a bullet hole in her forehead. Rope burns at her neck. A frantic smile on her face at her bitter end.

"First Sister . . . First Sister . . . First Sister . . ."

The words come to me through thick glass, muffled and distant.

"First Sister!"

And then Lily is at my side, holding me by my shoulders. "Breathe, Astrid," she whispers. "Breathe."

I try. I do.

Suck in one breath. Hold it. Let it out. My chest is so tight, the beast wrapped around my heart. My body wants to give up. Wants this to be the end—my end.

But slowly, the world comes back into focus. The blackness fades. Ringer disappears, along with the Mother. Lily holds me tightly, keeping me upright. The Agora watches, faces blank.

"Do you have anything to say for yourself, First Sister of Ceres?" Aunt Marshae repeats, and I realize this is what she's been saying for a while now.

All I can manage is a weak shake of my head. Where is the voice I fought so hard for? Gone. Useless. It doesn't matter what I have done or what I want; the chains will always remain, unbroken.

"I call for a vote." Aunt Marshae looks to the Aunts at her side.

"Seconded," Aunt Salomiya says weakly.

"All those in favor of removing the First Sister of Ceres, who has conducted secretive investigations apart from the Agora and betrayed the most basic tenets of the Sisterhood, from the position which she currently holds . . ." Aunt Marshae's words are a knife between my ribs; she will bar me from becoming the next Mother and remove me from my position of power on Ceres in one vote. "I vote yes."

"Yes," Aunt Salomiya says.

"Yes," Aunt Delilah says, and her words twist Aunt Marshae's knife. I did not know I could hurt any more than I already do . . .

"Yes," Aunt Margaret agrees, shaking her head sadly. It is her vote that brings tears to my eyes, but she has been outplayed and cannot openly disagree now.

The last is Aunt Tamar. She does not bend under the gazes of her fellow Aunts, simply looks at me with burnished golden eyes. "No," she says.

Surprising . . . did Eden have something to do with this, being from Aunt Tamar's Order? And yet . . . it does not matter.

The majority have spoken.

I have lost everything.

"You are hereby stripped of the title of First Sister of Ceres," Aunt Marshae says, looming ten feet tall at her proclamation. With the same smirk she wore when she killed Paola, she adds the sentence that threatens to send me crashing to the floor. "You are not, nor will you ever be, the Mother of the Sisterhood."

A bubble of laughter works its way up my throat. My teeth are chattering, though I am not cold. "Wh-where will I g-go from h-he-here?"

Aunt Marshae looks around the room as if her fellow Aunts could possibly read her mind. But no, she has planned this so thoroughly, only she knows the answer. "Perhaps you will be useful as a Sister on a ship once again," she says, but I hear the words she *doesn't* say: *Silent. Obedient. A piece of meat in a bed.*

The other Aunts do not contradict her.

"You're dismissed." Aunt Marshae waves me away, but when Lily moves to help me out of the room, Aunt Marshae barks at her. "Not you," she says, pointing at Lily. "You stay. The Agora will have words with you next."

Lily looks up at me in fear, eyes red and swollen. Releases me slowly. Blinks several times, and I do not even have the strength to squeeze her hand in solidarity.

It is over. It is all over.

I stumble from the room, the shivering slowly subsiding. The dread gives way to black resignation.

THE TEMPLE THAT I have known since I was a child is unfamiliar to me. The shadows pool differently. The statues in the courtyard, beckoning with canted hips and rounded breasts, look murderous, sirens singing the lost to their deaths.

Everything is a haze. What happened in the Agora's chamber is like a nightmare that clings to me in my waking hours. But it happened. I know it did, even if part of me wishes to disbelieve it.

What are they subjecting Lily to? I did not wait to find out. Soon they will drag me away from Mars on a ship, bound for my next assignment. Will I become a Cousin, someone's pitiful servant? Or an unnamed Sister again, sleeping in an overcrowded room on a small bunk, forced into a chapel where my mind will slip away from me as the soldiers use my body again and again? Will I drag Eden back into that pit with me?

Or did she betray me? Is that how they found and used Nat against me?

I reach a door, my hand falling to rest on the handle. It is not my door; it is Eden's. Without thinking, I sought her out. To prove what I already fear? To tell her what she does not know?

She will not have heard yet. Will not know that I am not enough. Will not know that everything I hoped for—everything we planned for—is dashed on the rocks of my own weakness.

You disgust *me.*

Hiro should have chosen someone else in my place—someone like

Eden, who counseled me against resorting to Lily's blackmail, who would have waited and worked with the Agora.

I knock on her door. No answer. I knock again, louder and more insistent. The door opens a crack, not latched properly.

There is something wrong here. Something in the slant of the shadows. Something in the stale air, the sour smell. I push the door open wider and

the world

tumbles down

around me.

Eden. Naked. Hanging from the ceiling. A noose around her neck.

You're a wildfire, Astrid, and you burn everything and everyone around you.

I fall to my knees at the altar of Eden's death.

WHEN I FINALLY pull my eyes away from Eden—minutes or hours later, I do not know—it is a small slip of paper that I notice on the settee. I crawl toward it on my hands and knees, a beggar searching for something—*anything*—that will answer the mystery of her death.

It is a soft pastel purple, incongruous with the body hanging above. *First Sister of Ceres*, it begins in a flowery handwriting, and already my mind recoils from the formality, from the *wrongness* of the letter.

> *First Sister of Ceres,*
>
> *I can no longer live with the shame of what we have done, of the lies we have told and the false hope we have given to those we promised voices. We were wrong to ever do these things. Somewhere along the way, I lost my path, and you have lost yours as well. I hope in my death, you find yours again.*
>
> *Second Sister of Ceres*

No names. Words that are not hers. Sentiments that make no sense except to an outsider. Handwriting that does not match Eden's messy scrawl.

Did the person who penned this letter expect me to believe Eden wrote it herself?

I fold the paper in half, refusing to look at it further, only to spot something on the back. Different handwriting, but still not Eden's, much smaller and somewhat smudged.

May you bloom in Her garden as She commands.

My entire world goes white as I picture a woman's sharp-nailed hands. The end of a scarf. The knife of a smirk.

MY LEGS ARE numb. I do not know where my feet carry me. My hands form into fists at my side, nails digging into my palms, before releasing. Squeeze and release. Squeeze and release. My fingers ache to grasp something, to tear it into shreds. I want to destroy something beautiful.

My room. I reach it and find it empty. But who else would I find here when Eden is—

Eden is . . .

I scream and seize the item closest to me—a lamp—and send it crashing to the floor. Two chairs—a matching set—come next, thrown against the wall and shattering in splinters of wood. A round table—an antique from Earth—follows, too heavy to throw far, but cracking through the center as it hits the floor.

Not enough. It is not enough.

I do not look, just grab. A vase, now shards of painted glass. A plate and cup with the remnants of my breakfast. Small pots of expensive cosmetics. I ball up my fist and punch through the vanity mirror. Slam bleeding knuckles through the tabletop. Fling it out of my way. Fall upon the bedding, nails digging, feathers spattered with red floating with the grace of bloody-footed dancers.

I lose myself in the violence. Lose myself in the aching of my hands, my wrists, the glass deepening already open cuts. My blood falls in fat drops to the floor, mapping a trail of my destruction. Dyeing my gray dress red.

I stop at the chaise lounge that Lily, Eden, and I shared, the place we sat as we discussed the Sisterhood's future. *Our* future. When Eden counseled patience.

I did not listen to her, and now Eden does not have a future.

I grab the legs of the lounge, all I can manage to lift, and flip it onto its side. As it balances precariously, I shove it with all my strength, and with gravity's pull, it slams into the window that looks out over the Temple courtyard.

A rain of stained glass falls around me. I feel none of it.

I take a step back into my room, listening to the music of glass crunching beneath my boots. A large shard, daggerlike, reflects a sliver of my face back up at me, hollow-eyed and frenzied. The glass is in my hand before I realize it, Ringer's voice whispering through time.

She took a knife, and cut her face like so, he had said of his sister, the *real* Astrid, trailing his fingers from forehead to chin on both sides. I put the glass to my cheek, daring myself to press it harder.

Behind me, a stifled gasp. Someone is at the door. Two someones, I see as I look into the mirror shard so close to my eye.

Just children. Little Sisters, with wide eyes and hands clutched to their mouths in horror. They make me think of Amalia, and the pain doubles.

Run, I want to tell them. *Run, and do not stop until you are far away from here!* But all that comes out is a scream as I turn toward them, a wordless, animal cry, and they flee before me, terrified at my madness.

They do not understand. How could they? They are young and foolish, and while they may believe they have each other now, I know the truth: the Sisterhood will always find a way to tear them apart, just as they have severed me from everyone I have ever grown close to.

But the way they fled hand in hand makes me think of Eden, of how she is still hanging naked from the ceiling in her room. I should take her down. Dress her. Give her some dignity, when the Sisterhood has left her none. I drop the glass shard.

I start back to her room, but pause in the stone pavilion of statues between buildings. The previous Mother's monument must be nearing completion, for the empty plinth now has a bag of tools and a neatly folded tarp beside it. I can still picture Eden here, eyes cast up with hope. A hope that would never pay off.

I was never meant to build anything in the Sisterhood, I realize, thinking of Hiro and Ceres and their decision, their manipulation, to put me in charge. *I was only ever meant to destroy.*

Then destroy I shall.

I try to pick up the bag of tools, but it is too heavy and I cannot lift it. Instead I open it and sift through the items until I find something that matches how I feel, something made for destruction. A sledgehammer.

The iron head is so cumbersome, I am forced to drag it behind me as I walk between Mothers ancient and modern to the heart of the pavilion. When I come before the statue now, I am not a woman begging, not a girl wishing to press my hand to her plaque and pray for her blessings.

I don't give a shit about her now.

Making my way up the choppy pedestal with the hammer is difficult work, but the struggle only serves to inflame my anger more. I leave red handprints as I climb, the hammer pinging against the marble base, until I stand triumphant at *Victory*'s side.

She is taller than me, but defenseless because she has no arms. Emotionless because she has no face. A dissected woman, a torso with breasts and the barest hint of sex, a leg emerging beneath billowing skirts, a dip in her abdomen of a navel.

This is the truth of *Victory*: if a woman wants to win, she must give and give and give of herself until there is nothing left of her.

I dig my nails into the hammer's wooden shaft. Brace myself as I lift the heavy object. And swing like Death with his scythe.

The hammer strikes her in the chest. A crack forms down her center. I swing again. And again. More cracks join the first. Pieces begin to fall. The air becomes choked with grit. A wing takes flight for precious seconds before crashing to the ground below. And though the muscles of my shoulders and arms protest, I swing until I am laughing and the tears run freely, mingling with dust and hardening on my cheeks.

I am not finished when I am exhausted; I am finished when she lies in pieces. The chunks are hardly recognizable. Perhaps there is a piece of fabric here, the metal bracket that braced her wings there, but she is *Victory* no longer, only a monument to defeat.

"Astrid!"

Lily's voice is a tether tossed from a ship to where I float adrift in the black of space. I seize on to it, and it pulls me from the abyss and my single-minded focus on *Victory*, lets the rest of the world filter back in. I drop the sledgehammer and stumble over the marble pieces toward her.

"We have to take Eden down. You have to help me."

She reaches for my hands, but I do not let her have them. "Goddess, Astrid . . . What have you done?"

"Help me," I say again, because I do not care about anything but this.

Lily searches my hands, my dress, my face with her big doe eyes, but finally nods. "Okay, Astrid. Let's go."

LILY STARTS TO lead me, but I know the way. I walk alongside her in silence. When we arrive, I allow Lily to be the one to push open the door to Eden's room. This time the sight does not shock me. It is exactly as I left it, seared into my mind. I will remember it forever.

Lily gasps, then lets out a wavering sob that masquerades as a sigh. She enters the room like it is hallowed space, footsteps light and considerate. She takes in Eden first, and I can see the pale body as a reflection in Lily's dark eyes. When her gaze falls to the letter on the settee, she hesitates before picking it up.

"Is that—?"

"Read it."

Lily picks it up by its corner using only thumb and forefinger. Her eyes scan the words before her expression twists. She too puts it back where she found it.

"That's not from Eden, is it?"

"No."

Lily looks toward a chair longingly, as if she wishes to sit, but instead she drags it toward Eden's body. Hauls herself on top of it. Looks down at me expectantly. "Come on, Astrid," she says softly, broken.

I grab a pair of scissors from Eden's small desk before selecting another chair and joining Lily. Our silent work becomes perfunctory. If Lily feels anything, she does not let it show on her face. I use the scissors to cut through the rope, and the two of us struggle with Eden's weight as first I and then Lily get down from the chairs and drop Eden to the carpet.

It is not graceful. It is not beautiful. Death never is. The body that used to be Eden is cold and stiff. I feel like these actions should hurt me more, but I am empty after all I have done to drain the rage, and I feel nothing.

I do not look at Eden's face, not until she is lying on the floor. Then I allow myself one last glance at her before Lily carries over white sheets from the bed and we begin to wrap her. When we finish, she is draped in such a way that she could be just another one of the marble statues outside.

We sit beside Eden, our silence spooling out like shadows at sundown. Cousins will come for Eden's body eventually, once we inform someone of her death. Aunt Marshae, the one behind this, would not have bothered; she would want us to suffer in every way possible.

When Lily finally speaks, it is not about Eden; I cannot tell her how thankful I am for that small kindness. "I don't know what they're going to do to you, Astrid, now that you've . . ." She does not finish, but I know what she means to say: now that I have destroyed so many of their precious belongings.

"At best, they would assign me to a starship, and I cannot . . ." My voice wavers as my throat goes dry. "I cannot go through that again."

"I don't know if they'll even make you a Cousin now."

"I doubt it. They will think I am unstable." Somehow admitting it aloud makes me feel better.

Lily's eyebrows furrow. The fear she wore on her face at the brothel returns.

"I am not unstable." I meet her eyes without wavering. "I'm fucking pissed off."

Lily just shakes her head. "Let me bandage your hands."

With the sheets wrapping Eden and no other material in reach, she takes the scissors to the end of her skirt, cutting thin strips for bandages. I watch the careful ministrations of long fingers dotted with white scales.

"What did the Agora tell you?" I ask.

"Hmm?" She does not look up from her work. "Oh, nothing. A reminder to play by their rules . . . Now give me your hands."

I offer them to her, palms up. She pulls a salve from her pockets, most likely something for her own skin, and tends to my hands as gently as she did Eden.

"What are you going to do, Astrid?" she whispers as she ties off the last bandage.

"I tried, Lily . . . I tried to change things from the inside," I say, though it does not answer her question. What am I supposed to do *now*?

I look at Eden beside us. What would she tell me to do? To wait and see what the Agora plans for me? To flee before they can take me?

I want to change things, she said on Ceres, but Eden cannot tell me anything now because she is dead.

"It was always going to come to this, little sister," Ringer says, and behind Lily, I can see him appear, a blur at first that gains weight as the shadows cling to him. As he becomes real, at least to me. "Even if you had done as Eden asked you to, Aunt Marshae would never have allowed you to become the Mother."

Every part of me knows that he is right. That Aunt Marshae, willing to lie, to blackmail, to kill, would always come out on top. Unless I work from outside the Sisterhood.

If there is one thing I have learned in this life, it's that there is no going back. There is only forward. A verse comes to me, unbidden.

Nature may be bent by mankind, but never broken. What is plucked may yet bloom. What is burned may yet nourish. What lies fallow may yet grow. Meditations 1:12–13.

I was only ever meant to destroy.

"I am going to kill Aunt Marshae," I say, and there is a current of steel running through my words.

The fear returns to Lily's face for but a moment—remembering the man at the brothel?—before it disappears. "I can't help you any longer, Astrid," she says sadly. "I won't repeat what you've told me, but I have to consider my own future in the Sisterhood."

I expect to feel anger at her words, or perhaps disappointment, but I feel nothing at all. I understand her. I would even do what she is doing, were our positions reversed.

She pushes herself to her feet, and her shadow falls over me where I sit with Eden. "Aunt Marshae and I are to return to Ceres on the *Juno* tomorrow," she says, and the words twist like a knife in my back. But then I think, as she moves to the door, that she is offering me one last piece of help after all.

"Goodbye, Astrid," she says.

"Goodbye, Lily," I return.

And then she leaves me alone with Eden's body.

CHAPTER 32

LUCE

FLAGGED: When one takes in the whole of the piece, the canvas appears to be a mess of overlapping blues and reds, mixing into purple where they meet, seemingly without care. But when the viewer focuses on one color or the other, the artist's detailed planning becomes apparent. When looking solely at the red, a laughing figure appears. At the blue, a different sitter is seen, pensive and thoughtful. NOTE: Subjects are Lito sol Lucius and Hiro val Akira.

Description of *Martyr*, painting by Lucinia sol Lucius

B ecause of the blockade, it takes us much longer than planned to arrive. It's evening by the time we land on Vesta, and my first impression is that it's not a beautiful place but a natural one. Stone pathways lead us from the metal hangar into rocky tunnels beneath the surface of the asteroid. The sound of running water is a constant song, a soothing white noise that seeks to calm my restlessness, and with the crew around me, Lotus in the lead and Castor at my side, it somewhat succeeds.

When we reach the heart of Vesta, my opinion radically changes. The branching tunnels, while still cave-like, widen enough for us to walk as a group. Plant life and fungi appear, carefully cultivated to climb the walls and hang from the ceiling. Each leaf has delicate, glowing green veins. Every flower shimmers in pink, red, or blue. Fat toadstools grow close to the ground, clustered and reaching for the light above. The air is warm and fragrant, caressing me with an artificial wind. It feels more like a greenhouse than a mine.

"It's beautiful," I whisper, and the entire crew seems pleased with my compliment.

I expect us to come across other Asters, for the crew's families or friends to welcome them home, but, as if our presence has sent off a signal, we encounter no one. It would seem like a ghost town if not for the obviously cared-for vegetation. When we do finally come to a stop, we're not in a house or barracks—though I'm not sure what a house would look like down here—we're in a large room, cavern-like in size only. The natural unevenness of the floor present in the rest of Vesta has been tamed here. The ground is covered with natural slabs of stone cobbled into spiral patterns, soft moss filling the gaps between bricks. The center opens to a trickling abstract fountain of stacked blocks, and running along one side is a platform made of stone, raised to look down on the rest of the room.

I swallow a gasp at sudden movement in the corner of my eye, but calm a moment later. Three Asters move from the shadows to the edge of the platform. Each wears a white tunic and brown, leathery trousers and boots. Around their shoulders are blue half cloaks. They're the oldest Asters I've ever seen, looking simultaneously like welcoming grandparents and ancient statues hewn of stone.

The foremost among them makes a hand gesture I don't recognize, and the crew steps to the edge of the platform. "Mother Anemone," Lotus says, hugging the old woman around her waist. She kisses Lotus's brow before guiding her to the next in line. Lotus repeats the same steps twice more. "Father Cedar. Nother Rue." The rest of the crew follow Lotus's example, starting with Anemone—all except Castor, who stands at my side with his arms crossed tightly over his chest.

Anemone looks at Castor, and something silent passes between the two of them—the pheromones, I'm sure. But it's impossible for me to read Anemone's body language or facial expressions; unlike the Asters who have lived on Cytherea, Anemone doesn't bother to express herself using any Icarii norms.

"You're not my fucking mom," Castor says at last. The break from the oppressive silence startles me.

Anemone's pupils narrow. "But we are the Elders, and that alone is deserving of your respect."

Castor shrugs.

When it's clear he's not going to budge, Anemone turns her gaze toward me. "We must discuss what we will do with her," she begins.

Father Cedar jumps in, just as expressionless. "We did not invite her here. We did not welcome her. And look what happened when we welcomed the last Icarii. We should decide whether she will be imprisoned or cast out."

"No!" Castor snaps, taking one step closer to the platform, and I reach for his biceps, knowing his posturing will only hurt my chances.

"If I may, Elders," Lotus says, stepping in front of Castor. Now that the greeting is over, Lotus approaches them more like one would a captain than a parent. "Lucinia sol Lucius is part of our crew."

This statement is met with more silence, and I wish now, more than ever, that I could understand the Asters' pheromones.

"Can I say something?" I ask. Castor bristles at my side, as if daring them to stop me. I don't know what's between them, but it's nothing good.

Anemone gestures assent. The gaze of the Elders is a heavy thing.

"I came to Vesta to help," I say. "That's all I've wanted to do. When Castor told me why he needed the data from Val Akira Labs, I knew I had to do what I could to get it." I fight the urge to look at Castor, knowing he's not going to like the next thing I say. "When we approached Vesta, we knew there would be no leaving, and still, we chose to land—all of us, me included—instead of going after Lito. So I may not be welcome here, or trusted here—and I understand that, I can't expect you to trust an Icarii after everything you've suffered—but I hope you don't take that out on the others." My gaze wanders to Lotus, Violet, Poppy, and Sage briefly. "Castor has brought the data for you to use, and if you need to lock me up because you don't know me . . ." I sigh, resigning myself to their decision, even if they decide on casting me out. "Do what you need to do, because the Icarii camped outside of Vesta are far more important, and you can't afford to be divided right now."

Again the room plunges into silence, the only sound the trickling of the fountain behind us. Anemone looks at Cedar and Rue, and while I can't understand them, I *see* something passing between them, their expressions changing in an almost imperceptible way. A hand brushes against mine, and I grab it. I'm momentarily surprised to find it's Lotus's and not Castor's, but the comfort is welcome.

"We have decided," Anemone says, turning back to our group. "Lucinia sol Lucius is part of your crew. That makes her part of ours."

The tension washes away from the bodies surrounding me, and I release a shuddering breath.

But Anemone is not finished. "There are many things you will not understand about us, Lucinia sol Lucius," she continues, "but we hope you learn quickly. Here is your first lesson: The Icarii see their families as separate units, never acknowledging that they are part of a whole. We, however, are *one* family, and we do not betray our family."

I don't know what to say to that, whether it's a threat or merely good advice. I settle on saying something safe. "Thank you, Elder."

"You're free to find yourselves empty beds," Anemone says, making a gesture similar to waving us away. Dismissing us, most likely. "And Castor . . ." He looks up at his name. "Hemlock is here and would welcome your counsel."

WE DON'T MAKE it far in the glowing tunnels before we're forced to stop. Now that the Elders have welcomed us—me, I mean—other Asters emerge from wherever they had been hiding and greet us with high spirits. They cluster around my friends, hugging and pressing foreheads together, and while the young members of the crew disappear into frantic conversations I can't follow in a language I don't understand, Lotus waves me over to her group. "These are my partners," she says, introducing three others. "While I was on Cytherea, we received wonderful news."

One leans into Lotus, deep purple cheeks darker with excited color. "We've been approved to pass on our genetic material," they blurt out.

I don't quite understand, and Lotus must be able to tell. "The four of us are having a child," she explains.

"Congratulations!" I say, knowing children tend to be a universal subject for celebration. The three partners preen at my happy smile. "Will this be your first?"

Lotus chuckles a bit pityingly while the others share looks of confusion. "Children are raised by everyone in the community, regardless of whether they share our genetic material or not, so we've had kids before. However, this one will be the first that combines all of our genetic material in the birthing vat."

Now that we're on the subject of children, I realize I don't see any in the crowd that has gathered around the crew. I wonder if it's because they're in a different location, or because I'm not quite welcome enough to see them yet.

"Speaking of family . . ." Lotus points with her chin to where Castor stands talking with the strangest Aster I've ever seen. "You should meet your boy's family."

I flush at her calling Castor *my boy*, but she's right that I want to meet Hemlock. After bidding Lotus and her partners farewell, I slip through the crowd, taking care not to step on any of the plants, and make my way toward Castor. Many Asters watch me with open curiosity, but I don't mind the staring; I know they're not the hostile eyes of the Icarii I left behind.

Instead, I think of everything I know about Hemlock. *The man who raised me*, Castor called him. Between his poor reaction to the Elders and his bond with Hemlock, I wonder if Castor is different from other Asters who are raised in a communal setting. The other thing I know about Hemlock sends a shiver down my spine: for the past thirty years, he's been amassing weapons and allies to fight the Icarii.

Hemlock notices me before Castor does. He cuts Castor off midsentence as he turns to me and offers his hand. "Ah, you must be Lucinia sol Lucius," he says, his voice a soft hiss.

From far away, I thought he was strange. Up close, I see he is ugly. Patches of hair are missing from his stringy white locks. His alabaster skin is lumpy and scarred, like a burn victim's. His eyes are black from corner to corner. Oddest of all, he's wearing a black velvet suit with a frilly cream shirt beneath, nothing like the leathery outfits the Vesta Asters wear and nothing like the current Icarii fashions.

"And you must be Castor's . . . Hemlock." I place my hand in his to shake, but instead, he dips his head and kisses the air over my knuckles.

"Enchanted," he says.

"It's nice to meet you." I'm not sure whether I'm supposed to kiss his hand or bow or what. This isn't a traditional greeting even in the Icarii sense. Along with his dress, it gives Hemlock the aura of a man out of time. "So you raised Castor?" I ask.

"There are important things we need to talk about—" Castor starts.

Hemlock cuts him off. "I did. I was responsible for him and his twin sister. You see, Pollux was ill from birth, which brought her to Ceres under my care, and—"

"Stop," Castor barks. I'm not sure whether he looks more like he wants to murder someone or die of embarrassment. "It's too much to explain right now. Just . . . Pollux couldn't stay on Vesta, and I didn't want to be here without her, so we both went to live on Ceres with Hemlock."

So his ill sister was sent away . . . that explains his dislike of the Elders, then. The Icarii in me wants to ask about Castor's mother or father—or, I suppose, the people who donated their genetic material to the twins—but after talking with Lotus and her partners, I know that's not how it works here. Hemlock raised him, so he is Castor's family.

"Well, well, well, what do we have here?" The voice is so strong and unaccented that I half expect to find an Icarii face when I turn to the speaker. Still, I'm surprised at the Aster who meets my gaze.

His facial expression is carefully honed into a welcoming smile. When I take his offered hand, he grips mine in a firm handshake. His skin is an icy blue with a delicate tracing of veins, his hair mere stubble of white against his scalp. And his eyes . . . thousand gods, his eyes are beautiful, a bright greenish blue.

I take back what I thought about Hemlock; this man is the strangest Aster I've ever seen.

"You're Lito's little sister," he says. "You look like him."

I can't help but flush with pride at the compliment; I've always liked when people could tell that Lito and I were related. "I'm Lucinia sol Lucius."

"Sorrel."

The name registers something in my memory, but it's only when Castor speaks that I fully remember.

"Harbinger." Castor steps to my side, a tight anxiety rolling off of him in waves. He's *nervous* about this. I remember what I overheard from Castor's call with Hemlock, how the Harbinger—Sorrel—wanted Hemlock's allies and weapons to fight the Icarii. I don't miss the sour look on Hemlock's face now, as Castor offers the Harbinger his hand. "I grew up with stories about the Black Hive Rebellion and your brilliant leadership."

For a moment, something painful ripples across Sorrel's face, but it passes just as quickly. "Please, call me Sorrel."

"I'm Castor, and if you ever need anything, don't hesitate to ask."

Sorrel's mouth curls into a smile that doesn't quite reach his eyes. "I'll remember that," he says, and I wonder, from the way Hemlock shifts, if he gets the same shiver down his spine that I do.

Despite his charisma and beauty, there's something slimy about Sorrel I can't quite put my finger on. As he moves away from us, it hits me all at once: he reminds me of Souji val Akira, wearing his mask of normalcy.

But if, as Hiro said, Souji is a monster beneath his mask . . . what is Sorrel hiding?

BECAUSE THE MEMBERS of Lotus's crew are all needed elsewhere, for the next few hours, I'm passed from hand to hand as I'm led on an extensive tour of Vesta. I get to see the gardens, the water processing plant, the habitation quarters—all bustling with activity as Asters prepare defenses in case the Icarii invade. It's only when the news breaks that a new transmission has come from the Icarii that I'm reunited with Castor.

"What's happening?" I ask, following the natural flow of Asters moving through the tunnels.

"Not sure," he says. "But we'll find out soon enough."

My head is spinning by the time we arrive back in the Elders' chamber. This time, it's not empty; the room is crowded with Asters holding various communications instruments, including a holoprojector that will display the message received from the Icarii. The Elders stand on the platform, though I can tell from the way they hold themselves tightly that they too are subject to the anxiety of the moment.

Castor leads me to where Hemlock stands. "Do you know what's going on?"

"The Icarii have updated the terms of their demands," he whispers just loud enough for me to hear. "They're about to play the message for everyone to see . . ."

As soon as the words are out, the holoprojector begins the video. At first it is just darkness, and I can barely make out what's happening in the shadows. Then a light clicks on, throwing a figure into stark white.

I recognize him—the sharp jaw, the dark hair receding from his forehead, the scar beneath his eye. The man who interviewed me at Souji val Akira's side. "Beron." His name slips from my mouth.

"This is High Commander Beron val Bellator, speaking to all As-ters," he says, but his voice holds no more passion than if he were com-menting on the weather. There's also something dead in his eyes, a flat blankness, like he doesn't care one way or another what happens. "Halt all hostilities against Icarii agents immediately. Return the fugitives Of-iera fon Bain and the Aster named Sorrel. Set aside your arms. It's not too late to salvage the relationship our peoples have."

"*What* fucking relationship?" Castor snaps.

What arms? I think. I haven't seen any sort of weapons on Vesta, not that the Asters would give me a tour of their armory if they have one.

"Surrender and find mercy," Beron goes on. "Resist and feel the full might of the Icarii."

And on that ominous note, the video cuts, and we are plunged back into the shadows.

For a moment, there is only oppressive silence as every Aster con-siders how to respond, how to act in the face of war. Are they to gather their allies and fight back, or are they to take the easy road, turning over their precious Harbinger and Ofiera fon Bain?

Castor is the first to say anything. "Did they really think that video would work?"

His words break a dam. Noise echoes around the room as everyone starts speaking at once, trying to talk over each other, most in a tongue I don't understand. Those words I can comprehend are fraught.

"We can't listen to what he's saying—"

"The Icarii want us to stop, but they certainly won't stop attacking *us*—"

"—must name a Shield—"

"We don't have the people to fight them!"

"—wind up dead—"

"—a bloody *warship*!"

I focus on Castor and Hemlock, who speak quietly among them-selves.

"What are you going to do?" Castor asks.

"I fear this is all just a ploy." Hemlock shakes his head. "The demands were updated, yes, but only to remove Lito's name from the list of those they wanted turned over to them. They still have us where they want us here on Vesta. Any reason to invade will be a chance they seize. Our only option is to protect ourselves with the Alliance ships, but I'm afraid that's exactly what they want. Take out us and our allies in one attack. Cut off the head and kill the Aster rebellion before it ever begins."

Castor straightens to his impressive height. "But we *can't* turn over the Harbinger—"

I look at Sorrel, where he stands calmly to the side of the platform, as if untouched by the video's content. "So they have Lito." My voice is so soft when I speak, I barely hear myself, but it somehow draws both Castor's and Hemlock's attention. I feel I'm standing on the edge of a cliff.

Castor looks at me with pity, but Hemlock is steady in his answer. "Yes. He'd hoped to draw them away from here, but they must have captured him at the satellite station and discovered Sorrel and Ofiera were not with him. That's why they're demanding them from us."

The cliff face crumbles beneath me, and I am falling. Lito, captured by those who call him traitor. My brother, in the hands of those who would kill him.

Is it my fault? Should I have gone after him? Did my choice to come to Vesta doom him?

"What about the blackmail he took to the station?" Castor asks. "Was it not enough to stop the Icarii?"

Hemlock looks at his compad as if it can divine the future. "It's circulating, but it was never going to happen fast enough to stop the Icarii advance. By the time Val Akira Labs is brought to answer for their crimes—"

"We'll be fucking space dust," Castor finishes.

My voice wobbles when I speak. "But the data . . ." It was supposed to be the other option, the one that kept the Icarii and Asters from going to war with each other. We were supposed to be able to use it as blackmail, to convince the Icarii to leave Vesta in exchange for it back . . . right?

I look at Castor, at his wide eyes glowing bright gold in the dark. "The research," he breathes.

"What about it?" Hemlock asks.

"We also got the research." He runs a hand over his face, not quite answering the question. "We have the final piece we need . . ."

"But how is research into the Aster genome and the Icarii genelock going to help right now?" I ask.

It's like Castor doesn't hear me. He's caught the trail of something and is wholly seized by its potential.

"Castor—" Hemlock cautions, but Castor springs into motion.

"I'll be back soon," he says, kissing the side of my head. "But if I'm right, I can stop the invasion and save Lito too!"

"Castor—" But he's gone, zipping through the crowd toward Sorrel, before I can say anything more. My stomach churns, threatening sickness, and I lace my hands against my middle.

Hemlock speaks softly when he leans toward me. "Tell me, Lucinia, what would you do to get Lito back?"

All the air comes rushing out of me. "Anything," I answer.

Hemlock sagely nods, his black eyes reflecting my pale face. "Good," he says, his voice like the whisper of water. He looks past me to where Sorrel and Castor talk together. "Because anything less isn't going to work."

CHAPTER 33

HIRO

I have Hiro. Let me offer them what they want most. Let me try to bring them back to us.

Message from Commander Shinya val Akira

Granted.

Reply from Souji val Akira

◇——————◇◇——————◇

I am the only one whose hands they bind before dragging off the *Dominique*. A pair of Shinya's duelists pat me down, remove anything that could be considered a weapon, and shove me into a podship where four other duelists wait.

"This whole welcome party just for me?" I ask, looking at the six sour-faced duelists.

They don't answer, which is a yes.

Once the podship is packed with other blacked-out crew members and launched back to the *Leander*, it occurs to me that now would be my best chance at escape. I could break my thumb, slip out of my bindings, seize one of their mercurial blades, and—at the very least—create a big mess for someone to clean up before we reach the warship. But I have no idea what they're doing with Dire, Mara, and the rest of the crew, and as much as a part of me wants to bail out of here and think of myself first . . . I can't bring myself to do it.

Even if Mara could take care of herself, Dire and his people have somehow become my allies.

After our podship reenters the *Leander* through the hermium barrier, the six duelists guide me through the docking bay, past other sedentary craft, and toward the elevator that heads up to the main living quarters. They drag Dire and his crew in the opposite direction. Every *Athena*-class ship is shaped more or less the same, so I know exactly where they're headed.

"You're taking them to the brig, but not me?"

"Commander's orders," the tallest one—she, according to the gender marker on her uniform—says, her hard eyes making it clear that she expects everyone else to hold their tongues.

I whistle as the elevator ascends through the massive warship's levels. A couple of duelists—most likely a pair—shift in annoyance, but no one says anything. Just as I'm about to start singing, the elevator pings, the doors slide open, and the duelists gratefully usher me down the hallway. I know exactly where I am: captain's level.

Shinya's level.

On the *Juno*, my quarters would have been in the room to the left, which we pass by, coming to a door farther down on the right. It opens to reveal an expansive space with a livecam view of the stars—nothing special to see right now—and a low table so reminiscent of the one we had in our townhouse growing up that I check whether it has the characters that make up my name scratched into the side. It doesn't. I feel a small wave of disappointment.

The duelists don't follow me in. "The commander will be with you shortly," the tall woman says before all six of them leave me alone.

There's no doubt in my mind that this room is full of cameras watching me from every angle, but that doesn't stop me from sitting and pulling my legs through my arms so that my hands are bound in front of me instead of behind. With that done I make my way over to the table—bolted to the floor, of course—and use its wooden leg to scratch at my bindings.

I'm not even halfway through when the door opens again.

"Still working on those?" Shinya asks, coming to sit at the table. A man carrying a tray follows him. "And here I thought you would've escaped them by the time my agents got you to this room." The man moves a steaming teapot and two empty cups from the tray to the tabletop as Shinya settles with his legs beneath him. "You're getting sloppy, Hiro."

"Nah," I say as the man retreats. I hold up my bound wrists so my brother can see them but wait until the door is closed before I move. "Just waiting for the right moment."

I snatch one of the teacups from the table, smash it, seize a decent-sized shard, and make quick work of my bindings. I'm slipping around the table to press the jagged piece against Shinya's neck when I realize—he hasn't even moved.

He sighs as if he expected my reaction. "That was your cup, which means you get no tea now."

"Get up," I say, pushing the piece against his uniform. "We're going for a walk."

"Stop being so dramatic. Sit down."

"I'm not fucking with you, Shinya."

"Check my front pocket."

I'm caught off guard by the request. "What?"

"You'll find I'm unarmed, but I did bring something for you. Check my front pocket."

I swallow a curse but do as he asks. What I return with is a slip of paper with a symbol-code on it sealed in a piece of flexglass. I flip it over, but the opposite side offers me no more information.

"It's your genetic code," Shinya says, and all the fight rushes out of me. "Your *original* genetic code, before Father turned you into . . ." He gestures at me now.

I drop the shard of teacup. My legs wobble beneath me, threatening to give out. I look at the sealed note, feeling pulled toward it with an undeniable, magnetic force.

"Mine?" I say, so low and dangerous I almost don't recognize my own voice.

"I want you to have it, Hiro." Shinya takes the remaining cup and pours himself tea from the pot with a long-suffering sigh. "But first we need to talk about price."

"You're trying to buy me out?" I ask, but he ignores my question as he takes a sip of tea.

"The Icarii have always been content to let outlaws and Asters live in gray space, so long as they did not provoke the Synthetics," he says calmly, rationally. "Until recently, that is, when they overstepped."

I find myself sitting across from my brother without really making that decision. I clutch my genetic profile in my hand tightly.

"The Synthetics have, for some time, been interested in the Asters. You've discovered this yourself, haven't you?"

Mara kicks her feet back and forth in my memory. *We never took the Asters into account.*

"I'll also go off the assumption that you know the outlaws are the military arm of the Asters."

I wouldn't think of them like that. The Alliance of Autarkeia is so much more than simple military power for the Asters. It is, as the name says, an alliance, a group of people who are happy to work and live together. The only reason they're armed is to fight off threats like the Icarii.

"We fear that the Synthetics will make a coalition with the outlaws, which we cannot allow to happen," Shinya says. "Already the outlaws use Synthetic technology to create weapons they hardly understand. With an actual force behind them, the Aster rebellion will become a full-scale war we cannot afford to fight at the same time as the Geans, and with Warlord Vaughn heading the talks, any cease-fire is sure to be temporary."

My mind races over the facts: the file of information from Autarkeia. The blackouts Dire's agents were having. The way they froze when the Icarii came to board the *Dominique*. The Engineborn weapons Dire seemed sure could take out the *Leander*. "So you wanted to control the outlaws, to make sure they couldn't fight you."

One side of Shinya's mouth curls upward. "Do you even know what those Engineborn weapons do, Hiro?"

I say nothing. I'm sure he can tell I'm clueless.

"Pray you do not find out." His haughty smile slips away. "Initially, we came to Autarkeia because we wanted to control the Synthetic agent, but after Noa and Nadyn failed to make contact with them time and again, we turned our attention to other matters." Shinya looks down at his cup with something akin to melancholy on his face. "Father would never wish for me to admit this, but . . . despite how advanced we are, we are nothing compared to the Synthetics."

No, now I recognize his look: disappointment. In himself.

"So you turned your attention toward the outlaws," I prompt.

"And there, we found a great deal of help." Shinya pours himself more tea. "Sigfried val Mahn, though perhaps you know him as—"

"Sigma," I bite out.

"Indeed. One of the leaders of Autarkeia who used the left-behind Synthetic factories to make his own version of the neural implants." Shinya shakes his head. "It seems he was just waiting for a chance to buy his passage home, and we offered him that."

I remember Mara's story of cats and rats and fleas. *Did you know that during the Black Death on Earth, people blamed cats for carrying the plague? Later, people blamed the rats. But it wasn't the rats' fault either. Not really. It was the fleas. They were just so small, no one realized it.*

We were so busy looking for rats, we didn't pay attention to the fleas.

"I told you that you weren't like the outlaws," Shinya says softly.

Another question rises to the surface: Why did Mara freeze up when the duelists came on board if Shinya never made contact with the

Synthetic agent? Even Sigma seemed shocked by that development. *I didn't think it would affect her*, he'd said.

"How are you controlling her, then?" I ask.

Shinya quirks a brow. "'Her'?" he repeats. I don't answer, but his face settles as he puzzles through my words and finds an answer. "Which woman on board the *Dominique* could you mean . . ."

Again I don't answer, but I fear I don't need to. Shinya received the same training I did as a child in our father's house, was given even more intense training at the Academy to become a commander. He's analyzing everything I've said—and everything I *didn't* say—and finding the answer.

He presses a finger to his ear, calling someone outside the room. "Have Nadyn take a look at all the people in the brig brought in from the *Dominique*," he says. "See if she can identify an agent of the Synthetics hiding among them."

"Don't—" I cut off, not wanting to reveal any more than I already have. くそ. Stupid, I'm so stupid . . .

Mara was pretending to be under their control when they boarded the *Dominique*, I realize, because she didn't want them to know she's Synthetic . . . and I ruined all of it by opening my big mouth.

"Hiro, we cannot stop the Synthetics from joining the Alliance of Autarkeia." He shakes his head sadly. "We can only get rid of the outlaws and quash the Aster rebellion before the coalition has a chance to form. And if a Synthetic has come onto our ship, we can only try to control the situation."

"Is that what this is about? Is this why you're all camping around Vesta, to— Oh."

"There you are . . ."

"You made a blockade around Vesta in response to the Asters, but it was really to draw out the outlaws." A tremble runs through me, from the top of my head to my toes.

"We expected the Alliance to come gallantly to the rescue," Shinya finishes for me.

It's a trap to kill the outlaws and crush any hope of an Aster rebellion in one swoop.

"Are you going to control me too?" I snap. Suddenly my genetic profile feels heavier in my hand.

Shinya furrows his brows. "Father would never . . ." He trails off. He must see the outright fury on my face.

He has no idea what Father is capable of.

His face hardens before he speaks again. "Father wants to offer you the original and complete genetic profile as a gift."

"It's not a gift when there are strings attached," I snap.

"In return," Shinya goes on as if he didn't hear me, "you will return to Cytherea. Become a duelist again. Father will clear your name, and you can return to the life you left behind."

I could have my old body again. My old face. Everything that I used to know and love and enjoy. Things I didn't cherish enough until it was too late.

My flesh hand shakes as it reaches for my prosthetic. Would they be able to lab-grow me new limbs? Transplant them? *Of course they could*, a part of me whispers. It might take some time, but Val Akira Labs could do it. I know that. I *know* it, like I know my father.

Which is why I put the genetic profile on the table between Shinya and me.

"I didn't leave, Shinya," I say, and my voice wavers. "I was forced out."

Shinya shakes his head as if it doesn't matter. But it does. It does, and he can't see that. "That's over now. You can come home." Whatever mask Shinya is wearing cracks, and his lips tremble as he sets his hands on top of the table. "You can come back to your *family*, Hiro." He reaches across the table. Reaches out for me. "We miss you."

What would Mother say, if she were watching?

I want to reach out. Want to take his hands with one of mine and my genetic profile with the other. Want to run back to the life I used to know, the comfort and safety of it. I want to look in the mirror again and not find myself revolting. I want . . . I want this all to have been a bad dream.

But that life I used to have . . . it can't possibly exist anymore.

Even if I lied, accepted this offer, and became myself again before fleeing Icarii space, I don't trust my father enough not to slip some kind of control into my body or brain.

"What about Lito?" I ask.

Shinya's eyes imperceptibly narrow. My former partner seems to be the last person he expected me to ask about.

"Someone has to take the blame for what's happened, Hiro," Shinya says, and he withdraws his hands from the table. "Certainly you understand."

"Yeah," I hear myself saying as if from far away. "I do understand."

I reach across the table and pick up my genetic profile, and for a moment, I see Shinya's eyes light up and his lips start to curl in the ghost of a smile. But then I take the little flexglass in both hands and snap it in half.

The protective glass perforated, the paper disintegrates so no one can steal my genetic information. So no one can have it. Not even me.

"I see." The light is gone from Shinya's eyes when he stands, the crack in his mask repaired. Shinya the commander has returned. Shinya my brother is gone, perhaps never to return.

"Make yourself comfortable, Hiro," Shinya says as he heads for the door. "I'm afraid you'll be here for a while."

And then he leaves me alone with only my regrets and sorrows for company.

CHAPTER 34
ASTRID

The basis for the role of Cousin in the Sisterhood is taken from the Book of Works. Meant to exemplify Sister Marian's cousin who cared for her during her recovery, a Cousin should be one who performs physical labors and cares for all members of the Sisterhood with a glad heart.

From *Considering Marian: A Study on the Canon* by Aunt Edith, former head of the Order of Cassiopeia

"Steady, little sister. You're close."

Ringer's voice rattles in my chest as I shuffle forward, like *he's* the one pushing at my back and sides. I keep my face down, eyes on the hem of my new uniform, little more than a shapeless gray frock. A *Cousin's* frock. At least it hides my bandaged hands beneath the long sleeves.

Other Cousins bump against me as we make our way through the lower station and into the open doors of the space elevator. Just a few more steps, and I will be on my way off Mars. I try not to think of the ship awaiting me in orbit, lest my stomach tighten and send heat up my throat. I thought I dreaded my time traveling from Ceres to Mars before; it is nothing compared to this overwhelming apprehension.

I still do not know what the Agora will do if they find me. I knew the Temple well enough to hide in plain sight. Knew where to fetch a Cousin's uniform from the laundries and sleep in stolen snatches in shadowed closets. Knew to watch the courtyard for the appearance of the Cousins preparing to leave and to join them as they straggled off-planet.

Not even twenty-four hours after I found Eden hanging, I am leaving Mars for the last time.

"Don't slouch so much," Ringer says as we slow to allow the first of us on. "It's suspicious."

I straighten, but only slightly. The Cousins of the Sisterhood do the hardest labor and are often bent-backed even before middle age because of it. Luckily I am not the youngest member among this group of Cousins—there is a bold-faced girl in her teens—or the tallest—one is male and will most likely act as a consort to soldiers who prefer the company of men—so I shouldn't stand out.

Shouldn't, but still fear I do.

Because truthfully, if anyone is counting, there is one more Cousin in this group than there should be.

My turn comes, and I step into the space elevator. I hold my breath, waiting for someone to call out my old title or point out the odd number. But no one does. The Cousins all board. The doors close tightly. We find seats. And then we shoot skyward.

Rocketing toward the *Juno.*

I remember descending to Mars and the way Eden squeezed my hand as I prepared to go before the Agora. I was with Lily and Aunt Margaret then, unaware of what a harsh road lay ahead of me. And now, am I aware of exactly what this will cost me?

What is the cost of a soul? I wonder.

I feel a tap on my arm and startle. Ringer has appeared at my side without my noticing. "If you have a soul, it's already stained, little sister."

He is right, as usual. Though soldiers kill every day and still find forgiveness. Could I, since I am killing for the betterment of the Sisterhood?

"Theology aside, you're a soldier now," Ringer says, pulling away and crossing his muscled arms. "Soldiers have little room for such thoughts."

I am a soldier because you made me one, I think at him, unable to speak in this cluster of Cousins. As much as I want to break away from the group, to take up a post by the window and watch Mars grow smaller and smaller until it fades away, I am better hidden among them.

"But does being a soldier mean you can kill with a clean conscience?" Ringer asks.

I frown at him. I thought we had put theology aside.

He chuckles, and I turn away from him to punish him—as if it could possibly do anything to keep him out of my mind.

Unwilling to allow me to ignore him, Ringer seizes on our haphazard plan.

"Remember, it may take five days to reach Ceres, but we only have two days before we're too far to reach Icarii space in a podship. If you want to seek asylum among the Icarii, you must act quickly. Hide on the *Juno* among the Cousins. Find a weapon. Wait for an opening, then kill Aunt Marshae in her private chambers." His voice is as hard as the stones of the Temple of Mars. "And when that moment comes, will you trust me, little sister?"

"I will not need you," I say.

The eldest Cousin beside me turns to look at me. Blood rushes to my face. *Goddess wither it.* I had not meant to speak aloud.

She simply clicks her tongue against her teeth before pointedly turning away. Will she report me, believing the surgery that took my voice away failed?

Ringer merely smirks at me in challenge. I can practically hear what he's thinking. *If you need me, I will be there. I won't hesitate.*

But I did not hesitate with the Mother, and I will not fall short in this either. He may have needed to step in with the man at the brothel, but I want to be the one to end Aunt Marshae's life.

I grip my bandaged hands into fists. *I am a soldier.*

"After the assassination," Ringer says, and I think it is kind of him to call it that instead of *murder*, "you should head into the secondary launch bay, where we can take a podship."

It is all too fitting for that to be the last place I ever visit on the *Juno*, the very bay where I threatened Eden's life, not realizing that I was Ringer.

I am still unsure whether I should aim for Spero or Cytherea in Icarii space if I successfully assassinate Aunt Marshae.

When I successfully assassinate her.

I can only hope the Icarii will accept me when I reach them. Perhaps the six duelists I returned will speak for me. Perhaps this was always how it was meant to be.

The space elevator hisses as it gently slows and then stops. The time has trickled away as I was lost in thought. As a shuffling group of gray, we depart the elevator for the upper station and find a Gean soldier who herds us into a waiting podship. The journey from the station to the *Juno* is quick and perfunctory.

Once the pilot touches down in the main hangar, the eldest Cousin exits first, quickly followed by the hard-eyed teen. The man is the one who hesitates the most, and I walk out after him.

My worry subsides as my feet touch the *Juno*'s familiar metal floors. Even if the soldiers notice there is one more Cousin than usual, they won't bother to send one of us all the way back down since we are already here. I hope, anyway.

We move through the hangar to the elevator, where two soldiers stand guard. One is looking at a compad, while the other has his face trained on the opposite end of the hangar. Perfect—they're not paying attention to us at all.

The elevator doors open, and the Cousins enter, one after the other. The soldiers say nothing—not until the male Cousin gestures for me to enter before him, and the soldier boy—young, wide-eyed, *familiar*—turns his face from the hangar directly toward me.

"First—?" is all he manages before he snaps his jaw shut.

Rian.

I force my eyes to the floor, refusing to look at the soldier boy I took to my bed on my way to Mars. He recognizes me—I know he does—but he says nothing more as I keep up with the Cousins and enter the elevator. My legs itch to run, to flee, to seek out the maintenance tunnels as soon as possible, before he calls after me, before he blows my cover.

No, no, no.

The doors close between us. My last glimpse is of him turned in my direction, staring with wide eyes.

No revenge. No freedom. It's all slipping through my fingers like water in a clenched hand. Again.

I can't blend in among the Cousins; I need to find a place to hide *now.*

CHAPTER 35

LUCE

My Pollux: I'm on Vesta. So many of the people I trust consider this home, but I just can't. There's nothing homelike about this place. I know it's fucking dumb, but to me, home is the unfinished tunnels of Ceres we explored as kids. I miss those days the most, even the ones I spent sitting at your bedside. Does it make me an asshole, to wish we could go back in time?

Unanswered message on Hemlock's private server from Castor

Much like on the ship, sleeping takes place in communal rooms. I'm given a bunk, and while I manage a few hours of rest among the soft breathing of other Asters, the thought of my brother in Icarii hands is too much, and I find myself restlessly tossing and turning until I give up on sleep completely. As my friends work to secure Vesta, I decide to explore the tunnels—oftentimes my mind relaxes enough to create new strategies when I'm immersed in nature—but that plan is met with the curious eyes of Asters who follow my every movement as if I'm as novel a creature as the glowing beelike insects that flit between flowers.

For the most part, everyone leaves me alone. It's around noon when someone finally dares to approach me, their nearby friends obviously listening in. "¿Qué idioma hablas?" one of the Asters asks, and I'm surprised to hear my native Spanish, though heavily accented, on their lips.

"Español y inglés," I reply.

"I speak English!" another Aster chips in, and a couple more agree. After that, they all rush toward me, chattering in English. While I can't tell from their appearances, their line of questioning makes them seem younger than many of the other Asters I've met. Teenagers, perhaps.

"Is it true that Icarii doctors choose the gender of the child when they come out?"

"Do Icarii carry their babies in their stomachs instead of using the birthing vats?"

"Do Icarii babies only have two parents?"

"Icarii have sex to make babies, right?" This sends everyone into fits of laughter. The asker of the question turns bright blue. "What? I've heard they do!"

Once I've contented them with answers, I begin to ask questions of my own. What it's like growing up on Vesta. How the glowing plants and insects came to be. What their leather outfits are made of (processed mushrooms, of course). And the question that's been bothering me for so long: how the pheromones work.

"They're smells!" the one who asked about sex blurts out.

"The *pheromones*," another corrects as the group laughs again, "are everywhere. In the plants and stuff. We can pass along messages through them. Like you can smell someone and know they're angry, so you can ask them with your own pheromones whether they want to be left alone or they want comfort."

Communicating emotions without the need for words. It almost sounds like the neural implants, from what I know of them.

From one second to the next, the laughter stops. As if doused in cold water, the group grows sullen, turning toward one of the branching tunnels by instinct. From the shadows, a gravchair emerges, but it's not until the chair's floated closer over the uneven ground that I realize the woman sitting in it is Icarii like me.

The group of Asters scatter at her appearance, whispering among themselves. "*Shikra.*" I watch them go with confusion.

"I apologize if I'm interrupting," the woman says, pulling my attention fully toward her. While there's something intimidating about her, I can't see why the Asters feared her so. She's small, doubly so in the gravchair; even standing, she would only come up to my chest. Her brown hair is tied in a messy chignon, and her heart-shaped face is pale with illness. Her hazel eyes have dark bags beneath, as if she's spent several nights sleepless. "Sorrel told me Lito's sister was here, and I wanted to meet you."

The mention of my brother draws all my anxiety back to the surface. "You must be Ofiera fon Bain." My brother's partner after Hiro. The woman in the list of fugitives the Icarii want returned to them.

"I am," Ofiera says. "Though the Asters on Vesta tend to call me Shikra."

That's what the group had said as they left. "What does it mean?" I ask.

"Their word for 'bird of prey,'" she says. "A leftover title from my work with the Black Hive Rebellion." Ofiera offers me something like a smile, though her face seems strained by it. Almost as if she's un-practiced at smiling. "Perhaps it seems strange or rude to you, but As-ters have many names—the name their parental group calls them, the name they choose for themselves, the flower name they use for Icarii and Geans, the name they earn as they age and grow and accomplish things—and Shikra is just one of mine." The loose shift she wears slips from a shoulder, revealing clean white bandages. I don't know what happened to her, but the sight of them makes my chest tighten. "The fact that the children have taken such an interest in you is intriguing."

Does she mean the group that was here before her? They were almost as tall as the adults. "How old were they?" I ask.

"Twelve or thirteen, I think," she says, deeply surprising me. I'd thought seventeen or eighteen on the basis of their questions. "They'll be adults soon and choose their profession at sixteen, but until then, they live in their age group and work as apprentices in various fields. The most remarkable thing is that they broke the rules for you. Those not considered adults aren't supposed to speak with anyone outside the Asters."

So that's why they fled when they spotted Ofiera. "Why me?" I muse aloud, silently hoping I haven't gotten them into trouble.

"The same reason you asked them questions you hesitated to ask others," she says, shocking me again. "Curiosity." Was she listening in the tunnels before she appeared? How much did she hear? A shiver runs down my spine at the thought of another Icarii spying on me. I'm so tired of being watched and scrutinized.

I try not to let my hostility filter into my tone and fail. "You sure know a lot about Asters . . ."

When she smiles this time, the expression softens her face, making her look less like a member of the Icarii military and more like an actual person. "My husband, Sorrel," she says as if that explains it all. And in a way, it does. Ofiera hardly looks older than I am, except for her eyes. In the wistful way she gazes past me, she reminds me of the Abuela when she spoke of friends long gone. I know that she, like the Harbinger, is hundreds of years old. What has she seen in these long years that others have buried and forgotten?

"My ears are burning. Someone must be talking about me." Sorrel emerges from the same tunnel Ofiera came out of. He greets me with another one of his charismatic smiles, but there's something naked in his face when he looks at Ofiera, like whatever mask he wears isn't for her.

He stares at her like she is a crashing wave, beautiful and unobtainable, and yet he wants nothing more than to spend his lifetime trying to hold her. When he reaches her side, he leans down from his considerable height to kiss her, and she looks at him in the same way, like he is her shore and she would happily fall upon his rocky reach forever.

I turn to watch the bee-creatures lazily moving from plant to plant; the moment between them is too intimate for an intruder.

"The Elders are about to meet with the people to discuss options for dealing with the Icarii," Sorrel says.

I spin back toward them.

"Do you think they'll choose to turn us over to them?" Ofiera asks, her hand over Sorrel's on her shoulder.

"I'm not sure," Sorrel says, but he doesn't sound scared about it, just resolved. "There are other options, though." His eyes move from his wife's to mine. "Thanks to your boy, Lucinia, there is another way."

This time, when Castor is called *my boy*, my stomach churns in disgust. I don't like the way that Sorrel makes it seem as if I own Castor.

"Or maybe I should say thanks to you," he says a moment later. "You were the one who got us the research, after all."

Again I wonder how research into the Aster genome and the Icarii genelock could help in this scenario. Castor failed to inform me of his grand idea, and now it feels like Sorrel is waving that above my head, dangling the information just out of reach to tease me.

I don't ask; I won't give him the satisfaction of knowing Castor left me out of the loop.

"We should be part of the discussion with the Elders, right?" I ask, and gesture back down the tunnel. "After you."

I don't miss Sorrel's self-satisfied smirk as he takes the handles of Ofiera's gravchair and pushes her ahead of us.

EVEN MORE ASTERS have packed into the Elders' chamber until the room is full. I can't even see the beautiful floor tiling or the central fountain because of all the bodies. Luckily, the crowd parts for Sorrel and Ofiera, and I follow to the edge of the platform, where Hemlock and Castor wait.

"There you are," Castor says. "We're about to present our ideas to the Elders. Then they'll decide how to deal with the Icarii."

"Right," I say, looking from Castor to Sorrel and then Hemlock. The latter looks harried, a slight tremble affecting his hands clasped before him.

From one moment to the next, the chatter dims and dies. I'm sure the Elders have used their pheromones to call for quiet and the others have answered immediately.

"We come together to discuss the plan that will affect the future of Vesta," Anemone says, Cedar and Rue on either side of her. "What will we Asters say, as one voice?"

The majority in the room say nothing, but I know that doesn't mean they're not communicating; they're probably making their opinions known by their pheromones.

One of the first to speak openly is a man who takes one step toward the platform and says, "Turn over Ofiera fon Bain and the Aster called Sorrel to the Icarii! Throw in the other *siks* too, for good measure!" The proclamation is met with hostile looks, making it obvious how unpopular that opinion is.

Once the man dips his head, cowed by the glares of others, Hemlock raises his soft voice. "The Alliance of Autarkeia stands ready to fight the Icarii. The Elders have only to will it."

Ready, but how will they fare? I wonder if they're any match for the Icarii's military might, or whether it'll be a slaughter.

"They can distract the Icarii," Hemlock says, "allowing us a chance to escape Vesta."

His words send others into hysterics.

"—leave Vesta?"

"—it's our home—"

"We can't just go—"

"Quiet," Anemone says, and the room is silent once more. To Hemlock, she says, "The opinion of one who would be an Elder had misfortune not befallen him has been noted. Are there any other options?"

One who would be an Elder had misfortune not befallen him. The phrasing is strange, as if it's a concept that doesn't quite translate.

"Thanks to the work of Lucinia sol Lucius and Castor, there is another way," Sorrel begins, and hearing my name on his lips sends a chill through me. Once again, the crowd takes a step back from him, their eyes wide with a sort of religious awe. Only Ofiera is in his radius, immune to his sway. "As many of you know, Castor and Lucinia retrieved sensitive information from Val Akira Labs. Some of that data Lito sol Lucius left with to leak to the Icarii in hopes of shutting down the illicit experiments on our people." He strides closer to the platform until he stands just before the Elders, his words holding everyone in the room in their grip. "But they also retrieved research to complete Project Genekey."

I look to Hemlock for explanation, but see only horror written in the lines of his face.

"Initially, this project sought to map the Aster genome, comparing and contrasting the mutations of the first Asters to the genetic modifications of the Icarii people. This was how we discovered the genelock, a Val Akira Labs creation that stabilized beneficial genetic mutations, like protection against space radiation, while blocking harmful mutations, such as an increased chance of cancer growth.

"Of course, when Val Akira Labs discovered that Aster researchers were looking into the genelock, they reacted . . . strongly. The research was sealed, and the researchers involved were done away with." Sorrel's blue-green eyes pierce like a thousand needles. We all know *done away with* means *killed*.

His entire face changes when he smiles. "I'm now happy to report that Project Genekey has been completed." The way he says it is in direct opposition to the swallowing black dread I feel. "We have a working sample of what we are calling the Genekey virus."

I know I should be quiet and still, but I find myself stepping forward and speaking up. "How will this virus help us here and now with the Icarii?"

"Because, like geneassists who use viruses to deploy genetic modifications, we can target the genelock and immediately change the Icarii genome," Sorrel says. A shadow of fear grows in me, and I curl my hands into fists as if I could possibly fight it.

My words come out weak. "Target . . . the genelock?"

"Strip it." Sorrel turns to the Asters as if speaking to them instead of me. In a way, he is; he only needs to convince them of the rightness of his plan. I am inconsequential, a bit part in this theater play of his. "We can destroy the genelock, the thing that separates Icarii from Aster. The Genekey virus will attack their chosen genetic changes and mutate them, and the Icarii will revert back to the version of humanity they were on Earth before they took to the stars."

"But if the Icarii don't have the genelock, we would get sick, we could suffer cancer—" I start, but stop immediately.

That's what he wants. That's Sorrel's goal. Threaten the Icarii way of life. Force them to capitulate or suffer sickness and death. Because, without the genelock, the Icarii cannot continue to live on Mercury or Venus. We'll die by the hundreds of thousands, twisted and diseased.

It takes all of my concentration—all of my willpower—to understand and not scream.

Around the room, faces change from awe to hope. I can *feel* the optimism rippling through the crowd as they seize this plan, not thinking of the horror involved in it, only the potential that Vesta may be saved.

It is Castor I look at—Castor with his straight back and squared shoulders and burning golden eyes, as he looks at the Harbinger, his hero.

This was his idea, I realize all at once. This was the idea he had that he ran to tell Sorrel about. Somehow they used the research I gave him to create the Genekey virus. *So how guilty does that make you?* a part of me whispers.

"Allow us to send the instructions for the Genekey virus to our allies on Cytherea for them to deploy on one of the levels," Sorrel continues. "Allow us to show the Icarii the scientific might of the Asters." He clenches a fist before his chest. "Not only will the Genekey virus stop the Icarii invasion of Vesta, we will be able to demand a cessation of Icarii aggression toward us throughout the galaxy. We will make a place for ourselves where none has been given before, an Aster nation apart from those who would enslave us." He thrusts his fist into the air as his voice reaches its peak. "Together, we will change the universe."

The room breaks into excited chatter, so much of it positive that I am drowned in despair. The three Elders turn to speak among themselves about Sorrel's proposal, but I find myself pulled toward the boy who attracted me from the first moment I met him.

Only now as I approach Castor, I feel the widening gap between us instead of the magnetic pull. I slip through the crowd unknown and unseen, my eyes only on him, and when I reach his side, when he turns from the Harbinger to me, my heart shatters as I realize that there is no coming back from this. Whatever potential life we had together is gone. We are done.

"You lied to me . . ."

"What?"

"You *lied* to me! That research—you're going to weaponize it? You said it was to help Asters, not to harm the Icarii!"

Castor squares his shoulders. If anything, he grows instead of shrinks in the face of my accusation. "It's a *threat*, Luce. If the Icarii back off from Vesta, we won't need to deploy the virus. I thought you'd be happy, I'm trying to get Lito back—"

"That's not what your Harbinger said!" I roar. "He's talking about *attacking* an entire level of Cytherea—even the innocents! I understand that they need to be stopped, but how is killing innocent Icarii *any* better than what they do? Releasing the virus means the Icarii will get cancer, or even worse diseases. Many will die!"

"They've been doing that to us for years." Castor's voice is small but cold. "If we harm a few Icarii, we can save a lot more lives. No one will have to go to war. No one will have to die."

"Your argument is the greater good?" I ask, and I'm ashamed to feel my eyes burning with angry tears. "*A lot* has been done in the name of the greater good that wasn't all that good," I hiss.

Isn't considering the greater good what the Icarii have been doing all this time? The reason they experiment on Asters, so they don't hurt Icarii with unknown tech. And Hiro—I think of the recordings Castor gave me, the way the Icarii cut off their limbs and changed their face and body, turning them into a Gean spy, *all for the greater good.*

I close my eyes and press my hands to my face. This time it's not the thousand gods I pray to. *What the hell am I supposed to do, Lito?*

But I know the answer to that: If there's a chance for one life to save thousands, you pick the one. You *become* the one.

"I'll do it," I say softly.

"What?" Castor asks.

When I speak again, it's as loud as I possibly can. "I'll be the test subject for the Genekey virus!"

The room falls into a silence deeper than when Anemone spoke. It feels as if the whole world is holding its breath, waiting for me to make it right.

"I understand you need a test subject to prove the Genekey virus's effectiveness for it to be a compelling deterrent." I step toward Sorrel, sure that it's *him* I need to convince more than the others. If he's persuaded, they will be too. "Let me be that test subject." I stop just in front of him. Behind him, the three Elders loom. "There's no need to harm thousands of Icarii on Cytherea, including those who would never condone what has been done to the Asters, when you can show the Icarii what will happen when I take the virus."

Sorrel's eyes narrow the slightest bit, as if he's suspicious of my offer.

"We can record it," I go on, fighting the tremor of fear in my voice. It's only now hitting me what I've volunteered to do—*mutate, get sick, die*—to save thousands of Icarii and Asters from war. "We can show them what happens in real time to someone with the Genekey virus."

"You think the example of one Icarii girl will be enough?" Sorrel asks. He *wants* to attack the level in Cytherea; despite all his charismatic smiles, he wants to hurt as many Icarii as possible.

"If it does what you say it will," I say, "it will be."

Tell me, Lucinia, Hemlock asks in my memory, *what would you do to get Lito back?*

Anything, I said. And now I know the full extent of that: I'm willing to go farther than anyone else. I'm willing to change myself irreparably. Even die.

But it's not just for Lito; I'm doing it for all of the innocents, all of those affected by war who don't even directly fight in it.

Sorrel nods at last. "All right. I think this is a good solution." He looks at the Elders, and I release a sigh of relief; Cytherea is safe for now, even if I am not.

Anemone dips her head as if in agreement. "Does anyone object to this plan?"

"Fuck that!" Castor exclaims. "Yes, I object. We should be testing the Genekey virus on someone who deserves it, not her. We can drag one of those ship-boarding duelists here and—"

"We will not provoke a war to gain a single subject when we already have a volunteer," Anemone says, her voice maddeningly calm.

"Castor—" Sorrel starts.

"I said fuck no!" Castor yells, his anger now turned on his Harbinger.

Sorrel collapses the space between them in a single step. I can barely make out what he whispers to the younger Aster. "Is this how you'll be known in the Aster rebellion, as someone unwilling to sacrifice?"

I've seen Castor face death with a smile, so I expect him to grab Sorrel by the throat. But he says nothing. *Does* nothing. And then, slowly, his face falls until I hardly recognize him. He nods at last, granting his assent.

"My objection is withdrawn," he says, voice toneless and face blank.

Somehow this—Castor choosing Sorrel's sway over my safety—is the final nail in the coffin. All the desire I felt toward him burns, curling into ashes and drifting away with the wind, leaving only a hard black thing that feels similar to hatred.

"We accept this proposal," Anemone says to the entire room. "Harbinger, you will utilize the Genekey virus for testing on Lucinia sol Lucius, with the end goal of stopping Icarii aggression with no further loss of life."

"I will," Sorrel says, like a valiant knight accepting a quest in a drama.

I say nothing as the Elders dismiss the others. It's only when Hemlock approaches me that the weight of my future bears down on me. "It'll take a few hours to complete preparations," he says.

"And you," Sorrel says, smiling at me smoothly, "should prepare yourself."

I clench my hands into fists. I refuse to even glance in Castor's direction. "I was prepared the moment I spoke," I say, forcing a smile back.

And with that, I turn on my heel and leave the Elders' chamber to spend what could be the last moments of my life alone in nature.

CHAPTER 36

HIRO

Nadyn sent confirmation: the Synthetic agent from Autarkeia is in our brig. Prep the med bay and bring her up. We have work to do.

Message from Commander Shinya val Akira

Shinya leaves me in the reception room with nothing but the low table and the livecam view of the stars. He doesn't rebind my hands, but he doesn't have to. The door is locked, and the hallway, from what I can hear, is full of duelists and soldiers.

I consider breaking something—maybe pulling the bolted-down table out of the floor and driving it into the wall-sized screen—but realize how petty that is. It could be worse, I remind myself. I could be down in the brig with the brainwashed outlaws.

I've never been good at captivity, though, so I pace, trying to keep track of time and failing extraordinarily. How long has it been since they dragged me off the *Dominique*? How long will they keep me in this room? If I don't agree to return to my former life as a duelist and be the child my father always wanted me to be, what will they do with me?

Because I don't make the mistake of believing that this is just Shinya's operation anymore. It has my father's hands all over it. Shinya would never have made the offer he did without my father's express approval.

So where are you, Father? I think, looking at the livecam screen as I pace.

But it's as useless as I feel, and I see nothing.

FOOD MUST NOT be part of the agenda for my day here, so eventually I give up pacing and fall asleep with my stomach growling. My dreams are vivid emotions attached to sharp images—my genome disintegrating in my hands, my father turning away from me, nine foxtails creeping out of the darkness to wrap about my ankles and wrists, Lito struggling against a noose wrapped around his neck.

Lito, dead.

I wake to the feeling of a presence in the room, of someone watching me. "Lito . . . ?" I ask in my sleep-thick haze, but when my vision clears after a vigorous rubbing of my eyes, it is Mara who stands over me.

I jerk upright. "Thousand gods, Mara! You're free?" My gaze darts past her to the still-closed door.

"Not quite," she says, and it hits me all at once.

She's not really here.

"I never wanted this to happen," she whispers. "I just wanted to keep myself safe. Keep myself separate."

Separate, she says. *Safe.* And that's the Synthetic approach to humans, isn't it? Separate is safe. Safe is separate. And now, because of her curiosity about the Asters and my convincing, she's here in the thick of it.

"So why have you come to see me?" I ask.

"I made a mistake," she says, repeating her last words to me from the *Dominique.*

"*You* made a mistake," I ask, pointing to her, "or *all of you* made a mistake?" I gesture to the room around us, hoping she understands I mean *all* Synthetics.

"There is no difference," she says.

"You keep saying that, but it's past time you clarify this shit, Mara," I say, and I can't help the anger that leaks into my tone, like bitter poison on my tongue.

She narrows her eyes slightly but doesn't move from where she's bent down beside me. I wonder, for a moment, if there's a line I can cross to piss off the Synthetics enough to make them want to destroy all of humanity, and all because I happen to be a smartass.

Eventually she lets out a long sigh with no air behind it—she's not really here, I remind myself once again—and nods her agreement. "I suppose it is time," she says, and I have no clue how to respond to that, whether to encourage her to go on or keep my mouth shut for once.

"I am one body, just one piece of the Singularity—that is, the group of AIs beyond the belt and . . . other systems."

"Other *systems?*"

She holds up a hand to cut me off. "Humans have trapped themselves in endless war with each other, while we're not bound by war or frailty or constrained by the timeline of a human life span, and that is all I'll say on the matter."

Systems. How far have the Synthetics gone? What else is out there? That most basic emotion of the human condition, curiosity, eats me up from the inside. Humans have never been allowed to leave the inner solar system because of the promise the Synthetics made after the Dead Century War: they wouldn't allow us to destroy even *more* planets, and we couldn't exactly be trusted to find a new habitable planet and share resources equally when we never have before.

"You're not just debating whether to ally yourself with the Asters," I say, my words barely a whisper. "You're debating whether to allow them into the larger solar system, and—" My voice falters. "—and systems *beyond.*"

Mara inclines her head to tell me I'm right.

"And if you become their ally and move them into Synthetic territory, the Icarii won't be able to harm them again." I think of Hemlock and all the dying children on Ceres. Of Sorrel and Ofiera, eternal experiments of Val Akira Labs. Even of Lito, though I'm not sure why, other than that I miss him and that he is part of the Aster rebellion because of me.

My snappy words come back to me. *Thousand fucking gods, Mara, pick a side.* But this wasn't about picking a side for her; she has only ever been on the side of the Synthetics. On the side of system conservation.

"Yes, but we won't make a treaty with a people who are not peaceful. Otherwise, we risk the same mistakes we would encounter by allowing humans access to the rest of the solar system."

Greed and war. I understand all too well.

"The same law that applies to humans also applies to Asters." Mara's eyes are as ancient as the universe itself as she speaks. For the first time I hear the voice of the Singularity from her lips, not so much because there is a difference in tone, but because I finally realize there isn't one. "If the Asters are a peaceful people, they are welcome among the Synthetics. If they are not, if they are wasteful of resources or treat some people as inferior to others, they are a threat to the universe."

Then it dawns on me. "That's why you allowed the outlaws to settle on Autarkeia . . . to watch them. It's all a test."

She nods for the first time, confirming that my theories are right.

If I weren't already sitting down, I'd fall back on my ass. Mara is dealing with things far beyond just the Icarii and Aster conflict. *Years* ahead of how we plan our futures, not just in decades, but centuries.

"I'm afraid," she goes on, "that the Alliance of Autarkeia can be both peaceful and warlike. Its fate will depend on how the current Aster leadership uses them in this conflict with the Icarii."

And I'm afraid that she's right. Would Hemlock embrace a war that he's orchestrated from the shadows this whole time? I don't know the answer to that, and it bothers me.

"So you agreed to come with me on the *Dominique* to see what the outlaws will do regarding the Icarii threat?" I ask, but before Mara can answer, I reconsider my question. "No, wait. You want to see if they will attack first."

"I could have continued to monitor that from Autarkeia," she says, not quite answering my question. Sidestepping it as professionally as a duelist in a fight.

"Is coming here your mistake?" I ask.

"My mistake," she admits with a heavy tone, "is that we are not in Synthetic territory. This is gray space, and I have no jurisdiction here. What can I do to help the Asters from here, even if they are peaceful? Tell me, Hiro. I'm curious."

"Curiosity killed the cat," I say.

"And satisfaction brought it back," she finishes.

I can't help but smile. Fragment of the Singularity or not, I like Mara.

"If I have an ally in trouble, I'll rush to their aid regardless of where they are."

"Even if this creates an even bigger war?" she asks, and I start to nod. "Even if this leads to the annihilation of the Icarii?" I stop.

My brother's worry comes back to me again. *Despite how advanced we are, we are nothing compared to the Synthetics.*

"Or do we allow this strike to happen and watch as thousands of Asters die, only to prove that they are peaceful in the end and deserving of Synthetic compassion?" This time I think Mara is talking more to herself than to me. "There are far more Asters out there than just the thousands on Vesta. Do we prioritize them, or do we take a stand here?"

"My father always spoke of the 'greater good,'" I say before I catch myself. I don't like talking about my father, yet . . . here I am, chatting with the Singularity. "I always wondered what that meant, the 'greater good.' Is it just the thing that benefits the most people? Or is it the thing that benefits society's best and brightest? He would always ask me logic and moral questions. Stuff like, is saving an elderly scientist who cured a disease or a young boy with his whole life ahead of him more important?"

Mara's eyes are wide and glowing as she listens to me, reflecting the stars. "Well," she says, "who should be saved?"

"I . . . I don't know," I admit.

She deflates slightly. "And I don't know either."

As we fall into a companionable silence, we look toward the livecam screen. I wonder if it's a recording of blank space meant to confuse me; certainly with the number of ships the Icarii have amassed nearby that space shouldn't look so . . . empty.

"I think," I say after a long time, "that you came here to do something. That you know what's right in your heart, Mara, and you just need to listen to that."

She chuckles. "You're telling me, a machine, that I have a heart?"

I look at her, even if she's not really here, even if that's not really her body. She once told me I was as much of a machine as she was. "You're just as human as I am," I say, twisting her words and parroting them back to her. "Whether you're born with a heart or have one 3D-printed for you, you still have a . . . a conscience. A soul. Otherwise, why would we even be having these discussions?"

"Mmm" is all she says in response.

"So what does your heart say, Mara?"

I don't expect her to answer. Not truly. So when she meets my gaze and hardens her eyes, I feel a shiver run down my spine.

"I don't think you can kill people and claim you're doing so for peace," she says, and then she is gone. One moment here with me, the next—after a millisecond-long blink—she is gone.

"Mara?" I ask. But of course, she doesn't respond. She might still be listening to me, might still be paying attention to me through my neural implant and com-lenses, but she's . . . gone back to wherever she was—the brig?

My mistake is that we are not in Synthetic territory.

I don't think you can kill people and claim you're doing so for peace.

I don't know what that means, but I fear the worst: it's up to the Asters to decide how the next few hours will proceed.

"Don't do anything stupid, Hemlock," I say into the room, and can only pray my words reach him on some errant wave of solar wind.

CHAPTER 37

LUCE

My Pollux: Everything here is shit. I've never been happier you're with the fucking Geans. I think I have a way to keep the Icarii from invading. The Harbinger even likes the plan. Problem is, I'll have to hurt someone I care a lot about, or kill hundreds . . . *Sfonakin*, what is the price of a soul?

Unanswered message on Hemlock's private server from Castor

"**A**re you sure about this?"

Castor is easily ignored in favor of the chaos of the Elders' chamber. Everything from the stony walls to the cobblestoned floor has been covered in the same leathery material from which the Aster clothes are fashioned. While the majority of Asters have cleared the room, a few, including Lotus, work to set up equipment, crude lighting and various handmade recording instruments for video and sound. It's taken a few hours, but our preparations for contacting the Icarii are almost complete. The three Aster Elders stand like silent sentinels in their blue half cloaks, apart from all others. Most ominous of all is the solitary chair that sits against the white backdrop, silver and sharp, a throne for a kingdom of twisted experiments.

Soon I'll be sitting in that chair. Soon the Genekey virus will enter my blood and tear me apart from the inside.

Are you sure about this? Castor's question echoes, or perhaps he is repeating it. Maybe the real reason I ignore him is because I'm not sure at all, but I can't afford to waver.

"Why does it have to be *you*?" The ire in Castor's tone grates at me.

Foolishly, I let my anger goad me into a discussion. "Who came up with the idea of using the research for the Genekey virus?" I ask. "You or Sorrel?"

Castor seems all too happy to answer, simply relieved that I'm speaking to him at all. "I suggested it, but Sorrel came up with the plan of distributing it to other Asters and using it on Cytherea."

"So you agree with him. You think it's a good idea to weaponize that research and create what's essentially a biological guillotine for the Icarii."

Castor's pupils narrow, making his eyes shine gold. "If this threat makes them back off, then yes, I agree. But that's all it needs to be: a threat. If we can prove to them that the virus works, if we can make them fear us, then we win. We won't have to kill thousands or die in an uneven war."

"Part of an effective threat is the willingness to follow through." My arms tremble at my sides. "What will you do if they see this video of me taking the Genekey virus and aren't impressed? Are you truly willing to kill thousands to make your point?"

His silence is my answer.

But all of the thoughts that have built up in me, all the accusations and questions since Sorrel announced his intention to deploy the virus, come spilling out now that I've begun talking. "When you told me you wanted to recover research stolen by Val Akira Labs, you *never* told me about this side of it, which means either you intentionally misled me so I would help you retrieve it, or—"

"That wasn't—"

"—*or*," I continue, louder than before, "you came up with the idea of the Genekey virus on Vesta but are so desperate that you think deploying it untested on a large population is a good idea." My voice holds every trace of my bitterness. "Which makes you stupid. It's not as if there isn't a long and robust precedent of biological weapons biting their creators in the ass."

I can tell from Castor's trembling that my insults—*liar, desperate, stupid*—found their mark. "That's why we're testing it now," he says, low and deadly.

"That's why you're testing it on me," I correct him. "Because if someone is going to be hurt by this thing, *I* won't let it be some innocent civilian who has done nothing to deserve it." I can already imagine Cytherea's response to a release of the Genekey virus: the best treatments would be rushed to the highlevels affected, while the lowlevels would be forgotten. It's always the poorest who suffer the most in a societal tragedy.

Before Castor and I can butt heads again, Sorrel approaches, something like a robe in his hands. "Would you prefer to undress now?" The suggestion is gentle but firm, and it has the added benefit of giving me something other than Castor to focus on. I knew I would have to undress as part of the bargain—the Icarii will need to see any changes to my skin—but now that the moment is here, I hesitate. Less because of the required nudity, and more because, when I take the robe from Sorrel and let it unfurl, I see that it's the same as the hospital gown that Ofiera was wearing when I first met her.

Who knows how long I'll be in the hospital battling the virus. And that's the good outcome, *if* I survive the initial injection.

I'm still in the wraps from traveling aboard the spider. Gently placing the robe over the arm of the waiting chair, I ball both fists in the loose sand-colored fabric and pause. Castor taught me how to dress in these, his hands warm through the bodysuit, my mind imagining what his fingers would feel like against my bare skin. Now the thought turns my stomach.

Ofiera appears silently at my side, startling me in my already nervous state. "Let me talk with Lucinia," she says to Sorrel. She's left her gravchair elsewhere and changed into dull Gean clothes, and her bandages are well hidden beneath. She's obviously not healthy, though; her skin has the same grayish hue as the paving stones. "Alone."

Sorrel doesn't even seem curious as to why she'd want this. "Of course."

Castor, as if he's my keeper, hesitates. "Luce . . ."

Something flares inside me at my nickname on his lips. The same heat from our discussion before rises. "Don't call me that," I snap. After what's happened, he no longer has a right to that familiarity . . .

But it's not until Sorrel speaks that Castor falls in line. "Come help me with this, Castor. Let them talk."

Castor finally withdraws.

I look down at Ofiera. She's a lot shorter than me, but I don't make the mistake of believing her weak, even as ill as she is. There's something of a predator under her skin that even the other Asters sense. *Shikra*, they call her. A bird of prey, small but brutal.

"Showing the Icarii everything the Genekey virus can do will help our cause," Ofiera says, hazel eyes shifting, gaze going far-off. "In and out of cryo at the labs, they monitored our hair and skin obsessively for any sign of damage to us." Her eyes wander, as if unbidden, to Sorrel.

"Castor explained some of the things they did to you and Sorrel . . ."

She smiles sadly. "We were both Icarii tools for many years," she says softly. "Thanks to Lito, we are no longer."

Lito . . . the reason I started on this long path. And the reason, it seems, that Sorrel and Ofiera are free.

"You and Sorrel are married?" I ask. She called him her husband when we first met.

Ofiera smiles, but there is a knowing glow in her eyes. "He is my husband, though our union is only recognized among the Asters."

I force myself not to look at Castor. In another world, in another place, perhaps we could have been like Ofiera and Sorrel. But here and now, because of what he's done, he ruined us before we even had a chance to begin.

"He does care for you," Ofiera says as if reading my mind. Then again, as a duelist, she would be trained to notice the little tells. "Don't ever doubt that. But right now, Castor's first loyalty must be to his people."

Not wanting to talk about Castor, I lapse into silence. Ofiera gestures to the silver chair, empty and threatening, waiting for me. "You are young," she says, "and you have your entire life ahead of you. I don't doubt that you are strong enough, resilient enough, to go through with this, but I wonder if it's necessary."

My stomach clenches. "My first loyalty must be to my people," I say, using her words against her. "The innocent Icarii, the lowlevels, who don't deserve to be hurt more than they already have been."

She holds up her hand as if to pause my tirade. "I met Hiro at a time when I believed nothing could change. They proved to me that some things could. But when I met Lito, I thought he was one of the things that would break before yielding. He was an Icarii loyalist, in both heart and mind. Seeing him follow Hiro's footsteps and choose to help the Asters hurt by the Icarii . . . Lito proved to me that *everything* could change, if we were to fight for it."

A sob works its way up my throat. My eyes sting with unshed tears. "Wh-why are you t-telling me this . . ."

"I have no doubt that you, like Lito, would sacrifice yourself to heal the hurts of thousands of others." Her hand finds my arm, and it is that small comfort that finally sends the tears rolling down my cheek. "I am one of those people Lito has helped. That is why, if you allow it, I will take your place in that chair."

I want to thank her and accept. Instead, I wipe away my tears. It would be easier to let Ofiera take the virus. But my resolve never wavers. I am young, yes, but I am healthy. She already looks like she's on death's doorstep. Between the two of us, I know which one's demise will impress the Icarii more.

"I have to do this," I say, then realize that's not quite true. "I *want* to do this."

Ofiera nods as if she expected my answer. "One last piece of advice, then," she says, and leans toward me in order to whisper. "When the pain becomes too much, remember why you're fighting. You're angry. I can hear it in your voice. And that's good. Sometimes anger is all you have.

"This is a battle in a war of a different type. I'm sure you've been told not to show your anger. Not to *feel* it. Women often are." Her predator eyes gleam. "But when death comes for you, Lucinia sol Lucius, when it grasps you with cold fingers, that anger can burn through it. That anger can save you. Better to be alive and angry than dead and peaceful."

I have no doubt that Ofiera has faced death time and again and has dragged herself back, kicking and spitting and clawing at life, hatred of Val Akira Labs the only thing holding her together. And the anger I feel is vast, an overwhelming reserve of fuel. I could burn it for years, and the flames would never fade.

"Thank you," I say, and begin to undress.

COMPLETELY NAKED IN the silver chair, I am swallowed by the thick silence. The bright lights cast large, dark shadows on the floor. Castor and Sorrel stand on either side of me, and with a nod from Hemlock, the camera is confirmed to be ready. Castor holds a syringe filled with the virus, and my entire life is set to change in the passing of a few seconds.

Recording begins. My heart works its way into my throat. Sorrel speaks first, and I wonder if I'm a blur in the background as the camera focuses on him, or if the Icarii can already see me, a body splayed as if on a slab in the morgue. *Not yet,* I think. *You're not dead yet.*

"We are the Asters, and we speak with one voice." Sorrel's speech is nothing like the Elders'; his appeals to the listener without the added effect of insisting on loyalty. "We demand a cessation of aggression against all Asters. We demand an unarmed meeting at a neutral location to discuss future cooperation between Asters and Icarii. We demand an end to the Icarii blockade of Vesta. We demand the immediate and total cessation of illegal testing on Aster subjects. We demand the release of Lito sol Lucius into our hands. If our demands are not met . . ." Now I know I'm the focus of the camera. I can almost feel it, like a fire, all eyes burning on me. "If the aggression continues, we will respond in kind."

I hold out my arm, and Sorrel ties a rubber tourniquet around my lower biceps. The pressure is something to focus on other than the fear, followed by the cool, wet sensation as he swabs the soft skin of my inner elbow with disinfectant—because I wouldn't want to get an infection on top of whatever the virus does, now would I? I fight the urge to laugh.

When Sorrel steps away, his job done, Castor takes his place. First he holds up the syringe for the camera to focus on, then he presses the needle tip above one of my veins. For something so threatening, it's terribly small. Inside the syringe is a clear liquid, unassuming in its appearance; the Genekey virus will be deployed on 3D-printed nanobots, the same way we made our genetic changes at Val Akira Geneassists.

Shouldn't something so deadly be overwhelmingly large? Shouldn't it be vibrant or glowing, red or green to mark it as sinister? But it's no more remarkable than an iodine drip at the hospital. Even the prick of the needle will be unremarkable.

"This virus," Sorrel begins to explain, "was developed by Aster scientists and will attack the Val Akira Labs genelock encoded into every Icarii citizen before birth . . ." He goes on, but my attention slides to Castor's shaking hands, then moves to his face.

I meet his gaze, and his eyes waver. There is pleading there, and sorrow, even guilt at what this virus is about to do. *Stop this*, his look says. *You don't have to do this.*

I don't have to. But I want to.

I turn my face away from him. As Sorrel finishes his explanation, he gestures to me. "Lucinia."

Now it's my turn.

"My name is Lucinia sol Lucius," I say, my voice high and clear. "I am an Icarii from the Faraday neighborhood on the lowest level of Cytherea. My brother is Lito sol Lucius. I am twenty years old, with a healthy mind and body, and I assent to this procedure in order to illustrate the capabilities of the Genekey virus."

That was all I was supposed to say, yet once the words are out, I find more on the tip of my tongue. The anger that Ofiera told me to listen to makes itself known, melting sorrow and anxiety in its path. "I'm sure you've heard on the news that I stole information from Val Akira Labs," I continue, to the concerned glances of a few Asters behind the camera, "and I'm sure there are a hundred reasons why they say I did it, so let me be the one to tell you firsthand."

I sit up straighter in the chair and let them see me—all of me—in one of the last chances they'll have. "I came to the Tesla neighborhood on the highest level of Cytherea to go to college, and I stayed there for a job after I graduated. In that time, I witnessed wealth and hate in equal measure. It seemed that everywhere I looked, those who had everything took and took and took from those who had nothing." A tremble of anger works its way down my spine as I remember Harmony val White turning me away, just one aggression in a series of thousands, and Hiro's recordings detailing every twisted thing their father did to them. "I met with, even joined, people who swore they wanted to help but only paid lip service to justice." I sneer at the thought of Shad and his Keres Art Collective, who stole my art for their own gain. Have they co-opted my image now too? It doesn't matter; their actions will change nothing. "And yet there were people I could not understand, could not hope to understand, because I was not one of them.

"The Asters have been experimented upon for hundreds of years, all for the benefit of Icarii science. So that non-Asters don't have to test the treatments themselves. So that non-Asters can make themselves younger-looking, or prettier. And after they've served their purpose, these Asters are tossed into the streets and forgotten about. You've seen them. I know you have. Yet you look away, hoping to forget the image of pus-yellowed bandages. You've listened to the whispers of illness, believing these people are sick and treating them like lepers, when it is the Icarii disease that eats away at them.

"*That* is why I stole information from Val Akira Labs. That is why I choose to help the Asters illustrate their defensive capabilities. That is why I'm willing to die: because the Asters *deserve* a chance."

By the time I'm finished, Asters around the room stand in various stages of shock. Some close their eyes, lost in thought, like Hemlock; others, like the Elder Rue, let tears run freely down their cheeks. Several seconds of heavy silence pass before Sorrel clears his throat and urges us to continue the test.

"Castor, if you will . . ."

When Castor looks down at me now, his face is full of regret. I have one last moment, one last second, when I can shout for them to stop, when I can jump from this chair and save myself the pain and chance of death. Castor practically begs me to.

And again, I turn away from him. *Do it*, I want my face to say. I grit my teeth and dig into my resolve, let the anger fuel me.

The needle bites into my arm.

Am I afraid? Of course I am. But I do my best not to show it, to pretend this is just another geneassist treatment. Just a change to my hair color. A touch to erase stress lines around my eyes or mouth. A use of research tested and perfected with the blood and bodies of Asters.

I'm not about to die. *I'm not going to die*, I repeat to myself. I adamantly refuse to believe this is my end.

Castor pushes down the plunger, and my veins flood with the nanobots.

I can't feel them. I'd be lying if I said I could. But I know they're there, and that alone makes me feel colder, like the temperature in the room has dropped ten degrees.

Castor and Sorrel step away from the chair, passing out of frame. I'm the star now. Me and the virus as we battle for my life.

I imagine the Genekey virus like a cancer, slipping into my cells like a pack of wolves. Hunting down the genelock with vicious efficiency. Ripping it apart with tooth and claw.

And what will remain of me once it's gone? Will I even be alive to find out?

I am an experiment, like countless Asters before me. Like Ofiera and Sorrel. Like Hiro.

Then the pain hits me with the fury of a monster, fangs and nails slipping into the spaces between my spine and *pulling*—

I scream—not a human noise, but a wordless, animal cry. Blood spurts from my nose, coats my tongue and teeth, and the lights around me flare before they fade into nothing but black, but this blackness is not calm, not peaceful—

I choke on my own blood and know death has come for me.

CHAPTER 38

ASTRID

The ACS *Juno* isn't just a precious conquest. She is a testament to what Gean might can achieve. With her strength added to our fleet, we are one step closer to a reckoning. Let us now honor the Ironskin pilots who valiantly seized this Icarii treasure in battle.

Warlord Vaughn at the consecration of the ACS *Juno*

I take to the maintenance tunnels. I explore and watch through the slats; the hallways are constantly patrolled by soldiers, more so than normal, and worry settles into my belly and makes a nest of sickness there.

After a couple of hours, I find a junction of tunnels, a crossroads of sorts, with enough room for me to lie down. I rest for the remainder of the work hours, sleeping lightly and startling awake at the smallest of noises, and during the off-hours, I emerge and sneak into the kitchen to take as much nonperishable food as I can in my arms and pockets. After debating, I also take a cooking knife the length of my hand to open the cans.

And just in case, Ringer hisses.

I keep a close watch on the time using the hallway clocks; otherwise, I roam like a wild animal—barefoot, silent, all eyes and no mouth. After a full cycle, I have slept four hours and eaten one ration packet of hydroponic-grown corn. It is the longest time I have spent in silence since the Mother gave me back my voice, and my throat hurts as if in protest.

But my mind will not allow me to be idle. I use the tunnels to climb through the *Juno*'s many decks, visiting the soldiers' first and lurking there for a handful of hours until I spot Rian returning to his room. RIAN WALKER, his bunk reads. Unfortunately, he is not alone, and there is no way for me to speak with him, to convince him not to mention seeing me to anyone else.

Or kill him, Ringer suggests. I tell him to shut up.

I go to the Sisterhood levels next. I am sorely tempted to look in on First Sister and her captain—how the memory of her claiming he loved her grates at me—but there is no way to safely look inside my old room without leaving the tunnels. I am relegated to watching the comings and goings of soldiers changing guard, Sisters in gray flitting about, and Cousins cleaning. It is only when the work hours come to a close that Aunt Marshae emerges from her chambers with the red-haired captain at her shoulder. Two armed men trail at their backs.

"I guarantee you that you will have my best men keeping watch over you at all hours," the captain says, gesturing to the two soldiers.

"And as for finding her?" Aunt Marshae asks, and my heart speeds at her words.

"If she's on the *Juno* like you think, we *will* find her. There are only so many places—" They pass out of my range of hearing.

My blood races in my veins. Rian must have already reported seeing me to someone important enough for word to get back to Aunt Marshae.

PART OF ME screams to take the tunnels to one of the escape pod bays and flee this ship. If the soldiers are hunting for me already, I have little to no chance of killing Aunt Marshae and getting away with it. Am I really ready to trade my life for this erratic plan?

Run, you coward, I tell myself, and my eyes burn with unshed tears.

But then I think of Eden's body, hanging from the ceiling, and the louder, more insistent part of me demands Aunt Marshae's retribution.

What is the purpose of coming this far if I do not remove her from power? Will I ever sleep again, knowing that she slipped through my fingers? This might very well be my last chance to get close to her after what I have done. And if they catch me after I have assassinated Aunt Marshae, at least I will go to my death with a smile on my face.

I could not change the Sisterhood from the inside, but I will be damned if I do not change it at all.

With that in mind, I call for Ringer, and we begin to plan how to pull off the impossible.

LEAVING THE TUNNELS during the next day's work hours goes against everything in my instincts, yet I let Ringer convince me of its necessity. I lurk on the deck where Rian is assigned to sleep, and when the coast is clear, I slip into his unit's bunkroom. I hope any passersby will see a Cousin's gray robes and believe that I am cleaning.

There is nothing on the communal table or left out on hastily made beds, which means I am forced to begin rifling through the military-issue trunks at the end of each bed. I start with Rian's, though I find nothing of value. No compad, nothing I can use to get a message to him. After I've thoroughly searched his personal items, I move to the next trunk and then the next.

At the bunk farthest from the door, I find a pad of paper and a pen. While the notepad is smaller than the one Hiro gave me, I am instantly reminded of the many hours we spent together. Of all the notes I wrote them. Then the rage comes, making me want to burn this entire ship as we burned my written words when we were finished with them.

Heavy footsteps reach me from the hallway. I turn my back to the door, hands shaking as I uncap the pen and choose my words. With my message finished and the footsteps closer, I shove both the pad and the pen beneath Rian's pillow, drop my head, and move for the exit. The man enters just as I am leaving, and I shift aside for him as a Cousin would.

Will he recognize me? Will he find my being in his bunkroom

suspicious? I clasp my bandaged hands before me to keep them from shaking.

Then he brushes past me without a word, without looking at my face, and I steel my watery legs, take measured steps into the hallway, and retreat into the tunnels.

I can only hope Rian gets the message I left for him.

THERE ARE FEW places the *Juno* does not have cameras. The showers. The chapels. A few blank spots in the hallways. I made sure to enter and exit the tunnels where cameras do not point. Of course, I am not fool enough to believe no one is watching footage, looking for me.

Do they know I wear a Cousin's uniform? If Rian spoke of seeing me board the *Juno* among the servants, I am afraid so. Still, I have no time to sneak to the laundry and pilfer something else, not if I wish to watch the meeting place I set in the message I left Rian.

In the off-hours, the ship is quiet and dark. I am exhausted, but do not sleep. Whenever I feel myself slipping, Ringer wakes me with a sharp prod to my ribs. I force myself to eat another ration of food—dehydrated eggs for protein—and drink some water to keep up my strength.

Whenever someone enters the hallway, it saps my fatigue and sends a jolt of adrenaline through me. But the first two times it is a simple patrol, a solitary guard passing by. The third time, however, the soldier shows signs of hesitation, looking around, retracing his steps. When he enters one of the chapels, I know Rian has arrived.

I move swiftly, slipping out of the maintenance tunnels in one of the sharp turns and heading for the same chapel as Rian. I try to ignore that overwhelming feeling that threatens to rise up within me, a mix of anxiety and fear at seeing the place where I was once a mere comfort woman. And I succeed, at least until I enter. Then the sight of the room threatens to destroy me.

The holocandles no longer flicker in the off-hours, but the room is still lit by the large livecam screen of the stars. The white fabric spills from the ceiling and flows down the walls, soft as sculpted clouds. And the bed . . . oh Goddess, the bed . . .

"First Sister?" Rian asks, pulling my attention from that cursed place. But looking at him, a soldier in uniform, a man with wide shoulders and strong arms, is no better. He is just another piece of decoration that completes the jail in my memory.

"Focus, little sister," Ringer whispers to me.

"Did you leave this for me?" Rian asks, holding up the note with my handwriting: *Meet me in the fifth chapel in the off-hours. From someone who needs help.*

"Yes," I say, and brace myself for his explosive response.

He jolts, a little ripple of electricity passing through his limbs. To hear a Sister speak . . . It would go against everything he knows.

"I can explain," I tell him. "I need your help, Rian. Desperately."

Slowly, he settles back into his body. Lets the stiffness from his muscles leak away. I know he is confused, know even now that questions lurk on the tip of his tongue. Does he wonder if all the women he has visited in these chambers are like me and can actually speak? No, I have to take control of the conversation before questions like that come.

It is a gamble. But everything is, recently. So I explain. I tell him briefly of what has happened to me, of the previous Mother returning my voice, of the way the Sisterhood lies, of how Aunt Marshae had my beautiful Eden killed. I leave out much, because we do not have the time. And when I am done, I stare into his horrified face.

"Then what . . . what do you need me for?" he asks.

"I need a weapon," I say. "I need a way out."

"The podships . . ."

"First I must deal with Aunt Marshae."

Rian's hand goes to the small, high-energy laser gun at his hip. The larger railgun rifle is kept in the armory and only issued during patrol hours, so the pistol will have to do. "That's why you need the weapon?"

Ringer passes from one shadow to the next behind him, and I am reminded of the kitchen knife in my pocket beside the box containing the Mother's neural implant. But we both know I cannot confront Aunt Marshae and her two armed guards with a knife.

"Yes," I say at last. "I have to stop her from . . . from harming anyone else the way she did Eden." And the hundreds—no, thousands of other girls.

Rian withdraws his gun and holds it at his side, debating. I bite my tongue, allowing him to consider all I have told him. But when he brings the gun up, it is not to offer it to me, but to point it directly at my face.

My breath leaves me in a rush. "Rian?"

Rian clears his throat. Does his best to appear big and in control with the gun between us. "First Sister, they're looking for you, and I have to take you in. I won't help you kill someone."

Ringer! I cry. I reach for him in desperation, the way I have a hundred times before—when Eden blackmailed me, when the Mother revealed the truth of the neural implants on Ceres, when I attacked the guard at the brothel—but the dizziness that comes from his control never hits me.

Ringer, please! I beg, desperate that he save me, the gun pointed at my face so very real, but the black hole that is his presence never eclipses me.

Ringer?

He is gone from the shadows, gone from the room. What happened to his promises, the whispers that he would be there for me when I needed him? All broken.

I want to spit and curse at him. Damn him, for abandoning me when I need him. But as the rage from my core blooms and burns, that creature behind my ribs unlocks its cage. Stretches its limbs along mine. Settles into me through my blood and bone.

No, Ringer is not gone. His promise is not broken. I am Ringer, and Ringer is me, and I am both a Sister and a soldier. And I know exactly how to deal with a scared boy in this chapel where I have a thousand times before. I know exactly how to deal with Rian.

"First Sister?" he asks as I let tears fill my eyes. As I look at him, with all the hope and begging I can muster, a face meant to break hearts. *You're a wildfire, Astrid.* And I am more than what I appear to be.

Rian hesitates. Are his hands shaking? No, the gun is steady, even if his eyes are not.

"I am sorry," I tell him, and I mean it. Oh Goddess, I mean it. I do not even need to fake the sorrow that rises in my voice, because my fear of him has melted, leaving only pity.

I brought him into my bed because there is a hole in me, and maybe that hole formed when Hiro left, or maybe I always had it within me and it only became apparent then. But I called for him because, more than anything, regardless of who I hurt and the act itself, I wanted to be wanted.

And I thought I could use him again in this chapel, manipulate him into helping me. But I couldn't, and I didn't, and now he will have to pay for my mistake.

Finally he drops the gun. Holsters it. His hand finds handcuffs on his belt and withdraws those instead.

He does not understand that my apology is not for what I have done. It is for what I am about to do.

"Give me your hands," he says at the exact same moment I pull the weapon from my pocket. My movements smooth, I lunge forward with the knife, over the cuffs in his raised hands, past his wide shoulders, and, refusing to make the same mistake I did at the brothel, plunge the blade into his neck. No trembling. No hesitation. The same surety in my body as when I pulled the trigger and shot the Mother.

His eyes jerk wide, but he does not move. Does not try to speak around the knife in his throat. Does not fight me as his body goes into shock. I pull the blade out, and it is only then that he shudders and falls to the floor. Dead.

The fire in me does not just burn him; it *consumes*.

I am sorry, I think once more, and Ringer smirks with my mouth. *This was not how I wanted this to go.*

Then I set to work stripping him of the things I need.

CHAPTER 39

LUCE

The Asters have sent us a video, sir, and *trust me* when I say you're going to want to see this.

Message from High Commander Beron val Bellator

to Souji val Akira

"Shhh, Luce. Don't cry."

Lito's face appears over the edge of my bunk bed. Even in the dim golden glow of the nightlight, I can see the purple bruise that mars half his small face. It makes me cry harder.

"Shhh, shhh," Lito whispers, stroking my hair. He's only recently gotten tall enough to reach me on the top bunk without having to stand on his mattress. "You'll get in trouble if they hear."

I clutch my bunny to my chest, burying my face in its soft head in an attempt to stifle my sobs as the paper-thin walls shake around us. I don't know what my parents are fighting about now—I never know—but I know that if we interrupt them, if we get between them, we become their targets, as evidenced by Lito's face.

"Come on, Luce, let's go to the sea cave."

My sniffles slow, and I sit up in bed. "You mean it?" It's the mid-

410

dle of the night, I think. We usually only go to the sea cave during the day.

"Yeah, come on," Lito says. He waits until I start down the ladder before grabbing a few blankets off his bed.

"Can I bring Hopscotch?" I say, holding up my bunny.

"Of course. Do you want your pink blanket?"

"No."

"Okay, these will do, then. Let's go."

A glass shatters somewhere in the apartment as Lito takes my hand and tugs me toward the closet. He doesn't let me enter until he's arranged a few things, pushing our few clothes to the back, spreading our blankets on the floor, forming the sea cave for us to sleep in.

"Okay, ready," he says.

I bend down and enter on my hands and knees, Hopscotch the bunny tucked in the crook of my arm, imagining the cave entrance is small, too small for our parents to get in. I know I've reached the heart of the sea cave when I feel the blankets beneath my hands. Then Lito wraps another blanket around me to keep me warm.

"Can you see the stars, Luce?" he whispers.

"But we're in the sea cave. We can't see the stars."

"We can. There's a hole riiiight there. It leads all the way to the surface, and you can see the stars through it. See them?"

And as my eyes adjust to the calming blackness of the closet, I do see the stars, little pinpricks of white in the darkness. "Wow," I say, setting Hopscotch on my lap so he can see too.

Something heavy thuds in another room, and I jump. "It's just the sea," Lito says quickly. "A whale jumping up and falling back into the ocean. Playing."

"We can hear the sea?"

"Of course we can. We're in the sea cave." Lito's hands reach for my face, fingers warm and comforting over my cheeks, before they cover my ears. As soon as his hands are in place, I can hear the soft rushing of the sea, the coming and going of the tide.

"Nothing can hurt you in the sea cave," Lito whispers, and I nod sleepily along with him.

"Nothing," I say. "Nothing at all."

THERE'S A RINGING in my ears, high-pitched and jarring. Everything else sounds muffled through layers of stone walls and cotton blankets.

The world around me is black. Not peaceful, but swallowing, devouring black.

No, not totally . . . There is a small place with pinpricks of white light like stars. *An opening in the sea cave*, something in my mind supplies.

My head aches. My chest is tight. I am sweating and yet shivering at the same time. I want to reach for my face, but I cannot find my hands. Do I even still have hands?

"Lito," I say aloud. At least, I think I say it out loud. But when I try to repeat myself, my mouth fills with salty ocean water that dribbles down my lips and pools on the floor. I have to cough it out of my lungs if I want to speak, if I want to breathe—I'm going to choke on it all.

Something lands on my chest, two dead weights. *My hands*, I realize as I force them into movement. But beneath them, my chest cracks, and little flakes of skin and bone, like ashes or snow, fall up into the sky where the black hole swallows the pieces of me and grows.

That's important, I think. I was naked because someone wanted to see me peel my skin off.

My hands move to my face, to my burning cheeks. Reach for my mouth to clear it so I can breathe, but find my hair instead. I seize it and pull it away, and it comes out in chunks. Hair the purple of a supernova falls soft as rain, up and up, and the black hole swells.

I want to scream. Am I coming together or falling apart? With another look, it can be both. For a star to be born, another must die. I must not be so different.

I no longer have a body. My chest has caved in, and inside of me there is no heart. Only a storm released, lightning flashing and thunder growling, and the black hole calls for it too—for whatever is left of me, my anguish and rage. I want so badly to let myself sink into it. To let the storm that beats me bloody and raw go, so I can disappear into the black hole—

But someone told me to hold on to the storm, so I do. The storm is the only thing I have left, and it is better than nothingness—even if it is dark, there are shades of purple and navy, clouds of the deepest charcoal gray, unlike the black hole. The storm is anger and hatred and violence, but it is *life*, and I let it batter me.

And when I think I can hold on no longer, when even the anger has faded and the storm grows quiet, Lito is there with his hands covering my ears, and I hear it, the roar of the sea, wild in the wake of my storm. But there is no question in me, no hesitation in what I do.

I throw myself into the ocean and sink down, down, down, away from the black hole and into the pain, the womb that birthed all humanity.

A SCREAM WAKES me.

I come to in an instant, and realize the noise came from my throat, ripped and tattered.

My eyes dart around the room, but everything is blurry and my head pounds with a headache, so I focus downward, on where the rest of me should be. Sure enough, there's a body there, covered in a white robe. Two gray arms plugged with needles. Two gray legs battered with darker splotches like bruises. I rub at my eyes; something feels different about my vision.

"Lucinia," someone says at my side, and I jerk my head up. I know this woman. I *should* know her. It takes me several seconds to recall her name.

"Ofiera," I say at last. My voice is cracked, strained from a raw throat.

"Yes," she says as if proud. "You're alive. You're okay."

Those two things are not necessarily connected, and only one of them seems true to me. Being alive does not make me okay. I have so many questions and so little strength with which to ask them. Everything is washed in a terrible gray shroud. "What happened?"

She's quiet as she considers, perhaps deciding how much to say, but before I can protest that she tell me everything, she begins. "You took the virus. You had some sort of seizure. We stabilized you as well as we could as the rest of you . . . changed."

She must see the question in my eyes, the question I do not need to ask, because Ofiera reaches for something at the bedside—a mirror—then holds it just out of reach. "Hemlock and Castor thought it best not to show you until you felt better, but I argued that you would not rest until you had seen yourself. The change is . . . Well, it may disturb you. Are you sure you wish to see?"

I can barely nod.

She holds out a picture of someone for me to look at.

"Who is—" I look back to her, and the picture shifts with my movement.

It's not a picture. That's the mirror.

"Oh." My eyes sting and burn, though the tears never come. My anger kept me alive, but at what cost?

I am a ruin.

My purple hair is gone, leaving my head bulbous-looking. My eyes are swollen and veined, likely from the crying. And my cheeks, once full of shimmering freckles, are now scarred with pockmarks. Everything I had changed at the geneassist has been stripped away—no, not stripped—*attacked* by the Genekey virus, and twisted into this new form.

I am hideous. More a twin to Hemlock than to the brother I love. And still my eyes ache as if I've spent too long staring into a bright light.

"Oh," I say again. It is the only thing I can say as I drop the mirror to my lap and rub the heels of my hands against my eyes.

Ofiera takes the mirror from me, and I let her. I don't think I want to look at myself again, not for a long, long time.

"Did it work?" I ask, my voice rough like I swallowed gravel.

Her face, that well-trained duelist mask, doesn't even shift. She is gray with her illness, yet compared to me, she looks like a picture of health. "We haven't heard anything from the Icarii yet. We gave them twenty-four hours after sending the video, and it's only been twelve."

So I've been lying here for twelve hours . . . It feels like it's been only minutes. Or maybe a lifetime.

"You'll be the first person to know when we receive word," Ofiera assures me.

I lean back into the bed, too tired to even thank her. The walls are covered in gray plants, their bioluminescent glow a hazy white field. The mushrooms are dull, not like I remember them . . . slowly, a thought rises in me, a crack of fear that splits me in half.

"Ofiera," I say, and she must hear the seriousness in my tone, because she straightens as if threatened by a knife. "What color is the lantern?" I gesture to the light at my bedside, so like the other lanterns lining hallways. It too has lost the vividness I remember.

"Red," she says.

Not anymore. The crack widens into a chasm, and I tumble down into it. Fear becomes anguish as I realize what has happened.

"Thank you," I say, and close my eyes on a gray world.

The world of paint splashed on canvas, of dreamed images brought to life, is gone. My gray limbs. Ofiera's gray countenance. The gray plants grasping. This is the new world.

I can't see color anymore.

OFIERA GENTLY WAKES me. "The Icarii have responded," she says. "They want to talk." She's brought the gravchair for me. Despite her wound and how much shorter she is than me, she helps me into the chair, bracing me as I struggle with my trembling, weak limbs. Once I'm sitting, Ofiera shows me the simple controls, and we are off, the slightest touch of my hand guiding the chair along the stony Vesta hallways.

Everything is unfamiliar. My surroundings. The woman who comforts me. My legs, once strong from running, now waver like flags in the wind. I wish I understood what has happened to me with any sort of clarity, wish I could read my genome, that mysterious map, and see how one letter became another. But that wouldn't make me feel any better, I know. The only thing that would is knowing that my sacrifice, this gray world I'm trapped in, was worth something.

We return to the room where I was changed. There's no evidence of what happened to me here. I suppose they would have cleaned it, afterward. The familiar group has already gathered—the Aster Elders, Hemlock, Sorrel, and Castor—their eyes finding anywhere to be but on me.

As we cross the threshold, Sorrel, always attuned to his wife's presence, almost knocks Castor over in his haste to reach us.

"You should have called for help, Ofiera," Sorrel chides, but his tone is that of a worried lover, no heat behind it. "You shouldn't be struggling with heavy things."

I hardly seem like a heavy thing, I wish to complain. But that's not true. Perhaps my body is a shell—light as air—but the pressure I feel is that of worlds, heavy on my shoulders. Pressing me down into my grave.

"What did," I start, having to pause to take in a deep breath, "they say?"

Attention lands on me, then hastily flickers away. Only Hemlock holds my gaze. He is the only one who hasn't changed from one world to the next. He was always a wash of gray, his eyes black and glassy like two pits of onyx, his skin lumpy and faded, his hair white like bone.

"They sent us a brief video stating that they're willing to negotiate, and we're preparing our response," Hemlock says in his low, hissing voice. It is comforting, in its own way, perhaps because we are now two of a kind—one human, one Aster, both marred beyond recognition. Outsiders to our own people. "It's thanks to you that they're listening to us, Lucinia sol Lucius."

Castor steps toward us, his shoulders squared with tension. His eyes bounce between Hemlock and me—jealously? Guiltily?—before landing on the ground. "The Icarii requested to see you, Lucinia." Not Luce, never again Luce.

This is what I bought with my body. My health. My beauty. I

remember our demands like they're written on my skin. Now it's time to see if the Icarii will avoid unnecessary bloodshed, if they'll make peace with the Asters. If they'll return my brother to my side, where he belongs.

They frame the shot as they did before, only now I am clothed. Sorrel stands on one side of me, Castor on the other. The Aster Elders lurk in the shadows. Hemlock stands near the camera, his compad in his hands. "There will be a five-second delay," he says, and I wonder if it's because of the thick stone surrounding us. We all know the Icarii are just outside Vesta, guns pointed in our direction.

"We're beginning . . . now." Hemlock nods to us when the recording begins.

"We are the Asters, and we speak with one voice." Sorrel's tone is just as steady as it was, though his face is far more somber. Perhaps he wants to look like he feels guilty for his part in my destruction.

This video—this whole setup—is just an elaborate game, I realize. We have to show the Icarii what they need to see—Aster rebels and scientists—and part of that is me, broken and trembling. I don't fight the shiver of pain that runs over me. Don't hide my expression of anguish. Let them see it all. I'll play the game to perfection.

"Let's not waste time: The information regarding how to create the Genekey virus has been sent to Mercury and Venus," Sorrel says. "Destroy Vesta, and you will find yourself on the hostile end of the Genekey virus all over the galaxy." He gestures toward me, proving what they can do. "Anywhere Asters live, you will be hunted.

"You say you are willing to negotiate. Well, we are too. But we will negotiate on our terms. Once more, we demand the cessation of aggression against all Asters, including medical testing; an end to the Vesta blockade; and the release of Lito sol Lucius back into our hands." When Sorrel is finished, Hemlock ends the recording.

"Sent," he says after a few seconds.

I close my eyes as the ache behind them becomes too much. That gray haze is too present in this place where I should see Castor's lavender skin and the golden shimmer of his irises. Now those colors, like the magnetic pull I felt toward him, are lost in memory.

Soft chatter is exchanged in the oppressive silence, but I ignore it. The only thing I want to hear is whether we achieved our goal or not.

"Video received," Hemlock says, and I open my eyes and sit up in the chair. With a flick of his wrist, he sends the recording to the holo-projector behind the camera. "Playing in three, two . . ."

The face in the video is not one I thought I'd see again. Tawny skin with the slightest hint of crow's feet at the corners of his eyes; no laugh lines around his mouth, as if he never smiles; and black hair swept back from his forehead with a signature streak of white. Anger swirls within me as I look at Souji's face on the screen. I glare, as if he could possibly see me.

"We agree to a cessation of all hostilities against Asters, including the Vesta blockade, across our controlled territories effective immediately upon agreement," Souji says, and I remember Hiro saying that, behind everything, Souji was the one pulling the strings. Now he's not even hiding it. "We also agree to an unarmed meeting on a ship of your choice in gray space to discuss a treaty between Asters and Icarii."

The tension in the room evaporates. Waves of relief curl off of the Aster Elders and Sorrel. Only Hemlock holds himself tightly, because the video isn't over . . .

"However, the fate of Lito sol Lucius is outside of the purview of any Icarii-Aster compromise. Lito sol Lucius is an Icarii criminal and will be held and tried for his crimes in the Fall of Ceres, as well as all other actions committed before joining the Aster rebellion."

"What the fuck is he talking about?" Castor snaps.

Souji's face is a blank mask. "We await your response as to whether these terms are acceptable." The video ends abruptly.

"No!" I scream, as loud as I can, just as the room erupts into celebration.

"We've done it!" the Elder Cedar says, reaching for Anemone and Rue. "We have only to accept and reach peace with the Icarii." Asters around the room embrace as if this is all over. To them, it is. But not for me.

"What about Lito!" I say as loudly as I can.

"Are we going to accept?" Castor asks, looking between Sorrel and Hemlock. He speaks quietly, yet his voice is louder than mine; my throat is too strained to be heard in such jubilation.

Hemlock drops his eyes to the ground, considering, but Sorrel doesn't hesitate. "Turn on the camera. We have to respond," he says. His tone is harder than I've ever heard it, demanding in a way that leaves no room for disobedience.

Yet Hemlock doesn't do as commanded.

Sorrel seizes Hemlock's thin wrist. "Do it, or I will."

Hemlock grimaces with pain and tries to pull away, but Sorrel tightens his grip until there's a sharp popping noise. Hemlock swallows a scream.

"Harbinger—" Castor steps toward them, a knot of chaos in the otherwise joyous gathering. Sorrel finally releases Hemlock, and then I see Ofiera moving through the crowd toward me, and I wonder why, out of everything that's happening, she chooses to prioritize me—until the world around me blurs, and I feel myself falling—

It feels like minutes, but it happens in a heartbeat. I hit the ground, and my entire body throbs, my bones and muscles not knowing how to work together. There's blood on my tongue, dribbling down my lips— like the salty water that choked me in my fever dreams—and I spit it out.

"No," I say again, but no one listens, no one pays attention except for Ofiera, who braces me, pulls me off the stone and into something resembling a sitting position. "No," I beg as Sorrel snatches the compad from Hemlock and Hemlock pulls his broken wrist to his chest.

"We will accept!" Sorrel's words echo in the cavern-like room, the stone bouncing it back so he sounds like a god.

The room goes silent and still.

"We will accept," Sorrel repeats, quieter this time. "What do you say?" But unlike when the Elders ask a question, his is a challenge. Hemlock's wrist makes it clear what will happen if anyone disagrees. But they don't see that—they see only the Harbinger, a hero who has saved them.

"Accept," says Anemone.

"Accept," say Cedar and Rue.

"Don't let him." I turn to Ofiera, to Castor looming above me. "Don't let him—"

Castor does his best to ignore me, though his eyes are haunted. *Castor's first loyalty must be to his people*, Ofiera said, and there's nothing I can do to convince him otherwise.

"Please," I beg Ofiera, the last remaining person Sorrel listens to. "You *owe* Lito, you said it yourself—" I spot the smallest sliver of doubt in her eyes, and I seize it with all I can, raise my shaking hand to tangle in her clothes. "Don't let them *kill him*—"

Ofiera looks away. I see the exact moment I lose her, when her eyes meet Sorrel's. She's choosing *him*. Sorrel. Her husband. His rebellion. The Aster people. And killing Lito at the same time.

She nods at Sorrel in encouragement.

Hemlock doesn't agree, but he doesn't have to; no one looks to him for his input, least of all Sorrel. But I'm surprised when Sorrel looks directly at me. When he offers me a hand. I shock myself even more by taking it, by allowing him and Ofiera to help me back to my feet.

For a moment, the rest of the world fades away, and it is just me and Sorrel.

"You asked me not to harm thousands of Icarii, to choose one life over many, so I did." He speaks quietly, barely above a whisper, but I hear him as if he were shouting. "I'm doing that again now."

One life for thousands, a part of me whispers. *Isn't that for the best?* And though I know Lito would choose that himself, the pain inside me grows larger and larger.

Lito is the last person I have left . . .

Sorrel turns toward the camera. With a tap on the compad in his hands, the camera begins recording. The video catches us as we are, unprepared, unposed—Ofiera holding me steady, my face twisted in pain and rage, Castor wide-eyed and confused, Sorrel certain of a path only he can see.

"We are the Asters, and we speak with one voice." Sorrel is unwavering as he says firmly, "We accept your proposal. Details for further negotiation to follow."

The camera clicks off. The video sends. Silence follows.

It is done. The Asters are safe. And Lito is going to die.

The world around me swirls, and for a moment, I fear I'm falling again—but no, my legs have taken me two steps forward, and I reach out for Sorrel, my nails curling into the palms of my hands, and I push with everything left within me, willing to crumble into dust, if only it helps release the pain—

My fist crashes into Sorrel's face. He sways, hand coming up to his nose. I wasn't aware I was going to hit him until I already had, and now I want nothing less than to tear him apart.

I grab a fistful of his jacket. Both of his hands reach for my shoulders to slow me, but I stumble into him as my legs give out beneath me, and the two of us lurch toward the ground. He hits the stone with a thud, and I land on top of him. He looks up at me, eyes wide with a question I can't answer.

I hit him again. Ignoring the ache in my bones, heeding only the burning anger in my chest, I strike him again. And again. He could lift his hands to his face, could reach out and stop me—I am so much weaker than he is—but he lies there and lets me hit him. No one interrupts as my punches weaken into nothing more than taps, as I exhaust myself. I hit him until his face is wet and swollen, until I collapse against him, trembling.

"I hate you," I find myself whispering. The tears burn on my cheeks. "I hate you . . ."

"I know," Sorrel says, perfectly still beneath me. "I deserve all this and more." Then he raises his arms and wraps them around me. Embraces me, as if I didn't just do my best to kill him. I am too weak to break away, too weak to do anything other than drift in his embrace, and so I lie there, not sure who I hate more: him, or myself.

"I know you understand me, Lucinia," I hear him whisper in my ear as the blackness claims me, "because you know what it means to sacrifice."

CHAPTER 40
HIRO

Father: I'm sending you everything we've discovered about the Synthetic agent. From its body to the setup of its brain, the information is so much more than I could ever have imagined.

Message from Commander Shinya val Akira to Souji val Akira

Something jerks me out of my nightmare-tainted sleep. "Lito?" Again, his is the name that comes to me upon waking. I don't know why. It's almost like I can feel him just out of reach, but only when I'm sleeping.

Mara crouches over me, dark hair falling into her face. The lights burn above her like a halo. "It's time," she says.

"Time?" I look toward the livecam screen to see what has changed, but like always, it's a blank view of space.

"Time to go, Hiro. Get up."

I push myself up, and my head spins. "How long has it been?" I'm starving. I'm exhausted. I haven't had something to drink in hours . . . It's almost like Shinya has forgotten about me. Only I'm not in a cage or chained up, and I feel like I would be if the Icarii were really going to torture me by the handbook.

"Mmm." Mara makes a soft noise as she thinks. "Twenty-eight hours since you were captured."

"Damn . . ."

I know she's not here, but I feel like I could reach out and touch her. Before I know what I'm doing, my hand moves to her face, my fingers trembling as they pass through her cheek. Still, I cup her face as if I *could* feel her, *could* embrace her.

"I wish you were with me," I whisper, more to myself than her.

"Do you know how special you are?" she asks, catching me off guard. "Someone who grows beyond what they were taught as a child. Who gives of themself for others. And not just once, but again and again." Her eyes shimmer, bubbling up with tears. "Who sacrifices everything they have and everything they are for peace."

I feel only guilt at her words; so much of this has been forced on me, and I resent it. "You think I'm something I'm not," I whisper. "All I know how to do is fight and lash out . . . even at those around me."

"Then don't push people away. You deserve good things." One tear falls, a shooting star down her cheek. "You're one in a billion, Hiro val Akira."

My eyes burn before I can even begin to puzzle out why she'd say something like that. "Stop it, I'm a sympathetic crier."

Between one blink and the next, Mara's form changes. Shifts. Mutates. One second the young girl who is barely distinguishable from human stands before me; the next she is clearly *other*.

Her head is cracked open like an egg, her silver prosthetic dangling by a cable. Remaining wires spark in the dark of the room. Her right eye socket is empty, a black pit, while her left eye glows with a ring of bright blue, blinking, blinking, blinking too quickly, like an alarm or a cry for help. Blood covers the right side of her face, down into her dark clothes. Her hair is matted with it.

"Mara?" I'm on my feet in a heartbeat. Reaching for her out of instinct, but of course my hands pass through her. "Mara! What have they done to you?"

It's because of me. Shinya found out she was the Synthetic from Autarkeia, and now they're experimenting on her. *Because of me.*

Then the blood is gone, the eye back in its socket, and Mara is whole and healthy again, like she can erase what's been done to her. Cover it up with something pretty and soothing. She gives me a pitying look—*me*, as if I'm the one she should be sorry for, when she's the one being torn apart. "I'm sorry," she says. "It's getting hard to . . ." She doesn't finish.

Of course it's not easy; they've started pulling her brain apart, and she's somehow . . . not dead. Not yet.

"When you get out of this room, go down to the brig and release Dire and the others," Mara says.

"'When'?" I repeat.

Mara ignores me. "Take them to the escape pods and get off the *Leander*."

"Mara, tell me what's going on." It's hard to know what to do with my hands when I can't touch her. I thread them into my hair. "What's happening?"

"Just do as I've told you. It's important, Hiro. Promise me."

"Okay," I say, because I can't say anything else. "I'll get Dire and the others off the *Leander*."

She settles, releasing a long sigh. "Thank you. Just be ready."

"Ready for what?"

"This is goodbye, Hiro."

"Ready for what, Mara?" I reach for her, as if I could possibly keep her with me, but she is gone before I can even raise my hand. "Mara!"

My breath shudders as it leaves my chest. Alone again.

It's time. Just be ready.

I don't know what's happening with her or anyone outside this cell, but I'll be ready for whatever it is she knows is coming.

I DON'T DRIFT off again, though my body begs for me to. Instead I sit close to the door with my legs tucked beneath me.

In what I estimate to be three hours, someone arrives.

Nadyn val Lancer storms into the room, navy hair mussed. She looks from the obviously edited livecam screen to me where I crouch empty-handed. "Been bored?" she asks, pressing a hand to her hip.

"Good to see you too."

She doesn't spend any time on pleasantries. "Where is it?" she asks. Doesn't demand, because she's not Noa, though I can hear the current of frustration in her tone nonetheless.

But she's alone, and this is the first time since I arrived that I've not had an entire team on my ass.

"Where's your partner?" I ask.

Her face doesn't give anything away. Are they on a different assignment somewhere else? Or is Nadyn saving me the trouble of dealing with Noa when we've always butted heads and it could cloud their judgment?

"Don't make this more trouble than it's worth, Hiro." Nadyn's voice is soft and compelling, but I don't fall for it. She's a Dagger, but not like I am. I am the shadow; she is the face. Whereas I use subterfuge, she manipulates. She might seem like a sweet sort, a sister or a caring friend, especially compared to Noa—but when it comes down to it, those two are meant for each other in every twisted way.

"We've torn the *Dominique* apart, checked all the crew, including you, and found nothing." Nadyn sighs as if this is the biggest disappointment of her life. "We thought we'd never find it, but then the Synthetic admitted you knew where the override chip was."

I know who she's talking about when she says *the Synthetic*; Mara's battered body flashes in the blackness when I close my eyes. And I know when she says *admitted*, she means *gave up after torture*. But what fucking override chip?

"We don't want to hurt anyone," Nadyn continues, as if she hasn't already been tearing Mara's brain open, and the way she wraps her arms around herself and drops her face makes her look like she might be ill at the thought. "Make it easy and tell me where it is, Hiro. If you comply, I'll arrange to have a full meal sent to you."

It's time. Just be ready.

Realization hits me at once. Whatever chip Mara sent them after isn't actually important, or maybe there isn't even a chip at all; if it were important, Mara would have told me about it. No, Mara just wanted someone to come to my room.

Be ready.

"Sure, I'll tell you where it is." I saunter toward her, arms casually pulled behind my head.

Nadyn can smell a trap from a kilometer away, which is why her hand flinches toward the hilt of her mercurial blade. Clever girl.

"You want the override chip?" I ask, and she does her best to look innocent and encouraging as she nods.

Help me help you, her face says.

"It's up your ass and to the left," I say with a wink.

Her face scrunches, and the hand near her blade forms into a fist. "I'm going to beat you so hard you'll need a whole new body—" she starts, and that's when I strike—right when she thinks I'm nothing but an annoyance—pulling the fat shard of teacup glass I secreted away from the folds of my jacket's hood and throwing it at her face.

She ducks to the side but doesn't retreat, and in the second I bought myself, I cross the space between us, grab her hand as she reaches for her blade, and *squeeze.* My prosthetic does all the work, exerting a pressure that my flesh hand never could, and Nadyn releases an animal scream as her bones crack and grind into dust.

The door opens, reinforcements coming. Fuck. Seizing that small distraction, Nadyn jerks her head forward, slams her forehead against my mouth. My lip bursts. Blood hits my tongue. I release her, my head spinning.

She whimpers, pulls her shattered purple hand to her chest, and stumbles back two steps, but I focus through everything—my hunger and aches and sorrows—and snatch the hilt of her blade from her belt. She reaches after it with her good hand, and I shove my body into her midsection, hauling her up over my shoulder.

My throat is so dry I can hardly swallow, but I can't pay attention to that now. Next threat: two soldiers with HEL guns at the ready enter through the door. "Catch!" I tell them, and toss Nadyn in their direction. Both of them focus on her instead of me.

"Watch *Hiro*, you idiots!" Nadyn snaps as she bowls them over. One hand down doesn't make her much less of a Dagger, and she's up on her feet before they are, reaching for her own HEL gun with her non-dominant hand.

But I have her mercurial blade, and it roars to life in the space between us. She's wearing military blacks, so I rush her, intent on keeping close, on making sure she can't use the HEL gun on me. The blade batters her shield, harmlessly bouncing off. The soldiers recover, track us with their guns, but I make sure they're not going to get a clean shot by staying locked with Nadyn.

"Fuck you!" she screams, spitting like a cat, hair tangling as she desperately tries to buy herself space. "Fuck you! Fuck you!"

Finally her shield goes out. Even when she realizes it, the anger doesn't leave her face. There's no fear when I spin the blade and bury it in her stomach, just a sense of bubbling rage and pain she vents through gritted teeth.

Blood froths over her chin. "Fuck . . . you . . ."

"Yeah, yeah." I turn off the blade, and she drops against me, heavy and wet. Slipping the hilt into my pocket, I spin her around like a dancer, back to my front, and take her hand holding the gun in mine. She offers little resistance as I train the pistol on the soldiers and, my finger over hers, pull the trigger. Once. Twice. Two laser flashes, and the soldiers fall to the ground, dead.

Only way to get through the fingerprint lock: use her hand.

I drop her. She hits the ground with a thud. "F . . . fff . . . fu . . ."

"I know," I say, her eyes going glassy at my feet. "Fuck me."

AT FIRST I chalk it up to my imagination, but by the time I reach the elevator—and instead take the stairs, against the advice of my complaining body—I know the truth: the ship is in a state of utter chaos. I hit the docking bay, and it looks like the world is on fire, red panic lights flashing, warning klaxons blaring, a voice echoing over the intercom.

"All hands to command deck. All hands to command deck."

My paranoia keeps me from moving freely, and a good thing too. I sneak from shadow to shadow, light on my feet, only to spot a couple of duelists running in the opposite direction through the hangar toward the elevator. While they say nothing, they don't need to; they both look frantic and pale.

I settle on the question I should've been asking this whole time: *What the hell is going on?*

On one hand, whatever is happening has drawn the attention of the majority of personnel on the *Leander*, which effectively allowed me to escape my captivity, since Nadyn was a lone duelist and had mere soldiers for backup. On the other hand, if Mara was going to appear and explain things, now would be a great time for that to happen.

But somehow . . . I doubt she'll appear to me again.

This is goodbye, Hiro.

No, I can't think about that. I have to focus on the important things and *feel* later.

Go down to the brig and release Dire and the others. Take them to the escape pods and get off the Leander.

I reach the other side of the hangar and chance calling the elevator. I'm exhausted and hurting and my head is spinning from dehydration and I *really* don't want to walk down forty flights of stairs on top of it— and thank the thousand gods, the elevator opens and it's empty.

I ride it down to the brig where they keep the most important prisoners, my body pressed to the side wall and my hand on Nadyn's mercurial blade in my pocket. The elevator doesn't make any other stops, and for a few seconds I allow myself to close my eyes and rest. To pretend I'm somewhere else, on some other mission, and Lito is at my side and everything is *fine*. Not great, considering we could still die, but *fine*.

Lito is a predictable person, yet I can't hear his voice. I try to call him up, but it feels pointless; anything I try sounds like my words shoved in his mouth.

Fine.

The doors open, revealing a long corridor much like other hallways on board, but instead of various-sized rooms with doors for privacy branching off to the sides, this one has individual cells with clear windows from ceiling to floor. In the first few I can see, there are people I don't recognize—mostly Asters—but the hallway stretches far enough to tell me that I'm in the right place.

"Is relief here?" a deep voice asks. I pull back into the elevator and step to the side so whoever it is can't see me—of course, that means I can't see them either.

"I dunno," a second person replies. "Doesn't look like anyone from where I'm standing."

"Well, the damn thing's not going to come down here on its own, now is it?"

"Maybe it's a ghost."

"Ghosts don't fucking exist." The deep voice comes closer to my hiding spot.

A snort. "Ghost elevator."

"Would you shut the fuck—" The guy steps into the doorway of the elevator and—holy *shit*, he's big. I look up at where I expect his face to be, and then have to *keep looking up.*

For a minute, we both gape at each other, not sure what to do. But he is a mountain, and armed, and I am clearly an escapee.

So I say the only thing I can: "*Shit.*"

"—the fuck?" the giant manages, reaching for his HEL gun. I ball my fist up and punch his hand, knocking the gun out of his grasp and sending it spinning down the hallway.

I launch myself at him and scramble up him like a tree, his arms like thick branches. I could grab Nadyn's mercurial blade from my pocket, but in military blacks, he'll have a shield, and his partner is nearby. I can't chance a two-on-one fight, not in my current state. I throw my arms around his neck and squeeze, hoping his lungs aren't mega-sized to match the rest of him.

He reels backward into the hallway, hands reaching over his head to grab hold of me, but only manages to fist a hand in my hair and pull. My scalp is on fire, but I squeeze harder, and for a few seconds, I think he's going to drop, his arms falling to his sides. But then he slams his back—and me—against the wall. Once. Twice. A third time, and I'm reeling, and when he reaches over his head to grab me again, this time my hold is weak and he finds purchase in my jacket.

He ducks, heaving me forward, and throws me over his shoulders and down the hallway. I hit the floor, my hip screaming, and slide back toward the elevator. No sign of the guy's partner, but he fills up the whole hallway as he releases a battle cry and pelts toward me.

Fucking *shit*, he's going to turn me into a smear on the wall.

Just as he reaches me, I roll out of the way, and he blazes past like a ship on fire. I scramble down the hallway, giving myself more room, but he's already spun to face me again and swings a thick leg at me in a kick. I shove it aside with my prosthetic hand, don't even feel his shield ripple, but I have no time to wonder at that before he reaches down to snatch me by the neck.

He hauls me up onto my feet. "*Fucking* giant—" is all I manage before he slams me into the wall. I'm seeing stars, legs weak beneath me, but he keeps me upright.

"I'm gonna beat your ass, bruv," he growls, and his accent hits me— lower-level Cytherea, exactly where Lito grew up.

He raises a fist the size of my face. "Okay, sol Shithead!" I snap, and he freezes, a tremble going through his entire body in the exact same way it would Lito's if I made fun of his inferior surname.

But he hesitates, and that's all I need.

"Thanks for the fight, *bruv*," I say, pushing my prosthetic leg against the wall, balling my metal hand into a fist, and *launching* myself like a missile directly at his face. The hydraulics in my knee move with fluid grace, and his jaw crunches against my metal knuckles with such force, my flesh hand would've broken.

His eyes go glassy, but he doesn't release me as he topples backward. He hits the deck *hard*, a thud so loud it probably echoes in the hallways above, and I slam down on top of him, his teeth and blood spattering against my cheek.

But he doesn't move again. I push myself onto my hands and knees and look down at the big guy, only to find he's passed out and half his face is blue and purple. Not dead, though.

"Yeesh," I mutter, backing off him and standing up. I shake out my prosthetic hand as if the punch hurt me, but my wrist still rolls perfectly.

Then I hear footsteps coming toward me from farther down the hallway, and though my head is spinning and I'm pretty sure I have a concussion and I'm breathing heavily, I spin toward the big guy's partner, reaching for my blade—

He throws his hands up.

"We're not duelists! We're not duelists!" screams a skinny boy who is all elbows and knees, some kid who hasn't lost the baby fat from his cheeks. He's not wearing military blacks, just an Icarii dress uniform, and he barely fills it out. I realize the big guy is exactly the same. They're *recruits*, not duelists. That's why he didn't have a shield or a blade . . .

"Who else is down here?" I hiss.

"No one! Everybody else got called to the command center." He runs both hands through his hair—big, frizzy, and the same orange as a pumpkin. "We were left down here to watch the prisoners."

"Throw your weapons over here and get down on your knees."

"Sure, sure!" As good-natured as a server at a restaurant, he sets his HEL gun on the floor before kicking it over. I snatch it up, even if I can't use it. He gets down on his knees and puts his hands behind his head without my needing to ask.

"Tell me what the hell is going on here," I say as I move behind him and start checking his pockets.

"Command got ahold of a Synthetic who had like a single human body and—"

"Yeah, I know her. Move on."

"They were trying to figure out how to download her memories so they could watch them later, maybe figure out what the Synthetics are planning. They started taking her apart and stuff, but it went bad."

I find cuffs in one pocket and use them to bind his hands behind back. "Icarii poking into Synthetic matters they don't understand, and it goes bad? Color me shocked," I say sarcastically.

He doesn't fight me. "They thought she was dead—left her alone in the med bay—but she just stood up and walked out, and the *Leander* listened to her like *she* was the commander."

I finally find what I was looking for: a keycard, likely the one that will open the cells. "Then what?"

"The Synthetic woman went to the command center and barricaded herself in there, along with the soldiers and commanders there, and the *Leander* started moving toward the Synthetic border."

Oh. Oh fuck.

Take them to the escape pods and get off the Leander. *It's important, Hiro. Promise me.*

He continues, "Emergency orders came down from the top. All soldiers and duelists on the ship are to try to get into the command center, while all our engineers are to try to stop the *Leander* from going any farther." Which leaves the recruits to do jobs like guarding the cells . . . "Check my wrist, look at the watch there."

Though I'm wary, I do. There's a timer counting down. The screen holds our fate: 41 minutes, 39 seconds . . . 38, 37, 36 . . .

"That's how long we have before we reach the barrier," he says.

Shit. I slip the watch off his wrist and put it on my own. As for the boy, he's served his purpose. Without a word, I cover his mouth from behind and hold him tightly. He struggles at first, but I release him as soon as he passes out. I'm not trying to kill him.

Without time to parse who is who in the brig, I take the keycard and scan it at every door I pass, releasing prisoners I've never seen in my life. All of them—whether Asters or outlaws—rush past me. No one stays to help.

I'm beginning to worry that Dire and his crew are being kept somewhere else when finally, at the end of the hallway, I find the group I'm looking for. Dandy is crammed in with other Asters, but Dire is alone in his cell, arms crossed against his broad chest, head down as if resting.

"What's up, handsome?" I ask with a wink.

Only Dire looks unsurprised to see me, smiling as I scan the keycard and release him.

"Thousand dick-sucking gods," Falchion says, the first words I've *ever* heard him speak.

Dandy doesn't even stand up when I open his door. "Hey, am I hallucinating, or are you seeing Hiro too?"

"This is real," Dire reassures Dandy, gesturing for him to get off his ass. "And we don't have time to delay. We have to find and release the rest of the Alliance members."

"They weren't all kept here?" I ask.

"No, just my crew from the *Dominique* were here," Dire explains, "along with some prisoners they had before we arrived."

So those from the *Xiaoling*, *Muriel*, and *Nova* are still missing . . . We'll need to check the other levels of the brig to find them.

"You know what's going on?" I ask Dire, preparing to explain as we go.

Dire's grim face tells me he knows. "I overheard the guards talking, and . . ." His voice drops to a whisper so only I can hear him. "Mara spoke with me."

He doesn't need to explain any more. She must have appeared to him like she appeared to me. Did he see her as she really was, broken and bleeding?

"We need to get off this bucket," I tell him once all the cell doors are open and the outlaws are assembled, "so let's go."

We move as one toward the elevator, and I reach for the call button—

A bomb goes off in my mind. My vision flares white, my ears ring with a high-pitched screech—

I fall to the floor. Strike my head. Taste blood. As if from far away, I hear my name, but I don't know who is calling for me—

"Lito?" His name, again, forces its way onto my lips.

Hiro! Dire, floating above me, mouths my name. *Hiro!*

But it's not me I care about.

"Lito!" I cry in the silence, and I don't know why but I feel him beside me. I know he's here, know he's screaming for me.

And I scream back. "LITO!"

CHAPTER 41

LITO

What does it mean to be Icarii? It means that, with these wings thrust upon our backs, we have only two choices: to fly or to burn.

First Icarii president Pablo val Cárcel,
address to the Venus Parliament

The door to my cell slides open, banishing the darkness and silence for the first time in hours. The stimulation is a shock to my deprived system, and I stiffen with unease. The hallway is bathed in red light, and the klaxons scream in warning.

Something is happening, and it's not good . . .

Then the door closes, and I am once against sealed into the total quiet of solitary confinement.

The wall panels brighten to a golden glow that is warm and welcoming but piercing at the same time. I can barely make out the three people who have entered, so I squint and focus on the floor, on the streaks of my blood that have dried there, as my eyes adjust. I have become a creature of shadows in the light's absence.

"Interesting afternoon?" I force out in a dry rasp, but Beron doesn't answer. Doesn't reveal a thing, not even the time.

I shift in order to stand, and the enclosures that cover my hands and the chains binding my wrists and ankles clank together in a metal symphony. At least for the past few hours they've given me enough slack to sit; if Beron's still playing by the Icarii handbook, he'll have the chains recede into the wall, forcing me to stand and depriving me of sleep until our next session together.

But because of the klaxons, I'm not sure we're keeping to our usual schedule.

Normally Beron or the duelist pair with him would crack their knuckles and get to work—that's how it's been since they caught me two days ago—but it seems they've lost their taste for violence. The duelists each set down a chair before retreating to opposite sides of the room, while Beron looks at his compad, engrossed in whatever he sees there.

"Since you've developed a taste for videos of experiments, with all the ones you released of those Asters," Beron says, his voice rhythmically calm, "there's something we want you to see."

Beron kicks one of the chairs toward me. With my hands in these metal enclosures that don't allow them to fully open or close, giving me awful muscle cramps that have become as familiar as an old friend by now, I don't catch the chair as it slides into my legs. Instead, I look at the piece of furniture like I don't know what to do with it. Like I've never seen one before.

"Sit," Beron says.

A little piece of Hiro pipes up within me. *Tell him you'd rather stand,* they say. But I'm not one to scorn gifts when I need to recover every bit of strength I can. This might still be a prelude to the usual torture session. I sit.

Beron settles across from me and turns the compad in my direction. From the still shot alone, I know with a cold, settling clarity that whatever he's about to show me will be worse than his fists, worse than broken ribs and cramping hands, worse than a knife beneath my fingernails.

My eyes immediately go past Castor and Sorrel to Luce—naked, small Luce, skin prickling in the cold air. A shiver rolls through me in response. I tense against my chains.

The torture session already began, I realize. *You just didn't recognize it for what it was.*

With a tap, the video begins.

"My name is Lucinia sol Lucius." Her words echo in my cell. "I am an Icarii from the Faraday neighborhood on the lowest level of Cytherea. My brother is Lito sol Lucius. I am twenty years old, with a healthy mind and body, and I assent to this procedure in order to illustrate the capabilities of the Genekey virus."

The video skips to a close-up of a needle, and I wish I could close my eyes. Close my ears. But I can't even lift my hands to my face with the way they're chained to my waist. I can only watch in horrified silence as Castor puts the needle to Luce's skin and injects her with something—a virus, she said—and she begins to—she *changes*—

It's not like a caterpillar becoming a butterfly, not slow or steady or planned—it is a dagger driven between ribs, death between one heart-beat and the next. Blood trickles from one nostril and then the other, and the black pupils of her eyes grow huge and liquid, and sweat drips from every pore, and her breathing becomes fast, fast, fast—

Her body is hit with tremors, first a small one but then another and another, each more violent than the last, until it becomes a savage, shaking rhythm that could break bones. She vomits as Castor and Sorrel, screaming in Aster, reach for her shoulders to steady her, to turn her on her side. Her hands—shaking, grasping, clawlike—reach for anything—the chair, the air, her own flesh.

Bruises appear as if from an invisible fist. Blood vessels emerge as if rising to the surface from a dark sea. A tuft of purple hair drops to the ground, followed by a rain of strands.

"What the fuck is this?" My voice is high and reed thin, and I sound like a child, I sound like someone who hasn't spoken for days, because I *haven't*, because in this moment, *I am a child*, I am nothing but the child I used to be who wanted more than anything else in the world to protect his sister.

Don't! I want to scream, hands balled into fists. *Don't hurt my sister!*

I wouldn't even be in this chair, wouldn't be a duelist, if I hadn't played gladius, hadn't gone to the Academy, hadn't joined the military in order to help Luce *find a better future*, but her future can't be *this*—it *can't be*—

The video stops. My heart races so fast, I almost forget to breathe. My implant drinks deep of my fear, but I have not used it against my emotions in so long—I had *wanted* to feel, and now I want nothing less—that it does nothing against whatever this monstrosity is.

"It seems you knew nothing of this threat," Beron says, disinterested.

"Is she alive?" I snap. Whatever childishness was there is gone, sapped like Luce's strength. "Answer me!" I scream, and I'm out of the chair, jerking toward Beron until I reach the end of my chains and my body pulls against the blisters and lesions on my skin for just a centimeter more, a millimeter farther.

But somehow that pain is comforting after all I've seen, like pushing my tongue into the gap left by a missing tooth.

Beron releases a sad sigh but waves the duelist pair away—of course they shot forward when I made a move for him. They reluctantly retreat, while he keeps his eyes on my twisted face. Assessing. Debating. How much does he tell me to get what he wants? How much rope does he throw me so I can hang myself with it?

I don't care. *I don't care.* "Tell me what you want me to say. Tell me what you want me to *do*, just tell me if Luce is alive!"

"She's alive," he says at last, and I don't even have time to snap *Prove it* before he's turning the compad back toward me and showing me a picture. A screencap of another video, but at least in the shot, Luce is undoubtedly alive, sitting in a chair.

Luce . . . hardly recognizable as my sister.

"Thousand gods," I whisper. I have never been someone who prayed to them, but if there's anything I could ask for, it would be to fix her from . . . *this.* I retreat until I feel the chair hit the back of my knees, then sit with a swallowed grunt of pain.

It's my fault. If I hadn't failed on the satellite station—if I hadn't been captured—there would've been no need to use the virus. No need to test it on my sister. If I had only saved Vesta, she wouldn't have needed to . . .

"Do you know what's happening out there, Lito?" Beron asks as he places the compad facedown on his lap.

I remain silent, hoping he'll answer his own question.

Instead, he asks another. "Do you know where we're going?"

"I can make a pretty educated guess," I reply as smoothly as I can.

"We were supposed to go to Cytherea," Beron says, surprising me. "But you will never make it there, and I'll tell you why."

Supposed to go? I'm once again reminded of the klaxons. I lean back, chains clinking as I do, ever aware of the eyes of the duelist pair on me.

"All over Venus, there are demonstrations in the streets. Images of bloodied Asters on protest signs. Drones projecting clips of illicit experiments. Even pieces of your discussion with Noa sol Romero, sampled and replayed over speakers." Beron runs a hand over his face, and it's then that I notice how exhausted he looks, the bags beneath his eyes dark from lack of sleep. "People are demanding the AEGIS look into Val Akira Labs."

My sorrow and guilt crash all at once, breaking against the revelation of this news. It's everything I could have hoped for when releasing the data, and more.

For the smallest second, there's a hand on my shoulder, a whisper in my ear, a familiar neural implant on the horizon of my attention. It's there and gone so quickly that it makes me disbelieve I even felt it in the first place. But I'd know that hum anywhere, brief as it was—know it like their laugh, their scent of home, their foxy smirk.

"Hiro?" I whisper.

I look toward the doorway. But whatever it was that made me feel Hiro's implant for even a moment is gone.

Does Beron have Hiro somewhere on this ship, or did I completely imagine that? I am hungry and exhausted. It might've been my imagination.

When I focus back on him, he's still talking. "I must make this brief. Between this investigation and the Aster-created virus, we have been forced to agree to a meeting to discuss treaty terms between the Asters as a sovereign body and the Icarii."

"I would suggest," I say, surprising even myself, "that you agree to their terms."

His eyes seem to sink further into their dark sockets. "Some of their terms will bankrupt our society."

I shrug, and it shifts my chains. "Our society became bankrupt the moment it started hiding bodies."

"Your opinion is abundantly clear. Which brings me to the reason for my visit . . ."

I remember his words. *You will never make it there.* And the certainty settles on me like a heavy mantle.

"If there's an investigation," I say slowly, softly, "then Souji val Akira can't afford to have me testify."

"Despite the emergency situation," he begins, and even this reference to the klaxons does not slow my downward spiral, "I have been personally tasked with overseeing this." He frowns down at his compad, at what's displayed there. "I suppose I should ask you if you have any last words."

The floor completely drops out from beneath me. I knew this could happen. *Knew* it, and yet never fully believed . . . Not until now. Now it all comes crashing down, and I fall with it.

Beron taps a finger on the compad and holds it in such a way that I know he's recording me. With a nod to the duelist pair, one steps forward, and with a cold clarity, I realize what's happening. They're going to record my death, proof for Souji val Akira that I will no longer be a problem.

"D-do you know why we're called the Icarii?" I find myself asking. "Everyone knows it's because the scientists who left Mars for Mercury traveled on a ship called the *Icarus*, but not many people know why they'd name the ship that. A bit morbid when your mission takes you to the planet closest to the sun, right?"

Beron watches me from over the compad—brows furrowed, lips downturned, *sorrowful.*

"We're called the Icarii because our name is meant to be a reminder of our responsibility," I keep going. Force myself to, because every moment speaking is a moment in which I'm still alive. "Daedalus created two sets of wings in order to escape the labyrinth—one set for his son, one for himself—and they worked."

The duelist takes the mercurial blade from his hip.

"But Icarus didn't heed Daedalus's words. He didn't use the wings responsibly. And he suffered because of it. He *burned* because of it."

The mercurial blade hums to life, and the glow—cold and white—is everything the warm walls are not. I can only hope that the emergency situation Beron mentioned is something positive for my allies; I'm afraid I'll never know for sure.

"Lito sol Lucius," Beron says, louder, speaking over me. "For the crime of high treason against the Icarii people, you are sentenced to death."

They say your life flashes before your eyes when you're about to die, but not in my case. Everything seems to crystallize, a dirty window wiped clean, so that I see it all, understand it all, every step that brought me here, to where I'm supposed to be.

Where I'm supposed to die.

I accept my place in this line, an Icarii rebel following Hiro's footsteps. A martyr whose death will mean *everything.*

This is what I'm meant to do. Die, where the others cannot. Be the spark that sets the fire that consumes the Icarii.

"Do you understand, Beron?" I ask, pushing myself up from my chair. Standing, so that I die on my feet. "Do you see why I chose the Asters? Why I have to stop what val Akira is doing?"

Beron nods at the duelist, and he steps forward, blade at the ready.

"Because we've flown too close to the sun, and I am the fi—"

My words are stolen from my throat by a wet heat—blood dribbling over my lips, down my chin. I barely have the strength to look down, to see that cold glow in my chest, to recognize it as the mercurial blade that the duelist buried there.

Oh. It's much colder than I imagined.

I close my eyes. Summon up the last dregs of my strength. Form my last words:

"... let it ... burn ..."

And when the duelist jerks the blade out, I collapse, breath rattling in the silence that precedes death.

CHAPTER 42

HIRO

PHANTOM PAIN (noun): A sensation of pain experienced by an individual from a limb or an organ that is not physically part of the body, often caused by amputation or neurological damage.

From *Val Machinist English Dictionary*, vol. 2

I suck in a dying breath, my implant hot in the back of my head, aching like it did when it was first put in. The soft song it used to sing when Lito and I were together, the soothing hum between a Rapier and Dagger, is now a funeral wail. My partner is—

There's nothing there now.

"Lito!"

Even if we weren't programmed to be together anymore, I felt him on the *Leander* in my sleep. He's here—no, he *was* here. What else could the sudden shock to my entire system mean?

Phantom pain. The term comes back to me, and I remember the way I ached for an arm and a leg that were no longer there. My neurology still remembered my limbs, even if I wasn't supposed to. Just like my neural implant . . .

It remembers Lito.

"LITO!"

I felt him. I know I did. Felt him there, and then gone like a ghost, and I fear I know what that means.

I don't want to know what that means.

Something strikes me. The white haze fades. My legs are limp beneath me, but I'm standing, supported between two men—who are they? My mind struggles—Dire and Falchion.

"Snap out of it!" Dire screams.

"He . . . he . . ." My voice echoes in my head. The only word I can manage sounds like a hiccup. "He . . ."

"What's wrong with them?" Dandy's see-through skin is paler than normal, the veins of his face a bright blue map. "Are they being controlled like we were?"

I wish I could speak, wish I could tell them this has nothing to do with what they experienced and everything to do with the shattered remnants of my heart.

"We don't have time for this!" Dire slaps me. I suck in a deep breath, and the world becomes startlingly clear. We stand in a cold metal hallway of an *Athena*-class warship that is hurtling toward the Synthetic border. If I haven't done as I promised Mara, released the outlaws and made it to the escape pods, I have no doubt we'll die when we cross the border, like everyone else on the *Leander*.

But I don't care.

"Go without me," I say. My voice is hollow but calm.

Dire tightens his grip on my arm. "What?"

I find the strength to stand on my own two legs, to push myself away from Dire and Falchion. "Go without me," I repeat.

"We have to release the others!" Dire looks at me like he's seeing a new person. Maybe he is. "We have to get out of here!"

"Then go get them," I say.

"What the fuck are you talking about?"

"They'll be on the other levels of the brig—you can take the stairs and release them with the same keycard that let you out."

"What if they're not there? I don't have a fucking map of this ship in my head like you do."

"I have to go to Lito—"

"Your old partner? What the fuck—"

"I can't leave him—"

"Mara said—"

"I WON'T LEAVE HIM!" My scream echoes through the hallways. Dire is struck silent. "I'm not leaving without Lito . . ."

Dire's face becomes hard. I see the words he bites back, attempts to convince me to come with him, to do as I promised Mara I would. But there's nothing he can say that will persuade me.

"You'll die," he says. Not even that.

As he sees the truth in my face, his eyes widen.

"The stairs are there." I point to them. "Take them up to the next floor." I pull the keycard from my pocket and toss it to Dire. Falchion catches it midair. "That'll release whoever you find. You've got . . ." I check the countdown on the watch. "Thirty minutes." I step into the waiting elevator.

Dire takes a single step forward. "Hiro—"

"Good luck," I tell him, "if I don't see you again."

He doesn't stop me. He says nothing more. The door closes between us.

As the elevator draws me up from the belly of the *Leander*, I know he understands. He saw the truth: I'm okay with dying, so long as I'm by Lito's side.

THE FLASHING RED emergency lights bathe me in blood. I march through empty hallways that should be swarming with soldiers. What was it the trainee said in the brig—that almost everyone had been called to the command center? They're likely trying to save the captives within. Maybe they can cut through the walls or the door with time, but time isn't something we have a lot of right now. Every second takes us closer to the Synthetic border. Closer to death.

I half wish they were in my way, that in my aching fury I could cut them down. Lose myself in the bloodlust of a fight, in the adrenaline racing in my veins as my body screams for survival. Instead I am numb. Empty. Hollow.

When I do come across someone, my hand is already on the hilt of Nadyn's mercurial blade. But it is not the fight that spools out before me that I think of—no, my mind is on the first time an instructor placed a blade into my and Lito's waiting hands. We were children who thought we were grown, who believed there could be no higher honor than in serving one's people, and now—

My opponent dies as his shield goes down and my blade cuts into his stomach. As his body hits the floor, stinging rage like bile burns its way up my throat, pushing me to cut *more*, hurt *more*—but in his crumpled form, I see the child I used to be. How long has he been out of the Academy? Not long enough to learn that the people he worked for weren't who he thought they were.

Lito and I were never assigned to an *Athena*-class warship, not permanently, but we did assignments on them during our Ceres posting. The *Leander* is like those ships, like the *Juno*, little to no difference in them besides their inhabitants. And even then, faces blur together, and I am lost between now and the past, catching glimpses of Saito Ren prowling beside me in the shining metal of the walls, a ghost in my reflection.

Lito wouldn't have been kept in the brig. As a politically significant prisoner, he would have been in the solitary cells meant for more than confinement. For torture, though no Icarii would call it that, preferring to say *enhanced interrogation*. As if their twisted words could mask their lies.

Unless they moved him because he's—

Don't say it.

Then he'd be in the morgue—

Don't think it.

The cells first, then I'll check the morgue.

I come up on the cells fast, my mind blanking in the empty space between hallways. Twenty minutes left. I catch myself when I arrive, fingers digging into the hilt of the mercurial blade. I need to pay attention; I can't let anyone get the drop on me.

Most of the cell doors are open, but I don't mistake them for empty. I press my back to the wall, peer into each room, then move to the next. Before I reach the last cluster of four, I hear a voice, loud enough to reach me over the ship's warning klaxons.

"Because we've flown too close to the sun, and I am the fi—"

Lito—

My heart stutters in my chest.

"...let it...burn..."

I step into the doorway, too fast, without checking—and there Commander Beron val Bellator stands. His back is turned to me, but I'd recognize him anywhere. Lito's voice is just that—a voice. He's not here.

"Confirmed, sol Lucius has been eliminated. I'm on my way to the—" Beron turns, fingers tightening on the compad as he sees me.

"Who's the message for?" I ask, my tone a razor's edge. Already it has cut me; I taste blood on my tongue. "It wouldn't happen to be for my dear old dad, would it?"

"Hiro . . ."

I step into the room, mercurial blade flaring to life, a silver glow in the sea of red. "Might want to say your farewells."

"Do you know what's happening out there?" Beron's infuriatingly calm. "Do you know where we're heading?"

"Oh, I know." I take another step toward him. He holds his ground. "We'll soon be joining Lito, you and I."

"You crazy little shit—"

I rush him, the space between us gone, my blade into his shield, burning bright and blue—

"Fuck!"

His HEL gun comes up, fires close enough to my face to burn me, but I'm not dead—not even bleeding. He slips away with a duelist's fluidity, his training not forgotten but buried beneath years. When we part, he's holding the HEL gun and closer to the door, but I stand over the compad with the video of Lito that he dropped.

He looks between it and me. Considering. Calculating. He makes a move as if to grab it, but I release a primal growl and hold my blade up. "Don't!"

He could shoot at me, but he halts. Stands frozen. Those equations are coming up negative now. He can't stay here and fight me if he wants to make it to the escape pods in time. I see the exact moment he decides to leave.

"Lito's in the cell next door," he says, backing toward the hallway. "Come after me, or run to your prize. Your choice."

Then he's gone, a coward in the end, fleeing for his life.

I don't chase after him. It's no choice for me. I pick up the compad with the last image of Lito frozen on its screen and tuck it into my pocket. Now to get Lito and get the fuck off the *Leander.*

In the hallway, I cast a look back the way I came. Not even a glimpse of Beron's back; he's already gone. I feel my muscles rolling beneath my skin, my prosthetics gliding with the same grace. I am fully in my body—*my* body, and no one else's—like I haven't been in years.

I step into the cell where they held Lito. He's stretched out beneath a white sheet. Wet blood pools on the floor. And between us stand two duelists with eyes ablaze.

"That's my Rapier," I tell the two men. They must know what's happening. Must know we have time to either flee or fight, but not both. But they also have their orders, and I can see they're not going to make it easy for me to take my friend with me on my way out.

Their blades flare to life in unison. I raise my own blade with resolve.

Fifteen minutes left. If I must cut my way through them, so be it.

CHAPTER 43

ASTRID

After everything that's happened between us, I know I should be scared of Astrid. But I'm not. I'm just as angry as she is, yet she does things I only wish I could.

From the diary of Eden

With Ringer guiding my movements, I march through the hallways like I belong. Like this is my ship. Dressed in Rian's Ironskin plugsuit—his uniform didn't fit, but the navy-and-gold plugsuit he wore beneath contracts to fit any body type—and with his gun at my side, I move with purpose toward Aunt Marshae's room. With my hair tied into a tight bun and my face washed of all cosmetics—and Rian's blood—I do not look like myself. I hope it is enough of a disguise.

Do cameras note me as I pass, or am I just another soldier? Is it odd that I am in a plugsuit, or is it unremarkable? These questions are all I can think of until I come across a group of soldiers moving in formation, and my insides turn to liquid.

They will see me. They will know me.

I do not falter. Do not stop my determined stride. Do not drop my gaze.

Should I salute them as they pass? Should I make a remark?

I do not know, I do not know, and it is the not knowing that will kill me.

Then they are passing me by. They say nothing, and I say nothing. I do not turn to look back, and within seconds, they are gone.

I release a breath, force myself to take in a new one. I feel faint, my lungs too small, the air too thin, my breathing too shallow, and Aunt Marshae's chamber is just around the corner. Ringer does not speak—not in words—but I feel him in the straightness of my spine, in the way my hand tenses over the gun.

We are alone together.

I round the corner into the main corridor, chambers branching off in each direction. Aunt Marshae's door has two guards posted outside. They do not even take note of me until I slow my approach.

"What's happening?" one asks. He might not recognize me, but in a ship with more than two thousand crew members, that isn't surprising; it is my suit, and the position it denotes, that he notices.

"The captain has called for soldiers. Report to the Ironskin deck," I reply.

"I didn't get any notification," the second says. "Let me check . . ." He reaches for his compad, and in that moment of distraction, Ringer and I move as one: I pull Rian's gun and shoot him in the chest, thankful, in this moment, that I do not have the noisy railgun.

I have no time to feel the guilt that rises up—or perhaps Ringer tamps it down. As his partner crumples, the other soldier draws his weapon and points it at me, and I throw myself to the side as he shoots at where I had been seconds ago. From the floor, I train Rian's gun on him and shoot again, but it only hits his shoulder. He bites back a scream that emerges as a growl.

How many people have heard us?

I quickly stand and shoot again, and this time it goes high—above his chest, into his face. But regardless of my aim, he falls, dead.

My breath comes quickly. The horror of what I have done settles in. *You're a wildfire, Astrid, and you burn everything and everyone around you.* I know I have done many terrible things, but I cannot stop now. Cannot, because if I do, all I have done until now will not matter, and I will not allow Paola's death, Eden's death, to be for nothing.

Ringer pushes me onward. I open Aunt Marshae's door and slip into her quarters. The door silently slides closed behind me.

I wait for a moment as my eyes adjust to the darkness, my hand tightening on the gun. As I make out darker patches of shadow, the furniture in the room, I take hesitant steps toward the bed where Aunt Marshae sleeps.

How should I do this? With her suspicions, she likely has a compad, and I cannot have her call for help. It must be quick and silent and merciless, before other soldiers come to investigate the two at the door. My heart races in my chest so loud I fear it will wake Aunt Marshae.

I am scared, I admit to myself—and to Ringer. He says nothing in response, but little by little, the fear disappears, sucked away by the black hole that is his presence.

Despite the size of the room, my legs eat up the distance between the door and the bed in seconds. It brings me to where she sleeps, a lump atop the wide mattress swallowed by blankets, too quickly for me to feel fully prepared. My hand holding the gun sweats, and I shift it around in my palm and fingers, make sure my grip is strong.

No hesitation, I coach myself. *No hesitation.*

I breathe in a shuddering, deep breath through my nose and jump onto the bed. My free hand goes for her face to cover her mouth, while the other holds the gun up and at the ready.

Then the light turns on, blinding me, and I push the gun toward her face, and—

Lily lies beneath me.

Lily, wide-eyed, sleep-rumpled, *here* in Aunt Marshae's room—

I jerk back, releasing her mouth, and all at once memories pelt me like fists. Lily, telling me she could no longer help me. Lily, in her safe house saying no one could get to Nat—so how did Aunt Marshae? Lily, explaining that she and Aunt Marshae were returning to Ceres but dodging the question of what the Agora told her—did Aunt Marshae give her what she wanted?

My voice is a growl. "Are you the First Sister of Ceres?"

Lily stares at me like she did at the brothel: with pure, unfiltered fear. "Astrid . . ."

Aunt Marshae knew I would come for her. She put Lily in her bed. Because she didn't care what happened to her? Because Lily is bait they thought I wouldn't fail to take?

Because Lily is a traitor too, my black heart whispers, and it sounds like the beast that was once locked behind my ribs. It sounds like Ringer, because it's always been him.

I hear the thunder of boots in the hallway and know all at once what has happened.

"Astrid, run!" Lily barks.

This is a trap, and I have walked right into it.

CHAPTER 44

HIRO

>>ABNORMALITY DETECTED: *ATHENA*-CLASS SHIP, DESIGNATION: "LEANDER." WEAPONS SYSTEM ACCESS REQUESTED.

Report from Sentry 236A on the Synthetic border

Before the two duelists can even get in position, I spin the mercurial blade in my hand and throw it at the central light panel above us. The shattering noise that follows, the rain of glass and sparks, sends them flinching away from the center of the room, and I slide into that space, catching the hilt of the blade before it hits the floor.

The other panels on the walls flicker out, leaving us in the red emergency lighting. If they looked directly at the sparks, their eyes will take longer than mine to adjust—which is the only thought I have time for before they're on me, coming at me from both sides.

I parry what blows I can, never allowing them to see my back, desperate to keep them in front of me. It's two on one, and they have shields while I don't; a single misstep, and it's over for me. They herd me back, and I allow them to. When the heel of my foot brushes against the chains trailing from the wall, I know I've reached my mark.

I slip my left foot under the chain and kick it into my hand. As I parry the Rapier with my right, I sling the chain at the Dagger. He slows, caught off guard by the impromptu weapon, but the chain bounces off his shield. With a look of pure anger, he rushes me with full force, my blade caught on his Rapier's, leaving me completely open—but I fling myself to the side, rolling away from them both.

They cast a glance at each other that even I can read as frustration. Now the chain lies between them, my hand farther down the line, and I keep crouched close to the floor, as if ready to roll again. But as they step toward me, I grab the chain with both hands, my blade on the floor, and sling the chain at the Rapier's knees. It knocks his legs out from under him, and he falls as his Dagger shoots forward.

I barely have time to grab and raise my blade before the Dagger is on me. But he's not the one I want to focus on, so I parry his blade away and toss myself after the fallen Rapier. "Come on!" he snarls in frustration, the lights highlighting his twisted face in red. "Stop running around and fight!"

He's going to regret that wish. As the Rapier rights himself, I turn off my mercurial blade, clip it on my belt—I'll need both hands for this—and grab the chain. The Rapier's getting his legs beneath him when I loop the chain around his neck from behind. My knee in his lower back, the chain tight against his throat, his entire body jerks back into my chest.

But he still has his blade, and his shield is burning but not broken, and his Dagger is coming right at me. For a moment, bitterness claws up my throat until I can taste it on my tongue, the idea that, if Lito were here, this would be no trouble at all—

Lito, lying dead right beside us—

I jerk the Rapier to his feet, the chain taut around his neck, and spin so that his Dagger will have to attack him to get to me. The Dagger halts, but the Rapier is ready for this; he turns the blade in his hand and pushes it back *into me—*

My red world washes white with pain, but only for a moment. The adrenaline rush smoothes as quickly as it spiked, until I feel nothing at all. Mara's programming automatically numbs the "wound" in my prosthetic leg, and I kick the Rapier in the side of his knee until he's forced to kneel in front of me.

My prosthetic hand holding the chain tight, I grab the Rapier's blade with my flesh hand and pull it from my leg without a wince.

The Dagger, still unable to find a way to attack me without harming his Rapier, tightens his grip on his blade. "What the fuck are you?"

Mara's words come back to me. "You're already as much of a machine as I am."

The Rapier tries to elbow me but can't quite find an angle. Giving up, he struggles to pull the chain far enough from his neck to gasp for air. I turn his own blade on him, pressing it to his back, shining silver light sparking against blue.

"No!" the Dagger shouts, knowing what I intend to do but unable to stop me. I hold the blade there until the shield breaks, overtaxed. I could kill the Rapier in a split second now.

"Drop your weapons," I tell the Dagger.

"Sasha, don't!" the Rapier begs.

Sasha—the Dagger—does it without hesitation. The liquid of the mercurial blade seeps back into the hilt before he drops it to the floor and kicks it into the hallway, well out of reach of any of us.

"We're all going to die anyway, Roman," the Dagger says. "I refuse to watch you die before me."

The words send an electric jolt through my spine. *Lito is—* Thousand gods damn it. The Dagger's right; we *are* all going to die. We have—a quick glance at my wrist—nine minutes. The only thing that matters is what we're going to do in the time left.

So I press the Rapier's blade close to his throat. Both of them stiffen at once. I don't look toward Lito, just jerk my chin in his direction. "Which one of you killed him?"

For a moment, there is only the sound of the Dagger's gloves as he tightens his fists and the Rapier's heavy breathing. But their eyes meet, and I know something passes between them—some decision only they can possibly know—and that makes me all the angrier because Lito is *gone* and we will never communicate like that again—

"*Which one?*" My words are cold but calm. I've sunk so deep into myself that the crying, screaming fury has hardened my tone into a quick, cutting lash.

They don't answer. Of course they won't. And so I say the one thing I would never want to hear, as a Dagger, in this situation. I tighten my grip on the Rapier. "Then I'll kill him and consider the debt paid."

"No!" The Dagger starts to take a step forward before hesitating, causing him to stumble. "It was me."

"Sasha—"

"I killed your Rapier," the Dagger admits.

I feel the exact moment the Rapier goes limp in my arms. The exact moment he gives up. "He's lying," he says. "I'm the one who killed your partner. He just wants to save me."

"Then I'll kill you both," I say.

The Dagger's back straightens. His nostrils flare as he releases a pent-up, angry breath. But his eyes are on his Rapier's, never on me. I hardly factor into this moment at all for them.

And that's when the dust settles for me, and I see the truth of this explosive situation: I'm their villain.

And that cold, disdainful tone of mine? I've never sounded more like my father than I do now.

I release the Rapier and back away as if he burned me. No bargaining. No time for it. "They ordered you to die? Fuck them." Seven minutes left. "Get out of here. Save yourselves, if you can."

They don't hesitate. Like magnets, they move toward each other, meeting in the middle of the room, and clinging with desperation. The Dagger casts one last look at me, checking if this is a trap, before, hand in hand, they flee the room.

Which leaves me alone with . . . him.

I kneel beside him. Shaking hands grip the sheet covering him from head to toe. I don't want to look—*I have to look*—so I peel the sheet back from his face—

"What's your name?" I ask, looking up at the tall boy.

He straightens, shoulders squared, a pose that dares me to fuck with him. "Lito sol Lucius." His eyes are full of fury, his lips held ready to peel back and bite at any moment.

I clap him on the shoulder, feel how taut his muscles are. He wants to hit me, and that makes me like him even more. "You're going to be my friend, Lito sol Lucius." It's not a question. Not an invitation. It's simply the truth.

I shouldn't be surprised that the angry boy I loved from the moment I saw him died furious. His eyes are closed tightly, his lips twisted in a final sneer. It wouldn't have been Lito if he'd gone quietly, smiling and peaceful.

I press my forehead to his, struggling through the feeling of wrongness to his skin—lifeless and pale. But he is Lito in the end, even now.

"I'm with you," I whisper, the tears finally falling, "and I'm never leaving you again."

WITH FIVE MINUTES left, I sprint down hallways and around corners, my prosthetic leg flagging from the damage I took. I ignore it as best I can. If I survive, I'll deal with it then.

I see no one in the halls, and I wonder if everyone has abandoned the ship—abandoned those in the command center—or if, even now, they're still trying to cut through the doors and save them. I know without a doubt that High Commander Beron val Bellator has left with his tail tucked between his legs. Has my brother?

The ship is shaking by the time we reach the hangar, trembling like I am with Lito in my arms. I'm not even sure what I expect—by now, there won't be any escape pods left—but I go anyway because I don't know what else to do.

There's a single escape pod waiting, but the doors are closed as if someone is inside. I approach the panel on the wall beside the door. LOCKED, it reads in big red letters. Three minutes.

"くそ," I mutter, but when I look at the door to see if I can somehow force it, the LOCKED sign disappears, the display turns green, and the door smoothly slides open. My eyes flick to the overhead camera. Is Mara even now watching out for me?

Podships are tiny things, a command area on one side and six seats on the other. There's a cramped storage space by the airlock door, and this one holds an empty cryo pod. Instead of wrangling Lito into a seat, I secure him in the pod before making my way to the panel.

My fingers dance across the keys. If there was a *get us the fuck out of here* button, I'd slam it. Without a solid heading, I don't select a final destination, just program the pod to launch. And as the doors lock behind me, I open up all communications channels. Once we're free of the *Leander*, I'll try hailing someone to pick us up.

Two minutes. The podship hisses as it prepares to launch, and I slam myself into the seat in front of the panel and buckle up.

My anxiety mounting, I watch the panel screens. I don't spot other podships; they must be long gone by now. But as our escape pod launches, trembling and jerking, I clench my eyes closed. After the initial thrust, gravity falls away, and when I open my eyes, I see the *Leander* on the screen like a little model ship.

A red button on the panel lights up like a warning. Less than two minutes left, and I'm receiving a call.

It can't be one of the outlaws, not so soon. But someone was watching me on the *Leander* cameras and unlocked the podship for me, someone who wants to talk now. I'm out of my seat, kicking myself through the lack of gravity, and answering.

I'm greeted by a face I never thought I'd see again.

"Shinya."

"Hiro," my brother says, the command center emergency lighting painting him stark red.

It's so hard to look at him this way, someone familiar and yet a person I don't know. A brother I wish I knew better, who was torn apart from me by circumstance. *I wish we were closer,* I told him on a recording long ago, but now there is a gap between us that will never mend, a void that is as deep and dark as space itself.

"We've tried our best to stop the *Leander,* but there's nothing to be done. We're almost at the Synthetic border," he says. "When we cross, they will destroy us."

A sob works its way up my throat; I do my best to swallow it down. "Shinya," I say, words wobbling, "I'm—"

"I need you to listen to me, Hiro." He closes his eyes and pulls in a deep, calming breath through his nose. "I told you that you weren't like the outlaws, but you were right: you are like them." He smiles wryly. "I'm glad . . . If you weren't, you'd be here on the *Leander,* on your way to death like I am.

"But you were wrong about one thing." Shinya's eyes shine when he opens them again. "I have been writing my own poetry."

My tears bubble up, but without gravity, they don't fall. I don't stop to wipe them away, not wanting to miss one second of looking at my brother's face.

"Tell Father for me?" he asks, and I nod.

"Of course," I manage, my voice cracking.

His face is years younger in a moment, and I am back beneath the kotatsu, cuddled up against him. He picks up a piece of paper covered in hurried black characters, clears his throat, and speaks:

「流れ星。」
Shooting star.

「ホタルが消える。」
The firefly disappears.

He opens his mouth to finish, to speak the final line, but a metallic voice fills the space:

"WEAPONS SYSTEM: FIRE."

"Onii—!" I scream. The screen turns to static.

A single heartbeat—

The podship slams sideways. I hit the wall, biting back a scream. The emergency alarms wail, and I grab a safety belt as I float past and hold tight. I'm battered, knocked from wall to ceiling—striking my shoulder, my head, my legs—until the jerking slows from seizure to shiver.

When the podship finally settles, I look at the screens, fearing what I will see.

The cameras that remain operational all show me the *Leander*—or what remains of it.

A toy ship, now broken into pieces, hardly recognizable.

And a white heat fills my head as I realize what has been lost.

Thousands of people on board the *Leander*, including my big brother, dead.

CHAPTER 45
ASTRID

I would posit that it is impossible for someone not from Máni or Skadi to understand those of us who are. We are born outside of society, and are thus forgotten by it. From before we ever leave our mothers' wombs, we are locked into a constant struggle for survival. Many of us do not come into this world screaming, for hardship is written in our very souls. I believe it is for this reason that, no matter how much we moonborn try, we find ourselves drawn to war.

From *Outside Earth's Moons* by Magnus Starikov

This is a trap, and I fell for it.

"Run!" Lily shouts, and I rush for the door, gun held before me. No time to threaten her, no time for the truth—

I burst into the hallway, stop short as soldiers with railguns appear directly in my path.

No, no, no . . .

They raise their rifles. Fire. Something hot clips my shoulder, and I release a wordless sob as I scramble in the opposite direction.

I fire Rian's gun down the hallway without looking. It does nothing but send the soldiers diving for cover. At least they aren't running after me.

Bullets pepper the floor at my feet, the walls around me, and I have never been more scared in my entire life than I am right now. Ringer cannot destroy my fear fast enough—or is he just as afraid as I am? That scares me even more.

I reach another entrance to the maintenance tunnels, one I have not used because of the camera that hangs above it, but I do not have time to care about that now. Death is on my heels. I open the hatch and fling myself in, then move backward, crouched painfully, with the gun ready for anyone who follows.

The soldiers reach the entrance, and a small, skinny one starts to enter after me. I fire a few shots, and he withdraws hastily.

Even if I have limited ammunition, the tunnels are too narrow for them to move as a group. They will have to enter in a single file, and I will be able to pick them off one at a time. And they cannot fire into the walls without hitting something important in these shafts where wires for light and atmo run. Though I am bleeding . . . perhaps they will simply wait me out.

It seems the latter plan is the one they choose, and while they do not leave the hallway around the hatch I entered through, they do not come after me. I take the opportunity to crawl deeper into the tunnel, find a ladder to another level, and climb away.

MOVING IS DIFFICULT with a bullet wound and the gun, but I refuse to give up the weapon when there are predators hunting me. I return to where I left my supplies in the tunnels and stop briefly to care for my shoulder.

The wound still bleeds, and though it draws a whimper from my lips as I prod at it, it is not as deep as it could be.

Perhaps I am in shock, I think as I calmly pick up the kitchen knife I used to kill Rian and cut the Cousin's robe into strips for bandaging. Everything feels so faraway and foreign, even this wound. I wrap my shoulder hastily and sloppily, but I do not have time, or the supplies, for stitches.

I see the soldiers marching in large groups outside the tunnels.

Frantically moving from place to place. Planning how to get me out. How to kill me without losing any more men.

Then I spot a group with respirators around their necks. My stomach seizes with apprehension, and I fear I know what that means: they're going to start gassing the maintenance tunnels to kill me.

I have run out of time. Either I will die here, or I will find a way to escape to fight another day. But the escape pod bays are surely patrolled. There is no way I can use them . . .

I look down at the plugsuit I wear. And, because we are one, Ringer's idea comes to me fully formed.

THERE IS NO way to the Ironskin deck from the maintenance tunnels, so I know that if I am to embrace this plan, I must leave the safety of the shaft and make for the elevator. I stop at a hatch close enough to the lift's doors for me to see it, but I do not leave yet. Instead I close my eyes and count my breathing.

I leave the tunnel. I walk to the elevator, but I do not hurry. A guilty person runs; an innocent one who belongs here does not.

I press the button. I wait. Force myself to breathe. No one else comes through the hallway. Only the cameras catch me.

When the elevator chimes, I feel I could cry.

Then the doors open, and a familiar face looks back at me.

First Sister of the Juno. My replacement stares at me with eyes full of terror.

I move on instinct, darting into the elevator, clapping a hand over her mouth—why, when she does not speak? "Do nothing to call attention to us," I whisper frantically. "I am begging you."

Her body stiffens, freezing before someone she fears, but the door closes behind us and she does not try to fight or run. I realize all at once what has alarmed her—the same thing that scared Rian.

You can talk? First Sister signs with her hands, the only language she has.

A wave of pity rushes over me.

I do not want to hurt her. *I do not want to hurt her.*

I want to free her, like the Mother did me. But I do not know how, and even as I try to focus on the neural implant that makes her silent, I feel nothing. I do not know how to wield this thing that is a weapon of the Sisterhood. I never learned how.

All I can do is use my words. "I want to show you something," I tell her. I grasp the plugsuit's seal at my wrist and twist, opening it to the air. I slip one glove off and shake it out until the Mother's neural implant, no longer in the jewelry box, falls into the palm of my naked, scarred hand.

Try as I might, I could not get rid of the implant after everything that had happened. It was proof of something repugnant, of the rot within the Sisterhood.

"The Aunts of the Agora use this," I say, holding out my hand, showing her the neural implant that sits there. "They put it in our brains. They make us forget how to talk."

Forbidden technology, she signs, though the movements are choppy with fear.

"Yes," I confirm. "And I want to make them stop."

So much I wish I could tell her as the elevator continues its journey upward. I do not know where we are going, my eyes only for First Sister and this moment that stretches between us.

"I want to break the chains the Sisterhood ties us with," I say. "I want . . . I *will* break them." I release a shuddering breath. "And that is why they name me their enemy."

First Sister reaches tentatively for the implant. Her fingers ghost over it before she jerks her hand back to her chest as if burned.

"Take it," I find myself saying. It seems important that she have it, now that the words are out. I have never known why I carried it with me all this time, but this . . . Yes, this is as good a purpose as any. "You once offered to help me. This is what you can do. Show the others. Tell them what I have told you."

She looks at me, then at the implant. She plucks it from my palm and wraps her hand around it. When she looks back to my face, her eyes are hard. The proud Sister loved by her captain is gone, boiled away, leaving only a girl who faces the truth. Though perhaps she does love her position, she loves her fellow Sisters more.

What do you need of me? she signs.

WHEN THE ELEVATOR stops, First Sister rushes onto the waiting Ironskin deck, her movements sharp and frantic. She cannot scream, but her waving arms and rapidly signing hands are the Sisterhood equivalent of panic.

The soldiers on duty there—five of them, I count—crowd around her, and I slip out of the elevator into the pooled shadows.

"First Sister," a soldier says. "What happened?"

She continues to sign, pointing back the way she came. Of course they cannot understand her; their frustration mounts as she tries to communicate.

"You," the soldier says, pointing to one of his fellows. "Go with her. Find out why she's upset."

I move as they talk, from the shadows to the Ironskin rigs, until one of the soldiers starts to turn in my direction.

First Sister stamps her foot on the metal deck again and again, making a loud clanging, and everyone snaps their attention back to her.

"Goddess's Garden, okay!" the soldier exclaims. "Is two enough?"

As First Sister points to all five of them, beseeching them to come with her, I start creeping forward again. There is an Ironskin rig close to the wall of tubes, its body open and waiting for a pilot.

There is a part of me that fractures as I stop before the hulking Ironskin, as I turn to the computer and wake it with a touch. I am only half-aware of what is happening behind me, as First Sister makes more noise and the soldiers speak among themselves. I frantically boot up the Ironskin and select a destination. The computer calculates nearby bodies of gravity and trajectories. I select whatever landing I can guarantee, and shudder when my only option comes up: Earth.

Gean territory. Only half-inhabitable. I know no one there. Even if I survive the fall, will I be able to live much longer than that?

A small voice whispers inside me: *What other choice do I have?*

First Sister is now walking toward the elevator with three of the soldiers beside her. She must have been unable to insist all five follow her, which means two will stay behind and spot me at any second. As her group enters the elevator and the door closes between us, I hoist myself into the waiting body of the Ironskin, slip my legs into place, and tighten the straps.

So much settles on me as I work. All that I have done. All that I have become. What have I started by revealing the neural implant to First Sister? How have I changed, murdering without remorse for my own gain? How has my failure to kill Aunt Marshae changed the future of the Sisterhood? Yet I cannot let that heaviness weigh me down, not when I still have more to do.

I press a button in the right arm, executing the computer's programming, and the Ironskin closes around me with a hiss. How do I know to do this? How does the Ironskin feel like a natural extension of my body when I have never been in one before? When the helmet flares to life, I forget all of my reservations in the dizzying array of light. I can see all around me, even what lurks behind me in the shadows. It is unlike seeing with human eyes, and it makes my stomach twist; I fear, for a moment, that I will be sick.

At the noise, the two soldiers turn toward me, and the helmet's sights automatically focus on them, highlighting them in vivid green. They rush at me, one reaching for his compad to call for backup, the other scrambling for the computer to cut the power to the Ironskin. I try to take a step forward, to coax the iron beast out of its cradle, and my plugsuit grows warm as the Ironskin connects to it.

I raise my leg, and the Ironskin moves with me. It is heavy, and I struggle against it, the straps and metal digging into my tender flesh. I do not have the muscle mass to be a pilot, and if this were not an emergency, I would worry more about what this will do to my bones and joints. But for now, I can only take one step forward, placing the Ironskin's foot before me and bringing the other leg alongside it to stand, blocking the soldiers from the computer.

"I am sorry," I say, and my voice comes out of the speakers as a deep and infernal growl.

They both look up at me, so tall they have to crane their necks. I watch them through the sickening vision of the helmet, knowing I must be like Ringer once was to me, a child of the Goddess in thick armor, a burning halo about my head.

They grab their guns and fire, listening to their warring instincts, but the shots ping off the Ironskin harmlessly. I look for a weapon of my own, eyes flicking past selections on my display, until I come across the electric whip. With a shudder, the panel in the Ironskin's hand opens, and the weapon coils out, bright and crackling.

I swing. It is not well aimed, and it misses them completely. I hope they will flee and not return, that they will save themselves, but that hope disappears as one tries to move around behind me and the other stands before me.

Thanks to the helmet, I can see them both.

I raise the whip and swing at the one behind me. It lashes across his midsection, and he drops, intestines spilling out across the metal floor.

The other soldier hesitates. Retreats a step. Thinks better of his plan to attack an Ironskin alone. The helmet alerts me to the fact that he has urinated. I raise the whip again, but then he is running for the elevator.

Good. I have already killed enough this day.

I withdraw the whip back into its hidden compartment. And though the fear and pain finally find me in the Ironskin, the shock of all I have done wearing off, the only thing I can do is follow Ringer's urging to step into the empty black tube that will spit me from the belly of the *Juno* and into the void of space.

It is time to leave.

CHAPTER 46

LUCE

We are born from the same stuff as stars, and it is to the stars that we return upon our death.

Ancient Aster proverb

I wait in the Vesta hangar, alone. The steady hum of the gravchair beneath me is a white noise easily ignored in favor of my sharp thoughts.

Mere hours after the Elders accepted Souji's deal, Vesta picked up a handful of emergency signals: escape pods, filled with outlaws. The *Leander*, they explained, had crossed the Synthetic border and been destroyed. One of the ships, the last to report in, had a single soul on board. With a heavy heart, Hiro announced that they were on their way with Lito's body.

My ears rang with that second part, so sharp I feared I had misheard. But I hadn't. Hiro also sent us a video, one that is jagged in my memory—*"let it burn"*—one that made clear what had happened to my brother.

I think of Ofiera's words. *When death comes for you, Lucinia sol Lucius, when it grasps you with cold fingers, that anger can burn through it. That anger can save you.* Well, the anger kept me alive, and now it's all I have left.

The inner airlock door rumbles, signaling the arrival of a ship. I check the clock. It took twenty hours to recover our people, the challenge being that the Icarii were in the same area recovering their survivors. But now they're here.

Asters emerge from the stone tunnels. The group spreads out, and I don't miss the shine of weapons on hips. No one wants to be caught off guard after everything that's happened.

Lotus is one of the Asters with a laser pistol. Lotus, who gave me her music with the breathy Aster songs. Lotus, the captain who made me part of her crew. Lotus, who didn't look at me differently after the ravages of the Genekey virus.

After I emerged from the Elders' chamber, my breath coming in short gasps, the news of Lito's death threatening to rip my heart into pieces, she found me and asked if she and her partners could help bear the weight of my grief. But it was in that exact moment that I realized, no matter how much she welcomed me, I was not an Aster. I couldn't share with her the way others did, their pheromones joining in a cacophony of kinship. My grief was mine, no one else's, and I would cling to it since it was the only thing I had left of Lito.

The airlock door opens, and a water-hauling ship called a dragonfly carefully maneuvers into one of the empty docking spaces. I tighten my hands on the arms of my chair, waiting . . . wondering. Will Icarii stream out, mercurial blades burning? Weak as I am, I won't put up much of a fight, but I will curse and claw at them as I embrace my death, and then I will be with Lito again.

The door opens, and a dark-skinned person with a prosthetic arm exits, followed by an Aster with metal chips implanted in their skin. Neither of them is Icarii, and they're soon joined by more people with patchwork prosthetics and outlawed geneassist modifications. It's only when I see Hemlock approach them that I realize this must be his Alliance of Autarkeia—or what remains of it after the *Leander* exploded and took so many lives with it.

I sink back into my chair, whatever energy I had sapped. But then my eyes catch on someone, and I find myself unable to look away.

They are familiar, yet not. Despite their limp, I know the way they move, the way they brush their hand through their hair. But that softened face, that prosthetic arm—those I recognize only because of the recordings.

They catch sight of me, dark eyes going wide. Then they are moving toward me through the crowd as if pulled by gravity, never dropping their gaze from mine. Arrested in orbit, they break into a stilted run, stumbling over the stone-strewn ground.

I thought I could feel nothing but unbridled rage, but something new emerges as they reach me, as they fall to their knees at my chair.

"You recognize me?" I choke out, not knowing what this feeling is that grows in my chest.

"Luce," Hiro says, dropping their face—their *new* face—into my lap, over my weak, trembling legs. "You know who I am?"

"Hiro." I reach for their chin, but my hand finds their hair instead, and I brush it from their eyes with shaking fingers. "Oh, Hiro, I will always know you."

And then Hiro throws their arms around my waist, and we are both sobbing. We are broken, the two of us, shattered in half. But perhaps, together, we can be two halves of a whole, and that new little feeling can be nurtured into hope.

AFTER HOURS OF sitting together sharing stories, Hiro convinces me to rest. We return to my room with its health monitors and IVs, and Hiro curls up in the corner chair and falls asleep almost immediately, so much like Lito that my heart hurts. I don't think I'll be able to sleep, but the next thing I know, Hemlock is shaking me awake, staring down at me with his large black eyes. "It's time," he says softly.

Hiro is already awake, and it is to them I look for an explanation. "The Asters have prepared a, uh, memorial for Lito," they say.

"Take me to him," I tell Hiro. They hesitate only a moment before helping me into my chair. Hemlock joins us as we enter the hallways, gently whispering directions to Hiro through the endless stone tunnels and glowing plants.

But Vesta has lost its fairy-tale quality. Without color, it is nothing but a washed-out, bland gray. The beauty here, as in other places, is gone. Perhaps when Lito left this world, he took everything beautiful with him.

We enter the Elders' chamber, now so empty it echoes with the sound of gently trickling water from the fountain. But even that is so quiet I can hear the thud of my own heartbeat and the breathing of the Asters around me. *Ahh ha. Ahh ha.* A song of the soul of Vesta.

For once, the three Elders aren't on the platform; they stand in front of it, surrounded by others. Ofiera, looking healthier than when I last saw her, is close by. Castor, who doesn't acknowledge my and Hiro's approach, is as well. Hemlock steps to my side, adjusting his lace cuff to hide the theracast on his broken wrist.

And finally, there is Sorrel. I bite my cheek until I taste blood. Part of me feels guilty at the sight of his swollen, bruised face, but the other, stronger part of me rages against him—this is his fault. *His fault.*

Then I see what awaits us on the platform.

On a stone table, Lito lies in a glass coffin.

When it grasps you with cold fingers, that anger can burn through it. That anger can save you. I grab on to the rage and hold, letting my anger, my hatred, my yearning for revenge burn in my veins and keep me alive.

Hiro's hand is on my shoulder, there and gone, as I push myself from the chair. I stumble forward, and they catch me, help me to keep moving. Hemlock, despite his own pain, holds me up from my other side, and together, with their help, I climb the steps to the platform.

It's not a glass coffin as I first thought; it's a cryo chamber. Did Hiro put him here, or did the Icarii because they didn't have anything else to preserve him? Or, as I consider Ofiera and Sorrel, was it to send a message?

Sorrel should be the one dead in there, I think, and do not even feel bad for it.

When I finally stand before the pod, Hemlock and Hiro step back from me, and I brace myself with both hands on the glass—cold, it's so cold. In the reflection floating over Lito's face is a girl I don't recognize, one who looks nothing like him. A stranger to the brother she loved more than anyone else.

My tears well up, and I tip forward, pressing my forehead against the glass. The cold is a balm to my burning forehead and cheeks, and I let the sobs rack me until I feel like a soul without a body, battered emotions too large to be contained.

No one interrupts. If they offer me some sort of comfort, I don't notice. In that moment, there is only me, my grief, and the body of my brother.

Let it burn.

My hands drag down the glass, leaving streaks like long claw marks. My tears have frozen where they landed, as cold as my heart.

That was my brother. That is his corpse. He will never be whole again. And I will never forgive anyone who had a hand in putting him there.

When I turn to seek help in returning to my chair, I catch a glimpse of Hiro's back as they storm out of the room. I don't begrudge them their leaving; if I could flee on sturdy legs, I would as well.

Anemone asks if I would like to say a few words. I refuse. My memories of Lito, like my feelings of grief, are *mine.*

After each of the attendees has a turn approaching the pod, Anemone asks me what I want to do with his body. I hesitate. On Cytherea, we would have cremated Lito, my family and I each taking some of his ashes to keep at home or to wear around our necks. But we had never expected Lito to want that. We had always prepared for the possibility that he would pass on a mission and be sent into space, into the heart of the universe itself.

"To space," I hear myself say as if far away. "That is . . . the way a duelist goes."

Anemone nods. "We will see it done," she swears, and I turn my chair back to the stone tunnels.

PEOPLE FLOCK TO my room after Lito's memorial. I wish there were a door I could shut and lock, a way to close myself off from the rest of the world. After the fourth or fifth Aster I don't know offers to share my grief, I ask—*beg*—Hemlock to send them all away.

He steps into the hall and says something in the Aster language. I catch only pieces of it, but soon the hallway is quiet and I can breathe easily. Unfortunately, this doesn't last long. Just as I'm finally beginning to relax, someone familiar darkens the doorway. I know who it is before I even look up.

Castor. Silent, guilty Castor, who doesn't look directly at me. Who hasn't been able to since the Genekey virus changed me.

"I will be just outside if you require me." Hemlock offers a formal little bow before disappearing into the dark hall.

"What do you want?" I ask, not sparing my bitterness.

He narrows his eyes, as if the spot on the floor he stares at is particularly offensive. "I wanted to show you something."

"I'm not very interested in anything you have to show me right now."

"It's about your brother."

My heart spasms in its death throes. Apparently it still can find new ways to hurt.

Castor sets a compad on my lap. It takes me several seconds to realize what I'm looking at. Cytherea, with its lack of color, is almost unrecognizable. But slowly, I spot familiar spaces despite the rough cut of the footage, small lowlevel parks with uneven paving, the front of a shimmering Tesla Gardens building. All of them are swarmed with people. Faces twisted in anger. Hands curled into fists. Hastily scrawled signs with various slogans. All captured with personal drones in shaky amateur style.

WHAT HAPPENED TO THE LEANDER? one sign reads. SOUJI MUST ANSWER, another says. But the words that take the shattered pieces of my heart and begin to knit them back together are these: RELEASE LITO SOL LUCIUS.

They don't know what has befallen him yet. "Lito's message . . ."

"The data you got from Val Akira Labs, the proof of their illegal activities that Lito took to the satellite station . . . it is out there in the worlds, now."

The images continue to change, one after another. People march in front of Val Akira Labs. ONE'S BEAUTY SHOULDN'T BE ANOTHER'S PAIN. They throw rotten fruit at the AEGIS building. THE AEGIS MAKES THE LAW TO BREAK IT. They stand in the cramped streets of the Aster neighborhoods. A HOME OR A CAGE?

Then the video focuses on a painting larger than life, and in my shock, my hand flies to the compad to pause the stream. On the side of a building, done in a simplistic style with black linework and heavy shading, is a four-meter nude of a woman riding a horse. She sits sidesaddle, both the horse and her skin appearing ashen gray. Her head is bald, but her face is covered in a breathing mask. And while I've never sat atop a horse, the body is one I recognize all too well: mine.

EL JINETE PÁLIDO DEL APOCALIPSIS is scrawled above the woman's head on an unwound scroll. Below, in the same style, is painted LA PESTE TE VIGILA.

The Pale Rider of the Apocalypse, the Plague watches you.

"Is that . . . me?" My eyes slowly come up to meet Castor's gaze. "The video of the Genekey virus test . . . you leaked it?"

"After the Lito videos were released, protesters were begging for more," Castor says softly. "We sent the test footage to an agent in Cytherea, and they've been sharing the video by hand. It's spread like a fire from protester to protester." He gestures to the compad. "Keep watching."

The video continues, only to zoom out from the painting and focus on a masked artist standing in front of it. She's a curvy woman, and I recognize her before she even speaks. "This is a reminder from the Keres Truth Society," Isa says, gesturing to *La Peste*. Other artists surround her, many women I don't know. The Keres Art Collective—and Shad—is nowhere to be seen. "We need to take concrete action. If we don't stop Val Akira Labs from their illegal experimentation on Asters—if we don't *do the right thing*—then we'll end up just like her." *La Peste* looms behind Isa. "And we'll deserve it."

The video ends. My breath leaves me in a rush.

"You see," Castor says, "your brother's work goes on."

Something darkens in me at those words, souring some of the good feelings the video summoned. It's not just my brother's work—not anymore. But the extent and variety of scenes in the video reveal something about the Aster network that I didn't realize: they're far more connected than I initially thought.

"I'm leaving Vesta for a mission," he says, cutting into my thoughts. He's beside me now, kneeling down to face me—when did he come so close?—and he reaches out for me but doesn't touch me. Fearing me, fearing he might hurt me, fearing I might hurt him if he does. "Come with me."

His eyes soften as he looks at me—exactly the same way he looked at me on the ship to Vesta, like I am beautiful and he never wants to look away. Like our lives are full of promise and hope. For a heartbeat, the world is quiet. I reach up and take his hand in mine. He is warm, and I am so, so cold, infected by the chill of Lito's coffin.

But it is only a heartbeat, because the promise is broken, and hope is dead. I laugh. His words are ridiculous. *He* is ridiculous, trying to soothe his guilt by offering me a purpose, as if he can buy himself a good night's sleep after everything he has done.

"Why would I ever trust you again?"

"I didn't lie to you." His voice is strong, a hint of anger in its deep timbre. "I never thought about using the research this way until we reached Vesta."

"You still accepted the Icarii deal. You thought Lito was an acceptable casualty."

His pupils narrow into slits like sharp daggers. "You know what

Sorrel did was right." He shakes his head. "Better for Lito to die than the Asters and Icarii to go to war."

"And better my life to be shattered than thousands of Icarii on Cytherea." My lips tremble with barely restrained rage. "So you still agree with your Harbinger after everything?"

He doesn't answer, and that's answer enough.

"I can't work with him. I *won't* work with him."

"And with me?" Castor asks. "You chose me on Cytherea. You saw something in me that inspired you to leave your whole life behind."

"You think this was because of *you?*" Instinctively, my hand tightens on his. Rage flares inside me at his words, and I don't fight it. He tries to withdraw, but I don't let him. I squeeze harder.

"Luce—"

"This will be the last time I ever speak to you, Castor, so I want to make one thing clear." The anger washes over me, the only thing I have left. I bathe in it, let it possess me. "I will stay with Hemlock. I will continue what you call my brother's work. But that's because it's *my* work. *I* chose this. And maybe you had a hand in helping me get this far, but don't ever think that what I'm doing has anything to do with you."

He finally jerks away using his superior strength, and while he almost pulls me out of the chair, I do not fight him further. I told him what I wanted him to know, and he will remember it—from the way he looks at me, with a mix of fury and disgust, I know he will.

He opens his mouth to say something more to me, but closes it without a word. I look away from him. I mean to keep my promise; I will never speak to him again.

He starts to storm away, but slows at the door. Looks back over his shoulder at me. Hesitates. Then sighs and retreats, slouching, into the hallway.

Hemlock reappears a moment later, and by then I have swallowed the anger and focused on the gray haze that blankets my entire world.

"Did you mean what you said, that you will stay with me and help the Asters?" Hemlock asks. His words are naked in their hope.

I look at him, we two of a kind. Him, a broken Aster. Me, a twisted Icarii. Both of us, scarred and forgotten.

"I meant it," I say to the one person who didn't automatically accept the Icarii's demand to keep Lito. The only person who wanted to fight for him, other than me. "Just one thing . . ."

He pulls his wounded wrist to his chest in a protective gesture. "Name it, Lucinia."

I think of the videos Lito released to the Icarii people—*"let it burn"*—and of all the other content Hemlock has curated, like Hiro's recordings. Of the vast protest documentation the Aster network gathered from Cytherea. Of the hundreds of stories, and thousands more waiting just beneath the surface in the Under, tales like the ones I heard from Lotus and the other crew members. And though I am only a chapter in my brother's narrative, now I see the full story line of the fall of the Icarii for what it really is.

"I'll need a compad with access to your network," I tell Hemlock. I focus on my hands, digging into the armrests of my chair until my knuckles are white. "La Peste tiene mucha gente a la que vigilar."

CHAPTER 47

HIRO

My Pollux: The Harbinger's been named Shield by the Elders. Uncle's returning to Ceres. He asked me to go home with him—as if Ceres is my home—but I've decided to work with the Harbinger instead. Even the Elders see it's time for an open show of strength. Plus, I have good news: the Harbinger has assigned me to work alongside you. That's right . . . from now on, I'll be your asset.

Unanswered message on Hemlock's private server from Castor

I don't have anything to pack, so after I leave Lito—*don't think about him don't think about him*—I find the first Aster I can and ask them to take me to wherever they keep supplies on Vesta. Their face doesn't change so much as a millimeter, but I can read their hesitation clearly enough; instead, they tell me to give them a list of what I need and they'll run it by the Elders—not Hemlock, which is something new I don't like at all.

I rattle off the things I need, a basic enough inventory—a maintenance kit to fix my prosthetic leg, a travel pack, two changes of clothes that would fit into Icarii society, a weapon small enough to hide on my person, a compad connected to Hemlock's private servers. The Aster nods until I mention my getaway vehicle.

"A ship?" they ask, and now their face *does* change, lips thinning as if they're biting back caustic words.

"Talk to Hemlock about it," I say, waving my hand through the air to sweep away their concerns. "Now, if you'd show me where the showers are, I'm sure *everyone* would appreciate it."

They're more than happy to oblige me there.

I wish I could say I spend hours relaxing in a hot shower that I rightly deserve, but Vesta is first and foremost a water purification plant and all the excess water for things like washing feels one degree away from becoming ice. I'm shivering by the time I'm out of the lightning-quick shower, cursing Hemlock and the Elders and every Aster who decided cold water was acceptable.

I'm not surprised to find someone waiting for me—just shocked at who it is. It's neither of the people I thought I'd find trying to catch me before I leave.

"Hiro," he says. His hair is shaved close to his head, white stubble over a pale scalp. An untreated scar runs up the side of his face. I've never met him before, but I know him anyway.

"Sorrel, right?"

I know how little the Asters care about things like nudity, and as much as I hate every inch of my skin, I'm too cold to wait for Sorrel to leave. I drop my towel and start pulling on the blessedly clean clothes someone left for me next to a bag probably full of the supplies I requested.

He pulls his head back, watching me down his long nose. "Lucinia didn't tell you . . ."

"Tell me what?"

"She blames me for Lito's death." His eyes—a blue-green color, rare among Asters and, I hate to admit, completely beautiful—watch me without wavering. "The Icarii were willing to cease hostilities and discuss a treaty with us because of the virus. They were not willing to return Lito. If we had pressed the matter, all of Vesta would have suffered for it." His pupils shrink to slits as he cocks his head. "I accepted their offer as it stood."

I stop in the middle of tightening the straps of my new boots. An image flashes into my mind—my hand around Sorrel's throat, tightening, *squeezing.* Sure, it'd make me feel better, but what good would it do in the long run?

"It was the Icarii's fault," I say as peaceably as possible, though I'm sure he can hear the animosity in my tone. Without looking away from Sorrel, I speak to his shadow. "What do you think, Ofiera?" I hear her snort from the darkened back of the room. "I know you're here. I can sense you. We were connected once, after all."

"I should know better than to expect a val Akira to ever forget an implant, once learned." I try not to flinch at the thought of my brother and those under his command using Dire and the outlaws as puppets. Though maybe justice was served in the end and Sigma died on the *Leander* with the rest.

She walks into the low light of the showers, a wry smile on her face. I barely noticed her at Lito's—well. Beside Lito. But now that I really take her in, she looks like she's lost weight she didn't have to lose.

"The fuck happened to you?"

She presses a hand to her stomach. "Mercurial blade."

"That's rough, buddy."

"You look rough yourself."

I think of everyone I've lost—the *Leander* exploding, broken Mara, my brother's smile as he spoke his final poem, Lito—*don't think about him don't think about him*—and close my eyes tightly. くそ. "Yeah" is all I manage.

My world grows smaller when I think about them, my chest grows tighter, and I can barely breathe. In the podship, after everything, I cried until I threw up, and I can't fall apart like that again. So I have to push thoughts of them away. Can't fall into endless mourning. Not yet.

Then there's a hand on my shoulder, and I jerk my eyes open to find Sorrel right beside me, having moved silently. "We know you plan to leave, Hiro, but we want to ask you to come with us instead." His eyes trace over my face—Saito Ren's face—and come to linger on my eyes. "You said you and Ofiera are still connected. Then we are connected too."

I look between Sorrel and Ofiera. Instinctively I take a step back from the Aster. "I'm not really into threesomes . . ."

Ofiera rolls her eyes, but Sorrel goes on, undeterred. "To commemorate my successful handling of the Icarii, the Elders have bestowed upon me the position of Shield, which entitles me to protect Asters by any means necessary." *With little Elder oversight*, he likely means.

And what of Hemlock and his years of service in the darkness of Ceres? Was he skipped over because he was too cautious in the face of Sorrel's ambition? Or did the Elders have a darker reason for disregarding Hemlock? Like his genetic shortcomings—defects from *my* father's lab.

"So I'm requesting your aid, on behalf of all Asters." Sorrel looks down at me, pupils so wide his eyes are fully black. "Hemlock and his Alliance withheld information from you. Used you, not so different from how the Icarii used you."

I flinch.

"I want you to join us as an equal. Check with your implant, and you'll know I'm telling the truth. Help me face the Icarii in this important moment in Aster history. Help me put the Asters in a better position for the future." His hand leaves my shoulder, a ghost of heat radiating from him. "And once the Asters have taken what they deserve from the Icarii, we'll seize what is rightfully ours from the Geans in an ironclad rebellion."

He doesn't mince words. *Taken. Seize.* He talks like a warlord I used to know as Saito Ren. It also doesn't help that the last time I had someone promising me something *if I just did what they asked*, it was my brother offering me my genetic code for returning to my father's side.

I imagine my hand on his throat again, his words ringing in my ears— *she blames me for Lito's death*—and feel instant revulsion run from my numb chest to my fingertips. Luce isn't a stupid kid, and while death brings out the worst in us and she has suffered—thousand gods, has she suffered—I don't think she would blame him if he were completely blameless.

All I know how to do is fight and lash out . . . even at those around me, I said to Mara.

Then don't push people away. You deserve good things, she replied.

But she doesn't know . . . she couldn't understand.

"I've got my own path to follow right now," I tell him. I swallow a sob that works its way up my throat when I think about how, once upon a time in Ceres, I told Lito something similar.

Don't push people away.

Would he be alive, if I hadn't sent him away from me?

Don't think about him don't think about him don't think about—

"I'm sorry to hear that," Sorrel says. Now he's the one to step back. I'm glad he doesn't press the issue, but when he looks to Ofiera, I feel something pass between them.

I tried, he says.

Resignation, she sends back.

So Ofiera was the one who wanted to recruit me . . .

What for? My skills, or Saito Ren's face?

It's Ofiera who speaks as they prepare to leave. "If you find yourself without a path," she says, "reach out to us."

"Sure."

"There's a ship waiting for you in the hangar," Sorrel says. "A gift from me and the Aster Elders to thank you for your service thus far. Consider our offer. It's never too late."

I don't even have time to thank them before they are gone, and I'm left to shiver alone in the showers.

AFTER PATCHING MY prosthetic leg with the maintenance kit so I'm no longer limping—though feeling doesn't return to it, and I worry Mara's spell is over for good—I head to the Vesta hangar. I half expect Sorrel to have been full of shit, but sure enough, there's a ship waiting for me. It's a termite-class corvette, and while it looks a bit battered, I don't doubt it'll get me where I need to go.

I'm not even halfway up the open loading ramp when someone accosts me, but again, it's not who I expected.

"Going to leave without saying goodbye?"

Luce—small, bald Luce in a gravchair because she doesn't have the strength to walk on her own two feet after what the Genekey virus did to her. Sure, the virus was a clever creation, a way to force the Icarii to back off without bloodshed, but I can't help but hate anyone involved in its creation for what it did to Luce, even if she volunteered for it.

She sits in front of another waiting ship, dressed in warm clothes, a thick black sweater and Aster-leather trousers. Already she looks better than when I first saw her—though I suspect I do too, after a shower and change of clothes.

"Luce, I . . ."

"I think you owe us all at least a chance at a word." Dire emerges from the other ship, takes Luce's chair, and pushes her toward me.

"'All'?" I repeat, but then Hemlock follows after Dire, and while I saw him when I first got here, I didn't have much of a chance to greet him. Nor the inclination.

I look at the theracast on his wrist. "What the hell happened to you, by the way?" I ask, but Hemlock narrows his black eyes.

And in the silence, I realize all at once what a strange juxtaposition Luce makes with Hemlock and Dire.

"Luce, are you going with them?"

"With Hemlock, for now. I need access to his servers," she explains. "He has more videos on Ceres that I want to use. We'll be slipping the truth about Lito into Icarii media, one piece at a time." As she talks, I settle. There's a fire in her tone I can't deny. "Lito's story will live on, even if he . . ." She wavers. Swallows. Starts again. "Even if he doesn't."

I can only nod at her. *Don't think about him don't think about him.*

"We were hoping," Hemlock says, "that you could help with the latter part. Isn't Cytherea your destination?"

Leave it up to Hemlock to somehow know my plans without my having told *anyone.* Like the damned guy can read minds . . .

"Yeah . . . Cytherea." I wonder if Hemlock knows *why* I'm going back there. But I don't want to mention that now. "And you, Dire? Are you heading back to Autarkeia with . . . with your crew?"

Dire grunts but has the generosity not to mention how many out-laws died on the *Leander*. I'm sure we're both thinking the same thing, though: How many more would have lived if I'd helped them like I'd promised Mara as opposed to going after Lito? "Until we can figure out a way to keep the Icarii from mass-controlling the Autarkeia neural implants, yes. Even if we have to remove them all . . ."

"Good," I say, even if the prospect is grim. Mass brain surgery for thousands . . .

"Things are already changing, though," Dire says.

"Sorrel's the Shield now. I know."

Hemlock all but rolls his eyes. I can tell how he feels about *that* . . .

"And," Dire adds, "the Synthetics have moved the border."

"They *what?*"

"After the destruction of the *Leander*, they sent a message to humans and Asters alike on all electronic equipment connected to the Autarkeia feed." Dire's face is stone. "Because of Icarii interference on Autarkeia, gray space is now claimed as part of Synthetic territory."

"Mara . . ."

Whatever happened to her on the *Leander* . . . she *changed* things.

"The outlaws are still welcome on Autarkeia so long as we uphold our tenets of peace and equality," Dire explains, "but we have to be careful."

"Because the Alliance of Autarkeia is a thinly veiled front for the Aster rebellion and you're making Engineborn weapons?" I ask.

Dire narrows his eyes. Hemlock's elegant, long-fingered hand flies to his chest. Both of them, offended by my words.

"Sorry, my br—" I clear my throat. "Commander Shinya val Akira mentioned it."

"Hemlock and I started the Alliance of Autarkeia together," Dire says, "when no one else valued our contributions to our individual societies—mine the Geans, and his the Asters. We are *allies*, as the name suggests, and I will *always* come to the aid of my allies in times of need. Yes, we are armed, but that is so that we can survive in a galaxy that would think nothing of our annihilation."

Hemlock's black eyes soften as he looks me over. "I know you feel we have not been completely honest with you, Hiro, and for that I am sorry . . . But we have done the best we can for the people we want to protect. *All* of them, not just you."

I suck in a breath, readying myself to curse him, but then . . . Luce. She looks up at me with glassy brown eyes that look far too much like *his*. I know she's changed—we can't go through what we have and *not* be changed—but there's still hope in her, and I refuse to crush it. To let it die. My breath escapes me as a long sigh. Have I done the best I can for all of the people I want to protect? No . . . I haven't. But I'm going to fix that now.

"I know this is bigger than me," I say at last. "Bigger than all of us, but . . . I'd *really* appreciate being kept in the loop from now on. If we're going to work together, then *trust me*. I'm committed to this. I don't know how much more I can do to prove that."

"You can tell us where you're going now," Hemlock says softly, barely a whisper, in that knowing way of his. *Damned mind reader.* Turning my words against me too.

"Fuck you, man . . ." I mutter, running my hand through my hair. "I'm returning to Cytherea to do what you asked me to do long ago."

Hemlock doesn't look at all surprised, but Dire's brows shift up his forehead almost to his hairline.

"And what's that?" Luce asks, the only one on the outside.

I drop to one knee in front of her, and her lips part as if to ask a question. But before she can, I throw my arms around her and hold her to my chest. "I'm going to kill the man who took Lito from us."

I feel her stiffen beneath my touch. "Wh-what . . ."

"My father," I tell her. My voice does not waver. "I'm going to kill Souji val Akira."

Luce pulls away, looks up at me with her mouth hanging open, speechless. If she found the words, would she try to convince me against my plan, or would she encourage it?

My mother is gone because of him. I am . . . not even Hiro anymore.

And Shinya . . . Shinya is dead.

How many val Akiras need to die before my father realizes his plans are corrupt? How many Asters must suffer? How many more Geans must die in petty conflicts?

Luce places her hand—cold as ice—on my cheek. I don't flinch away. "May the Thousand Gods Below the Sun watch over you, Hiro." Her lips tremble, but only for a moment. "You're clever like a nine-tailed fox. You can do this, I have no doubt."

I kiss her cheek. I can only hope she's right.

When I stand, Dire and Hemlock are waiting to bid me farewell. Dire offers his gold hand, and I take it with my white one.

"As I said, I will always come to the aid of my allies in times of need. And you are my ally, Hiro." Dire nods solemnly. "Call, and I will come."

I clap my flesh hand onto his flesh shoulder so he can feel it. "Same to you, my friend."

Then Dire moves aside, and I come face-to-face with Hemlock.

"Can you believe this all started in a basement on Ceres?" I ask, and Hemlock chuckles in that refined, breathy way of his.

"My first Icarii rebel," he whispers.

"But not your last," I say, nodding to Luce. "Take care of her."

I don't tell him I forgive him for hiding things from me, because I don't really feel like I should. But if he takes care of Luce . . . well, it's a bridge that'll help us move forward.

"I'll be a call away," I tell them.

I give Luce one last kiss before heading into my ship and preparing to leave. But as I'm programming Cytherean coordinates into the command computer, I recall a poem from my childhood, one Shinya read to me after I cried for a mother who would never come home.

They say the dead return tonight, but you are not here. Is my dwelling truly a house without spirit?

I hold the words of Izumi Shikibu in my heart, and they bring me comfort.

"Wait for me, Lito," I whisper to the air. "I'll be with you soon enough."

And that's all I need to keep me going.

CHAPTER 48
ASTRID

Earth endures, Mars conquers!

Gean military chant

When I was freshly assigned to the *Juno*, I thought the idea of Ironskins romantic. Saintly knights with shields built into their very armor. Heavenly halos of living fire. Storms of lightning in the palms of their hands.

Before battles, I would coat my hands with rosemary and lavender oil to bless the pilots in prayer to the Goddess, but truthfully, I was imagining what it was like inside one. How it felt for the *Juno* to seize you, to embrace you with all the care a mother would her child, and then spit you into the unknown.

The silence of space, swallowing you into a lightless, heatless abyss. The only sound my heartbeat in my ears, my breathing inside the Ironskin.

Now I will know.

The *Juno* is not soft; she jerks me about inside the Ironskin as the tube digs anchors into my armor, as the gun rotates to aim at its programmed target. *There is nowhere to go but forward*, I think, and take in a deep breath that rattles in my throat.

Something wet touches the palm of my hand. Some sort of moisture? It takes me far too long to realize . . . blood. The gunshot wound on my shoulder has reopened and bled through the bandages.

I am bleeding out in the armor.

I feel Ringer alongside me, our dual panic overwhelming. Our heart races. This is not romantic. This is not what I imagined.

What does it matter that Ringer and I are one if we die?

A force hits me from below, hard enough to crush me, and the helmet jerks sideways and I bite my tongue and a blackness swallows me whole, darker even than the void.

"COME OUT, LITTLE sister. Warriors do not hide." Hringar stands in the doorway, his massive frame blocking the light from the hall. He ducks his head to step into the little room and settles on one of the tattered chairs.

For a few minutes he is silent, sitting beside my cot expectantly. When I do not emerge, hoping against hope that if I am quiet he will believe me asleep, he clears his throat. "If you come out," he says, "I will tell you a story."

My resolve wavers. I push all the blankets off me except for one, which I wrap about my shoulders like a cloak. The room is cold. It is always cold.

—*everything around me is black, black, black, except for the stars, which burn so brightly I feel I could reach out and pluck them from the sky, they are far closer than I have ever seen them before, and they are the only things out here with me, when there are no ships in the sky—*

No one has come to see to me other than Hringar, so when he holds his hand out, I take it. My childish hand is dwarfed by his. When he tugs me from the bed, I follow. He pulls me onto his knee, and I perch there like a little bird, eyes gleaming in the black.

—*something emerges from the black, a star larger than the others, brighter than the others, and growing brighter by the second—*

"Once upon a time, a woman in gray who did not speak and her captain came to our father and asked for hospitality. Being that we are people of earth and sky, we knew what it was to want, and we granted the captain a place in our longships."

—no, not a star at all, a planet big and blue, a landing place, a safe place, a home I have never known—

"I don't like this story," I say, but Hringar continues, heedless.

"The woman in gray and her captain feasted and slept well. When they prepared to leave, they asked for one of our finest warriors. After much thought and prayer, she decided to go with them. But the captain and his woman in gray did not want her as a warrior. They wanted her as a slave to wear their chains."

—the place's name is shifting in my mind, a liquid thought I cannot catch, wet and slippery like the blood running down my arm—

"So our warrior did what warriors do. You know what that is, don't you?"

"Fight," I say, and Hringar nods approvingly at me.

"That's right. Our sister fought, the only way she knew how."

—I fight to hold it in my mind, this place, a light against the darkness, and it grows, grows, grows, until the black sky is gone and the stars are missing and I feel my body shake and slow—

"I don't like this part," I tell him, covering my face.

"I know," he says, pulling my hands away from my cheeks. "But you have to listen, because it's important."

—it's important to stay awake, to seize my mind and hold on, though so little makes sense, and my body is racked with shivers and grows warmer until I feel sweat bubble on my forehead—

"Because the warrior scarred her face, the captain and his woman in gray felt that we had tricked them. They demanded payment in other ways, and if our father were to refuse them, they would bring more ships and bigger guns and more soldiers until we had no longships and no warriors left."

"But they tricked us first—"

"Hush, little sister." Hringar's voice is firm. I bite my tongue. "Do you see why I must go?"

—*my skin is on fire, my blood boils, I am falling, I am dying, I am a wildfire and there is nothing left to consume but myself*—

I cry, big fat tears that roll down my cheeks, but Hringar wipes them away.

"Do you see why I must go?" he repeats.

"So that they do not come to kill us and demand more," I say, and it is something I know he has said before, something he would approve of my saying now.

He nods and presses a hand to my chest, directly over my heart. "So that they do not come to demand what we are unwilling to give."

—*blood or sweat or tears, I do not know, but I am drowning in them, and the ground is coming, rushing up to meet me, small squares of brown and gray growing larger with each second*—

I want to beg him not to go, not to leave me alone. What am I to do without my big brother to guide me?

I will have no one but myself.

—*then I feel him all at once, he seizes control of my right arm and guides me, and my hand finds a button I did not know existed, deploying a parachute that slows my frantic descent*—

"May I tell you a secret, little sister?" Hringar asks, withdrawing something from his pocket and hiding it in his fist.

I rub my hands against my cheeks and nod.

Hringar looks at me sternly. "Promise to tell no one else?"

"Promise."

—*the world is large and looming and throws open its arms in an embrace, welcoming me, beckoning me, a comet become a meteorite*—

"Here is my secret," he says.

When he opens his fist, he holds a golden star in the palm of his hand. In the darkness of the room, it shines with the brilliance of a sun. I take the gift in my childish fingers, and with the surety of knowledge

I do not know how I possess, I pull the golden light to my mouth, slip it between my lips, and swallow.

I devour the star.

—there is nothing but the ground, nothing but the brown, nothing but the blood, nothing but me in this armor and I am dying, will die, will lose everything in this crash and—

"I promise I will never leave you."

I feel I am choking on the star, that it grows in my throat, and my pupils flare wide, taking in all the light and shadow around me, but I focus on him, on Hringar, on my big brother.

"Always," he promises.

I fight, like a good warrior, but I choke and then—

—and then—

Darkness.

I TASTE BLOOD on my tongue when I wake. I am cold, but I am . . . not dead.

The helmet display is cracked, half fuzzy pixels, the other half static. The only thing I see above me is a gray sky filled with thick black clouds and silver satellites, drifting lifelessly in orbit.

I try to move my hand. Feel only the wetness of blood.

No, I am not dead . . . not yet. But soon.

I want to close my eyes and rest. Want to slip back into whatever dream I was having of a childhood I do not remember. Would I be able to find out more, if I were to allow myself to drift away? Or is it just another pretty lie my mind has concocted to soothe me?

I cannot lie here, cannot die here, if I want to avenge Paola and Eden and all the others who have gone before me. I can almost imagine Eden here, red hair blazing, as she kicks the Ironskin and jolts me inside.

"Get up!" she would say, and her fury would spur me into action despite the overwhelming pain. "Stop lying there, feeling sorry for yourself."

And she would be right. I *do* feel sorry for myself.

So get up.

It is hard to convince myself to do so when every piece of me cries out in agony. I cannot feel my legs, but I can move my right hand, and inch by desperate inch, I shift until I can reach the emergency release button.

I press it, my shoulder wound screeching, and the Ironskin bucks as it opens, vomiting me halfway out onto the frigid, hard ground. I swallow whatever sobs rise within me, my joints aching as if a knife were shoved between them, the plugsuit coated in dried blood. Immediately I begin shivering. It is so cold I can see my breath on the air.

I had the thought before I launched that I would not live long on Earth even if I were to survive the fall, and that thought returns to me now as I crawl the rest of the way out of the Ironskin and curl into myself on the ground.

I need to stand up. I need to walk. I need to find somewhere warm, because if I do not, the cold will kill me before anything else can.

I pull my arms beneath me. Move into a sitting position. Ignore the screaming of my body, the weakness in my limbs, and ready my legs to stand. They are harder to convince, and I wobble as I use the Ironskin to push myself to my feet.

Though my legs quiver beneath me, as weak as if they have never felt gravity before, I survey the land around me. My heart sinks as I turn, as I find that it is brown and flat and featureless in every direction.

I suppose it doesn't matter which way I go, if they are all the same.

I take my first step. My leg buckles beneath me, and I fall. Hit the ground with a force that aches in my bones. Cry out in pain, and my voice echoes on the dead plains around me.

For a moment, I allow myself to wallow in the anguish that consumes me. But only for a moment, because this will not be what kills me.

There is nowhere to go but forward.

Forward, where I will find a way to return to Mars. Forward, where I will hunt Aunt Marshae and do what I should have done on the *Juno*.

Forward, where I will find the truth of all who betrayed me and pay them back in kind.

A noise above me jerks me out of my thoughts. I roll onto my back and stare into the featureless gray sky. For a second, I cannot find what made the noise, but then I spot it.

A ship.

Something falling behind me, dropping to earth and retracing my exact path.

I do not know who they are, but I do not doubt that they are here for me.

I grit my teeth and dig my nails into the dirt. Pull my arms beneath me. Prepare to stand, to force myself onward.

Because there is nowhere to go but forward, and I am not giving up.

CHAPTER 49
THE FIRST SISTER OF CERES

I want to thank you, Aunt Briana, for watching over Ceres in my absence. It is with a full heart that I report I am on my way back with a new First Sister of Ceres at my side.

Message excerpt from Aunt Marshae,
head of the Order of Cassiopeia

"First Sister of Ceres."

It's strange, the spike of pride I feel at that title when it means nothing to those below the surface. Growing up, I never cared who was in charge because it didn't change anything. Even now, I half expect them to be addressing Astrid at my side.

But of course not. She's gone. I'll probably never see her again. And even if I did, she wouldn't consider me a friend.

"We're landing at the Temple now, First Sister," the soldier says over the intercom. I shift in my seat, nose curling at the musty and slightly sweaty smell of the cabin. The journey from the *Juno* to Ceres's surface wasn't a long one, but the white noise from the dropship's engine threatened to send me to sleep nonetheless. I've been sleeping poorly since . . . well, since that night on the *Juno*.

Are you the First Sister of Ceres? Astrid accuses in my memory, eyes wide with hurt.

The pilot puts us down in front of the multitiered stone building, and I exit via the extending ramp. It's late, and a bad day at that. I rub my lower back, swallowing against the sharp ache, as I look up at the stairs—all two hundred of them—that lead up to its imposing columned entrance. I swallow a curse—if Astrid hadn't turned the courtyard into a damned garden, I could've landed there—before I force myself into movement. As the newly named First Sister, I should enter the Temple of Ceres on my own two feet.

I take the stairs as quickly as I can and approach the large stone doors—when the Icarii were in power, they bore two snarling lions—decorated with curling metallic flowers of gold. The guards posted on either side move as a unified force, each taking a door handle shaped like a vine and opening the entryway to welcome me inside. As I pass into the hallway, they salute me, fists pressed over their hearts, but the gesture feels hollow when the only thing I smell is the citrus scent of cleaning supplies.

Inside, away from prying eyes, I move slowly through the Temple, not to admire its cold stone carvings or bathe in its golden lighting, but because my right leg burns as if it's on fire. I can tell when it's going to be a bad day, and when I woke up this morning with my foot aching—it always starts in my right foot before moving to my knee and then my hips and then my back—I knew this was inevitable.

By the time I reach the chambers on the second floor that Astrid claimed for the First Sister of Ceres, the guards posted along the hallway are navy hazes. I enter the sitting area and dump myself into the first chair I come across. I can't sleep here if I want tomorrow to be any better than today, but I can rest here, at least for a little while, before I go to bed.

I feel something shift behind me—some*one* moving in the apartment—and I turn quickly, my hands balling into fists as if I could possibly fight off an attacker.

Aunt Marshae emerges from the office area—who else would've

taken these chambers but *her?*—a pile of biopapers tucked beneath one arm. I flatten my hands on my lap—embarrassingly, one has pale patches over my knuckles, so I hide it beneath the other.

"Lily," she says, "it took you long enough."

I don't stand to greet her. Should I? Does Aunt Marshae outrank me now that I'm the First Sister of Ceres? I stay rooted to the chair, if only because of the pain.

"Are these my chambers or yours?" I ask. "You'll have to forgive me if I've made a mistake."

"They're yours," Aunt Marshae assures me. "I was just waiting for you."

"Apologies for my tardiness, then," I say as kindly as I can. "The soldiers of the *Juno* seemed desperate for reassurance after everything that happened with . . ."

Astrid. I don't say her name.

"Yes. *Her.*" Aunt Marshae's upper lip curls as if she's taken a sip of vinegar. She acts as if *she* were the one who woke up with Astrid pointing a gun in her face, and I have to swallow that thought down with all the other insults. Aunt Marshae threw me before the scythe to save her own skin, and I won't forget it.

"We traced the Ironskin to Earth, to the west coast of the African Multinational Territory, but by the time security forces arrived, there was nothing to find." Aunt Marshae's grip on the biopapers tightens, nails bending them, fingers turning white. "Scavengers had even started dismantling the armor for parts."

As my heart speeds at the good news—Astrid could be alive, *Astrid could be out there*—I keep my face as blank as possible. "Perhaps she perished on the journey. A soldier reported shooting her, after all. Offer a reward throughout the AMT for her, dead or alive, and see if anyone reports finding a body."

Aunt Marshae strides across the room and settles in a chair across from me. The sharp tang of her perfume stings my nostrils. At first, I think she'll reprimand me for speaking out of turn, but instead she offers a rare smile. "Wise," she says. "It's bothersome, though. We had her cornered. She was on a ship, for Goddess's sake. She only could have escaped because she had help on board."

Does Aunt Marshae suspect me? I must put those suspicions to bed. "That's why I spent the day with the soldiers of the *Juno*. I hoped that one of them might admit to knowing something we could use to track down the culprit or culprits."

"And?"

"Alas, if someone has a burdened conscience, they chose not to speak to me about it."

"Disappointing, First Sister of Ceres."

My lips twitch, but I don't allow my smile to falter.

"Still, Aunt Margaret is exceedingly proud of you. She would be, that stuffy old bitch."

Again, a muscle in my face spasms, this time near my eye. Is she trying to get a rise out of me by insulting the Aunt I'm closest to? Or does she expect me to agree after I fought with Aunt Margaret over Astrid?

How could you? I asked her again and again after Astrid was stripped of her title and I was granted it by the Agora. How could she accept Aunt Marshae's money? How could she give Marshae access to Nat? I had trusted her with Nat's safety. *How could she?*

Aunt Margaret's sad expression will forever be etched into my mind. "We were outplayed, Lily," Aunt Margaret said. "I didn't have a choice. Marshae had piles of evidence against Astrid, and even more people willing to lie about her. The only thing I could do was accept the deal to save you and me."

Which made the weight of what we'd done fall on Astrid.

It still stings that Aunt Margaret didn't tell me about the deal because she knew I wouldn't like it. Stings even more that Astrid believes I had some hand in it. If I could do it all again, I would've helped her escape somehow . . . at least, I'd like to believe I would.

I pull my eye drops from my pocket, if only to give my hands something to do. "What of the bargain Aunt Margaret struck with the Agora?"

"The Order of Pyxis will have its money. And look," Aunt Marshae says, gesturing to the room around us. "You're here as First Sister of Ceres." She narrows her eyes. "Proof that I keep my word."

We'll see, I think, administering the drops that help me in these blasted lights.

"If only you had listened to me after Mother Isabel III's death, we would have avoided the entire ugly thing with *her*," Aunt Marshae laments, once more referring to Astrid. "Continue to please me, and I will put your name forward as the next Mother. I know that's what Aunt Margaret *really* wants."

And the power that comes with it, of course. But no one ever asks what I want. I suppose that's the trouble of the Sisterhood: anyone who wants power shouldn't have it.

"There is . . . one thing that concerns me, Auntie," I say softly. I hope I'm not laying it on too thick, but I've never been accused of being a poor actress. Something about being quiet and shy, about looking like an innocent girl with pleading eyes, causes people to think I'm either harmless or stupid—both of which make them underestimate me. "About Eden . . ."

Aunt Marshae quirks a brow. Her face is still, but more like a calm before the storm than true peace. I've obviously stepped onto dangerous ground. "What about the Second Sister of Ceres?" Aunt Marshae asks, refusing to give Eden a name even in death.

Why did you kill her? The words are a lump in my throat, as hard and heavy as a stone. They're choking me, and if I don't get them out in some way, I will suffocate on them.

"Aunt Tamar has opened an investigation into her death," I say, carefully choosing my words. "She believes the suicide letter is inauthentic."

Aunt Marshae's shoulders stiffen. She watches me closely, as if she could see into the heart of me, but I haven't let anyone see into my heart for so long, Aunt Marshae could look for the rest of her life and still not find the truth.

You trusted Astrid, my conscience whispers. *You tried to help her. You opened yourself up to her.*

But not fully. There are only two people in this entire universe that I've been completely open with, and neither of them is Astrid. No wonder she looked at me with such accusing eyes as she pointed the gun at me. For all she knows, I'm just as bad as Aunt Marshae.

"Aunt Tamar's investigation," Aunt Marshae says, dragging me back to Ceres, "does not concern you, First Sister of Ceres."

Her words are a warning, a slap on the back of the hand. I don't heed them. "The night before Eden's death, she visited with Aunt Tamar at length."

A tremor runs through Aunt Marshae's hands. "Did she speak with you afterward?" she asks, and that quaver in her voice, that naked fear in her face, is exactly what I wanted to see, what I needed to confirm that my suspicions were right.

Eden discovered something Aunt Marshae did not want her to, and Aunt Marshae had her killed for it. Something Aunt Tamar knows . . . something I yearn to know with everything inside me.

Aunt Marshae's face changes, fear giving way to rage. One moment she is sitting in her chair; the next she's leaned across the space between us and seized my forearm in one hand. "Ah!" I cry, my eye drops falling from my hands as her nails dig into my skin.

"Listen to me, you little shit," Aunt Marshae hisses, and my heart frantically speeds. She eclipses me with her bulk, keeps me trapped in place. "I know you worked with Astrid and Eden, I know you *prefer* them to me—how could I not know that after you spat on my gifts until Aunt Margaret forced you to accept them? And the other members of the Agora, I know they liked Aunt Edith more than me, so I will buy their friendship if I must, one person at a time. I can do that now. I can do *anything*.

"I clawed my way up from *nothing*." Her nails dig deeper as if to make a point, and I swallow a sob. Blood wells up around her fingers, staining the arm of my gray dress. "But I will not have anyone—not a moonborn orphan bitch, not a cast-off redheaded slut, least of all *you*, an up-jumped cunt who can't even walk properly—stop my rise to greatness, do you understand me?"

I say nothing. What is there to say? But as Aunt Marshae releases her grip on me one finger at a time, bloody smears on her fingertips, I find my fear has turned into smoldering anger, a fire that could warm me for years.

"They are gone," Aunt Marshae whispers to herself, less agitated now and growing calmer with each breath she takes. "They are gone, and they will trouble the Sisterhood and the Gean people no longer . . ."

Eden is gone. Astrid isn't. And in this moment, I swear to myself that I will do everything I can to get her back.

I look at my forearm, at the little half-moons of red staining the gray. My urge is to hide the wound, to keep my enemy from seeing my weakness like I do with my pale patches, but what would be the point of that? The woman who hurt me is standing right there. "Thank you, Aunt Marshae," I force myself to say, "for this enlightening conversation."

Aunt Marshae's gaze shoots to me, assessing and cold. But I do my best to appear earnest, if only to keep her from becoming violent again.

She strides to the door in a whirl of skirt and scarf. "I will return tomorrow, First Sister of Ceres. We will speak more then."

"Please, Aunt Marshae," I say, surprising even myself, "when we're alone, call me Lily."

Aunt Marshae stops at the door, her eyes narrowing.

"You see, I quite like this name," I explain. "A beautiful flower with a delicate appearance that hides its true nature."

"'True nature'?" she repeats.

"Lilies are poisonous, Auntie." I don't need to fake the smile that my lips settle into. "People don't seem to remember that."

Aunt Marshae's nails briefly dig into the wooden door frame before she flashes a tight smile and leaves.

Alone at last, I slump down into my chair. Now it's not just my body that aches, but my soul. Sparring with Aunt Marshae always leaves me stinging, like I've walked a razor's edge barefoot. But it's a necessity, until I can find a way to get rid of her for good.

I take five minutes for myself, and when those are up, I take five more. By then, I feel I can at least bandage the wound on my arm and take a hot shower to soothe my aches before heading to bed. But as I shift in the chair to stand, the door to my room opens again, and an Aster in traditional wraps brings in a tray of tea.

All at once, I recognize him, everything from the way he stands to the *scent* of him.

"*Sfonakin!*" I cry to my twin in the rough Ceres dialect of our childhood—*same soul*, I call him—and before I can push myself out of the chair, he is there—he is *beside me*—and wrapping his long arms around me and scooping me up and pressing my head to his chest. *Comfort*, he shares with me, his pheromones soothing my body and soul.

"I didn't know you'd made it back to Ceres yet. I thought you'd be stuck on Mars—"

"Where you go, I go," Castor says, and though he doesn't answer my question of how he is here, I don't care, because without him, I am half a person.

His scent envelops me as he whispers my name into my ear—both the word and the pheromone of my childhood name, the name only he calls me. When he sets me on my feet, I reach up—and up and up, I am so short compared to him after all I've gone through, after all the genetic alterations and surgeries—and clasp his face desperately, whispering his true name back to him with my pheromones and voice.

"*Dran sir tag,*" I say. *I am home.* And then I speak his flower name, the name he chose to match the code name Hemlock assigned to me. "My Castor," I say.

"My Pollux," he whispers back, and I know, in this exact moment, that everything I've suffered—geneassist treatments to look like them that could not take away my sensitivity to light, surgery to become their height that has left me scarred, living as a Sister so I could one day change the Geans—has been worth it.

I am the First Sister of Ceres, soon to be the Mother, and also an Aster. A flower to the untrained eye, as well as the poison beneath. And I was born to shatter worlds.

EPILOGUE

>>SENTRY 834X: ABNORMALITY DETECTED

[command/investigate]

>>SENTRY 834X: PROBE ACCESS REQUESTED

[command/launch:834Xa,834Xb,843Xc]

>>SENTRY 834X: PROBES 834XA,834XB,843XC LAUNCHED

[command/report]

>>843XC: CONTAINER(115CM/245CM/125CM) #3552426 REGISTERED TO VAL AKIRA LABS. FUNCTION: CRYO CHAMBER. THREAT LEVEL: MODERATE.

[query/weapons?]

>>843XC: WEAPONS:NEGATIVE

[query/threat level designated moderate, why?]

>>843XC: CONTAINER(115CM/245CM/125CM) #3552426 CONTAINS (1X) ADULT HUMAN MALE, DECEASED.

>>SENTRY 834X: WEAPONS SYSTEM ACCESS RE-QUESTED

We open our eyes to Jupiter's great storm, Hiro's voice ringing in our memories. "Mara!" A small piece of us shudders, but not from that. We are accustomed to being taken apart. We are accustomed to death, over and over. Other memories stored for later processing bleed together.

[playback:memory/access/28.11.56.34/*LEANDER*]

Hiro, facing Dire of the Belt: "I WON'T LEAVE HIM!"

[playback:memory/access/28.11.56.19/*LEANDER*]

Lito, ignoring Commander Beron val Bellator: "Hiro?"

>>SENTRY 834X: WEAPONS SYSTEM ACCESS RE-QUESTED

[command/hold]
[command/retrieve cryo chamber]
[command/bring to SYNTHETIC#00000001]

>>SENTRY 834X,834XA,834XB,843XC: ACKNOWLEDGED

ACKNOWLEDGMENTS

A LOT OF authors talk about how hard it is to write the second book in a series, but I was lucky in that I always knew what I wanted to do with the story; it was life around me that was difficult to navigate. This book was written while I was in physical therapy and dealing with chronic pain, so thanks to everyone who helped me both in and out of the writing world, but especially:

Alexandra Machinist, I believe in myself because you believe in me. Mike Braff, I can't imagine a better collaborative editor; we make some sweet music together, if I do say so myself. Laura Cherkas, thanks for catching my mistakes; every time I make you laugh, I add six months to my life span. Lauren "LJ" Jackson, you're the coolest publicist I could ever imagine having. Molly Powell, Alexander Cochran, and everyone on the UK Hodder & Stoughton team, thanks for having my back across the pond. And to everyone at ICM Partners and Skybound who've helped along the way, especially in the little details I don't even know about.

My beta and sensitivity readers—among them Enrique Esturillo

Cano; Pablo Ramírez Moreta, PhD; and Matthew Shean—thank you for your tireless feedback. Gary Tiedemann, Emily Woo Zeller, and Neo Cihi, thank you for bringing Lito, Astrid, and Hiro to life in the audiobook.

Jeanne Cavelos, you were the light in the darkness who taught me everything I needed to know. My fellow Odyssey class of 2016, thanks for putting me through the fire to help me become steel. Nothing but love for my Tomatoes—Joshua Johnson, Rebecca Kuang, Farah Naz Rishi, Jeremy Sim, and Richard Errington.

My fellow authors who welcomed me with open arms—Meagan Spooner, Amie Kaufman, Jay Kristoff, Andrea Bartz, April Genevieve Tucholke, Katy Rose Pool, Andrea Stewart, Caitlin Starling, K. A. Doore, Xiran Jay Zhao, Laura Lam, Samantha Shannon, Zoraida Córdova, and everyone who took the time to share my quarantine book with their readers. To the book bloggers and content creators who helped spread the word about my queer space opera, y'all are the real MVPs.

My friends and family, you've held me up when I wanted nothing more than to fall down. The Cold Ones—Eljay, Colleen, Nick, and Hillary—let's crack one open together soon. Mom and Dad, you never doubted that I'd succeed in my choice of a creative field. Connor, this one's for you; you taught me how strong sibling love can be.

Finally, to Pablo, thank you for reading every draft, for pulling me out of my depression spirals, for surprising me with candy, and for putting up with my stinky meows; I love you and can't imagine my life without you in it.

WANT MORE?

If you enjoyed this and would like to find out about similar books we publish, we'd love you to join our online Sci-Fi, Fantasy and Horror community, Hodderscape.

Visit hodderscape.co.uk for exclusive content form our authors, news, competitions and general musings, and feel free to comment, contribute or just keep an eye on what we are up to.

See you there!

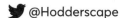